A LONG COLD FALL

"ENGROSSING AND CREDIBLE"

Chicago Sun-Times

"AN IMPRESSIVE MYSTERY DEBUT . . .
Surprising . . . well-paced . . .
Grabs attention with its opening chapter
and never lets up"

Publishers Weekly

"GRITTY . . . HARD-BOILED . . .
DEFTLY CRAFTED AND CRISPLY WRITTEN . . .
ONE OF THE BEST FIRST NOVELS
IN RECENT YEARS"

San Diego Union Tribune

"Sam Reaves writ̲͟e̲͟s̲͟ ̲͟ ̲͟ ̲͟ ̲͟ ̲͟ ̲͟ ̲͟ ̲͟ ̲͟ ̲͟ ̲͟ ̲͟ ̲͟ ̲͟iscent of
a John D̲͟ ̲͟ ̲͟ ̲͟ ̲͟ ̲͟ ̲͟ ̲͟ ̲͟ ̲͟ ̲͟ ̲͟ ̲͟ ̲͟ ̲͟ ̲͟ ̲͟ ̲͟ ̲͟ ̲͟way . . .
A tightly̲͟ ̲͟ ̲͟ ̲͟ ̲͟ ̲͟ ̲͟ ̲͟ ̲͟ ̲͟ ̲͟ ̲͟ ̲͟ ̲͟ ̲͟ ̲͟ ̲͟ ̲͟ ̲͟ ̲͟st clip"

REAVES I̲͟ ̲͟ ̲͟ ̲͟ST NOVELIST WHO WRITES
AS IF HE HAS BEEN DOING IT FOR YEARS."

Stuart Kaminsky, author of *Red Chameleon*

"The most difficult task of fiction
is to create living, breathing characters.
Sam Reaves accomplishes this with ease."

Gerald Petievich, author of *To Live and Die in L.A.*

A LONG COLD FALL

SAM REAVES

AVON BOOKS ◆ NEW YORK

AVON BOOKS
A division of
The Hearst Corporation
1350 Avenue of the Americas
New York, New York 10019

First Avon Books Printing: December 1992

AVON TRADEMARK REG. U.S. PAT. OFF. AND IN OTHER COUNTRIES, MARCA REGISTRADA, HECHO EN U.S.A.

Printed in the U.S.A.

RA   10 9 8 7 6 5 4 3 2 1

This book is for my father.

Many people have contributed in large ways or small to the making of this book. Particularly deserving of thanks are: Lisa Curcio for advice about the law; Lieutenant Lee Hamilton of the Chicago Police Department for patient answers to endless questions; and Al ("just Al") for the good stuff about driving a cab in Chicago and for thoughts on surviving Vietnam. The mistakes, of course, are all mine. Finally, thanks are due to Kim for . . . everything.

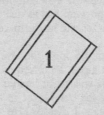

1

IT WAS A long way to fall, a very long fall through the cold night air, and she fell the whole way without making a sound. At the end there was a sound, a sudden sick sound, but after a minute of stillness no one had come to see what had made it. All the way down, all through the long journey from high in the night to the last precious inch above the ground, she had possessed lungs that breathed, a heart that beat, and a mind that knew. The moment of her death was the longest of her life. After the fall she lay still, slowly growing as cold as the earth. Cars passed near her but nobody looked.

High above her, a light burned.

By the time he reached 26th Street, Cooper was hoping he hadn't made a mistake. Things were too quiet in the back seat. The man had been congenial enough at the start, as they headed south out of the Loop, but he had fallen silent as the hotels and high-rise apartments on South Michigan gave way to weed gardens, FOR LEASE signs, and boarded-up gas stations. Cooper's last two attempts at light talk had been met with grunts.

Bad sign, bad sign, Cooper thought, and then told himself it was paranoia. The man had a right to keep his thoughts to himself. It wasn't a cheerful neighborhood and he probably didn't like it much either. At Cermak, Cooper looked right toward Chinatown and saw the projects looming, twenty stories of shelf space for poor black votes. Michigan was one-way now and almost deserted, and Cooper took it fast, over the expressway and past Mercy Hospital and into the Urban Renewal Land, new high-rises and townhouses built for the doctors and professors and such who staffed the nearby hospitals and schools. They were stark box-like buildings, too far apart to form much of a neighborhood, projects for the well-to-do. The streets were just as deserted here. Good stick-up territory. Cooper eased his grip on the wheel, making himself relax.

Cooper had given the man the eye before nodding and starting the meter, making a conscious decision. He had decided the man wasn't wasted or hostile or even just poor. He had on a nice black leather jacket in the late October chill and he wore tortoiseshell glasses. He wanted to go to King Drive and 35th, which was a long way from where most of the hold-ups happened, down past 61st. So Cooper had broken the rule and flicked on the meter.

The unwritten, quietly spoken rule said you didn't take a black male into the South Side at night. Cooper had broken the rule before, on the basis of judgments like this one, and never had any trouble. It was a rule he wasn't too comfortable with, liking to think he was no racist. The trouble was, drivers got killed a couple of times a year, mostly on the South Side. The word among drivers was that venturing into the South Side at night was a good way to wind up sitting in your cab with your head lolling on the back of the seat, bleeding all over hell.

Rein in your imagination, Cooper told himself, checking the mirror. He couldn't see the man, over in the corner. *He's tired and thinking of bed and he's got no use for idle words with a bored cabbie. He's going to pay and get out of the cab and I'll wing it over to the Drive and get back north. Maybe call it a night.* It was nearly one in the morning and he'd been driving off and on for sixteen hours. He needed to unfold his lean six-foot frame from the cab, get it stretched out on a bed. He passed a hand over his face, scratched at his ragged brown moustache.

"Make a left here, man." The words from the back seat were softly spoken, startling Cooper a little. He braked, checking the street signs. *33rd Street. Close enough.* King Drive was a couple of blocks east. Cooper was always wary when a fare changed destinations, but if the man lived along here somewhere, 35th and King would be the approximate address he might give a cab driver. No need to be suspicious. He turned east on 33rd.

He drove for a block and there was a big square stone

church, the Pilgrim Baptist Church. There were trees along the blocks right and left and the houses didn't look too bad. There were lights on; people lived there. *Terra incognita*, thought Cooper. Past the church there were vacant lots, with weeds coming up through gravel. The sudden open space brought back a bit of Cooper's tension; he liked having lit windows nearby.

"Next right," said the soft voice from the back. Cooper nodded and put on the turn signal. This wasn't as bad as some South Side blocks he'd seen, the ones with more vacant lots than houses, with weeds the size of trees. Or the West Side ghetto, the real badlands. This looked like livable middle-class territory. He made the turn and cruised down the narrow street, waiting for instructions.

This, however, wasn't a very nice-looking block. There were fewer lights, more weeds. He caught a glimpse of smashed-out windows as he passed. The houses were ancient here, old narrow brick relics of the last century, crumbling. There was some rehabbing going on, though; he went by a porch held up with new planks and adorned with a contractor's sign. "Where to, pal?" Cooper said.

"Just keep driving," the man said, still quietly. "This is the block." Cooper didn't like those words, just keep driving. He heard the man shift on the seat behind, reaching for something. *Money. Let it be money,* Cooper thought.

It was a long block and Cooper went down it slowly. There were a few cars parked along the way. There was no word from the back seat. More than half the houses looked empty. "What's the address?" Cooper said, getting the wind up.

"We're there," the man said. "Right here's just fine." There was more rustling from the back seat.

Cooper pulled over to the curb behind a rusting Chevy van. He looked at the house he had stopped in front of. It was dark but the windows looked intact. It looked habitable. Cooper's heart had accelerated a bit. He put the cab in reverse and put his foot on the brake. He reached over to turn off the meter, barely noting the fare.

"Don't turn on the light." The voice was a soft purr. Cooper twisted to look over his shoulder.

The gun looked about a foot long and the same caliber as an elephant gun. It was about six inches from Cooper's face.

Where the hell did he pull that out of, thought Cooper. He sat still for that eternal moment that always comes with the start of an adrenaline rush, and then his first response was rage at his stupidity for driving right into it. For breaking the rule.

"Pull it out, my man, all of it. I want the wad you got in there." Cooper saw a faint reflected gleam on the glasses over the dark face when his eyes finally left the muzzle of the revolver.

It took him a moment to find his voice, and then he nodded once. "You got it, pal." He dropped his gaze from the face and looked studiously at the dashboard as he eased his hand slowly in the unzipped front of his old leather flight jacket. There was a rustling behind him and the muzzle of the gun touched him lightly on the side of the neck, sending a chill down his spine.

"You don't wanna do nothing stupid now, do you?" said the man in his soft deep rumble.

"No," said Cooper, carefully. He had the roll of bills in his shirt pocket between two fingers now, and he slid it out with great caution. The first shock was past, and thoughts were starting to come, the main one being 'Don't do anything stupid.' He held the roll up, the bills clasped lightly between his fingers, offering it to the man, looking out the windshield at the back of the van. The muzzle of the gun was still at his neck. He felt the money leave his fingers with a little pang of bitterness.

"Don't be holding nothing out on me now, man," the man said. "This don't look like a lot for a night's driving."

Cooper stared at the back of the van for no more than a second before deciding that lying wasn't worth the risk. He always split up his cash for just this reason, so as not to lose it all, but the man had expected that. "I got more in the side pocket," Cooper said. "I'm gonna reach in and get it. Don't get nervous, OK?"

"I ain't nervous. You the one shouldn't be nervous, man. You move good and slow and we'll get along all right."

It cost Cooper more to reach in and get the bulk of it in the side pocket of his jacket. This was the whole load, the whole two hundred, the fruit of a long day's labor. But the light touch of steel on his neck made it easier to part with.

He had a brief vision of what a round from that gun would do to his neck and he was suddenly anxious to get rid of the money. He brought the roll out, wrapped tightly in its rubber band, and held it high for the man to take it. The gun muzzle left his neck just before the roll was plucked from his hand.

"Well shit, I knew you had to have a little more on you somewhere. But you wasn't gonna give it to me, was you?" said the voice behind him.

"I gave it to you when you asked," Cooper said. He didn't like that tone of voice.

"Yeah you did. You did just fine."

Cooper could hear him moving across the seat, toward the door on the left side, directly behind him. He didn't like that at all and another chill went through him. This was when it always happened, when the guy had the money and didn't want to leave a witness.

"I didn't get much of a look at you, did I?" said Cooper. "I avoided looking at you, right?" He hoped the man got the point. All Cooper could picture were the jacket and glasses, nothing that would help him identify a photo or pick someone out of a lineup.

The man sat still for a moment, a bad moment, right behind Cooper. "Hey. What you worried about, man? You think I'm gonna shoot you just like that?"

"I just want you to feel safe, pal. I couldn't begin to give a description. Couldn't describe you for a million bucks. OK?" Cooper hoped that removed any doubts. He figured the man was getting out on the street side so Cooper would be less likely to get a look at him.

The man laughed, a little contemptuous puff, and Cooper heard the door come open. The sound gave him a little rush of hope. He heard the man push the door all the way open and slide out. His eyes went to the side mirror and he saw the man come out of the cab, saw the nice leather jacket shine in the streetlights. "Thanks for the ride," the man said.

"My pleasure," said Cooper softly. He was still looking in the side mirror; he could only see the man's torso through the window of the open back door as he stuffed Cooper's money into a pocket.

And then in the dark distorted image in the mirror he saw the other arm straighten, rising up slowly with the gun at the

end of it. His heart bucked and he knew the man was going
to kill him after all. For a frantic instant he was frozen, as
the arm came up and stopped moving, and then he knew it
was try something or die. So he tried the only thing his re-
flexes could come up with.

Cooper threw himself violently to his right across the seat
as he took his foot off the brake and stomped on the gas. The
gun went off, deafening him, as the tires screamed and finally
bit and the cab lurched backward. From his half-prone position on the seat Cooper gave the wheel a twist to the left
and the cab swerved out into the middle of the street as the
gun went off again. Cooper felt the breath of the bullet on
his face as it came through the seat, scattering stuffing. Frantically Cooper jerked the wheel back and then the cab jolted
over something and there was a scream from near the left
front of the cab.

Cooper jammed on the brake and came upright. He looked
out the windshield and saw the man on the ground fifteen
feet in front of the cab, one leg stretched out on the pavement, supporting himself on one elbow, the gun still in his
hand. The foot at the end of the leg was twisted. The man
dragged himself backward a foot or two and then sagged and
gave a half-growl, half-gasp of pain. Cooper saw what had
happened; the open back door had swept him off his feet and
the front wheel had caught him as Cooper had swerved.

Cooper just stared for a moment, astonished to be still
alive, before thinking of flight. He wanted to get out of range
of that gun.

Then he remembered his money in the man's pocket, two
hundred plus dollars that belonged to him. He hesitated for
a moment, watching the man fight the pain and struggle to
drag himself out of the cab's headlights. He was fifteen feet
away and he still had the gun.

It's only a pistol, Cooper thought. He considered matters
for a moment and then swung open his door and leaned out
just enough to speak to the man on the ground.

"Drop the piece," he said.

In answer the man let himself collapse onto his back and
raised the gun, aiming at Cooper. Cooper ducked back into
the cab, rammed it into drive, and shot forward, keeping his
head low, his aim only approximate. The man fired again,

the windshield spider-webbed, and then there were two jolts as front and back wheels went over something in the street, and another scream.

Cooper stopped and leaned out carefully, looking backward. The man had been twisted around by the impact and lay still on the pavement, face down. The gun was still in his hand.

"Drop it," said Cooper. The man slowly raised his head. The glasses were gone and Cooper could see white teeth shining in a grimace. "Throw it. Toward me," said Cooper. He put it in reverse and backed it about a foot toward the man.

The man waited only a second and then with a convulsive motion slid the gun along the street toward Cooper. Cooper put the cab in park and got out and walked to pick it up. It was a big revolver, a Smith & Wesson with a wooden grip. He stood over the man, looking at his legs. He would need some time in a hospital bed. Cooper cocked the revolver. He reached down and grabbed a shoulder and abruptly turned the man over on his back, bringing a cry of pain. The man raised a hand to ward off whatever he expected to come. Cooper held the gun close to his face.

"You were going to kill me, weren't you?" he breathed.

The hand fell back to the pavement. It took a moment for the man to get the words out. "No . . . no I wasn't. Swear to God." His eyes were wide and his breath was coming in short whiffs.

Let him *be scared for a while,* thought Cooper. He bent over and reached into the side pocket of the leather jacket where he'd seen the man put his money. Wrong side; he'd seen it in the mirror. He tried the other pocket and pulled out the roll and the fold of loose bills the man had taken from him. The man lay panting, staring past the muzzle of the gun into his eyes.

Cooper stood up, the cocked revolver still pointing at the man's face, controlling the fury that wanted him to pull the trigger. "The money's one thing. Killing me for no reason is another," he said. He put the money in his pocket and stood for a moment watching the man suffer, pain contending with fear for his life. "You deserve worse," Cooper said, and turned away.

Walking quickly back to the cab he took a look around and

saw figures in the shadows on the sidewalk nearby. He glared at them. He stopped to slam the back door of the cab and then got in. He uncocked the gun with his thumb and laid it on the seat. He spun the tires a bit pulling away.

By the time he was on the Ryan heading south he was trembling a bit. He took deep breaths to suppress it and made himself slow down; it was hard to see out the windshield and it wouldn't do to get stopped for speeding with a recently fired revolver on the seat beside him. He was calmer by the time he reached 51st and took the exit, coming down from the adrenaline high.

He pulled into the drive of the sprawling somber brick complex at Wentworth and 51st, the main police station for the South Side. He stopped in front of the entrance, unsure where to park. Someone would tell him, he thought.

Cooper switched on the inside light, picked up the revolver and looked at it. It was a .44 special, a big deadly gun. He thought about how to walk into a police station holding a gun without getting shot or arrested. He broke out the cylinder and shook the shells onto his palm, the three empty ones and three others with flat-nosed slugs still in place. *The son of a bitch,* thought Cooper, feeling how close he'd come to being left there in the cab bleeding all over hell.

He got out of the cab and walked to the entrance, holding the gun with his finger hooked through the trigger guard, the cylinder out, the shells in his left hand. He pushed through the door.

The cops behind the counter watched him intently as he approached, eyes flicking from his face to the gun and back again. One was black and one was white, and he had their full attention. He laid the gun gently on the counter and put the shells beside it. "I just took this off a guy who tried to stick me up," he said. The black cop was sitting at a desk; he stared at Cooper for a moment.

"Where's the guy?" he said.

"Lying in the street. 33rd and . . . I don't know, just east of Michigan. Prairie, one of those streets in there."

"Lying in the street."

"I ran over him with the cab. Broke his legs. Cab's outside with three bullet holes in it."

The two cops looked at one another, then back at Cooper.

"Sounds like you've been having an exciting evening," the black cop said.

Two other cops took him back to 33rd and Giles in a squad, but when they got there the block was deserted. Cooper showed them the tire marks he'd left and told them exactly how it had happened. The figures in the shadows were gone and all the houses were dark.

"Somebody dragged him off, I guess," said the older cop, a tired gray-haired man.

"He sure as hell didn't walk away," said the other. "Not if you ran over him twice." He gave Cooper a long veiled look in the light from the streetlamps, chewing hard on his gum.

"No. He won't be walking for a while," Cooper said quietly.

"We'll find him. He's probably still lying in the emergency room, up at Reese maybe," said the older one, starting back to the squad.

"Maybe you should have run over his head," the young cop said. "Save us all a lot of trouble."

Back in the squad car heading south the younger one said, "You gotta be nuts, driving down here. Fucking shines—if I was a cabbie I'd never go south of the Loop." Cooper made no comment, staring out the window at the projects marching by above the expressway, lights shining through the wire grills on the walkways. He was weary and still on edge and in no mood to play champion of liberalism.

"You're a lucky man," said the older cop.

"I guess so." Cooper knew it was true. He was conscious again of the grace of survival granted him by a blind universe.

"You got balls, too, sounds like," said the young one. "Lotta cab drivers been in your place before and wound up dead."

The older cop stared at him over the seat back for a moment. "This kind of thing ever happen to you before?"

Cooper watched the city fly by in the night. "More than I care to remember," he said.

2

T HE MAN IN the phone booth said, "What'd you get?"
"Easiest job I ever did," said the deep voice at the other end of the line. "Took me half a day to find him. He's not hiding from anybody."

"No. We'd lost track of him, that's all."

"Yeah. Well, I sent a complete report to your office, along with an itemized bill about two items long. I wish I could charge you more, but I didn't hardly get warmed up before I found him."

"I appreciate the quick work. Listen, I'm not at the office now and I need the dope. Can you read me his coordinates?"

"No problem. He's hanging out at some female relative's place, exact relation I don't know but that's where they tell me he sleeps. 1521 North Spaulding, right near the park. The lady's name is Maria Cruz."

"Got it," said the man in the phone booth.

"I waited for him to come out and followed him to the place where he drinks, on North Avenue. Bar called the Río de Bayamón. That's B-A . . ."

"Yeah, I know. Bayamón."

"I went in and had a beer. Pure PR but nobody hassled me and I got a close look at him, to confirm the description and all. He got himself a nice tattoo inside. You know, one of those crude blue ink jobs? You'll love it. I put all that in the report."

"OK. Thanks a lot. You do good work."

"Just put in an honest day. Hey, listen."

"Yeah?"

"I'd handle this guy carefully if I were you."

"Meaning?"

"Meaning he's a rough customer. I don't get the impression his time away reformed him very much."

"We'll handle with care. We think he'll agree to cooperate. We've got an offer he can't refuse."

"Well, I don't know how much stock a jury's going to put in what this guy says. He's a shitbird. Know what he was inside for?"

"Yeah, we know. We're not dealing with John Q. Citizen here."

"Not by a long shot. Let me tell you, I don't deal with the nicest people all the time, but this guy scares me a little."

After he hung up, the man in the phone booth thought for a moment, just letting the jitters subside, replaying it all. His voice had been fine, calm and nondescript, and a cheap private detective wasn't going to be recording all his calls.

He stepped out onto the pavement. The itemized bill would bounce around the offices of the very large and very respectable Loop law firm for a while until someone asked who the hell had hired this guy and then maybe there would be some trouble about paying him. Too bad; he really had done good work.

"So would you do it again? Pick up the same kind of guy, I mean, and take him down there?"

Cooper put down his coffee cup with a mild thump and looked at Diana across the table. She sat with arms folded across the front of her terrycloth robe, a loose strand of auburn hair curving gracefully past the corner of one eye, down a faintly freckled cheek and around the chin. The look in her dark Latin eyes was grave, inquiring. Cooper told her what he had decided while lying next to her sleepless in the early morning.

"Sure. If I decide he looks OK. That's what it's all about, making the judgment calls. When you stop making the hard judgment calls and just say 'no more blacks,' that's when you become a racist."

Diana swept the strand of hair behind her ear, gave a dubious shake of the head, and rose to clear dishes. "I hope to God you don't make any more bad calls," she said.

"Me too," said Cooper, pulling the paper toward him. "Know what it was, I think? The glasses. Who the hell expects a guy with glasses to stick you up?"

"You should get out of that cab, get yourself a job sitting on something that doesn't move."

Cooper looked at her with amused eyes as she dumped plates in the sink with a clatter. Aware she had stepped over the boundary, she shot him a sheepish glance, came over, and ran a hand gently through his brown curling hair and down his shoulder, then passed both arms around his neck and bent to embrace him gently from behind. "Sorry. But I worry about you, Coop." The faint trace of her Puerto Rican upbringing was back in her speech, as always when she was disconcerted.

"Good to know somebody does." Cooper laid the paper and placed his hands over hers.

"I'm glad you came over," she said.

"You're the only person I knew I could wake up at four in the morning."

"Come over some morning when you haven't been shot at. Just for fun."

"Sounds good. I like fun." He smiled.

She squeezed. "You were a bit shook, weren't you?"

"A bit." Cooper closed his eyes and felt her breath on his neck, remembering the need he'd felt after finally speeding back north in the shattered cab, done with the cops, done with the claims adjuster. He'd needed Diana's warmth, and she'd taken him into her bed, unfettered, fierce, finally tender, the comfort Cooper had wanted. Now in the late morning light, the ambiguity was back.

Diana kissed his unshaven cheek, straightened, and returned to the sink. Cooper watched her slender form beneath the robe for a moment and then took up the paper again. He turned without great interest through its pages. Election buildup he avoided on principle, reports of continuing crisis in Poland bored him, Chicago politics was beyond his grasp in its Byzantine perversity. He scanned the crime reports, knowing his adventure would not have made it into the paper but looking anyway. Rapes, a knifing, a sixteen-year-old convicted of murder. Misery, despair, disintegration. HIGH-RISE SUICIDE STUNS NEIGHBORS.

Cooper had almost turned the page when the name caught his eye. He stared at it for a moment, frozen, then carefully cleared a space on the table and laid the paper down to read the article. Before he could begin he had to stare at the name again.

Vivian Horstmann. It was unmistakable. Cooper knew immediately that he had found news of her at last. His brow contracting slowly, he read.

Residents of 3472 N. Lake Shore Drive struggled to understand Thursday what drove gallery owner Vivian Horstmann to leap from the balcony of her 23rd floor condominium to her death on the pavement below. Horstmann, 36, was found early Thursday morning by a building security guard, apparently shortly after jumping to her death.

Cooper had to raise his eyes from the page. It was too grotesque, to hear of her like this, after—what, fifteen years? The age was right. Vivian had been twenty-one or thereabouts in 1973. Grimacing, he read on. Police had investigated. She'd left a note; apparently there was a son. Mention was made of an estranged husband. Cooper doubted for a moment—if Horstmann was her married name, it was not the same woman. And yet he was convinced that chance would not give the same name to two different women. This woman had owned a gallery, something he could well imagine his Vivian doing, and professional women usually kept their maiden names, he thought, especially after a divorce. He read more. Following quotes from the bewildered neighbors there was terse speculation that she had been driven to suicide by depression over her failing gallery and the recent breakup of her marriage.

Cooper sat rereading the article and then staring at the table until Diana noticed his stillness and asked what was wrong.

"I know this woman." He tapped the article with a finger. "Knew her," he corrected himself.

"God. The woman who jumped off her balcony?"

"Mm. I knew her in college."

"How awful." Diana came over from the sink and rested a hand lightly on his shoulder.

The past was the correct tense, Cooper reflected. For the Vivian he had known to have ended her life like this, unfath-

omable changes had to have taken place in fifteen years. He
gave a quick shake of the head and turned the page.

"Were you good friends?" asked Diana with her habitual
gentleness.

Cooper had to look out the back door at the sunlit bricks
across the alley and think before answering. "No, I guess we
never really were," he said.

Cooper had decided to give himself a break for the weekend; he wasn't anxious to step into another cab right away.
He'd had a good couple of weeks and could afford to coast
for a while. He left Diana with a promise to call her and
drove his old Valiant to the bank to deposit his hard-won two
hundred dollars. Then he went home.

Cooper lived near the lake in a neighborhood that was
about as mixed as Chicago ever gets. There were blacks and
whites, Russians and Haitians, Mexicans and Koreans, and a
little of everything else. There were students from Loyola and
Northwestern and black families taking the first step up out
of the projects and yups who worked downtown and even
some well-to-do families hanging on to sizable houses. There
were a lot of people like Cooper, neither rich nor poor, neither professional nor unemployed, without families but not
always lonely. There were those who insisted the neighborhood was the next great frontier for gentrification and those
who were sure it was about to slide into abysmal poverty.
There was a fair amount of petty crime, a lot of litter, and a
good deal of tolerance making the whole thing bearable.
Cooper liked it because he could live near the lake cheaply
and he kept running into people he knew on the street.

He made it home to the brick six-flat just west of Sheridan
Road and took a shower and lay on his couch looking out at
the yellowing leaves tossing outside his window. The books
sat in stacks on the old oak desk in the corner, reproaching
him. Progress had come hard in the last month. Cooper's
resolution had flagged: he had begun to doubt that the world
was in need of another scholarly commentary on war. He
reminded himself that it was for his own therapeutic benefit
that he had begun the project, then finally rose from the couch
and approached the desk, where the titles leapt at him with
the promise of enlightenment: *Fire in the Lake, The Rise and*

Fall of an American Army, The Open Society and its Enemies.

Cooper turned away from the papers and meandered across the worn carpet back to the window. He wasn't ready to sit and work. There was a bright autumn afternoon outside and the lake nearby. And things to think about. Cooper came away from the window, admitting at last his need to be sure. He went to the milk crate at the end of the couch that served as telephone stand and pulled out the directory. On second thought he set it down and hauled out the Yellow Pages, and under ART GALLERIES, DEALERS AND CONSULTANTS he ran his eye down the columns. HORSTMANN GALLERY THE had an address on Superior. Cooper hesitated for a moment and dialed the number. He was suddenly daunted, uncertain what to ask, uncertain how to identify a dead woman over the phone.

The phone at the other end gave five rings and Cooper realized that the gallery would naturally be closed in the wake of the catastrophe. He was on the point of hanging up when there was a click and the soft whirr of an answering machine.

"You have reached the Horstmann Gallery. The gallery is closed at this time, but you may leave a message after the tone. The Horstmann Gallery is open Tuesday to Saturday from ten to six, Sunday from noon to six, and Monday from eleven to five. Please leave your message after the tone. Thank you."

Cooper sat chilled with the phone to his ear as the beep went off and a gentle hiss came over the line. He cut off the connection with his thumb, waited a moment, and dialed again. He listened to the message once more and hung up.

Unmistakable. The voice was Vivian's, the accents well-remembered, the fluid unhurried diction distinctive. Even after fifteen years, even in the impersonal reading of a prepared message, he could not mistake it. He sat for a time uncertain of his feelings, bemused by the sound of a dead woman's voice. Finally he rose, took his jacket, and left the apartment.

Autumn had set in and the breeze by the lake had a bite to it. The sky held only a few high trails of cloud and the lake was a cold bright gray. Cooper wandered north along the deserted beach at the water's edge, looking for bits of colored glass ground smooth by the sand, wasting time, staving off memory.

Eventually he made his way south again and walked out on the long breakwater with the light at its farthest point. The fishermen had packed it in for the year and there was only a solitary cyclist at the end where Cooper liked to stand and look at the distant skyline of the Loop or turn away from the city and imagine he was at the prow of a ship, forging toward an unknown continent. The bicyclist, his solitude disturbed, wheeled around, mounted, and left Cooper alone.

Cooper was prone to attacks of memory. When he felt an attack coming on he liked to occupy himself, find company, or drink himself to sleep. It was not that all of his memories were bad, only that they left him too conscious of his help-lessness in the face of time. They made him feel like a man who has lost some valued object over the stern of a ship and sees it bobbing on the surface behind, farther and farther away. But Cooper had learned that when memory attacked, it was hard to fight it; he could only remember.

So Cooper remembered. He remembered the fall of 1972, the season of his reentry into the world. The time in Germany had provided valuable decompression. The bright green of the jungle and the smell of bodies had receded, muted by the tedium of peacetime soldiering. He had needed to be insulated a bit from the unconcern of the world, its staggering indif- ference to the price he'd paid in the A Shau Valley; two years in Mannheim had allowed him to cool a bit and glimpse a future beyond the Army. The future was called College.

In 1972 he was almost twenty-three and a freshman, anx-ious to claim what most of his peers had been given at eigh-teen. The college was a prosperous little liberal arts institution that drew heavily from the Chicago area, a cluster of red brick buildings in a little Illinois town. Cooper let his hair and beard grow, put on a little weight, let the easy life round off some of the hard edges. He hit the books hard, glad to feel his mind working again. He had survived and he was free.

He didn't quite fit, however. He was a lifetime older than the seniors who had gone on from high school at eighteen. He despised the men and made half-hearted efforts to chase the women, whom he called girls; his world-weariness put them off and after a month he began to despise them, too. He despised them all because they'd been flirting in the library while he was rotting in the monsoon rains.

Cooper didn't like being a political symbol, either. The war was winding down, but they were still bombing the North, and there were enough small-time radicals on campus to produce an occasional ragged demonstration. Cooper did his best to ignore them, not yet able to discuss the whole thing dispassionately but aware that if he let the hostility get to him he wouldn't be able to stick it out. Nobody spit on him or called him a baby killer or any of the other classic mythical abuses, but there were a couple of accusatory approaches to debate, which Cooper sidestepped. Worst were the couple of profs who, while never actually baiting him, trailed significant glances at him while voicing outrage at the abuse of American power. *Say what you want,* Cooper smoldered silently, *but don't talk to me about power.* The Soviet and Chinese firepower he'd walked into in the A Shau—they never talked about that power, and while Cooper was willing to grant them, from bitter experience, a lot of points on the senselessness of the war, he remembered too well that all the power he had wielded had barely sufficed to get him out of Vietnam alive.

He fell in with the few other vets on campus, men like himself who had been there, who were back with the same chip on the shoulder. They wore old field jackets and cultivated thick moustaches and spent a lot of time stoned. Most of them were phony vets, guys who concocted great tales out of nice safe tours in Chu Lai or Cam Ranh Bay. The one other guy who Cooper knew had seen a lot of hard combat was an ex-marine named Owen who moved in a catlike nervous silence and drank till his eyes watered. He disappeared quietly sometime in the second semester and Cooper was left to lounge with the others on the long sagging porch, with the conviction slowly dawning that he would never quite fit again, ever.

It was then that he met Vivian Horstmann. He met her at the house of a prof who had invited the class over on a Sunday evening. It was a 300-level elective that Cooper had taken to meet upperclassmen, and most of the others were juniors

and seniors. Vivian was not in the class but she came tagging
along with a friend who was. It was a genteel sort of evening
with white wine and earnest conversation, and Cooper had
been feeling uncouth for requesting beer and largely left out
of the swirling social currents. He was perched on the arm
of a chair morosely surveying the proceedings when Vivian
walked in, and as he watched her move across the room and
heard her speak, the evening was suddenly salvaged for him.

Vivian was a slender but rounded five-six or so with light
brown hair that fell in waves to her shoulders. That night she
wore brown corduroy slacks and a white angora sweater that
clung tightly enough to outline her figure. The single feature
of her face that Cooper was later aware of as having captured
him, more than the wide blue eyes, was the full lips. Cooper
could never adequately describe the face to anyone and in the
depths of his infatuation even found himself unable to clearly
picture it in her absence. He knew only that it was distinctive,
absolutely unique, incapable of being typed.

Cooper watched her surreptitiously and when she moved
out of the room it was not long before he felt propelled to
follow. He trailed her with quiet cunning for a while, eaves-
dropping and stealing glances, until he was finally introduced
to her by a classmate and smiled at her. Her returned smile
was his first reward, and it sealed his fate.

Cooper spent a good deal of time later unhappily musing
on love, but he was never able to understand the alchemy that
kindled his passion for Vivian. If sheer physical beauty were
the standard Cooper would have named four or five other
women first. It was a complex of things—the grace of her
movements, the music of her speech, mostly perhaps the good
will that she radiated. In a scientific mood, he supposed there
was some mechanism for fixing the psyche on what it needed
most. Cooper knew only that it had begun the moment he'd
seen her.

His first thought when he woke up the next morning was
of Vivian, and he knew he was lovesick. At first it was cause
for optimism; at last he had met someone worth pursuing.

But Vivian proved elusive. He began to watch for her on
campus and to see her everywhere, but the disease was working and he had become clumsy, tongue-tied, and dull. He
descended on her as she sat alone and spoke inanities; she

was far too courteous ever to repay him with coldness, but he knew from the start that he was making a poor impression. He raged at himself and planned new strategies; she slipped away with her friends and left him standing, looking urgently for something to do to cover his discomfort.

Vivian lived with four other women in a white frame house three blocks from campus. The women had lots of visitors and Cooper became one of them, dropping by late at night or on idle afternoons, hoping to see Vivian, lingering for hours making small talk with her housemates. It was not a bad strategy; the context was informal and he could disguise his intentions. He was not the only hanger-on and he became an accepted figure at the gatherings in the living room, passing the wine bottle or the roach, listening to the Doors or the Stones or the obscure folk singers favored by the women, listening to talk about *Gravity's Rainbow* or Einstein or hitchhiking to Peru. Cooper liked the people because they almost never talked about politics or the war. He sat quietly peering across the room at Vivian through the cigarette haze, trying to memorize her features. She sat with her particular grace, her wavy hair pulled back in a ponytail, sipping wine while her bright wide eyes surveyed the room over the rim of the glass. She was never bored or drunk or sleepy; occasionally she flashed the smile that haunted Cooper. He never succeeded in catching her alone.

Cooper heard references to an absent suitor of Vivian's that plunged him into a mad jealousy. Cooper's rival had graduated the year before and gone off to business school; when he came back for a visit and Cooper saw him hand in hand with Vivian, Cooper stared at him dumbly, wounded by Vivian's affection for this prosperous and confident man.

After that Cooper pursued Vivian hopelessly, sinking deeper into misery. Grateful for crumbs, he came by fits and starts to be on ordinary speaking terms with her. She was the daughter of a professor of economics and had grown up in Evanston, Illinois. That Chicago suburb was forever sanctified for Cooper. She was a senior English major and she loved Faulkner. Cooper labored his way through *The Sound and the Fury* one week just to have something to talk about with her.

He wanted desperately to impress her, but he had nothing

to impress her with except his survival. She knew more than he did about everything except death. She had grown up in the city, in sophistication and erudition; he had grown up in a little Indiana town, the son of a Presbyterian minister. She could discuss Rilke and Mann and Kandinsky and Braque; he was still in Western Civ 102. He sometimes wished he could tell her about the war, but he realized he had no idea whether her regard for him would grow or diminish if she knew about the A Shau Valley, about his Bronze Star and his Purple Hearts. He knew she wasn't the type to be impressed by heroics, and he wasn't sure he could tell her about the war without getting agitated anyway. When she finally asked him why he had joined the Army, the first personal question she had favored him with in two months, he told her the simple truth—he had joined to show people that a preacher's kid didn't have to be a sissy. He knew it had been a stupid reason and he told her so, watching the wide blue eyes blink at him, wondering if she thought he was still stupid. She smiled faintly and fell silent and that was the end of the conversation.

In bed at night Cooper felt the deep dull pain of her remoteness and wondered why it had to be that way. He knew that if he could only win her the nightmares that still woke him would slack off and his hair-trigger temper would be tamed and he wouldn't feel compelled to drink so much. He believed that only if he won her would the hard, mean, dark part of him be subdued.

He confided in no one. There was no one he would entrust the secret to except Vivian herself. His solitude made things worse. All the classic symptoms plagued him: he ate little and found it hard to concentrate on his books and walked with a weight on his chest. When he awoke from one of his nightmares gasping, he thought immediately of her and wished fiercely to feel her in his arms and tried vainly to make her face appear clearly to him.

It was never sexual; Cooper never lusted for Vivian. This was something else. He knew dispassionately that he would want someday to take her to bed, but that was not what he daydreamed of. His passion was bound up with her beauty, he knew, but its satisfaction would not be physical, not first. He wanted first and above all her acceptance. He wanted her to feel for him what he felt for her, just a part of it, just a little, just for a moment.

He knew it was impossible, and he was bewildered and angry. He took refuge in a hurried and humorless affair with a sophomore girl. It was a relief of a sort but without destination, and they dropped it after three weeks. After that there was a series of trysts with a townie divorcée that ended quickly in a drunken scene. Cooper wanted no one but Vivian.

As the spring of 1973 drew on toward summer, Cooper felt the world ending. Vivian was a senior and would be graduating. He paced the campus in numb despair. He was getting by in his classes but he wasn't sure he wanted to come back in the fall; college had lost its appeal, and he thought of heading out to the West Coast to sit by the ocean and forget. Without Vivian there was no reason to stay.

Worst was the fact that he had still never managed to make his feelings clear to her. He had not once, not even by his slyest stratagems, succeeded in finding himself alone with her for the time necessary to declare himself. There was always someone else there or not enough time. He had asked her out directly twice, to be gently, sweetly refused. Having abandoned hope of winning her, he had decided to try for just telling her. He had begun to think that if only he could tell her, however abjectly, it would release him. But she was leaving.

Then he was suddenly given a reprieve. Vivian and two of her friends from the house would be staying in town after graduation. Granting themselves a final summer of comradeship before dispersing to take up adulthood, they had gotten themselves jobs waitressing at the country club. They would have to move out of the college-owned white frame house, but they had agreed with a professor to stay in his house while he was in Europe.

Cooper revived. There was a factory on the edge of town that made prefabricated steel buildings and hired a lot of summer labor. Cooper got himself a job and called his parents to tell them he would not be home for the summer. He had been looking for an excuse in any event; he could not abide his parents since his return from the war. He arranged for a room in a boarding house and planned his campaign.

Vivian and her friends graduated with honors and moved into the professor's house. Cooper anticipated a summer full of opportunities to be with Vivian.

The flaw in his plan became evident immediately. Vivian worked nights and weekends; Cooper worked days in the welding department, which went six days a week. His opportunities to see Vivian were reduced to Tuesday and Wednesday night, her nights off, or Sunday morning, when Cooper was too exhausted to lever himself out of bed even for love.

With time and a half on Saturday, Cooper made a fortune that summer. He enjoyed none of it. He got through the days as best he could, feeling as if he were in the Army again, fighting tedium doing something he hated. At night he made his way slowly down the block to call on one of his veteran friends who was still in town. They sat on the porch drinking beer, watching a ball game on the portable TV or just watching people drive by. He shot pool on the worn tables in Duffy's Bar on the bad side of town and acquired a cut over his left eye in the scrap that got him warned off the premises. He took long walks by night along the railroad tracks, past the ragged edge of the town and out into the country, brooding, feeling his sanity dribble away, waiting for another Tuesday night.

On Tuesdays and Wednesdays he dropped by the professor's house without fail, to find Vivian just leaving to go play tennis, or having a dinner party with friends who had come in from out of town, or absent altogether, out somewhere with unnamed companions who stoked the fires of Cooper's jealousy. A few times he was lucky; he sat for an evening in the living room or out in the backyard with Vivian and her friends or accompanied them to a movie. He tried his best to be bright and interesting, to contribute to the conversation, to make Vivian notice him as a man, as a person who knew things and had traveled and was sensitive to the kinds of things she was sensitive to. Too often, he knew, he was merely a melancholy presence in the corner, uninvited and politely tolerated.

He lingered until the household readied itself for bed, hoping for a chance to isolate Vivian, take her outside for a walk, corner her in the kitchen, collar her on the porch. She was cleverer than he and always slipped his grasp. Driven to boldness by his desperation, he called her and once again asked her out point-blank; she thanked him graciously and produced an excuse. He was on the point of blurting out his declaration over the phone, but he was unable and the moment passed.

A couple of times that summer his rival came into town to see Vivian, and Cooper's misery plumbed the depths. The rival's name was Nick something or other and he was hearty and tanned and making a lot of money doing something in New York and he wore his hair short and neat and wore sports shirts and slacks. Cooper was physically pained by Vivian's preference for him and had to stay away while he knew Nick was in town. Cooper was obscurely aware that he just couldn't compete with the Nicks of the world, just wasn't really in Vivian's league.

One fine night as he sat on the railroad overpass outside of town waiting for the Santa Fe to come roaring along a yard from his toes and scare the hell out of him, Cooper was finally able to put his finger on the reason. Ever since he had stepped off the plane coming back alive from Vietnam, Cooper had considered himself an adult. At nineteen he had felt as old as war itself, having been shoved right out to the far edge of things and learned the fundamental lesson that the really significant thing about life is how close death is. Cooper knew that he was older in one way than Vivian or Nick or anyone else he knew would ever be. But that night he realized that in other ways he was still the pimply preacher's kid who'd had to sweat over the phone for a half hour before working up the courage to ask a girl for a date. Vivian and her friends were adults in all the ways that mattered back in the world—they had learned the ropes, had spent four years getting together, breaking up, learning the signals and codes and rules of love, learning to handle desire and jealousy. Meanwhile, Cooper had been learning to handle pain and terror. He'd learned it about as well as it can be learned, but the knowledge was useless to him now.

Two people got him through that summer—Mack McKee and Ellen Sims. McKee was the other veteran, Cooper's porch drinking partner. Cooper hadn't much liked him at first but McKee grew on him over the summer. McKee hadn't had an especially tough tour over there, as far as Cooper could tell, but at least he never tried to get mileage out of horseshit stories. He was a cheerful cynic and he knew everybody on campus and half the townies as well, and he was good for Cooper's spirits. Cooper actually confided in him about Vivian toward the end of the summer, downplaying or omitting the more degrading aspects of his condition, and McKee chuckled and handed him another beer and told him it was bad to ever let a woman get under your skin. He advised Cooper to get out of town and as far away from her as he could.

Ellen Sims was one of Vivian's housemates, a plump, quiet, angelic girl who had taken a Summa Cum Laude in philosophy and was going on to the University of Chicago to do great things in the fall. Of all Vivian's circle she was the one that Cooper actually felt the most comfortable with, the one who occasionally seemed actually to welcome his presence at the professor's house, who talked to him directly in an effort to include him in the conversation. Cooper took to going by the house sometimes on Thursday evenings, when Ellen was off work and alone, just to sit and talk with her comfortably and hope for crumbs of information about Vivian. Ellen talked to him with genuine interest, asking him about the factory, about his background and his plans, even eventually about the war. Cooper blessed her for her friendship and slunk away guiltily, knowing that what he really valued Ellen for was her proximity to Vivian.

June passed into a sluggish July, which expired and gave way to a worn tired August. The summer was ending and Cooper's passion was still undeclared. Ellen Sims packed up and left for Chicago and Cooper knew that the end was near. There would be no more reprieves. He sat in astonishment, realizing that he had impotently let the summer slip away.

All Cooper's desires had come down to one thing; simply to tell Vivian what she had done to the last six months of his life. He had no more illusions, no more fantasies; he only wanted to let her know how much she had made him love her, and then let her go off to her future with someone else.

On a stifling August night Cooper sat on McKee's porch with his feet up on the rail and half-listened as McKee listed the virtues of a thirty-six-year-old peroxide blond he had met at a roadside tavern just out of town. Cooper had had no chance to talk to Vivian in the past few days. The remaining housemate had left, and then Vivian's parents had descended unexpectedly for a short visit. Cooper had feared they would take Vivian away with them, but they had not. They had left Vivian with a car she was to drive to New York, to join Nick. Cooper knew she was intending to leave in the next couple of days.

At eleven o'clock he took his feet down, crushed the empty beer can and tossed it in the box with the other empties, and stood up. He took his leave of McKee and turned his steps toward the professor's house. On the way he rehearsed. He stood for a moment under a sycamore across the street from the house. A light burned behind the curtains in the living room. The night vibrated with the electric hum of insect noises. Cooper crossed the street slowly and mounted the porch. He was through worrying about making a fool of himself; he'd been doing that for six months anyway. He rang the bell and waited.

Vivian came to the door dressed in the calico housedress that was far out of style but fell about her hips so gracefully. She stood motionless for a moment in the doorway looking at Cooper. Her face showed no surprise, no welcome. "Hi, Vivian," said Cooper quietly.

"Hello, Coop." She stood aside to let him come in. She watched him with what he imagined was dread as he passed by her; she had run out of defenses at last.

Cooper turned to face her in the middle of the living room. The room was lit by a single lamp at the end of the couch under the front window. "I was afraid you'd leave town before I got a chance to talk to you." He felt weary; he would tell her quickly and be done with it.

"I'm leaving tomorrow," she said. She stood looking at him, blinking slowly. His heart sank as he looked into her eyes; the usual gentle tolerance, the courtesy that had borne all his importunate arrivals for half a year, was gone. She looked resigned, exhausted, run to earth.

"Driving alone all the way to New York?" asked Cooper. He could not bear to come to the point.

She nodded and walked across the room to the cabinet

against the far wall. "Want something to drink?" She picked up a tall glass half full of a clear iced drink. The doors of the cabinet were open and the professor's liquor stock gleamed on the shelves.

Cooper nodded slowly. "Sure." He'd never seen Vivian drink anything but beer or wine.

She waved vaguely at the bottles. "Rum, vodka, that's scotch I guess . . . What do you want?"

Cooper didn't answer and she looked back at him, waiting for his answer. "No, I guess not really," he said. "Vivian, I have to talk to you."

She came slowly away from the cabinet on legs that suddenly looked unsteady to Cooper. She walked to the couch on bare feet and sank onto it and stared into her drink. "I'm listening," she said.

Cooper knew he had done this to her; she had known he would come and steeled herself for it with drink. He was still standing like a rube in the middle of the floor with his thumbs hooked in the pockets of his jeans. He moved stiffly to the other end of the couch and sat down. Leaning forward with his elbows on his knees staring at the Persian rug, he knew there was no elegant way to say what he had to say. "I've been in love with you ever since I first saw you," he said, his voice to his chagrin going husky. He looked up to see her eyes rise to his. He wasn't sure what he saw there, whether it was pity or apprehension or scorn, but it wasn't surprise. She looked down at her drink again.

"I know," she said.

"Yeah, I guess it must have been pretty obvious." Cooper passed a hand over his brow and felt the words coming, the relief that had been a long time coming. "Vivian, I'm sorry. I know there's nothing I can ask from you, nothing you can give me. I know you're involved with someone else and all that . . . I know even if you weren't you might not give me the time of day. I'm not here to ask anything. I just have to tell you I think . . ." He ran out of words and spread his hands helplessly as she looked up again, alarmed perhaps. ". . . just that I've never . . ."

"It's all right, Coop."

"I've never known anybody like you. I . . ."

"It's all right." Vivian sat forward and stretched out a hand to touch his knee. He stopped, knowing he could babble all night if she'd let him. He looked down at his hands shamefully and then into her face again. This time he was sure it was pity as she let her hand fall back and leaned back again. "I knew. I understood. I'm sorry I couldn't . . ." She smiled, just a little, and her gaze wandered out over the carpet.

"I'm not asking for anything."

"I know. I know how it is."

"I know it couldn't have been too much fun with me hanging around like a sick dog and I'm sorry for that."

"It's all right, Cooper, it really is."

He wanted to tell her just a bit more and then he would leave her alone. He had to tell her what she meant to him, what he imagined she could mean. She was still staring at the floor. She took a drink and as she swallowed with a gulp, he realized that she had drunk a lot.

He was calmer and his voice was back. "Vivian, I've never been like this over anyone before. You can't imagine . . ."

"Yes I can." She set her drink down on the coffee table and leaned toward him. She put her hand on his forearm and rested it there. They looked at each other for a moment, Cooper astonished at her granting him that intimacy. Her long undulating hair was unbound, falling past the face he had tried to picture over the months. He looked at her in suspense, slowly realizing that it wasn't just pity in her eyes, but something else—sadness, maybe. Her mouth was slightly open and Cooper wondered how he hadn't seen right away that she was drunk. They went on looking at each other and Cooper saw her struggling. He waited for what she would say, sorry for causing her distress, wanting now only to tell her he was sorry and get out.

Vivian shifted around slowly on the couch and switched off the lamp. Cooper sat as still as marble. He heard Vivian come scooting slowly along the couch toward him, and felt her arm go around his shoulders. There was just a bit of light coming in around the edges of the curtain and as his eyes adjusted he could make out the dark outline of her face.

"You want me." She breathed the words close to his ear and Cooper caught a whiff of something, whatever she was drinking. He was motionless. She had both arms around his neck now and she was pulling him gently toward her.

Cooper was too stunned to do anything but go along, to let himself be pulled down alongside her on the couch, wrapping his arms around her. A detached part of him told him that this was not what he wanted, but he didn't find the wherewithal to resist.

Vivian put her lips to his and kissed him. Her tongue was cold and tasted of drink. He pulled back for a moment and tried to look at her through the dark, bewildered. She kissed him again and whispered, "You have me."

She slid a hand slowly up his back under his T-shirt. She tugged at it gently and Cooper, in shock, sat up and took it off. Vivian pulled the skirt of the dress up with both hands and Cooper could just see long pale legs in the darkness. She arched her back to get the dress past her hips and he made out the white of her panties. He felt no arousal, only astonishment.

"Help me," Vivian whispered, struggling to sit up. He pulled her upright and helped her get the dress off over her head. He felt one bare breast brush against his chest. Vivian pulled him close and found his mouth with hers again. He lingered, trying to enjoy the kiss as much as she apparently wanted him to, as much as he had dreamed of enjoying it. The detached part of him was saying that this was all wrong, but the rest of him was trying hard not to embarrass himself.

Vivian lay down and waited for him to undress. He laboriously got out of his shoes and socks and pants and then sat on the edge of the couch and pulled her panties down with great concentration, all the way down the long pale legs and off past the ankles. He dropped them on the floor and knew his last chance to stop had come and gone.

He felt no real arousal until Vivian reached down and gently took his penis in her hand. All the foreplay was on her part; he was too reverent with her body to touch her the way a lover would. On top of her and inside her at last, he felt sure he was going to be impotent and then he panicked and began to fantasize furiously, thinking of the whores in Saigon and the barmaids in Mannheim who had given him sexual pleasure, knowing he was sullying his experience but knowing at the same time that it should never have happened.

After release he lay holding Vivian on the narrow couch and trying not to feel cheated. One of his voices said he had gotten exactly what he wanted while another truer one said this wasn't it at all, not by a long shot; she'd given him exactly the wrong thing.

Vivian did not say a word afterward, not a single word. She lay breathing heavily into his ear, motionless. Cooper lay looking at the faint bands of light on the ceiling for a long time and then disengaged himself from her. She was either asleep or pretending to be, maybe even passed out. Cooper dressed quickly, getting angry. When he was dressed he knelt by her head and said simply, "Good-bye, Vivian." She stirred, pushed out an exploratory hand in the dark, and said drowsily, "Bye." Cooper clasped her hand once, found no desire to kiss her, and left.

He walked across the deserted town in a fever of conflicting feelings. By the time he got back to his house anger was dominant again, anger with Vivian for thinking that that was what he wanted, anger with himself for not telling her it wasn't, for taking another crumb from her. That was what it had been, just a bigger crumb. The biggest, soggiest of all. It had spoiled once and forever his passion for her.

He never saw Vivian again.

The chill was starting to get to Cooper's feet, dangling over the edge of the pier five feet above the cold green water of the lake. He was stiff as he hauled himself up and climbed back through the restraining cables. The sun was sinking low over the trees at the edge of the park behind him. It was time to go someplace warm and have something to drink.

The whole business had left him with a bad taste for a long time, made him wince at the memory until other successes and failures in love had finally washed it out. He'd finally forgiven Vivian and forgiven himself. Her conduct no longer mystified him; she had been drunk, tired of his lurking presence, hoping to put an end to his infatuation, maybe even, Cooper sometimes dared to think, a little bit attracted to him after all. He would never know.

Cooper didn't like funerals and he wasn't even sure how

to go about finding out where this one was to be, but he knew he had to go. Reading of her death in the paper, hearing her voice on the phone, he had again felt the hook she had put into him. He wanted to give Vivian a better good-bye than before, now that it was too late.

3

RICHIE WAITED IN the Camaro until Bobby came and rapped on the window. "Nobody home," said Bobby. Richie got out and they walked down the alley together and went up the back stairs.

"Perfect," said Bobby quietly. "The way this place is built, can't nobody see us except from that one window way down at the end." He had the masking tape out of his pocket and was already peeling strips off it and putting them on the window in the back door. "Just stand there blocking the view and look casual. Somebody looks out, they'll think we're fixing the door or something."

Richie leaned on the rail with his arms folded and watched Bobby work. He'd never gone in much for breaking into places but Bobby claimed to be an expert. Richie looked over his shoulder at the one window at the far end of the porch.

"For Christ's sake quit looking around," breathed Bobby. "You know better than that."

Richie looked at the little white guy with the blue bandanna around his greasy blond hair and thought again how he didn't much like him except he did come up with good jobs.

"All set." Bobby put the tape back in his pocket and turned to face Richie. He had a bored look on his face but Richie knew he was feeling the same nervous high.

Bobby pivoted away from the door and raised his elbow and then twisted back, driving the elbow into the glass hard. There was a crack but the masking tape kept the big pieces of glass from falling and it wouldn't really sound like a window breaking to anyone who heard it. Bobby pushed at the glass and caved in a section of it. He stuck his arm in up to the elbow and started feeling for the lock, frowning with the effort. "Move over a bit, right here next to the door," he growled. "Just in case somebody looks out."

There was a click inside. Bobby pushed in a little further and wrenched at something and the door gave way slightly. Bobby smiled at Richie like he was some kind of genius, waiting for Richie to applaud. "Just the one lock," said Bobby. He pulled his arm out carefully, moving glass out of the way with his other hand so it wouldn't tear up his jean jacket. Then they went in.

They closed the door behind them and stood listening for a moment, just to make sure. The kitchen was small and there were dishes piled in the sink and it smelled like a trash dumpster. There was an empty Jim Beam bottle on the counter.

After a few seconds Bobby turned back to the window and pulled out the tape again. "You go up front and watch. I'll fix this up a little, in case somebody comes down the steps." He was talking a little louder, but still quiet. Richie left the kitchen and went slowly through the place toward the front. The apartment didn't have much furniture, just a few beat up chairs and a table, and up in the front room a couch that looked like the rats had been at it. Richie took a look out the front window and then had to go look in the bedroom and bathroom because he liked the feeling of poking around in people's houses when they weren't there, thinking how pissed off they'd be if they knew he was doing it. The bedroom didn't have much more than a mattress on the floor with some sheets crumpled up on it. Indians, Richie thought. The guy'd probably rather be living in a teepee.

He went back to the front and stood well away from the window, looking out onto the street. This was the worst part, waiting out the first few minutes, waiting to see a squad car pull up out front, getting ready to run like hell if they had to. Fifteen minutes, Bobby had said. If they don't come in fifteen minutes they ain't coming.

Waiting around doing nothing had gotten a lot easier in the joint and it didn't seem too long before he heard Bobby come into the room behind him. "Fuckin' guy must put away a gallon of whiskey a day," Bobby said. "That's where the money goes."

"Indians, man," said Richie. "Can't handle the firewater."

"Yeah. Let's go back in the kitchen."

"The bedroom's better, man."

"Naw. The kitchen. They always come back to the kitchen when they get in, sooner or later. Him for sure, he'll be needing a drink. And there's more to work with back there."

In the kitchen Bobby showed him a coil of rusty wire he'd found by the back door. "We can use this to hold him. Whack him, truss him up, piece of fuckin' cake."

There was one chair. Bobby took it and Richie poked around some more, opening the refrigerator, looking in cabinets. "He got hisself a whole bar up here, man. Want a drink?"

"Why not? He ain't gonna be needing it."

Richie handed him a bottle of vodka and took down a nearly empty flask of Myers for himself. He hiked his butt up on the counter and sat with his feet dangling and took a drink.

"Take it easy. Could be a little wait," said Bobby.

Richie looked at him deadpan. Someday he was going to have to ask this little white shit how come he treated him like he was stupid or something. "Hey, man. I could finish this off and it wouldn't do nothin' to me."

"OK. All's I'm sayin' is we may be here a while. He comes in anytime after five, they tell me. Maybe as late as eight or nine. We gotta be ready."

"I'm ready." Richie reached across to the stove and picked up the cast iron skillet. He hefted it and smiled, his gold tooth flashing. "You can break one of these fuckers if you slam it hard enough on a rock or something. I wonder if you could break it on a knee. Or if the knee would break first."

"I'd bet on the knee," said Bobby. They laughed briefly and Bobby took a swill out of the vodka bottle. "But I don't know. We can do like product testing on it, see if we can bust it."

Richie scanned the kitchen in the growing dark. "When he comes in I'll be by the refrigerator there."

"Just if you use the pan don't hit him too hard the first time. We gotta talk to him."

"Yeah, yeah."

"They says to me, 'Get the money if you can, but if you can't, just make sure he don't get any deeper in.' "

"OK, we make sure. Fuck the man up big time."

"Use the dishrag there for his mouth. I'll tape it in, cover his eyes too."

"Got all kind of mildew and shit growin' on it."

"Nice and tasty."

They sat in silence for a long time. The light slowly faded. Richie finished the rum and set the bottle on the counter beside him. The rum sat in his stomach and sent heat waves out through his body. He was feeling all right. They heard footsteps and faint voices in the apartment upstairs and cars honking out in the street and kids yelling in the alley.

Richie was glad it was too dark now to see Bobby's face. He had that kind of feeling you get when you go to the pussy flicks and you're standing around in the lobby about to go in, joking around but kind of embarrassed to look at one another because you can't hardly wait to get in there and see some action and you don't want to admit how much you're going to like it.

"What's the guy's name?" Richie said softly.

"Mankiller. Believe it or not. One of them goofy Injun names. You believe that shit?"

"Mankiller, huh? Hey, we show him who's the mankillers, huh?"

"You just let me do the talking, man. If we do get the money out of him and leave him we don't want him telling nobody about your accent."

"What accent, man? You the one with the accent."

"All right, shit. You talk English pretty good, you just got the accent, that's all."

" 'Course I talk English pretty good. I fuckin' grew up here. I ain't been on the fuckin' island since I was four years old."

The scratching of a key in the lock came through the darkness from way up at the front of the place. Richie could just make out Bobby standing up and waving a hand at him. He found the handle of the frying pan and eased off the counter. The creak of hinges came down the passage and then someone was inside, muttering to himself. The door closed and a light went on two or three rooms away and Richie was hiding

by the refrigerator, ready, knowing Bobby was right. They
always came back to the kitchen.

His heart was going thump-a-thump-thump and he was
saying to himself silently, *please God don't let him have the
money, don't let him have the money.*

The interior of the church was somber and much more vast
than Cooper had imagined looking at it from outside. Vertical
slashes of stained glass between solid square columns rose
high into the gloom on either side. The coffin, draped in a
white cloth bearing a cross, lay at the foot of the steps up to
the altar. Above hung a vault of imposing dimensions. The
priest stood at the altar facing the cluster of mourners scattered through the first few rows. Cooper sat alone in the back
of the church and listened to the Mass.

He had forgotten that Vivian had been a Catholic. He remembered one brief allusion to her faith, a remark on the
peculiarities of German Catholicism that Vivian herself had
let drop once. It had been one more thing for Cooper to
admire in her, the way she apparently believed yet wore it
lightly. Cooper had been an apostate by then, but still ad-
miring of principle.

He wondered if there had been any problem over the funeral. He knew the church no longer buried suicides at the
crossroads with a stake through their hearts, but as far as he
knew suicide was still a mortal sin. With his Protestant background he was ignorant of Catholic policy in such cases, but
apparently the priest had no reservations about commending
Vivian's soul to her Maker. It was a worship service, without
a eulogy; Cooper's father would have sternly approved.

When the funeral ended Cooper sat and watched as the
coffin was borne back past him, then waited as the mourners
followed. There was a fair number of people, he realized,
lost in the cavernous church; he counted thirty or so and
stopped with more still coming. There were a couple of elderly women, tottering slowly and looking dazed. There were
people Cooper suspected were connected with the gallery,
people whose great attention to their clothing showed even at
a funeral.

Near the end of the procession came a gray-haired woman
in a navy-blue dress. Cooper had seen Vivian's mother once,

fifteen years before, and he imagined he recognized her. With her were five or six others, several women and a man in a dark suit.

Cooper sat still in the last pew after they had passed, trying to decide why he'd come and if he wanted to see any more or talk to anyone. He'd vacillated even after calling the gallery again and reaching an employee who had told him where the funeral was to be.

Cooper rose and went out onto the porch of the church, into the fall sunshine. He paused at the top of the steps, watching the people mill on the sidewalk below him. He knew he looked shabby compared to this crowd, in his old corduroy jacket and broad green tie, even having shaved and trimmed his moustache.

Hands in his pockets, he went slowly down the steps, watching the little group gathered at the bottom. He was certain now that this was Vivian's mother, remembering the face from graduation day 1973. She was older, of course, and just now looking about her with a good deal of composure but a tight-lipped look of holding things in. The man in the dark suit was at her elbow. He was in his late thirties or early forties, a dark blond starting to go gray, a bit heavy through the torso and around the carefully shaven jowls. Cooper gave him a look and recognized his old rival.

Nick Dennison. The name came to him easily despite the passage of time. Nick had been a lot younger and brighter-looking when Cooper had last seen him, his fingers laced with Vivian's across the kitchen table at the professor's house. So they had married after all, then divorced recently, according to the paper. Nick bore the blank tired look of the bereaved; however the divorce had gone, he looked as if Vivian's death had hurt him. His eyes swept over Cooper, lingered for the half-second necessary to decide he didn't know him, and went on.

And next to Nick was Ellen Sims. Cooper recognized her immediately despite the fact that the long straight tresses had been shorn and styled into something conservative and quietly attractive, despite the gray-checked, nicely cut suit that served to disguise somewhat her still-plump figure, despite the late-thirties maturity of her bearing. Ellen's eyes met his and she paused, uncertain, then smiled very faintly as she recognized him.

Cooper stepped toward her and she held out a hand. "Cooper," she said.

"It's nice to see you, Ellen. It's been a long time." Cooper felt he'd said the wrong thing but he shook her hand and returned the smile fleetingly.

Ellen held his hand for a long moment. She opened her mouth to speak but could not, and let her gaze drift away to the high trees over the street that were losing their leaves.

"I read about it in the paper," said Cooper.

Ellen released his hand and nodded. "Her mother called me yesterday. I flew in this morning."

It was not the time to ask her from where. She was already turning to catch up with Vivian's mother and her party, who had begun to move away.

"Coming to the cemetery?" she asked.

"I suppose so." Cooper followed her, uncomfortable. Vivian's mother and the other women and Nick had stopped to wait for Ellen. They watched Cooper approach with blank looks. Nick was closest to Cooper, and he was giving him a second look.

"Remember Cooper?" said Ellen.

Nick's face said no, but he nodded slightly. Cooper held out his hand, shook Nick's briefly, and said, "I'm very sorry." Nick squeezed his hand and tried to smile.

Ellen had turned to Vivian's mother. "Mrs. Horstmann, this is Cooper MacLeish. He knew Vivian at school."

Cooper was uncertain if he should offer his hand but he did, and she took it. She was not elderly, though she must have been approaching or already in her sixties; she was still in a handsome middle age that allowed glimpses of the beauty she had possessed. Cooper saw Vivian in her face. "I'm sorry," he said again, and hesitated. What had Vivian been? "Your daughter was a very fine person." It sounded trite but it was the truth, Cooper decided, and damned if there was anything better to say at a funeral.

"Thank you." Mrs. Horstmann's voice was quiet but well under control. Her eyes showed she had been crying but she was bearing up.

Cooper was perfunctorily introduced to Vivian's sisters,

younger than she and not at all resembling her, and then the
movement toward the waiting limousines resumed. Cooper
told Ellen he would see her there and slipped away to retrieve
the Valiant. He decided to tail the procession at a discreet
distance so as not to lower the tone.

The cemetery, it turned out, was miles away, a vast tract
of land cleverly hidden in suburban sprawl. There were too
few trees and the impression was of barren land strewn with
stones. *Cemeteries need trees,* thought Cooper. There were
patches of ground where stumps had been torn out; there had
perhaps been elms once, lost to the plague and not yet replaced.

They hiked from the cars and stood in a cluster around the
grave as a further short service was read. On the stone next
to the open grave Cooper read the name of Charles Horstmann and dates that would make him Vivian's father. He had
died only a couple of years before.

Cooper stood shivering a little at the edge of the gathering,
watching the people. The crowd had dwindled en route from
the church but there were still a good dozen present. Vivian
had moved in moneyed circles. The suits were immaculate,
the dresses discreet but whispering of great sums.

As people began to drift back to the cars, Cooper maneu-
vered his way to Ellen's side, needing a familiar face. She
was still on the fringes of the family group, marching with
her eyes on the ground, drying her eyes with the tips of her
fingers. Cooper gallantly dug a Kleenex out of his pocket and
offered it to her.

"Thanks." Ellen used it on her eyes, then blew her nose.
"And thank Heaven that's over."

Cooper walked beside her in silence. When they reached
the cars he asked her, "Where are people heading now?"

Ellen dabbed at her nose and drew herself up straight, red-
eyed but steady. "I think Mrs. Horstmann is having a few
people in. I can't stay, though. I have to get out to O'Hare.
It's maddening, but I have to chair a meeting at nine o'clock
tomorrow. I'd skip it, but there's several million in grants at
stake, and I've gotten to the place where I have to dance to
the tune the money plays. I can't even mourn a friend de-
cently."

Cooper grunted in sympathy. "Where are you these days?"

"Palo Alto." She looked at him blankly for a moment, seeming to remember suddenly that they hadn't seen each other for fifteen years. "Hiding in a think tank. That's where philosophers wind up these days, instead of at the royal court."

"How are you getting to O'Hare?"

"Nick's running me out there. I hate to bother him, but my plane's in an hour."

"I'll take you. I'm marginal to all this anyway. And I'd be grateful for a chance to catch up a bit. It's been a long time."

She looked at him as if to make sure the offer was sincere and then thanked him. "It has, hasn't it?" she said.

He nodded. "No luggage?"

"No. Just let me just make my good-byes." Cooper stood awkwardly nearby while Ellen spoke with Nick and then held Vivian's mother in a long embrace that brought tears again. Nick's gaze wandered over the gathering and settled on Cooper, and while Ellen lingered with the sisters he came uncertainly over the ten feet that separated them to offer his hand.

Nick said simply, "Thanks. Good to see you again." His lips tightened in a brief attempt at a smile. Cooper looked at his old rival, seeing only a tired man in the middle of a personal tragedy. Nick had very light gray eyes, and the eyes were not really settling on things today; they touched lightly here and there and went on, trailing a numb pained look. *Nick Dennison has some rough nights ahead,* thought Cooper. He suspected that Nick still had no idea who he was.

Running fast down a suburban boulevard with Ellen silent on the seat beside him, Cooper breathed deeply with relief. "Have you at O'Hare in twenty minutes with some luck," he said, moving out to pass a dawdling Cadillac. "If we hit the lights on Cumberland."

Ellen had been staring out the window; she seemed to come back from far away and turned toward him. "You sound like a cab driver."

"I am a cab driver." Ellen made no response and he smiled. "I did get that degree, yes."

"And all you've done is drive a cab?"

"No. I've done a little of everything. Drove trucks for a while. Worked as a security guard, fry cook, gas station attendant, motel clerk. Chauffeured for a Hollywood producer, bounced people out of bars, managed a restaurant. Even sold insurance for a month. There's a dishonest living for you. I wound up in a cab because I like the independence. Never did a thing with the history degree except read more history.''

''That's more than most people do with their degrees.'' She watched the road as Cooper swung over a lane and stepped on it a bit, impatient with the traffic. ''Have you been here in Chicago all along?''

He shook his head. ''I was out in L.A. for a long time, a couple of other whistle stops, here for the last seven years.''

Ellen was silent for a moment and then said, ''Did you ever see Vivian? She never mentioned hearing from you.''

''Huh-uh. I had no idea where she was until I saw her name in the paper the other morning. The last time I saw or heard from her was in August '73.'' There was a silence and Cooper wondered if Vivian had ever confided in Ellen about that night. ''I'm surprised now she never got in my cab. Maybe she did, and I just didn't recognize her.''

They rolled to a stop at a red light. Cooper stole a glance at Ellen and saw her gazing at him. Her round face was grave. ''You were in love with her, weren't you?'' she said.

Cooper looked out the windshield and nodded slowly. ''It was obvious, huh?''

''It was, after a while. You were somewhat of a figure of fun, but not much. We all liked you, really. We felt sorry for you.''

Cooper smiled. ''I got over it, but I never forgot it. That's why I came today.''

They sat in silence until the light changed. Cooper wanted to ask her if Vivian had ever said anything about him but realized that that would throw him back into his old role with her. He checked his mirror and changed lanes, then took a deep breath.

''So, Ellen,'' he said. ''What happened to Vivian?''

Ellen sighed, a long slow release. ''I don't know, Cooper. Nobody does. Not even the people closest to her. I still can't believe it. Not Vivian, never. I could never ever have believed it. She had had some rough times, but I would never have believed she would kill herself.''

"There's no doubt it was suicide? She didn't fall by accident?"

"She left a note."

"Huh. That doesn't square with the Vivian I knew. But then a lot can happen in fifteen years."

"It doesn't square with the Vivian I knew either, and I talked to her on the phone a month ago. She was still depressed about the divorce, but we laughed a little and made plans to get together in California next year. She wasn't suicidal."

Cooper frowned at the traffic and thought. "When did she and Nick get divorced?"

"The final settlement was just a month or so ago, but they had separated before that. They were having troubles last year, before Nick moved back to New York. I think Vivian's reluctance to go back there with him was part of the trouble, but she would have gone if the marriage had been in good shape otherwise. Things had started to fall apart before then. I think the idea at first was that he would move there, and there would be a cooling off period or something and then she would come to join him. But then last spring she went to see him and told him she wanted a divorce."

"So Nick's in New York now."

"Yes. He got the position he'd wanted for years, in one of the big investment firms. Chicago had been a way station for him all along."

"How long had they been here?"

"Eight or ten years, I think. They started out in New York."

"When did they get married?"

"Fall of '73. Right after she went out to join him there."

Cooper mused on that while he drove. She had fled straight into Nick's arms, the prodigal fiancée returning. "The paper said something about her gallery. How long had she been involved with that?"

"Just a couple of years. It was something she'd wanted to do for a long time. She came into some money when her father died and she put it into the gallery. But she would have sold out and gone with Nick if the marriage had still been sound."

"The paper made it sound like she might have been depressed about the gallery not doing well or something."

"Well, it wasn't doing very well, of course—that sort of thing is hard to get off the ground. But she was taking it in stride. She wouldn't have killed herself over that."

After a silence Cooper said, "So what would she have killed herself over?"

Ellen sighed again. "I don't know. Personal failure, maybe." Cooper eased through a yellow light and waited for Ellen to elaborate. She was silent for a block or two, her face turned away from him. Finally she spoke. "Vivian thought of herself as a very moral person. She wasn't a letter-of-the-law Catholic, but she tried to live by principle. I think she saw the divorce as a major failure. I know it bothered her a great deal. And then there were the problems with Dominic—I think she may have seen herself as a total failure."

"Hang on a second. Who's Dominic?"

She looked at him in surprise. "Her son. Didn't you know they had a son?"

"Oh yeah, that's right. The paper mentioned him. But . . . where was he today? I didn't see anyone who looked like he could be their son."

"Oh God, you don't know the whole story." Ellen waved a hand vaguely, speechless for a moment. "He ran away. Right after he came home from some school expedition and found out his mother had killed herself."

"Jesus."

"He had been away for a couple of days on a field trip with the Latin School. He got back Thursday and found the police in possession of the apartment. Mrs. Horstmann was there by that time, too, fortunately. She broke the news to him. And then that afternoon he disappeared."

Cooper shook his head. "Just ran off?"

"Mrs. Horstmann had taken him to her house in Evanston. Nick had been called and was flying in from New York. When Mrs. Horstmann went up to check on Dominic in the afternoon, he had gone, taken the bag of clothes he'd brought from the apartment and slipped out. They notified the police, but no one's found him. A policewoman came and talked with Nick and Mrs. Horstmann today before the funeral. Apparently they've learned that Dominic called a friend from school Friday night but didn't say where he was, only that he was staying with someone he knew in Lincoln Park and didn't want to talk to his father—you can imagine how Nick took that. And since then no one's seen or heard from him.'' Ellen was wiping at her eyes again. Cooper was out of Kleenexes. He drove in silence for a while, reaching the expressway and sliding into the traffic bound for O'Hare.

''So you think Vivian was depressed about her failures as wife and mother,'' he said after a while, when Ellen seemed in control again.

''That's all I can think of to explain it. Making the marriage work and raising Dominic were the most important things to her. And the marriage had broken up and Dominic was having problems.''

''What kind of problems?''

''Skipping school, running around with kids she didn't like, taking drugs, things like that.''

''He's not the only kid on the block doing that kind of thing,'' said Cooper.

''No, I think it wasn't as bad maybe as she thought. But Nick and he had some ferocious fights about it, and that bothered Vivian, too. They didn't get along very well.''

''How old is Dominic?''

''Let's see. He turned fourteen in May, I think.''

''Huh.'' Cooper eased into the right lane and thought. ''Still. If she was upset about all that, I still can't see her killing herself. Especially being a Catholic and all.''

''That's what we've all told ourselves, Cooper. I wouldn't believe it if I hadn't seen the note.''

''What'd she say?''

''She apologized to Dominic and told him he'd . . .'' Ellen's voice went as she choked up. ''. . . he'd be better off . . . without her.'' She gave a few brief sobs, her eyes squeezed shut, one fist tight against her face. Cooper raged at himself for asking her and stepped on the gas.

In a few minutes he was snaking around the upper level concourse fighting traffic to get to the United terminal. Ellen was dabbing at her face with the same crumpled Kleenex.

''Here we are. In plenty of time.'' Cooper pulled over behind a limo and put the Valiant in park. Ellen looked up at him, composed if a little red around the eyes.

"Thank you, Cooper. It's been good to see you after all this time." She gave him a brave smile.

Cooper could think of nothing to say but platitudes, so he kept quiet. He reached into his pocket and took out his notebook and pen. "Let's keep in touch. Can I have your address?" She wrote down her address and phone number in Palo Alto and he scrawled his quickly on another sheet and tore it off and gave it to her. She held out her hand and he clasped it briefly before she got out of the car and he watched her disappear into the terminal.

Cruising home along Devon, Cooper brooded. He would never quite be at peace with Vivian Horstmann's memory now. The ideal had been shown up as merely, sadly, human.

He was rolling through the forest preserve when the thought struck him, so forcibly that he had to slow down and pull off the road into the shadow of the trees and sit for a moment. Cooper could do arithmetic as well as anyone, but it had taken his mind a while to work around to calculating that if Vivian's son had turned fourteen in May, he had been born in May 1974, and thus conceived sometime in August 1973.

4

"**W**HAT THE HELL happened to you yesterday?" said the man in the phone booth. "You give me a safe number to call you at and then you're not there."

"Take it easy. You gonna get a ulcer, man." Slight Spanish accent, belligerent tone, fuzzy diction from alcohol.

The man reminded himself to keep his voice calm, unremarkable, unidentifiable. "You're a hard man to get in touch with. I almost wrote you off yesterday."

"I was busy. I hadda go give an Indian a haircut."

"You what?"

High wheezing laughter came over the line. "I had a job. Took all afternoon."

"All right. Listen."

"No man, you listen. What I said yesterday still goes. I don't take a job from nobody I don't know who it is."

"You'll take this one."

"Hey man, you wastin' my time."

The man in the phone booth said quickly, "There's a bar on Montrose called Duke's. Montrose just west of Broadway. Go into Duke's and ask for a bartender named Harlan. He's got an envelope for you. Whether or not you take the job, what's in the envelope is yours. If you want more of it, follow the instructions in the envelope. You know how to read, right?"

There was a short pause. "You keep on talkin' like that, I'll cut your fuckin' tongue outa your head."

"You're never going to lay eyes on me. Stop by and talk to Harlan. I'll be in touch."

"Hey, Bickle! Travis Bickle!"

Cooper drained the styrofoam cup of coffee and turned

around. Marsh came into the office, big and black, grinning a wide white grin.

"There he is, my friend, Taxi Driver with a capital TD, the meanest bad-ass cabbie in Chicago. Hey, Travis, tell us how you shot up that punk the other night."

"I didn't shoot him. I ran over him. You got the wrong movie." Cooper pitched the cup into the trash can.

"Ran him over twice, I hear. Now that is mean shit. One time wasn't enough, huh?"

"He was still moving." Cooper brushed past Marsh and headed for the door.

Marsh laughed. "He was still movin', shit. You a hard case, you know that, MacLeish? He ain't movin' now, huh?"

"Not out of Cook County Hospital, anyway. Not till his trial date comes up."

"And you wasn't scared a bit, was you?"

Cooper halted and faced him, deadpan. "Scared? All he had was a .44 Special. I had my trusty Impala."

"Shit." Marsh shoved him away. "Seriously, man, you gotta learn who you can pick up and who you can't."

"Tell me about it. Got any pointers?"

"Body language, man. I can drive up and look at a guy and I know."

"One look, huh?"

"Seriously. It's from growing up with 'em, watchin' that shit all my life. I know who's gonna fuck with me and who ain't."

"Maybe you can write up a brochure on it, help us all out."

"Yeah. With diagrams. 'This motherfucker is planning to blow your shit away and take your money. See figure two.' "

Cooper shook his head, reminded too vividly of the .44 going off, and headed for the door. "I gotta go drive."

"Yeah, well watch yourself out there. You got a rep now."

Just what I need, Cooper thought. He pushed out into the sunshine and made his way across the lot to the cab they'd given him. This was the first time he had driven since the incident, and he was feeling like the kid climbing back on the horse. He knew he had to do it but he wasn't going to enjoy it particularly.

The cab sounded and felt all right and the brakes worked.

Cooper headed down Clark Street, slipping back into the stop-and-start rhythm, watching the sidewalks with one part of his brain and reading the traffic with another. One good fare would help him get over the jitters. It was early afternoon, clear and cool, nice driving weather. Not the best day to make money, since people would be more inclined to walk, but a good day to drive and watch people and think. A good day to run downtown, cruise the Loop for a while, maybe pick up a run out to one of the airports, O'Hare preferably. When night came, he would take a dinner break, relax a bit, and be very careful about whom he picked up. He told himself he wouldn't hustle very hard, just ease back into things.

With the unoccupied part of his brain he went back to the question. Is this kid my son? The question had kept him intermittently awake the night after the funeral and come back to him often in the day or two since. Cooper had had a couple of pregnancy scares with former lovers, but neither had proven to be more than a scare. The simple calculation he'd made on the way back from Vivian's funeral had presented him with the most vivid possibility yet.

It was simple egotism perhaps, thought Cooper, but the mere chance that Vivian's son was also his was enough to give him an interest in the boy that he couldn't shake. Perhaps it was his sneaking fear that he had blown all his chances to leave an heir. Now suddenly it seemed as if there might be a bit of his genetic material walking around after all.

He wondered if the boy had been found, or come slinking home. If so, that was pretty much the end of it. He could hardly intrude himself into the boy's grief on the off chance that he was his long-lost father, especially not with another father already on the scene. There was too much he didn't know. Young Dominic could be Nick's son after all—it wasn't impossible that Vivian, fleeing to Nick in late August, had gotten pregnant by him in time to produce a May birth.

Cooper decided not to waste energy on fantasies of finding his son. It was mid-afternoon and things were starting to pick up. He drove steadily until nightfall, almost enjoying it again, outwitting traffic, bantering with fares and making money. At eight o'clock he was out on the West Side, and he headed back east and north, feeling he'd earned his dinner, needing to stop for a while and psych himself up for the evening. He was starting to remember the last nighttime fare he'd taken on, and getting the creeps a little.

Cruising east on Irving he thought of the boy again. This kid was having a rough time. First his parents break up, then his mother kills herself. I'd probably have split too, Cooper thought. If the father wasn't around and the kid came home to find cops all over the place and his mother dead, running away would be pretty natural.

Where to, though? Ellen had said none of his friends had seen him. There had to be friends somewhere they didn't know about; kids always ran away to friends. Unless they did a complete bunk and hopped a Greyhound for New York or something.

Cooper didn't like to think of that—he knew what happened to kids who disembarked in Times Square. For that matter, Chicago had plenty of Times Square action, along Halsted or in Uptown, where Cooper had seen kids selling themselves. Boys and girls.

But a child of Vivian Horstmann's wouldn't get into that kind of thing, would he? That was for hard-core abused and abandoned kids. Young Dominic had to have enough going for him that he wouldn't get sucked into that kind of morass, didn't he?

Sometimes kids couldn't help it. Cooper made a left on Western and headed north, vaguely looking for a place to eat. He was suddenly aware that he wasn't going to rest easy until he knew more about the kid and what had happened to him.

A call to 411 would get him Mrs. Charles Horstmann's number in Evanston. There was a place to start.

But start what? Nick was still in town, no doubt, and whatever Cooper was, Nick was the one who had the best claim to being the boy's father. All right then, he could explain that he was merely a concerned friend, offer his help in finding the boy. Except why would they take him, a complete stranger, into their confidence?

There was another way he could approach it. Cooper looked at his watch; the time seemed about right. It was a bit of a drive and he would waste time he had paid for with the cab, but he just might catch Valenti at dinner.

He cut over on Peterson and hit the lights going up Broadway. There were two squads parked outside the Starlight as usual, lit by the lurid yellow sign above the door. Cooper took a right and parked halfway down the block in a trash pile in the gutter, then walked back. The place was what Cooper thought of as a typical Formica restaurant, with plastic countertops and booths upholstered in maroon fake leather. It was open twenty-four hours a day, which Cooper knew from his restaurant experience was a bad sign as far as sanitation was concerned. The menu was standard for a Chicago lunch counter taken over by Greeks, with spinach pie and Athenian-style chicken added to the usual starches. The waitresses were always tired and testy and the owner brooded over his domain from a stool by the cash register like Odysseus in exile. It was not a terrific restaurant but Cooper ate there occasionally because he knew the value of staying on good terms with policemen.

The cops sat in the back room. Cooper had never been in the place without seeing at least two cops having dinner. It was a rendezvous for policemen from all over the 24th District, in which Cooper lived, and he could always count on finding a cop there if he needed one, although sometimes it was hard to convince them that whatever trouble was going on was more important than their dinner.

Cooper went into the back room, hoping Valenti was as much a man of habit as always. He was pleased to see him in a booth with two other cops, next to the window. Valenti's gold-banded lieutenant's cap lay on the seat next to him. Valenti had been a homicide detective when Cooper had met him several years before, in connection with a killing Cooper had taken personally. Since then Valenti had made lieutenant and been assigned to the 24th District, and Cooper had dealt with him in one way or another here and there. Valenti looked up as Cooper came down the aisle, swallowed, took a drink of water, and said, "Stay away from me, MacLeish. I got enough work to do."

Cooper smiled. "Good to see you, too. Just came in for a quick bite and thought I'd stop by and say hello."

Valenti looked from Cooper to the other two cops and then back again. He was going a little gray, getting a little heavier, but still looking formidable with his thick black moustache. "Bullshit," he said. "Every time I see you you're in some kind of trouble. What is it now?"

Cooper sat down on the edge of the seat across the aisle from Valenti, dangling the cab keys from a finger. "No trouble. Haven't been stuck up in almost a week and haven't been in a fight in months."

Valenti looked at the other two cops again. "MacLeish here has kind of a nose for trouble, you might say." He took another bite of chicken.

"It's never trouble I start, though, is it? I just don't drive on by, like everyone else."

Valenti finished chewing and smiled, with just a touch of malice. "I thought we could have had you for battery a couple of times."

"You mean the kid I hit with the pipe? Self-defense, man. He had just used it on the old man and tried to use it on me."

"Yeah OK, you're a credit to your race." Valenti exchanged a look with the two cops across from him, then looked back at Cooper with the little smile. "You're just in time to hear a story. Kenny here was telling us about a dead Indian they got down in Uptown. Tell him about it, Kenny. Tell him what makes our job so special."

Kenny was a big gray-haired man with very light blue eyes and a broad pale face on the brink of middle-aged sag. He took a drink of coffee and stared at Cooper for a moment with that complete impassivity that cops have after enough years. He looked as if he couldn't care less whether Cooper heard the story. "Yeah, we got a real nice one last night," he said. At his side the third cop belched softly, looking bored.

"I'm listening," said Cooper.

"Guy named Jake Mankiller. Terrific name, huh? Menominee from up on the reservation. Should have stayed up there. Got himself in trouble gambling, we hear, owed somebody big money for too long and they came by to get it. Looks like two of them. Came in through the back while Jake was out, middle of the day probably, and just sat and waited for him to come home."

The big cop took a sip of coffee and Cooper glanced at Valenti to see him picking at his chicken, still smiling faintly. "When Jake got home they wired him to a chair in the kitchen and gagged him and hit him a few times with a cast iron frying pan. Hard enough finally to kill him. But you know what they did before they killed him?''

''What?'' said Cooper.

''They scalped him.'' Cooper blinked into the big pale face with the washed-out eyes, eyes that had probably seen worse. ''Not very neatly, either. From the amount of blood all over it looks like he wasn't quite dead when they did it.''

Valenti was waiting for his reaction. Cooper said, ''Dinnertime must be your favorite time of the day.''

Valenti snorted with a mouthful of chicken. ''You know it.''

Cooper turned back to the other man, met his stare and said, ''So what did they do with the scalp?''

Over the rim of the coffee cup the cop said, ''We haven't found it yet.''

Cooper shook his head. He'd never had any trouble understanding why cops drank. ''I'm glad I don't have to look for it,'' he said.

''So,'' Valenti said. ''Now that you see how much fun we have, what do you want? I got a busy schedule tonight, starting with eating this pigeon here.''

''Just a question.'' Cooper stood up. ''If you have a moment between coffee and liqueur I'd appreciate it if you could stop by at the counter for a second.'' He nodded at the other two cops and went back to the front room. Hell with them. Cooper had seen worse than that, too.

Twenty minutes later he was reminding himself never to order veal parmesan except in a quality Italian restaurant when Valenti appeared at his elbow, cap and black leather jacket in place, looking very much the police heavyweight. A toothpick was nestled in the corner of his mouth. ''All right, MacLeish, you got thirty seconds. What do you want?''

Cooper pressed the napkin to his mouth and said, ''What happens when a kid runs away and the parents call the police?''

''Not a lot usually. Know how many kids run away every day?''

''I mean does an officer get assigned to the case, do you just put out a bulletin, what?''

Valenti shrugged. ''Depends. Any reason to think someone helped the kid run away? Like against the kid's will?''

"No. The kid just ran away. But you must do something, fill out a report at least."

"If the parents take the trouble to call the police an officer talks to them and then turns it over to a youth officer, probably. Who adds it to the zillion other cases he's working on. With a little luck, he might find a kid or two before they show up in the main feature at the Admiral or the Bijou."

"So suppose you people give up and someone else, like me for example, wants to keep on looking. How could I find out where a case stands?"

"You couldn't, unless you were family. What do you think we are, a news agency?"

Cooper considered for a second and decided to say it. "I'm the kid's father."

Valenti stared at him and then the toothpick shifted as the corner of his mouth twisted upward slightly. "I didn't know you were a family man."

"I'm not. The kid's all the family I've got and he's never met me."

Valenti gave vent to one little silent puff of laughter. "Like that, is it?"

"Yeah, it's like that."

Valenti took out that toothpick and examined it. "The mother raising the kid?"

"The mother's dead. She killed herself last Thursday. The adoptive father lives in New York. He's not going to be able to spend a lot of time looking. That leaves me."

Valenti gave him a hard stare. "Who was the mother?"

"Vivian Horstmann. The woman who jumped off the high-rise."

One of Valenti's eyebrows went up. He put the toothpick back in his mouth. "You used to hang around with a better class of people, huh?"

"I used to be a better class of person. Now how could I find out what you know about the kid?"

"I don't know shit about the kid." Valenti was losing patience.

"I heard a policewoman talked to the father—the adoptive father I mean—and the grandmother, the day of the funeral. Maybe you could find out who that was, put me in touch with her."

Valenti chewed on the toothpick for a few seconds. "How do you know the kid hasn't split completely? Lot of 'em like to go to L.A. for some reason. For that matter, how do you know he hasn't come home yet?"

"I don't know. But I'm sure the officer could tell me. According to what I heard the kid told a friend he would be staying with someone in Lincoln Park. That's a lot closer than L.A."

"If you heard all that, how come you need to talk to the officer?"

" 'Cause that's all I heard. And my contact with the family's left town."

"You're not on the best terms with the family, huh?"

"Not any kind of terms at all, really."

Valenti shook his head and worked on the toothpick a little more. "And just what do you plan to do?"

"Look for the kid, what else?" Cooper stared Valenti down this time, a little surprised at himself for putting it so explicitly.

"All right." Valenti gave a little what-do-I-care toss of the head and turned to go. "Catch up with me tomorrow sometime." He slapped the counter in front of the morose Greek, who growled at him in reply, and strode out of the restaurant.

Cooper sat up with Diana till nearly dawn over a bottle of Roditis. She was still in her high-class waitress clothes, white blouse with black bow, sleek black skirt, hair pulled back in a ponytail. She leaned on the kitchen table with her chin in her hand and looked at Cooper with sleepy skepticism. "Your paternal instincts have been awakened, huh?"

"Such as I have, I guess." Cooper yawned and scratched at the stubble that touched his cheeks with a hint of gray. "He might not even be my son. But there's a good chance he is. And if he is I want to meet him."

"Even though you mean nothing to him."

"Yeah. Wouldn't you be curious?"

Diana shrugged. "Sure. I don't think I'd let him know I was his father, if he'd grown up with another one."

"I don't plan to."

Her look lingered: thoughtful, wary perhaps. "So what do you tell him when you find him?"

"I don't know. That I was a friend of his mother's, I guess."

"And what do you do with him? Take him back to daddy?"

"I don't know that either. Just see if he's OK, probably, for starters. Too much can happen to runaways. And this is not the world's happiest kid right now, remember. I don't think this is just a lark, living it up with his pals for a few days."

Diana took a drink of the wine, slowly, her tongue coming out just a bit to explore her lips as she set the glass down. "You want to know what I really think? I think this is other people's business, not yours."

It was about what Cooper had expected her to say; she couldn't be too happy about the whole thing. He looked past her. "If he is mine, this is the only kid I've ever had. Or probably ever will."

She gave him a long steady look then, dark brown eyes in a serene, feline face, and he wondered if he had just broached a subject that Diana pondered in secret. Cooper knew it was there all the time, the question of how far he and Diana were going together. They'd had a good comfortable time for the better part of a year and he hadn't wanted to think past comfort. So far nobody had brought up any indecent words like love, but he wondered uneasily sometimes what she was thinking. Cooper was coming up on forty and Diana had left thirty behind; decisions couldn't be put off forever anymore.

For the moment, however, they could. Cooper rose and went slowly around the table. He felt weighted with fatigue and creaking with age. He stood behind Diana and her head fell back against his stomach. He ran a hand tenderly over her cheek, traced the line of her throat with a finger. He bent and touched her lips lightly with his, teased a response from her, bit her lower lip very gently. He pulled her to her feet and they went in to bed.

Cooper took a coffee break on the near North Side in mid-afternoon and called 24th District Headquarters from a pay phone. He was informed that Lieutenant Valenti was out on the street. Cooper kept driving and called twice more. The second time he got Valenti, who told him brusquely to meet him at Delmar's at eight.

The booths at Delmar's were lime-green instead of maroon and the effect was less lugubrious than at the place on Broadway, but the cuisine was similar. Valenti was sitting by himself in a booth back near the kitchen with a half-eaten small salad in front of him. Cooper slid into the booth across from him and ordered coffee. The radio clipped to Valenti's jacket sizzled with static barely recognizable as human speech.

"Don't like lettuce, huh?" Cooper said.

"Cow food. I'm a carnivore."

"Thanks for taking the time. I appreciate it."

"Just don't make it a habit. I'm not a public relations officer." Cooper nodded and splashed cream into his coffee. Valenti shoved the salad away. "Not that I have a lot to tell you. This is gonna be one of those kids you find by sheer luck. Or else he comes home when he gets tired. Like most kids."

"You talk to the youth officer?"

"Uh-huh. She told me everything she knew in about thirty seconds. Your boy didn't leave much of a trail."

My boy, thought Cooper. The waitress appeared and set down a plate of veal parmesan in front of Valenti. "Let me know how you like that," said Cooper. "So what is there to know?"

"Not much more than you knew already." Valenti sawed off a piece of veal and chewed for a while. "The kid talked to a friend on Friday night, on the phone. He said he wasn't gonna live with his father and he was splitting. He mentioned this person in Lincoln Park, nobody the friend knew. No name given. He said he'd be in touch but he hasn't been. The friend has been very cooperative, listing all kinds of places we might look, people we might talk to, the kid's usual haunts. A complete blank. Except we found one person, the brother of another school friend, who had seen your kid at the Galaxy on Sunday night. Didn't talk to him, just saw him. And that's it."

Cooper grunted and watched Valenti go at the veal again. The Galaxy was a dance hall on Clark Street. Cooper thought it was a New Wave sort of place, but he had a very rough notion of what that meant. "What the hell was he doing at the Galaxy? He's under age. By seven years or so."

"Probably one of their underage shows, no liquor served."

"Was he with anyone?"

"You got me. I'm giving you what the officer gave me, verbatim."

"Mm-hm." Cooper took a sip of coffee and winced at the taste. "This friend in Lincoln Park. Someone must know him. Canvass Dominic's friends and you'll find someone who knows the guy he's staying with. Have to."

Valenti chewed and gave Cooper the look of a man who has been offended but is too weary to protest. He swallowed and said, "You wanna be a cop, give us lessons, you gotta apply and go through the academy first. There's a waiting list."

"Just thinking aloud. Can I have the name of the friend Dominic called?"

"No."

"OK. How about the name of the youth officer?"

"She's a busy lady. She's working hard on it, along with the zillion other cases I mentioned. She doesn't need your help."

Cooper drank more coffee, watched Valenti, and thought. After a minute he said, "Would you happen to know if the kid's father is still in town?"

Valenti spoke out of the corner of a full mouth. "I thought you were the father."

"Adoptive father, I mean."

"Went back to New York yesterday. But I understand he's hired a private investigator to find the boy. I think you'll have lots of competition."

Cooper nodded slowly. "I don't suppose you could give me his name, either."

"I was not privy to that information, as they say."

Someone swore in Spanish in the kitchen behind Valenti. Cooper turned the coffee cup slowly on the saucer, around and around. Finally he nodded and said, "Thanks, Valenti. I owe you."

"Yeah. Pay me by staying out of trouble. Don't bother the family, don't get in our way."

"I'm going to find him." Cooper looked into the policeman's sour gaze and smiled.

"Fine. Just stay the hell out of trouble." Valenti set the

knife and fork down on the edge of the plate. "When am I gonna learn?" he said.

"About the veal parmesan, you mean."

Valenti looked at him sharply. "Uh-huh."

"Don't ever order it in a place like this," Cooper said, picking up his check and sliding out of the booth. "An Italian like you should know better."

"You speak English?" the man bellowed into the cab through the open back door. Cooper turned his head to look at him. He saw a flushed face, heavy brows drawn close together under a receding hairline. Type A personality, thought Cooper. "I'm not getting into a cab with anyone that doesn't speak English," the man shouted at him.

"You number one, GI," Cooper said. "Chop-chop."

"What the hell is that supposed to mean?" The man's neck was swelling against his tight collar and red power tie.

"It means hop in," said Cooper. "The longer you stand out there, the wetter that nice suit gets."

The man glared at him a moment longer and then managed to bundle himself, an attaché case and a raincoat folded uselessly over his arm onto the back seat of the cab. "McCormick Place," he barked.

"You got it," said Cooper, switching on the meter and pulling away from the curb. He nudged through traffic toward the Drive, windshield wipers beating time against the drizzle. Fall had turned nasty, with a treacherous wind slicing in from the gray reaches over the lake, and people walked tensed and wary of the driven rain.

Cooper fought his way out to the Drive, where the lake tossed dark and empty under the rain, and turned south. The man in the back seat had lapsed into sullen silence. Cooper's last couple of fares had been garrulous and he was glad of the silence, glad of the bleak weather, glad to keep his thoughts to himself.

He had told Valenti he would find the boy. Now, a day later, he was starting to think it had been empty bravado. First because it was impossible, next because he had no role in the play. A father and a private investigator were already on the scene; who needed him?

Maybe the kid, he persisted in thinking. Maybe his kid needed him.

Sooner or later Dominic would have to come in from the cold. When the panic wore off, when the grieving was done, when he woke up from whatever bad dream had driven him out the door, the kid would want to come home, wherever home was.

If Cooper could find him, he could offer two things. He could be a messenger, just carrying news to his father or his grandmother. In that role he saw himself aiding both parties; he could reassure the family without betraying Dominic. Runaways needed a mediator, someone to keep the lines of communication open. The private investigator was working for Nick and would thus be suspect.

The second thing Cooper could offer was a refuge, in case Dominic didn't find life on his own to be what he had hoped. Cooper was suspicious of friends that were so detached from the boy's family and social circle that the cops couldn't run them down in a couple of days. He'd seen the kind of friends kids could make in bus stations and parks.

So he had to find him. He had to find the boy, and he didn't even know what he looked like. He had a name and one piece of information. He was competing with an experienced investigator who had the cooperation of the family. He was out of his league.

He climbed the ramp to the huge black monolith of Mc-Cormick Place and dropped his fare, then cut over to Michigan Avenue to head back north. Maybe he wasn't so far behind the private eye after all, he thought. If the cops hadn't found Dominic, it meant that everything the family and friends had been able to tell them hadn't helped, and the investigator would be starting about where Cooper would be. And the investigator's mission would be different. He had to find the kid and bring him in to earn his fee. All Cooper had to do was set out a line, do a little fishing, let Dominic come to him when he was ready.

In fact, thought Cooper, he could hire an investigator himself.

The next day it took Cooper a couple of hours to find his investigator, an hour or two of spare time spent cruising and pounding the pavement along Halsted, Belmont, Clark, past the Oriental gift shops and the discount clothing stores and the tattoo parlor and the Indian and Japanese and Thai and Greek restaurants and the seedy hotels and the storefront church. He finally found him in a video game room on Belmont, an inspired guess. He pushed the door open and went into a den of vice scarier than any bar he'd ever been in, a long dark room filled with beeps and buzzes and roars and flashing screens and mesmerized children. He was the oldest person in the place by twenty years, but no one noticed him at first. Cooper moved slowly down the room checking faces. He found the one he was looking for near the back, lit by the sci-fi display on the screen in front of him, the same Peterbilt gimme cap still worn backward over his long dirty blond locks. Cooper watched over his shoulder while the boy rocked and lurched and slapped at the joystick and the buttons, intent. When the game finally ended and the boy swore and thumped the console and straightened up, Cooper said, "Got a minute, Mickey?"

Mickey started and looked at him and smiled. "Cooper, man. What the fuck are you doing here?"

"Looking for you. I got a job for you."

"Shit. Your kind of jobs I can't hack. Sorry, man, but I couldn't work for that guy at all."

"So I understand. No, this is different. Look, let's get out of here, huh?"

Outside, Cooper steered him toward the lunch counter at the corner but Mickey shook his head. "Uh-uh. I can't go in there no more." Cooper shrugged and took him across the street to a Mexican place. Mickey was lean and high-cheekboned, with dark brown eyes. He wore jeans and black high-top sneakers and a jacket with the name of a video store on the back. He was sixteen or seventeen but he had the hard wary look of someone with a bad case of street smarts. He walked with a hard-guy spring to his step.

The Mexican place sweated grease from between the tiles on the wall. They sat in a booth and Cooper ordered tacos for the boy. "I heard you were out on the street again," said Cooper. "Martha said you didn't adjust real well to the shelter."

Mickey leaned against the wall, put one foot up on the seat

and shook his head. "Look man, I appreciate your help, especially after you could have turned me in to the cops and all, but you really aren't gonna be able to make a straight person out of me, OK? I just ain't cut out for it." His eyes avoided Cooper's.

"OK, I'll stop trying. How are you supporting yourself these days?"

"Same shit. Whatever I can manage."

"You selling again?"

"Sometimes. Hey, listen. It's money. A lot more of it than your guy was willing to pay me for unloading trucks. And nobody fucking with me all day, either."

"You get busted again, they'll throw you in jail this time."

"No they won't. I'm still a juvenile."

"You won't be a juvenile forever. Where you staying?"

"Here and there. It's not too hard to find someone who'll take me home for the night."

Cooper looked at him for a moment and shook his head. "You're going to get AIDS, you know that?"

"I probably got it already."

The kid's a lost cause, thought Cooper. The tacos arrived and Mickey tore into one and took half of it at a bite. After a moment Cooper said, "So you interested in this job?"

"Depends on what it is. If it ain't too much work and I don't have to cut my hair, maybe."

"You told me once all the kids on the street around here knew one another."

"A lot of us, yeah."

"Could you find someone for me?"

Mickey swallowed. "Maybe."

"This is a kid that ran away last week. The cops think he's still around. He was seen at the Galaxy Sunday night. His father's hired a private eye to find him. He doesn't want to go back to his father. He doesn't know me or have any reason to trust me. All I want to do is get a message to him. Could you do that?"

"What do I get out of it?"

"Twenty bucks right now, fifty more if you get the message to him."

"Yeah, I could do that." The first taco was gone and Mickey started on the other one. "Rich kid, huh?"

"Fairly well-off, yeah. His mother just killed herself, so he's probably not the happiest kid in the world right now."

"Who the fuck is, around here? Shit, at least he's got a father that wants him back."

"Yeah. His name's Dominic Dennison. He's fourteen years old."

"What's he look like?"

"You're going to tell me that when you find him, so I know you didn't just blow it off and make something up to get your fifty bucks."

Mickey chewed and stared at Cooper. "How am I supposed to find him without knowing what he looks like?"

"The name. How many kids named Dominic can there be running around? And you said you get to know everybody."

"I wouldn't fuck you over, man."

"Here's the twenty." Cooper slid the bill across the table.

"All right. What's the message?"

"I'll write it down." He took his notebook and pen out of his pocket, thought for a moment, and wrote:

Dominic—
    When you get tired, call me. I was a friend of your mother's.
                                                        Cooper.

He wrote his phone number at the bottom, folded the note, and passed it to Mickey. "Just see that he gets that. I don't need to know where he's staying, you don't need to pump him or anything. Don't scare him off. Just give him that. Dominic Dennison. Got it?"

"Yeah." Mickey opened the note and read it, then stuffed it in a shirt pocket. "I can't guarantee you anything."

"And I can't guarantee the fifty bucks. But if you call me with a good description of him, you'll get it. Copy my number off the note."

"What's this kid to you?" Mickey said.

Cooper picked up the bill and slid out of the booth. "Like the note says, I'm an old friend of his mother's."

It took two days. Cooper was heading out the door when the phone rang; he heard Mickey's voice when he answered. "I found the kid for you."

"Yeah? All right, what's he look like?"

"I'll tell you the way he looks to me, OK? Pretty wimpy looking kid, if you ask me. Skinny, brown hair hangin' in his eyes, got some zits. That good enough?"

"Light brown or dark brown?"

"Shit, don't trust me, huh? Dark. Oh yeah, and he's got a pierced ear but he ain't wearing nothing in it."

Cooper knew that was as good as he was going to get. "Sounds like him. Good work. How'd you find him?"

"Just asked around. He started hanging with these people I know. I think he's got another daddy somewhere, 'cause he ain't sleeping on the streets. I don't think he'd last a week on the street. Anyway, this guy I know points him out to me in this coffee shop over on Diversey and I just go up and ask if he's Dominic whatever. I thought he was gonna shit, but he just says yeah, and I give him the note. He reads it and says 'Who is this guy?' and I'm like, 'Shit, don't ask me, some guy who paid me to find you.' And then I split. Can I have my fifty bucks?"

"You don't have any idea who this person he's staying with is?"

"You told me I didn't have to find out. Now what about my money?"

"Yeah, you're right, you earned it. Listen, I'm going out to drive now. Where can I meet you in about half an hour?"

"You name it, man. My schedule's pretty flexible these days."

5

THE SKIES CLEARED up and a hard clean autumn chill set in. Election Tuesday came; Cooper voted without passion and shrugged at the result. He had a run of two or three bad days in the cab, making a pittance, bored stiff. He did a bit more work on his magnum opus, sitting at the old oak desk tussling with grand ideas.

And he listened for the telephone. It rang a few times: Diana, on her way over; Emilio, looking for a game of pool; a cheerful woman trying to sell him the Brooklyn Bridge. But no Dominic. Days passed, and Cooper began to resign himself to never meeting his son, though he still scanned the sidewalks along Halsted, Belmont, Broadway as he drove looking for a skinny kid with dark brown hair, a kid who didn't look like he'd last very long on the street.

Cooper was not thinking of Dominic when he picked up the phone on a Thursday night and heard the voice, a tenuous young man's voice at the other end, say "Is this Cooper?"

He was speechless for a moment, then said, "Yeah. Yeah, this is Cooper." There was nothing but silence at the other end. "Dominic?"

"Uh-huh." There was another pause, and then the voice said, "Who *are* you?"

Cooper sat down on the couch. "I was a friend of your mother's. Listen, Dominic. Do you know a woman named Ellen Sims? She and your mother were best friends."

"Yeah . . ." Cooper could hear him doubting, debating whether to hang up.

"All right. Call Ellen Sims. Ask her about me. If she tells you you can trust me, call me back. I'll give you the number. OK?"

There was another eon of silence. "OK."

"It's in California. Call her collect. Let me get the number . . . Shit." Cooper's jacket with the notebook in it was halfway across the room. "Hang on a second, will you Dominic?" Afraid of losing the boy, Cooper scrambled to the jacket, tore out the notebook, and made it back to the phone in two hops. "Just a second . . . here it is. Got something to write with?"

"I can remember it."

"OK." Cooper read him the number Ellen had given him. "Got it?" The boy said it back to him perfectly. "Great. Give her a call. She'll tell you who I am."

After another pause the voice said, "What do you want?"

Good question, thought Cooper. "I thought you might need a place to stay or something. I won't take you back to your father, if that's what you're worried about." Cooper waited, his heart pounding.

"I'll call you back," Dominic said, and hung up.

Cooper laid the phone in its cradle and sat staring at it. He scratched at the stubble on his neck and then got up and went into the kitchen and put water on to boil. He had time to make a cup of tea and drink half of it, standing at the front window looking into the street, before the phone rang again.

Cooper got it before the second ring. "It's Dominic," the voice said.

"Yeah. What's the story?"

"I talked to Ellen."

"And?"

"She says you're not really a friend of my mother's."

After a moment Cooper said, "I was. In college. I hadn't seen her for a long time, that's true."

"Why are you looking for me?"

"Because I liked your mother. Because I know what can happen to runaways."

"Did my father hire you?"

"No. He hired some other guy. I'm just an amateur. If you don't need any help, fine. But you should at least let your family know you're OK. Your grandmother if not your father. If you want me to, I'll call her. I won't tell her how I got in touch with you if you don't want me to."

Cooper made out the faint sound of a car horn in the background at the other end of the line. He stood patiently with the phone to his ear while Dominic considered.

"I might need a place to stay," the boy said finally.

Cooper sat down again, slowly. "OK, cool. Where do you want to meet?"

"I don't know . . . Let me think." Several seconds passed. "There's a Dunkin' Donuts on Clark Street."

"Clark and Belmont, right?"

"Uh-huh. We could maybe meet there. Except . . . I don't know what you look like."

"Same here. Look, here's what we'll do. You set a time. I'll be there. I'll be reading . . ." Cooper cast his eyes about the room. "I'll be reading the *Sporting News*. You spot me, take a look. If you change your mind or you don't like my looks or something, you walk out again and I still don't know you from Adam. Fair enough?"

"I guess so."

"What time?"

"I don't know . . ."

Cooper could hear him having second thoughts. He looked at his watch. "How about ten o'clock? A little under an hour from now. I'll wait till ten-thirty. Can you do it?"

"Uh-huh."

"Good. I'm glad you called, Dominic. See you in a bit."

Cooper threw the rest of the tea into the sink, jammed his feet into his Dingo boots and grabbed his jacket before realizing he had all kinds of time. He made himself sit down again and think about the next step or two. Then, with great calm he folded up the *Sporting News* and stuffed it into his pocket and walked out trying to remember where he had parked the Valiant.

The Dunkin' Donuts was out of place in the neighborhood, a bright new franchise outlet in the middle of old tired brick and concrete. It had big plate glass windows and the people inside looked like fish in an aquarium. Cooper figured the boy had chosen it to get a look at him. Inside there was fake blond wood everywhere and the bill of fare in hot colors on black posted over the counter. The smell of old doughnuts pervaded the place. There were a couple of old Sad Sacks at the U-shaped counter, smoking hard and drinking coffee out of official Dunkin' Donuts cups and worrying in poverty-stricken silence. A couple of Latin guys in a booth on the side were laughing about something. Cooper ordered a chocolate doughnut and coffee and took them to an empty booth on the far side and sat facing the door. He pulled the newspaper out of his pocket.

In ten minutes he had finished the few articles he had not already read, except for the golf news, which he could not bring himself to read even to pass the time. He made a pretense of going back through it, trying not to look up every five seconds. He drank coffee and stared at the doughnut crumbs. A couple of plump, nicely made-up girls came in and sat at the counter. One of the old Sad Sacks put out his last cigarette and pulled his Bears stocking cap down around his ears and left, muttering. Cooper looked at his watch and saw it was ten-twelve. He convinced himself Dominic had gotten cold feet. He would give him until ten-thirty and then give it up, forget about the kid. He opened the paper again.

"Are you Cooper?"

He looked up with a start at the voice. He had not heard the boy come in. "Yeah," he said.

Cooper would have put the kid who slipped into the booth opposite him at sixteen or seventeen. Mickey's description was about right: he was in the five-nine, five-ten range, thin and angular, with a bit of acne but not too much. He had one of those haircuts that was shaved on the sides and piled up on top with a lock that fell directly into his face. He had on a long dark wool overcoat and underneath it a gray sweater. He had big brown eyes; that was the youngest part of him.

"Dominic?" Cooper said. The boy nodded. Cooper just stared at him for a moment, unable to connect this vision with the thought of his son, and then folded up the paper and laid it on the table. "Want a doughnut?"

"I ate already." Dominic's eyes flicked from the paper to Cooper's hands to his face. He brushed the strand of hair out of his eyes with a long slender hand, stuffed the hand back into the pocket of his coat and leaned back in the seat. It was only his size that was misleading; a close look at his face suggested the down side of sixteen. It also suggested a kid who'd missed sleep and spent the nights worrying recently. "How well did you know my mother?" he said.

Cooper looked at him and decided on the simple truth. "I was in love with her a long time ago," he said.

Dominic blinked slowly. "I never heard her talk about

you," he said. The voice, too, was young. It was a voice that probably still broke occasionally.

"That doesn't surprise me. She never paid much attention to me."

Dominic was silent while Cooper drank some coffee. "How come you came looking for me?"

"Curiosity. Concern." That wasn't going to do it, Cooper felt. The boy kept staring at him past the dangling lock of brown hair, a fourteen-year-old skeptic. "Maybe it's just a middle-aged need to worry about someone. Ellen told me about you and because I'd known your mother I started worrying."

"Are you going to tell anyone about me?"

"Of course I'll tell someone. You owe it to your family to at least let them know you're all right."

"I don't have a family anymore." Dominic's eyes darted away to the corner of the place. "My dad doesn't count. He hates me."

"Maybe he does. I don't know. There's still your grandmother."

Dominic shook his head and tried to sneer. "I'm not going to go live with her."

"Fine. Just give her a call, tell her you're all right. Then you can worry about where you *are* going to live. I don't think you'd be here if you had that all worked out."

The boy stared into space, looking worn and sullen in the corner of the booth, the collar of the overcoat turned up around his cheeks.

"Look," said Cooper. "I'll just run messages. I'll tell your family whatever you want me to tell them. Sooner or later you're going to have to get back in touch with them. You don't just cut people out of your life like that."

Dominic stared for a while longer and said, "So I can crash with you a while?"

"Sure. What happened to the friend you've been staying with?"

"Which one?" Dominic's eyes wandered.

"I only heard about one. The one you told your school friend about."

"Oh him. He's kind of weird. I left there."

"Where have you been staying?"

"With these people I met. One of them has a van. We sleep in the van."

"And you're getting tired of not being able to take a shower."

"Yeah. And . . . they steal stuff. I didn't want to like get busted or anything."

"No, you don't want to do that. OK, we can go anytime you're ready."

"There's one thing."

"Uh-huh?"

"That first guy I stayed with? My stuff's still over there. My clothes and stuff."

"OK, we'll go pick it up."

"I think he might be kind of mad."

"How come?"

"I kind of walked out on him. He . . ." Dominic gave a little hiss of disdain. "He started coming on to me. Like I owed it to him, for letting me stay there."

Cooper shrugged. "So he'll be mad. We'll just get your stuff and go."

Dominic blinked at him a few times and said quietly, "All right." Cooper folded up the newspaper and Dominic extracted his long-limbed frame from the booth and they went out to the parking lot and got in the Valiant.

The place Dominic directed him to was on a narrow street that ran south from Diversey, in a mixed block of old stone houses, a big courtyard apartment building and a couple of newer high-rises. It was a prosperous block of prosperous Lincoln Park, and like all Lincoln Park streets, it was permanently lined with parked cars, leaving no space for outsiders. Cooper circled the block once after Dominic pointed out the house and then gave up and parked illegally at the corner.

"How'd you meet this guy?" he asked Dominic as they were walking back to the house.

"He works in a bookstore I hang out at sometimes. He used to like recommend books to me and stuff and we just got to be friends. I guess I won't be able to go there anymore."

Dominic led him up the steps to a porch. There was a front door with two doorbells at the side; beyond the door was a little foyer with the door of the downstairs apartment and a steep staircase leading up to the second floor. Dominic rang the upper doorbell; after a few seconds a voice came from the speaker above the bells. "Who is it?"

The boy leaned closer to the speaker. "It's Dominic."

There was no reply. After a second or two the buzzer went off and Cooper pushed the door open. When they were half-way up the stairs the door at the top opened and a man appeared. He was bald on top with a gray moustache. "Dominic. I thought you were gone," he said.

"I just came back to get my stuff," the boy said. He halted on the steps and stood looking upward. Cooper could feel his tension.

"Who's this?" said the man, nodding at Cooper.

"Cooper," said Dominic.

"A friend of the family," Cooper added, putting a hand to Dominic's back and urging him gently on.

When they got to the top the man stood aside to let them pass, but he was looking hard at Cooper. Cooper slipped past him and found himself in a long living room that stretched to the front windows. The entire wall opposite him was lined with books. A second man sat on a couch to Cooper's left. He was younger, black-haired and bearded.

"Dominic's not on very good terms with his family now," the bald man said. "How do I know he really wants you here?" He hadn't yet closed the door. He was about five-ten, a little stocky; the remaining hair around his shining crown was gray like his moustache. He had bright blue eyes and a squarish face. He wore an old limp epaulet shirt with the sleeves rolled up.

Cooper turned to the boy. "Do you want me here?"

He nodded. "Uh-huh."

"Why don't you go get your stuff? I'll explain to your friend here how things stand."

Dominic moved toward the back of the apartment with dispatch. The man watched him for a second and turned back to Cooper. "I don't know who the hell you are, but I can't let you just walk off with that boy. He's having a very tough time right now and he needs people who care for him."

Cooper wandered a little farther into the room. It was a good warm-looking room, with the original woodwork bare and oiled, a thick blue and dark orange carpet showing smooth wood floor around the edges, plants under the windows, and all those books. Cooper nodded at the man on the couch. His impression was that he would probably like someone who lived in a place like this. A little sadly, he turned back to the bald man, who was glowering at him from near the door, his hands on his hips.

"I care about him. I'll see that he gets in touch with his family and gets all the care he needs."

"You'll take him back to his father, won't you? That's just what he doesn't need."

Cooper had no time to deny it before Dominic was back in the doorway, looking at the man. "Where's my stuff?" he said, with surprise, a bit of outrage perhaps, in his voice.

"Dominic, I can't let you run off with this man. How do you know where he's going to take you?"

"Check closets and places like that," said Cooper to Dominic, who spun on his heel and left.

"Don't you go rooting around in my closets," the man said, starting after him.

Cooper had spotted the phone, on a table at the end of the couch. He walked to it and picked up the receiver. The man on the couch was looking bewildered. The bald man had stopped at the sound of Cooper's steps and stared at him as he punched out 911.

A cop answered and Cooper said, "Could you send a squad around to. . . ."

"Put that down." The bald man was striding toward him. The other man stood up, still looking lost. Cooper hung up in the cop's ear.

"All right, let's talk sense then. The boy's going to get his things and we're leaving. And that's it. No one's making any trouble."

The bald man turned to the other man. "Would you go ask Reggie to come up here, please?" he said. The man hurried out the door.

"You try and stop us from leaving, it's unlawful restraint," said Cooper.

"And if you take that boy away, it's kidnapping."

"I'm not coercing him."

"You could be deceiving him. From the looks of you, you're no friend of *his* family's."

"There's the phone. Call the cops. We'll wait till they get here and talk to them."

The man appeared to consider it for a moment, and Cooper hoped he wouldn't actually do it.

"I lent that boy money," the man said. "How am I going to get it back?"

Cooper sighed. "How much did you give him?"

"Two hundred dollars."

"It wasn't that much," said Dominic, coming into the room with a dark blue carry-all in his hand. "And you didn't say anything about paying you back."

"How much did he give you?" said Cooper.

"Maybe fifty or seventy-five. It wasn't two hundred."

"Do you have any of it left?"

"Maybe a few dollars."

"Give it back to him." Dominic dug in the pocket of his trousers and pulled out a handful of wadded-up bills and held them out to the man.

"If it's just pocket change don't bother, Dominic. You owe me two hundred. And how many of my things have you put in that bag?"

Cooper took out his wallet. "Here's . . . forty-five. That's all I got. Take it and check his bag if you want. Then get out of our way."

The man took the bills from Cooper slowly, his eyes blazing. He folded them and turned to Dominic and said, "Dominic, I took you in and provided for you. I would think you'd show a little gratitude."

"Say thank you to the man, Dominic," Cooper said, deadpan. "Then let's split."

"Thanks," Dominic said, warily. Cooper walked past the bald man and shepherded Dominic out onto the landing. The man followed them to the doorway.

"Some people are giving people, Dominic. All you do is take, is that it?"

Dominic's mouth was a thin tight line. "Let's go," Cooper said softly, starting down. Dominic followed him.

"Congratulations, Dominic. You're learning how to live off people," the man said. "But if you're going to be a whore, you have to put out sooner or later."

"Ignore him," said Cooper, controlling his voice. He had

almost reached the bottom when the door opened and a big man appeared. He was over six feet and broad, partly fat, partly not. His hair was bleached blond, and he had a black goatee. Behind him stood the younger bearded man.

"What's going on?" barked the big man.

"We're just leaving," said Cooper.

"The boy's running off with him. He won't pay back the money I lent him," the bald man called from the top of the stairs.

"You got paid," said Cooper. He turned to the big man below him. "Dominic has decided he doesn't want to stay here anymore. I'm a friend of his mother's and I'm taking him home."

"He's stealing from me," the bald man said.

"I'm afraid I'll believe Walter before I'll believe you," the big man said to Cooper, filling the doorway.

Cooper turned to Dominic. "Go up and use the phone. Call the cops, tell them to get over here and sort things out."

"No need to get the police in on this," said the big man. "You pay back what the kid owes and there's no problem."

"You might mention unlawful restraint when you talk to the cops," Cooper said to Dominic. Dominic started uncertainly up the stairs, then stopped when he saw the bald man blocking his way.

"No police," said the big man. "Let's be reasonable. If the boy owes him money, he should pay him, right?"

"The boy doesn't owe him a thing. Now would you stand aside, please?"

"I will *not* stand aside until Walter tells me to."

Cooper knew there was a slow and patient and responsible way out of this, one involving a lot of talk and time and trouble, especially if the police came. He didn't think he had the patience. And he really didn't like these people.

"You're forgetting something very important," he said.

"What's that?" said the big man.

"I'm standing several steps higher than you," said Cooper, and kicked him in the face with the heel of his boot, hard.

The man's head flew back and he sat down heavily in the foyer, then slumped back against the door frame and put his hands to his face. "Jesus!" said the bearded man, pressed against the wall.

"Let's go, Dominic," said Cooper, stepping down into the foyer and across the big man's feet. "Excuse us," he said to the bearded man, who stared at him with wide eyes. Blood was starting to seep through the big man's fingers and he groaned softly. Cooper pulled the door open against the weight of the big man's shoulder and made way for Dominic to pass. "You have a broken cheekbone, maybe the nose too," he said to the man on the floor. "Should heal in a few weeks. Don't be so anxious to play the heavy next time." He stepped out into the cold air.

Cooper was already feeling remorseful as they strode down the block, knowing he should have taken the slow patient way. Maybe Valenti was right; maybe he did look for trouble.

"Uh . . . shouldn't we be like running or something?" Dominic said.

"Nobody's coming after us."

Dominic considered that in silence and seemed to concede the logic of it. "I never did like that guy downstairs," he said after a moment.

"You're not lying to me about the money, are you?"

"No! I swear to God. He never gave me any two hundred dollars. And he didn't say it was a loan, either. He just said 'here, you'll need this' or something like that."

Cooper looked at the boy's face and nodded. "OK, just checking."

"I guess I owe you money now."

"Yeah. I guess you do. Write me an IOU when we get home."

They reached the car and got in. Cooper headed down to Fullerton and out to the Drive. Hustling north, snaking past slower sets of tail lights while watching for cops with a practiced eye, Cooper stole glances at the silent boy beside him and saw his eyelids droop.

"Had a rough couple of weeks, huh?"

Dominic didn't answer and Cooper realized he could have chosen a more tactful remark. Dominic continued to stare out the windshield and finally said, "People keep turning out different than what I expected. Maybe you will, too." He huddled in the far corner of the seat, not looking at Cooper.

Cooper couldn't think of anything more to say and they kept
quiet until he got them home.

Inside his place, Dominic stood for a moment just taking
in the old desk, the board-and-brick makeshift bookshelves,
the director's chair, the threadbare wing chair with the magazines stacked on it, the brass floor lamp, the old mosslike
rug, the faded reproductions of Gauguin and C.M. Russell
tacked on the wall, the long couch with the old steamer trunk
serving as coffee table in front of it.

"The couch is a bit narrow but pretty comfortable," said
Cooper. "I've spent a lot of nights on it myself when I didn't
make it in to bed. Throw your stuff there—we'll make this
your corner. I'll get you a sheet and a blanket. There's a
spare towel or two behind the door in the bathroom."

Dominic dropped the bag and sat heavily on the couch.
"How long can I stay?"

Cooper hung his flight jacket on the closet doorknob and
considered. "As long as it takes you to get straight with your
family, one way or another. I hope it won't be too long."

Dominic's eyes were fixed on the rug. He sat that way in
the muted lamplight while Cooper went into the bathroom
and pissed, then came back in and sat down on the couch to
lever his boots off.

"What am I supposed to do?" said the boy. "My mother's
dead and my father might as well be, the way we get along.
It's like who am I supposed to go back to?"

Cooper tossed his boots toward the door. "I don't know,"
he said. "But it looks to me like you've had enough of the
street for a while. Work something out with your Dad so you
don't have to live with him, I don't know. Have him put you
in a boarding school. Find a friend or relative you can live
with. But start using your head. You need support."

There was no reply. Dominic closed his eyes and they sat
in silence. After a minute or two Cooper went and found a
sheet and an extra blanket in his bedroom and threw them on
the couch. "At least take off your coat," he said. The boy
didn't move. Cooper went into the kitchen and found one
beer in the refrigerator. He debated whether to offer it to the
boy, an obscure sense of responsibility telling him he would
be contributing to the delinquency of a minor. A feeling that
the boy had ingested far worse things won out and he took a

glass into the living room with the beer. "You want to split this?" he said.

Dominic opened his eyes and gave the beer a sidelong look. "No. Thanks." Cooper shrugged and went back into the kitchen. He sat at the table with an old issue of *Parameters* and drank the beer, listening for noises from the living room. He heard none. When he finished the beer he looked into the room from the hall and said, "I'm going to bed. The bathroom's down the hall here. You need anything?"

"No," the boy said softly. Cooper looked at the back of his head, that ridiculous haircut, for a moment longer, then said good night and left.

Lying in bed he listened, thinking about Vivian Horstmann and wondering if Dominic was really his son. He had closed the door to the bedroom and he heard no noises in the living room. He went to sleep eventually and slept soundly until the sobs woke him up.

They were coming through the door and Cooper sat up in bed, listening. He sat in the dark and listened for a time as the boy cried, cried like the end of the world, cried like a child without a mother.

Cooper got up and dressed and went softly into the living room. The lamp was still on but Dominic was prone on the couch now, still in his overcoat and black shoes, face to the light shining tears.

Cooper sat on the director's chair and spoke quietly. "You need anything? You want me to go away? Say the word."

"She didn't kill herself," sobbed Dominic through the thickness of his grief. "She didn't kill herself."

Cooper sat and watched him until he quieted down, until his eyes were closed and his breathing was smooth. After a while he turned out the lamp and went back to bed, but he didn't fall asleep again until it was beginning to go gray beyond the windowshade.

6

COOPER ROSE AT eleven and looked into the living room. Dominic was asleep; he had finally shed the coat and shoes and lay wrapped in the sheet, wheezing slightly as he breathed. Cooper stole out and came back in half an hour with provisions. The couch was vacant, and the sound of the shower running came from the bathroom. Cooper made coffee and sat with it over the paper until Dominic appeared in the doorway with wet tangled hair, dressed in baggy khaki trousers and a shirt that looked like a long undershirt dyed black. "I don't have any clean clothes," he said. He stood diffidently, hands in his pockets.

"There's a laundromat down the way. Want some eggs?"

The boy stared at him. "I usually have tofu or granola."

"Sorry, I'm out. You're too young to worry about cholesterol anyway. Have a seat."

Cooper scrambled the eggs with onions and tomato and they ate, mostly in silence. If Cooper had expected some immediate bond of sympathy between them, of genetic origin perhaps, he was disappointed. Dominic stared at the tabletop or pawed without interest at the sections of the paper Cooper shoved his way. He ate the eggs and toast and drank the coffee Cooper poured him. His hair was drying and the forelock was already drooping to obstruct his vision. Cooper watched him surreptitiously, looking for a resemblance beneath the trappings. He, too, had been a skinny teenager with brown hair, brown eyes, but he wasn't certain that this was his son just by looking at him.

Cooper cleared the dishes and went to hunt up his spare keys. "That's the door downstairs, that's upstairs." He tossed them on the table in front of Dominic. "You can come and go as you please. I'm working today so you'll be on your own. There's food in the refrigerator. We're two blocks from the lake. There's bookstores and coffee shops and such on Sheridan Road a block east.''

Dominic put his hand on the table next to the keys but didn't take them. "I don't have any money," he said.

Cooper stood still for a second and then smiled. "No, you don't, do you? Here." He put a twenty on the table. "That makes what, sixty-five you owe me?''

"Yeah. Thanks. I'm not sure when I can get the money."

"Maybe you can think about that today. While you think about what to do with your life.''

"You think I'm like a real fuck-up, don't you?'' He stared at Cooper past the lock of hair.

Cooper sat down at the table. "I think you're young and you've had a rough experience. I think you have a lot of pride. But you shouldn't have too much pride to do the smart thing. Rest up here for a couple of days and think things over. Then call your grandmother, let her know you're all right, and start negotiating. I gotta run. I'll be back late tonight." Cooper left him at the kitchen table, staring at the twenty-dollar bill and the keys.

Cooper found driving hard that day, keeping his mind on his business while tasting anticlimax. He had found his son and there was no recognition, no revelation, no satisfaction. No confirmation, no reward for those stunted paternal feelings. He wasn't even sure he liked the kid. What he had on his hands was just a traumatized fourteen-year-old with family problems.

He gave up near midnight and stashed the cab under a viaduct. When he walked into his place he saw Dominic stretched out on the couch with one of the old Horatio Hornblower books. The boy swung his feet to the floor and sat up as if waiting for a reproach.

"Hi," he said.

"Hey. Like the book?"

"It's all right."

"Did you eat?"

"I made a sandwich."

Cooper went into the kitchen and got a beer. "I wouldn't turn you in if you wanted one of these."

"I don't like beer."

"That's good. Keep it that way." Cooper sank onto the couch. "What'd you do today?"

Dominic laid the book on the floor beside his pile of clothes. "I called my grandmother."

Cooper nodded. "And?"

"I'm gonna go see her soon. When I figure stuff out."

Cooper nodded some more and drank. "That's good."

"I didn't tell her where I was."

"That's OK by me."

"She says the private investigator is costing my father two hundred dollars a day." He laughed through his teeth, briefly.

"He can probably afford it."

"Yeah. He can afford pretty much whatever he wants."

Cooper grunted. After a silence Dominic said, "Are you writing a book? I looked at all that stuff on your desk."

Cooper considered. "I guess it's a book. Or might be someday, anyway."

"What's it about? It looked like philosophy or something."

"Philosophy, history, politics. It's about what I did when I was eighteen and why I did it and whether it was worth it."

"What did you do when you were eighteen?"

"I ran off and got myself into a war."

Dominic considered that and then said, "How long have you been working on it?"

"About three years now."

"When are you going to be done?"

"Probably about the time they figure out how to prevent wars. I figure it's going to be a long job. But it helps me sleep nights."

Dominic slouched down until his head was resting on the back of the couch. "My father stayed out of the war by going to college."

"He wasn't the only one." Cooper drank and watched the boy blink at the wall. "What is it with you and your father, anyway?"

Dominic closed his eyes and then opened them again, slowly. "He hates me."

"How come?"

"I don't know. It's not like I try and make trouble for him

or anything. He doesn't like my friends, he doesn't like what I do, he doesn't like my hair . . . nothing.''

"Sounds like every other father in the world. Sounds like mine.''

"Uh-uh. I get an A minus in school, he's like 'How come you didn't get an A?' instead of 'That's nice, you didn't get a B.' I can't do anything right for him.''

"He wants you to excel.''

"Yeah. He wants me to be just like him, wear suits and stuff and make a lot of money.''

"Fathers get over it, not having their sons turn out like them.'' Cooper knew that was a lie as soon as he said it. He took a drink of beer and tried again. "He has a different idea of who you are than you do. That doesn't mean he hates you.''

"He tells me stuff like I'm going to be a junkie, I look like a queer, stuff like that.''

"Huh.'' Cooper shook his head once. "What'd you do, smoke a little dope?'' The boy turned a blank gaze on him and he wondered if his slang was out of date.

"Yeah. He threatened to call the cops on me. Some father, huh?''

"Drugs scare people. They panic.''

"You don't even know my father and you're defending him.''

"I'm not defending him. I'm just saying don't assume he hates you.''

"I'm not assuming anything. I know. He started to hate me when things started to go wrong between him and my . . . my mother.''

Cooper picked at the corner of the label on the beer bottle. "That can happen. If he saw you as your mother's ally he may have had a hard time with it. But if he hated you I don't think he would have hired that guy to find you. Anyway, things may change now.''

"Now that my mother's dead, you mean.''

"Yeah.''

Dominic's eyes were closed again; his head was turned away from Cooper. He said nothing and Cooper drank and stared at the wall above the desk. After a minute the boy said, "She didn't kill herself, you know.''

Cooper finished the beer and set the empty bottle on the floor. "You said that last night."

"She didn't."

"You mean someone else killed her?"

"Uh-huh."

"How do you know?"

"I just know. She wouldn't ever do anything like that. She was too religious. Not like she went to church all the time, but she was, really. She wouldn't have killed herself."

Cooper hesitated a long time before responding. "That's what a lot of people thought. But I thought she left a note."

"Somebody could have made her write it. Or copied her handwriting. There are guys who forge checks and stuff, aren't there?"

"Why would anyone kill her?"

"A robbery or something. Did the cops check to see if anything was taken?"

"I don't know." Cooper picked up the beer bottle and took it into the kitchen and threw it into the trash. He wandered back into the living room. Dominic was still slouched at the end of the couch with his eyes closed. Cooper stood watching him, thinking about Vivian, trying to imagine her on the twenty-third-floor balcony looking down.

"Besides," Dominic said suddenly, "there was someone there with her that night."

Cooper's frown deepened and he said, "How do you know?"

"The curtains were open when I got home. She always closed them when she was alone at night. She said it gave her the creeps to have them open. Only she'd leave them open if someone was there. People liked the view and stuff."

Cooper walked slowly across to the director's chair and sat down.

"Couldn't she have . . . I mean if she was really upset . . ."

"You mean like if she was upset enough to kill herself she would have forgotten stuff like that. No. If she was upset that was the first thing she would have done. She was weird about that. The only way she would have left them open was if someone was with her. Then it didn't bother her. And if someone was with her but left, she would have closed them.

If they were open, that means someone was there when she died.''

"Maybe the cops opened them. Or your grandmother. They were there when you got home, right?''

"They didn't touch anything. They hadn't even taken the note down. It was still taped on the door to the balcony. They wouldn't even let me touch anything at first.'' The boy's eyes were still closed.

"Did you tell the cops this?''

"Uh-uh. I didn't think of it until later. After I split.''

"Why didn't you tell them then?''

"I don't know. I didn't want to talk to them, I guess. I was kind of out of it for a while.''

Cooper leaned back in the chair and stared at the boy. After a minute he said, "Maybe it's time to tell them.''

"Think they'd believe me?''

"I think they'd listen. They'd have to. You could be wrong, I guess. But you would know something like that.''

Dominic opened his eyes. "Do you believe me?''

"I'm not sure. But I think the cops ought to hear it.''

The next day Cooper called the 24th District again and asked for Valenti. He was lucky this time and the lieutenant came on the line.

"What the hell you want now, MacLeish?''

"I found the boy, like I said I would.''

"Congratulations. He recognize you?''

"Listen. I want to talk to the officer who investigated his mother's death.''

"Christ. Is this what you do when you get bored?''

"Listen, Valenti. The boy thinks he can prove that someone else was there with her when she died. In other words she didn't kill herself.''

There was a silence. "Oh he does. Terrific. Every time, MacLeish. Every time Grandma sticks her head in the oven there's a relative right there saying she didn't kill herself, someone murdered her and covered it up, you can't let 'em get away with it. And you know what? We waste time looking into it and we never ever find anything different from what the initial investigation shows. If it's a faked suicide it shows up. Usually it ain't. People kill themselves, MacLeish. They

do it all the time. Do me a favor and help the kid face up to
it, all right?''

"Just put me in touch with the officer. If he thinks it's a
waste of time, OK.''

"Look, the lady left a suicide note, if I recall. What more
do you want?''

"The boy thinks it was faked.''

"Of course he does. What else would he think? If my
mama killed herself I wouldn't want to believe it, either. But
it happened.''

"Who would I call, Valenti?''

"Call the fucking non-emergency number and tell 'em
what you want. Don't waste my time. I got four rapes and
an attempted murder with a Lady Kenmore steam iron to deal
with right now.''

"I called you 'cause I know you'd take me seriously. Have
I ever wasted your time before? All the times you've dealt
with me, didn't you get arrests out of them?''

"Exactly two, if I recall correctly.''

"Three. That's three more than most people ever do.
Christ, if you had a district full of citizens like me you could
sit in Delmar's all day and plan your retirement.''

"OK, shut up for a second. I'll get back to you in a while.
Just sit tight and don't do anything stupid. Just don't do anything in fact.''

"Fine. Got my number?''

"I got your number from the last seventeen emergencies
you called me about.''

Cooper had to laugh. "You're a skeptic, aren't you Valenti?''

"I'm a cop. I've heard it all, MacLeish. All of it.''

The call didn't come for another day. When it came, at
eight the next morning, it wasn't from Valenti. It was from
a homicide detective named Shostak who had a deep voice
and a slow, patient way of speaking.

"Lieutenant Valenti up in Twenty-four says you have some
information about the Horstmann suicide a couple of weeks
ago?''

"Yes. The victim's son is here with me and he is convinced
his mother didn't kill herself.'' Cooper knew he sounded like

every other crank in the city but he was determined to get the boy a hearing.

There was a silence and then Shostak said, "She left a note. There was no question it was suicide."

Cooper took a breath. "I know about the note. The boy thinks it's a fake."

"It was in the woman's handwriting. That was established."

Cooper pressed on. "The son is sure someone was there with her that night, at the time she supposedly killed herself."

"How does he know?"

Cooper knew he was about to get brushed off. He said, "It was clear to him from certain things involving his mother's routine at night. I think you should hear him explain it. May we talk to you in person?"

The sigh at the other end of the line was just audible. "OK. Bring him in. You know where Area Six is?"

"Belmont and Western. We'll be right there."

They talked to Shostak and his partner in a room with cinder-block walls that held a table and four chairs. Shostak was a tall man with very neat gray hair and dark bags under his eyes. His tie was partially loosened and pulled to one side and the top button of his shirt was unbuttoned. He stared mournfully at Dominic as if he knew the kid could make nothing but trouble for him. His partner was a light-skinned black named Harrison who had big bright black eyes and a moustache that curled around the corners of his mouth. He wore a gray suit and he sat in a corner of the room with one leg crossed over the other, holding a paper cup of coffee.

"So she couldn't have been alone," said Dominic. He had spoken steadily, sitting with his hands folded on the table, looking a little intimidated by his surroundings but not wavering. He passed a hand over his forehead occasionally to get his hair out of his eyes.

Shostak nodded when Dominic finished. He sighed again and leaned back on his chair. He carefully pushed the ballpoint pen he had laid on the table an inch or so forward and then pulled the knot of his tie even looser. "I see," he said.

"You said you didn't open the curtains, and neither did the

policemen who got there first. So I know there was someone else there. It doesn't sound like much, but I know my mother," Dominic said.

"Yes. Sure you do." Shostak drummed his fingers on the table, briefly, and glanced at the impassive Harrison. "But I have a little problem with this whole thing. And that is that I can think of a whole bunch of reasons the curtains didn't get closed. Like she was on the brink of suicide and all her routine went out the window. She was full of alcohol, you know. She probably wasn't thinking about things like curtains. Or maybe she wanted them open. Suicides are sort of exhibitionistic sometimes. Especially ones that jump off high places. Maybe . . ."

"She didn't kill herself." Dominic was looking at the tabletop now, desolate.

Shostak leaned across the table and put a hand on Dominic's forearm. "Son, she left you a note. Did you read it?"

For several seconds no one moved. Then Dominic said quietly, "I read it. Someone could have imitated her writing. There are people who do that."

For the first time Harrison spoke from the corner, in a soft, unexpectedly high voice. "People who know compared it to samples from her papers. It was her writing, son. You can forge a signature, but it's hard to fake a whole note."

"We didn't even have any notepaper like that, that yellow paper it was on."

Harrison looked bored as he said, "We found a pad of it on your mother's desk. The next sheet had the impression of the note on it."

Dominic looked up at the detective for a moment, then at Cooper. "They're not going to believe me," he said.

Cooper said nothing. The detectives' account of the note had started to seem conclusive to him. He watched the boy, saw him glowering from under his forelock, hunkering down.

"I'm sorry," said Shostak. "I've seen a lot of murders and a lot of suicides. I know a suicide when I see one. That may be hard to accept. I can't help you with that." He picked up the pen and put it in his shirt pocket and stood up. "I get paid for catching killers. Nothing I like more. If I thought there was a killer still loose on this one I'd be busting my ass to get him. But there's no killer out there, son. I'm sorry."

"We didn't have any paper like that around the house. If you found some, it means whoever faked the note put it there."

Shostak looked down at him, a patient long-suffering man. "She could have bought it that day, couldn't she? While you were gone?"

"Why would she? We had tons of paper sitting around. Besides, did you check to see how many sheets had been torn off? If she had just bought it, there would have been only one or two, right? Did you check?"

Cooper thought at first that the detective was about to lose his temper, as his expression froze. Then he realized the cop was thinking, just thinking back. Shostak looked at Harrison in the corner and Harrison chuckled, one little spurt of bogus amusement. Shostak looked back at Dominic and said, "Why didn't you bring any of this up before? Why do you keep throwing it out a piece at a time?"

"I like keep remembering stuff. I just started thinking about it in the last few days. I'm not making it up."

Shostak sat down. He looked like a man who has just been told he has to work overtime on Christmas Eve. He looked from Dominic to Cooper and drummed on the table again. "This death has already been written up as a suicide. If we're going to do anything more on this we'll have to talk it over with the chief and with the medical examiner. If we decide there's good reason, we'll get back to you." He tugged absently at his tie again and stood up, Sisyphus returning to his boulder. Harrison drained the coffee cup and stared into it.

Cooper had been thinking, too. "What happened to the note?" he asked.

Shostak said, "It was returned to the victim's mother with the other effects we examined. She'd have it, I guess."

"Thank you," said Cooper, rising. "We appreciate your taking the time."

Shostak gave one jaded toss of the head and said, "Time is what I got, friend. Sometimes that's all I got."

Sitting in the Valiant while it warmed up, Cooper looked over at Dominic, who was staring out the windshield, and said, "Could you get into your mother's apartment?"

"Sure. It's my apartment, too. I have the keys."

"Want to go take a look? See about this pad of paper for example?"

Dominic gave him a long look. "Yeah. I guess so."

"That was smart, about the paper. I think that got his attention."

"It just occurred to me sitting there. I had never seen any paper like that around."

"Let's go have a look. Thirty-four something Lake Shore Drive?"

"Thirty-four seventy-two."

"You didn't run very far when you ran away, did you?"

"No. I knew the area and stuff. I thought I could hide out for a while."

It was almost a straight shot east on Belmont, but the traffic was the usual and it took a while. Cooper parked on a side street and they walked through the cold damp gusts to the building, which was separated from the eight freeway lanes of the Outer Drive by a low rail and the two lanes of the Inner Drive. It was one of the big concrete and glass stacks put up in the fifties when the Drive was put through. Cooper ran his eye up it and saw all the terraces. He didn't have time to count up to twenty-three. He glanced at Dominic and saw the boy marching resolutely, eyes on the sidewalk.

In a sudden fit of morbidity, Cooper looked up again and tried to estimate where Vivian would have landed. The terraces on this side filled the right angle between two main structural columns of the building. His eye ran down to a small yard at the side of the building, enclosed by a wrought iron fence, which belonged apparently to the massive brick house just up the side street and extended to the corner. Cooper looked at the hard dull yellow of the dying lawn; there was no sign that a body had ever lain there.

There was a canopied entrance with the address written in gold leaf script beside the glass doors. Inside the white lobby with its brass fixtures was a uniformed doorman. He stopped pacing when he saw Dominic and stared at him as if he knew him, but he said nothing. Dominic went straight past him to the elevators at the back of the lobby and punched the up button. He turned to face Cooper and said, "I haven't been here since that morning." His hair was hanging in his eyes and he looked as if he were trying to look bored.

It was a good fast elevator, an Otis deluxe. They stepped out on twenty-three and Dominic led Cooper to a white door thirty feet or so down a carpeted hallway, pulling keys out of some hidden place under his coat. He stopped in front of the door with the key poised and for the first time he wavered, paralyzed in front of the door, his poise suddenly gone.

"We can call it off," said Cooper.

"No. I'm OK." Dominic put the key in the lock and turned it. He pushed the door open and Cooper followed him into the apartment.

The first thing he saw was the broad gray sweep of sky and lake. The far wall of the place was mostly glass and the view beyond it dominated the room. The lake lay steel gray and menacing under the dirty sky, brooding on the concrete fungus that had grown on its shore, promising to outwait it. The second thing Cooper saw was the woman rising startled from a chair at the table in front of the window. She stood with her hands clasped on a white handkerchief and she stared at Dominic and then called his name.

"Hi, Grandma," he said in a dull small voice. He had stopped just inside the door, almost making Cooper bump into him.

"Dominic, I'm so glad to see you, honey." Mrs. Horstmann stepped away from the table. Her purse was on the table and her overcoat lay draped over the back of the chair at its head. Dominic crossed the room slowly toward her. Cooper closed the door behind him and stood uncertainly while the boy and his grandmother met. The woman reached for his hands. Dominic allowed them to be taken and then bowed his head as his grandmother pulled him to her in an embrace. He was a couple of inches taller than she. "We were so frantic about you," she said, and gave in to one quickly stifled sob. Dominic still had not put his arms around her; he stood stiffly, imprisoned in the hug.

"I'm all right," he said, very quietly.

Cooper moved stealthily around the edges of the room, past bookshelves and large cool abstracts on the wall. Behind him he heard Mrs. Horstmann shaking with the vain attempt to control her tears. He heard Dominic murmur something in a voice that sounded a lot younger than the one he used on Cooper, and then all he heard were the woman's sobs.

Cooper surveyed the place as he went. It was one long room, though divided into living and dining areas. They had come in past closets in the entrance area and seen Mrs. Horstmann standing at the glass-topped dining room table by the windows. The living area stretched to the left, and it in turn was divided by style into two distinct areas: one, closer to the windows, light and modern with a white roll-arm sofa and matching chair and a low glass cocktail table and sleek brass floor lamp, and the other, nestled in the corner away from the windows, darker, solider, older in feel, with a brown leather wing chair and mahogany sideboard and maroon upholstered library chair on a dark Persian rug. There were pillows from the sofa on the floor, and magazines and books lay haphazardly on an end table. Dust had started to collect on the surfaces and in corners. Cooper made his way toward the windows, noting the hallway to the right of the entry door that seemed to lead to bedrooms and such, and the counter that separated the dining area from the compact kitchen.

Dominic and his grandmother were still in their embrace, though the woman's tears were abating. Cooper stood with his back to them. He had reached the door to the terrace. It was a sliding glass door and through it Cooper could see the small balcony, no more than five by eight, that occupied the corner of the building, the corner he had looked at coming in. The two open sides of the terrace were protected by an iron railing. Beyond it was nothing, a great screaming expanse of chilly air with a slice of park and harbor and lake far below.

Cooper had to resist a strong urge to open the door and step out into the wind and look over, to see what Vivian had seen just before she died, before she went over the rail and sank through the night, building up speed until she hit. Cooper remembered things he'd learned in the airborne; from twenty-three stories up she wouldn't have had time to reach terminal velocity at around a hundred and twenty-five miles an hour. She'd probably hit the hard earth of the little yard at about sixty or eighty. Cooper shook his head and turned around.

Dominic and his grandmother had drawn apart, though she still held him by one hand. She was dabbing at her eyes with the handkerchief and he was wiping tears in the fierce, furtive way boys do. Mrs. Horstmann looked at Cooper and nodded gravely.

"Grandma, this is Cooper. He's letting me stay with him."

"We've met," she said. "How do you do?" Cooper nodded and murmured a greeting.

Dominic said, "What are you doing here, Grandma?"

Mrs. Horstmann walked slowly back to the table by the windows. She put the handkerchief in the purse and snapped it shut. She was wearing a dark green suit over a blouse with a lace collar and her white hair was styled close about her head. "I came down here to go through things. But I've just been sitting and thinking." She stood erect facing them, her composure regained, her eyes red but her breathing steady. "I'm glad you came by. It's been hard for me. Your Aunt Stacy was staying with me but she's gone home. It's been hard to be alone."

"We've been talking to a detective," Dominic said. "Mom didn't kill herself."

Her mouth opened and she froze looking at the boy for a long moment. Then she looked at Cooper, closed her mouth, and sat down. "What do you mean?"

Dominic's words came out in a rush. "She didn't kill herself. I'm sure. She couldn't have. I've been thinking about it a lot. There was someone with her that night. I know because she didn't close the curtains. She always closed them if she was by herself. And that note. We didn't have any paper like that around the house. It was a fake."

Mrs. Horstmann stared at him a moment longer and turned to Cooper. "You mean someone killed her," she said calmly.

Cooper, the mature voice of reason, said, "Dominic thinks there's good reason to believe that. I don't think the police are convinced."

"And what about you?" she said.

After a moment Cooper said, "I'm not sure yet."

"You don't believe me?" said Dominic.

"I believe you. I'm just not sure what it means. The curtains, OK. What about this paper, though? Are you sure your mother didn't have any?"

"I'm sure. That yellow notepaper, Grandma? Did you ever see any of it before?"

Mrs. Horstmann shook her head, very slowly. "I don't know."

"The detective said they found some here, on her desk," said Cooper. "Where would that be?"

Dominic wheeled and strode toward the hallway at the other side of the room. "In here," he said. Cooper followed him. The first door on the right down the hallway gave onto a small carpeted room fitted out as an office. There were muted gray and brown prints on the wall, a small sofa to the right of the door, and, in the corner, an antique ball-and-claw desk with brass fittings. The top was covered with the organic mess of paper and pens and clips that denoted a working office. "She did all her business stuff here," said Dominic. "More than down at the gallery. He stood poised for a moment, still in his overcoat, looking at the desk, and then pounced. "Here." He picked up a pad of yellow notepaper from the corner of the desk and held it out to Cooper. "I never saw this before."

Cooper took the pad. It was plain yellow notepaper, about four by six inches. He was aware that Mrs. Horstmann had joined them and was standing in the doorway.

"See?" said Dominic. "It's not new. At least half the sheets have been torn off."

Cooper ran a finger over the fringe of gum at the top of the pad and nodded. He tilted the pad to catch the light; he could make out the impression of cursive writing but couldn't read it. "So could you swear that you had seen all your mother's things? Didn't she have anything you didn't know about?"

"I knew about paper and stuff like that because I used to come in here to do homework. I borrowed paper from her all the time. And when she left notes for me it was on this paper we kept in the kitchen. This stuff." He darted forward and fished a sheet of paper out of the pile on the desk. It had a blue border and the heading READ IT AND WEEP at the top. On it was scrawled, near the top, 'Dr. Melvin,' with a phone number, and further down 'See Lauren Tues.'

"This is what she always left notes on." Dominic brandished it at Cooper and then slapped it back on the desk. "She didn't have any paper like that," he said, pointing at the yellow pad.

"I don't think you'll be able to convince the cops of that," said Cooper. "She must have several different kinds of paper in here. They'll never believe you could be sure she didn't have any like this."

"OK, if she did, then there should be a few sheets in the wastebasket, right? Look." He grabbed the woven basket that sat in the corner by the desk and put it on the desktop. "There's paper in here she's thrown away. Some of that . . ." He pulled handfuls of wadded-up paper from the basket and scattered them on the floor. ". . . and that. Look. Her good stationery. Some more of that notepaper from the kitchen. Some typing paper. No yellow paper." He set the wastebasket down abruptly and rushed out of the room, brushing past his grandmother. Cooper traded looks with her and moved out into the hall. Dominic had gone to the kitchen; Cooper heard thumping noises and then the rustle of paper. "Come here," called Dominic.

He had pulled the big plastic garbage can from under the sink and was rooting in it. "More paper. Come here and look. None of it is that yellow stuff." He straightened up and scattered paper and sent a challenging look at Cooper.

Cooper stood at the entrance to the kitchen with Mrs. Horstmann just behind him, the yellow notepad in his hand. He looked at the boy for a long moment.

"All right," he said. "She carried it in her purse. It's small, just the size you'd carry around to have paper at hand whenever you needed it. That's why you never saw it. She carried it with her."

"Why would she write a note on that when there was all this paper sitting around the house?"

"Maybe it was closer to hand."

Dominic stared at him. "You don't want to believe me either."

Cooper laid the pad on the counter. "I'm just telling you what the cops will tell you. You want to get them to investigate a death they've already called a suicide, you better have good reasons."

"I've got good reasons. Number one. My mother would never kill herself. That, I just know. You do too, don't you Grandma? Number two. She wasn't alone that night. Number three. This so-called suicide note was written on paper that didn't belong to her and had never been in this place before. Isn't that enough?"

Cooper leaned on the counter and thought. "Why would the person who faked the note bring his own paper to write it on? Why wouldn't he just use paper that was here?"

"It was a forgery. It took a long time because he had to work carefully. He did it somewhere else and then made sure to bring along the pad so the cops would think it was her own paper."

Cooper gave the boy a long look as he stood defiantly with his ugly haircut in the middle of the mess he'd made. Finally he said, "Maybe." He turned to Mrs. Horstmann. "Where's the note?"

She reached slowly for her purse. "I have it here. I was going to burn it when the police returned her things to me. But I couldn't. Then I couldn't decide what to do with it, so I just left it in my purse and I've been carrying it around with me."

"May I see it?"

Dominic and his grandmother exchanged a look. "Let him see it," said Dominic.

She opened the purse and sorted through the contents of one of the compartments with long graceful fingers. She pulled out a sheet of the yellow paper, folded in half, a little rumpled now, and handed it to Cooper.

With a sudden onset of something like awe he unfolded it and read the words written neatly in blue ink.

Dominic,
   Forgive me for what I've decided to do. I'm sorry to hurt you but I'm deadly tired and you'll be better off when I'm out of your life.
   Forgive me.

There was no signature.

Cooper folded the note reverently and handed it back to Mrs. Horstmann. "Keep it safe. I think we'll be talking to Officer Shostak again."

Mrs. Horstmann walked slowly to the table by the windows and sat down. She stared out the window for a moment and then began to tremble. She lowered her head and pressed her hand to her face. "I don't know which is worse," she said in a voice just under control. "Thinking she killed herself, or thinking someone killed her."

Dominic kicked at the trash on the kitchen floor. Cooper leaned on the counter, his eyes on the yellow notepad.

"At least," he said, "if somebody killed her, somebody's going to pay for it."

M RS. HORSTMANN SAT erect on the couch, her purse before her on the steamer trunk, looking in the midst of the bachelor disorder of Cooper's place like the lady of the manor dropping in on one of her poorer tenants.

"It is kind of you to offer, Mr. MacLeish, but I must admit I have my reservations. Nick does too, though I think in view of Dominic's attitude toward him he's more likely to agree to the arrangement for fear of sending Dominic off again. I took the liberty of giving him your number. I hope you don't mind."

"No." Cooper sat in the director's chair, a little stiffly. "Nick called here this morning. When I told Dominic who was on the line he went right out the door. There's a lot of bad blood there for some reason. I told Nick how things stood and he agreed that it would be a mistake to try to take Dominic to New York right away."

"I agree. But I have to admit I feel it would be best if Dominic came to live with me."

"It probably would. But he says he won't do that either."

"What on earth does the boy think he's going to do with himself?"

"He doesn't really have any clear idea. He talks about getting a place with friends, that kind of thing. With whose money, I don't think he's given much thought to. The reason I offered to let him stay here is that I think what he needs is a face-saving formula at this point. He doesn't want to come slinking back after a two-week bunk and just take up where he left off, going back to school and all."

"He can hardly just resume life as usual, in view of the circumstances." Mrs. Horstmann spoke with dignity, a bitter light in her eyes.

"No. Of course not. But I think he needs to assert his

independence in a pretty big way. I think that's part of dealing with his mother's death. After a couple of weeks with
me, on a pretty tight leash financially, he'll start to get a
more realistic idea of where a fourteen-year-old stands in this
world. Then I think he'll be ready to talk to his father or
move back in with you. In any event I've told him he's got
to make up his mind by January.''

"What about his schooling?''

"He's missed so much school now I think this term's a
write-off anyway. He told me he's willing to go back in January.''

"You seem to have given things some thought.''

"I have. I don't want to usurp Nick's role or yours. But
I'd rather have Dominic here for a month than see him take
off again. That's what I told Nick. I think he saw it my way.''

She stared at him for a moment, with soft blue eyes that
looked like Vivian's. "I'd have to clear it with Nick, with the
school, perhaps with my lawyer. There are truancy laws and
so forth to think about.''

"I understand. If you insist on taking him back with you
I'll put what pressure I can on him. I just don't want to send
him out into the street again.''

Mrs. Horstmann nodded slowly, taking a long look around
the room. "I see.''

Cooper knew what she was thinking. "If I were in your
position I'd want references. I can give you the names of a
couple of people who have known me for a while.''

"No, that won't be necessary.'' A faint smile touched her
lips. "Let me discuss this with Nick again. I'll call you tonight if I may.''

"Sure. I told Dominic to be back by six. We can get it all
settled.''

"There'd be the question of money if Dominic were to stay
here. I wouldn't expect you to support him.''

"You paid back what I spent on him already. For the rest,
give him whatever allowance Vivian gave him.''

"I'll discuss it with Nick.'' She rose and took her purse
and Cooper got her coat from the closet and helped her on
with it. She turned to face him and said, "I can see from
your bookshelves you're an educated man. I take it you don't
plan to spend the rest of your life driving a taxi?''

Cooper smiled. "That's a question I ask myself every so often."

"Remember the deal," said Cooper. "In January you move in with your grandmother if you haven't straightened things out with your father. In the meantime, what do you say I get you a job?"

"A job?" Dominic blanched. *As if I had suggested radical surgery or a vow of chastity,* Cooper thought.

"Sure. You don't want to sit around here all day. And it'll mean you won't have to depend on your grandmother for money."

"What kind of job?"

"I have a friend who runs a restaurant. I called her this morning and she said she needs a busboy." Cooper could read the incredulity and the affront on Dominic's face. "You've never had a job before, have you?" he said.

"Uh-uh."

"Well, you might like it. Let's go see my friend, huh?"

They went and saw her. Rose Connolly owned a health-food restaurant in the neighborhood, a wood-panelled, plant-hung, tea-scented place with windows misted in the cold and old Che posters on the walls, a last outpost of the sixties. Cooper had worked there for a time in what seemed like a previous life and had wound up sharing Rose's bed until the two of them became convinced that, despite all the will in the world to let bygones be bygones, a two-time winner in the Purple Heart lottery and an ex-SDS strategist were never going to make it as lovers.

Rose welcomed them with her glowing colleen's smile and showed Dominic around the place before handing him an application to fill out. "It's not a lot of money, but the servers give you a part of their tips, too. If you hustle. You can make decent pocket money. Can you start Wednesday night?" Dominic nodded bravely, resigned.

As a reward Cooper took him to play pool. The pool hall on Sheridan Road was nearly empty in the early afternoon. They took a table in the back of the place, dark except for the single light over their table. Dominic insisted he knew how to play but he shot like a blind man fending off a dog with his cane. Cooper showed him how to hold the cue, the stroke, the way to figure a shot. He had him just knock the cue ball around the table a few times to get the feel, then had him go through a rack by himself.

Standing watching the long gangly frame stretched out over the table, Cooper wondered if he was up to helping put the boy's psyche back together. There had been another midnight crying jag, and Cooper had wanted to call Mrs. Horstmann and tell her to come get the boy. It was going to be a long job, and family was what Dominic needed. Cooper watched the boy's face move through the shadows, thinking that paternity was a hell of a lot more than biological.

They shot a game or two, then headed north on Sheridan through a sharp chill. The sun was almost down already; the short fall days depressed Cooper. "Know what I think you should do when we get home?" he said to Dominic above the noise of the traffic.

"What?" The boy was wary, his eyes on the sidewalk.

"Call your father."

They walked a few feet in silence. "My grandmother already talked to him."

"Yeah, I know. But it's you he needs to talk to."

"He won't be home yet. It's not even five in New York and he works till eight or nine at night."

"Call him at work."

"He won't want to talk to me."

"Bullshit. He may not like everything about you, but he'll want to talk to you. Especially now. Look, you try and stay mad at him forever, it's going to take more work than it's worth."

Back in the apartment Dominic slumped on the couch while Cooper went into the kitchen and ran an eye over the supplies. He made a list and came back out to the living room. "I'm going out to get groceries. You know where the phone is." Dominic looked up at him and said nothing.

Cooper took his time shopping. When he got back to the apartment Dominic was still on the couch, but sprawled on his belly now, face to the back of the couch and a hand trailing on the floor. Cooper took the groceries into the kitchen and dumped them on the table. He was stashing them away when Dominic appeared in the doorway.

"I called him." He looked a bit tender around the eyes.

"How'd it go?"

There was a silence while Cooper shoved things into the refrigerator and then Dominic said, "OK. He says we have a lot to talk about."

"I guess." Cooper shut the refrigerator. "How do pork chops sound to you?"

"I told him about talking to the cops. About how my mother didn't kill herself."

"Yeah?"

"I don't think he believed me. But he said he'd call that guy Shostak."

"Huh."

"He's coming to see me in a couple of weeks."

"That's good."

"He can't make it this weekend 'cause he says he has too much work. It's like that's what's really important to him, making money."

"Maybe he just doesn't want to crowd you."

"Yeah, I thought you'd be on his side."

Cooper sat down at the table. "The only interest I have in the whole thing is that I knew your mother. I don't even know your dad. It just seems to me that in the long run you'll be better off if you learn to live with him. Fathers can be a pain in the ass, I know. Why the hell do you think I ran off and enlisted? But you need a father. Especially now. So give the poor bastard a chance."

Dominic stared at him for a moment and then wheeled and left the room. "I'm going for a walk," he said.

"You want any pork chops, make it a short one," Cooper called after him.

He heard the door slam.

Cooper eased down onto Diana's sofa with a sigh and took a pull on the beer. "Thirteen hours for a lousy seventy bucks," he said.

"At least you get to sit while you work. I bet I walk ten miles in a night." Diana was curled up at the end of the sofa, feline and feral in a slinky dark blue robe.

"Yeah, you don't hear me complaining. I could never wait tables. First trouble anyone gave me, it'd be 'Get your own damn meal.' "

"I've been tempted, believe me. Tonight this guy sent back his tournedos three times and then stiffed me, like it was my fault the chef couldn't get it right."

Cooper drank and said, "The world is full of assholes."

"You say that a lot, you know."

"It's the summit of human wisdom. I had a guy try to stiff me tonight, too. The old you-mind-waiting-a-couple-of-minutes thing. I said sure, if he wouldn't mind leaving his watch with me. Suddenly he decided he didn't need me to wait. I thought for a second I was going to have to chase him down, but he came up with the money. No tip, of course."

She brushed the strand of hair aside, that little amused lift at the corner of her mouth. "I don't see why you guys need tips anyway, if you're just pocketing everything above your lease fee."

"We don't, not like waitresses, anyway. But don't spread it around, OK?"

Diana laughed and settled deeper into the cushions, squirming her feet in under Cooper's thighs. "So what are we going to do when we grow up?"

"Me, I'm going to wear tweed jackets and write history books. What about you?"

"Seriously? Go back and get some more schooling and be the next Gregory Rabassa."

Cooper looked at her for a full three seconds before giving up. "Who's he?"

"A translator. He did García Márquez's books. I could do that." Arms folded, her gaze serene, she gave off quiet confidence in the lamplight.

"Yeah, I bet you could. So when does that happen?"

"A couple more years of waiting tables and I'll have enough. How about you?"

Cooper shook his head, drank some beer. "I don't know. Any time now, I guess."

After a silence she said, "So you're letting your boy have the run of the place tonight, huh?" There was a light of amusement in her dark eyes.

"Well hell, I wasn't going to invite him along. He'll be fine. He was going to be out with friends of his until late anyway. That's a good sign—getting back in with his school friends again."

"Would his grandma approve of your leaving him like this?"

"I don't know. I don't check things with her. I figure the kid needs a fair amount of independence or he'll take off again."

"How long are you going to have him on your hands?"

Cooper looked at her and found nothing in her expression to betray her thoughts. "Till January, like I said."

"Isn't he supposed to be in school or something?"

"Probably. The grandmother and I agreed to finesse that part of it for now. The important thing is to get the kid patched together again."

"The father didn't have anything to say about it? Sorry, I mean the stepfather."

"She cleared everything with him. He's coming in in a couple of weeks to see Dominic."

There was a silence during which Diana picked at a loose thread on the sofa. Finally she said, "How does that go down with you?"

"Fine. How should it go down?"

She frowned at him, faintly, and said, "He's your rival again. You've been getting into this fatherhood thing."

Cooper looked at the patch of lamplight on the worn sepia rug and shook his head slowly. "I've satisfied my curiosity. Done my good turn. Even if I actually fathered the kid, he's the guy who changed the diapers. If I can get him and Dominic back on good terms I'll have played out my role." He turned to see Diana staring at him, gravely. "You never liked this much, did you?"

"No." She shook her head and a smile touched her lips.

"You're jealous, huh?"

"I know. I don't have any right to be. Especially of a dead woman."

"But you're still jealous."

"It's been a little hard, seeing you caught up in this."

"It's been weird, yeah. But it'll be over soon."

Cooper stretched out a hand and Diana took it in both hers, squeezed, caressed it, still looking at him from the depths of her Caribbean remoteness. "You really think somebody killed her?"

"I don't know. The kid makes out a pretty good case. But

whether it really stands up, I just don't know." His eyes left hers and they were silent for a time.

Shostak reached him the next day just before he went out to drive. Dominic was out somewhere; Cooper stood looking out the window at the tree branches while he listened to the detective on the phone.

"So now I've got the husband on me, calling from New York, same thing. Who killed my wife? He talked to the kid, now he's convinced, too. He wants to know why we're not investigating it. Know why? Because nobody buys it down here. If you want to get a suicide call reversed, you have to have a lot more than what you've got. We have an authenticated suicide note, no signs of struggle, no visitors, nothing, we have reasons for the lady being depressed. It's a suicide."

"What about the notepaper? That made you think for a while, didn't it?"

"Yes, insofar as the kid's right that if it was recently bought it wouldn't be half used up, like it was. But who says it wasn't there all along? The kid. All you have is that the kid thinks his mother would have closed the curtains and that she didn't have any paper like that. You want me to reopen an investigation on that? Think for a second about what you're asking us to believe. Someone gains entry to the apartment. How? Did she know him? Maybe. But she had no visitors that night. There's a doorman in that building twenty-four hours a day. We talked to the guy that was on that night. Nobody came to see her."

"Nobody from outside the building, anyway."

"OK, right. Say it's one of her neighbors. Think about it. You ever tried to pick someone up who didn't want to be picked up, much less carry her across a room and out a door and throw her over a rail? There would have been signs of struggle."

"Unless she was passed out drunk. Or someone hit her over the head. A bump on the head might not show up after she fell twenty-three stories."

"The note. She left the kid a note. In her handwriting. Indisputable."

Cooper grunted, suddenly weary. "OK. I'm just playing

devil's advocate here. The boy had some ideas, I thought they ought to be heard."

"I've heard 'em. Believe it or not, I think about this kind of thing, too."

"Can I ask you one more question?"

"Shoot."

"The paper said Vivian jumped onto the pavement, meaning sidewalk I guess. But when I looked at the building, it looked to me as if she'd have to hit in that yard at the side of the building. I was just wondering where she was actually found."

"She was in the yard, yeah. Newspapers never get a damn thing right. They send out some kid who thinks he's going to win a Pulitzer for getting in our way, and he gets everything wrong. They said the guard found her shortly after she jumped. But the guy didn't find her until it started getting light out. The medical examiner said she could have been there for a couple or three hours. We're trying to find someone who heard the noise. A body falling that far makes a hell of a thump. But then grass is softer than concrete and what with traffic noise on the Drive and the fact that everybody was in bed we'd have to get real lucky to find someone who heard it and could pin down the time for us."

"Huh. Well, thanks for listening."

"You taking care of the kid now? Take my advice. Get him to face the facts. His mother killed herself. People deny it, and you can't blame them, but the sooner they face it the better. This one's got suicide written all over it, friend. In capital letters. Underlined."

After he hung up, Cooper stood for a time with his fingers just touching the receiver, thinking of the thump at the end of the fall, thinking of Vivian Horstmann's body lying unnoticed on the grass in the cold hours just before dawn. He stared out the window at the branches tossing in the wind, a few leaves still clinging.

The man in the phone booth waited a long time, hearing the slow country and western bass beat coming faintly over the line. Finally there was a series of thumps and the Puerto Rican said, "Yeah?"

"You really take your time, don't you?"

"Hey. Don't nobody own me."

"If I pay you to be available, you make damn sure you're available."

"Available for what? For sitting on my ass watchin' a bunch of white chumps fall off the bar stools? If it wasn't for my partner being the right color they'd run me outa here. The other place was better, man, where Harlan was."

"We're through with Harlan. You just make sure to spend some of my money in this place and keep out of trouble."

"Hey talk louder man, I can't hear you with this fuckin' hillbilly music."

"You listen harder. I got a job for you, if you think you're up to it."

"You know, I wanna talk to you just once, face to face, see if you still got the balls to talk the same way. People like you, man, I don't like 'em too much."

"You don't like my money, huh? The job's worth five hundred."

There was a short pause. "What's the fuckin' job?"

The man in the phone booth smiled. Money really was magic; the best magic there was. "Are you a good shot with a pistol?" he said.

Cooper sat in the office with Rose while Dominic finished his tasks for the evening, filling salt shakers, upending chairs on tables, sweeping up.

"He's all thumbs, but he tries," said Rose.

"He's never had a job before."

"Gotta start somewhere. At least he didn't break anything."

"He will. But this'll be good for him."

Dominic appeared in the doorway of the office, a damp stained apron in his hand. "What do I do with this?" he said diffidently. A white sweat band held his hair out of his eyes and his black cotton shirt was limp.

"Put it in the laundry hamper at the end of the counter in the dishroom. Then punch out and take off. Good work, kid."

Dominic was silent as they walked to the cab, which Cooper had double-parked outside. "How were the tips tonight?"

"I got about twelve dollars. And I was there for like forever. That doesn't seem like much."

"It's not. But there will be better nights. And you'll get a paycheck too, remember."

"I could make more than this on one little bag of weed."

Cooper shook his head and started the cab. It was a short ride home but as always he had to cruise for a while before finding a place to park the thing. Finally he left it under the viaduct again and they walked the half-block home. "Try and think of it as an education," Cooper was saying. "Like George Orwell in Paris."

"Who's George Orwell?"

"You're kidding." He looked at the boy, to see only the truculence of the ignorant caught out in his ignorance. "A great writer. I'll show you the book I'm talking about upstairs."

Cooper had his keys out and was starting to push through the outer door when the crack came. Something burned his upper arm and the hole appeared in the glass door just in front of him. He wheeled in time to see the flash of the second shot and feel it zing past his head, and then he was hauling Dominic down into the bushes with him and the car was tearing away with a squeal of tires.

As soon as the noise faded away toward Sheridan, he was up on his feet yelling "Son of a BITCH!" electrified. He couldn't see the license plate, had only the vaguest impression of the car, maybe an old Camaro; as he watched, the tail lights disappeared onto Sheridan and headed south. Beside him Dominic rolled out of the bushes and said with a quaver, "What happened?"

"We just got shot at. Let's get inside. Where are my fucking keys?"

The cops who showed up half an hour later looked with mild interest at the holes in the door, found the splintered place in the inner doorjamb where one of the slugs had buried itself, and followed Cooper upstairs to his place. Cooper had taken his shirt off and wrapped a towel around his upper arm; once inside he sat on the couch and took off the towel to show the cops the inch-long gouge the bullet had taken out of his flesh. "Tore up my good jacket, too," he said, indicating the flight jacket over the back of the chair, now sporting two small holes in the upper left sleeve. Dominic had effaced himself and sat in the darkest corner of the room.

"I'd say you got off easy," said one of the cops, a heavy sandy-haired man. "You can buy yourself a new jacket. An arm's harder to replace."

"Flesh grows back. That jacket cost me seventy-five dollars used," said Cooper, putting a brave face on for Dominic.

"And you can't give a description of the car or the occupants," said the other cop. This one had gray hair and an acne-scarred face under the fur cap with the badge pinned to it. He had sat at Cooper's desk to fill out the report.

"Not really. Like I said, maybe a Camaro, one of the old seventies type. Occupants male. I think. And that's about it. I have the impression that the one who fired had light-colored hair. But I sure as hell couldn't pick him out of a lineup."

"You think it was random, just driving by, or you think they were waiting for you?"

"They weren't parked in front or anything. I think they came down the block behind us as we walked. It might have just been random, yeah."

"Well if it wasn't, you'd be the one to know," said the cop.

Cooper let out a long whistling sigh and dabbed at his wound with the towel. "If it has to do with anything, it has to do with a matter I was discussing with Detective Shostak at Area Six."

"Shostak. Violent Crimes, right?"

"Yeah. Though right off the bat I can't see why anyone would take a shot at me just because I talked to him. All we talked about were suspicions and he wasn't even convinced."

The cops looked at one another. The one at the desk said, "That'll do it sometimes. I think you should get in touch with him."

"Yeah, I think I will." Cooper's arm was still bleeding slightly and he pressed the towel over it again.

"You should get to an emergency room and have that looked at," said the sandy-haired cop. "That gets infected, you'll have a hell of a time."

"In the morning," said Cooper. "When it's nice and light outside."

The cop grunted, understanding. "This ain't the first time you've been shot, is it?" He was looking at the moonscape of scar tissue on Cooper's torso.

"No," said Cooper. "But with any luck it's the last."

When the cops had left, Dominic came to sit on the couch beside Cooper, who had dabbed at the wound with alcohol, taped gauze over it and put on a sweatshirt. "Who do you think it was?" the boy said.

"Your guess is as good as mine."

"You think it was the same person who killed my mother?"

"I couldn't tell you, Dominic. It could have been two drunks having a party." Cooper got up and went to the kitchen to get a beer.

When he came back Dominic said, "If it did have something to do with my mother, how did they know who you were?"

"Try this on for size. Maybe they were shooting at you." Cooper saw the boy go white, saw his mouth come open, watched him while he sat stonelike for a long moment. "Yeah. It's a hell of a feeling, isn't it?"

Dominic clasped his hands between his knees and shivered once. "They were trying to kill me?"

"Could be. If it's any comfort, the guy is obviously a lousy shot."

Cooper drank the beer slowly, coming down from the nervous high, feeling the arm start to ache, thinking about the two doors to the apartment and wondering how likely it was someone would come back for a second try. Not very, he decided, but without total confidence.

"You sleep in the bedroom tonight," he told Dominic. "I'll take the couch." *With the Louisville Slugger down on the floor beside me,* he added silently to himself.

There was no response from the other end of the couch. Cooper turned and saw Dominic's wide eyes fixed on the wall, skin pale, fear settling on to him. "Who is it? Who's doing this?" the boy said.

"I don't know," said Cooper. "But we're going to find out. That I can tell you."

8

DRIVING BACK FROM the hospital the next morning, Cooper asked Dominic, "Who knows you're staying with me? Me by name, I mean, so they could find us. Who have you told?"

"Nobody. I mean I've told like a couple of friends about you, but I didn't give them your name."

"All right, so who knows? Your grandmother. Your father. The two detectives. Another cop named Valenti. A couple of friends of mine. No one else I can think of. So how did whoever shot at us, assuming it had something to do with your mother's death, find out where you were?" Dominic had no answer and after a minute Cooper went on. "I doubt the cops gave anyone the information, though you never know. Your father's in New York. I think we should talk to your grandmother."

They drove down the block once, looking for suspicious cars, before parking and walking back to the apartment. Mr. Kim, Cooper's squat Korean landlord, was standing in front of the building looking at the bullet holes in the glass. When he saw Cooper he waved a hand at them and shouted "What happen?" with his customary belligerence.

"Somebody shot at us last night," said Cooper, pushing past him.

"Shoot at you? Why dey shoot at you?"

"I don't know," said Cooper, turning to let Dominic slip in past him. "Maybe we were the only thing moving."

"You hab ducks in dere? You hab ducks I sow you out." Mr. Kim stared at Dominic in suspicion. "Who she?"

"Look," said Cooper with dignity. "If I had drugs I wouldn't have called the police, would I?" They left the landlord planted on the porch, staring after them as they climbed the stairs.

107

Cooper wasn't looking forward to the call but he went straight to the phone and got Mrs. Horstmann. "We had a little trouble here last night," he said after greeting her.

"What kind of trouble do you mean?"

"Somebody took a potshot at us."

"Someone . . . shot at you?"

"We're both OK. They missed."

There was a silence. "Where? What happened?" She sounded bewildered, as if someone had told her of an embarrassing stain on her dress.

"Right outside my door. Two shots from a car. We talked to the police but I couldn't give them much to help them."

"Dear God. Just a moment." Over the line, faintly, came the scraping of a chair. "Do you think this had anything to do with . . . with my daughter's . . ."

"I think it's possible. If it does, there's one big question to ask. Besides the whole question of what the hell's going on, I mean. That is, how did whoever shot at us know where to find us?"

There was a considerable silence this time, and then Mrs. Horstmann said, "I see."

"I was wondering who you have told about our arrangement."

"Goodness, not that many people. And certainly no one who would . . ."

"No, of course not. But if this isn't just a random shooting it means word got around somehow to the wrong people. Tracing how that happened would be pretty important."

"Certainly. Certainly. Excuse me, but shouldn't we be discussing this with the police?"

"I plan to do just that today. I thought of calling you just now to try and pin down this point before I talk to them."

"Of course. Well, give me a moment, then . . . I've talked with Dominic's father, of course, and the people at his school. But I hardly think . . ."

"No, of course not. Anyone else?"

"A number of friends. But you see, I didn't mention you by name."

"Then that wouldn't mean anything, no. You can't think of anyone else?"

"I don't believe so."

"Hm. Who did you talk to at the school?"

"The principal, a Mrs. Helms. And then yesterday a man called, one of Dominic's teachers, wanting your address so he could send Dominic some materials to keep him busy."

"Ah." There was a pause.

"Oh dear," said Mrs. Horstmann.

"What was his name?"

"He . . . he did tell me, yes, though I didn't make a note of it. I didn't see any reason to. But I think it was Stevens or Stevenson, something like that. I'm sorry, I thought nothing of it."

"There wasn't any reason to. And it may be completely on the level. But you might want to call the school and try to confirm it. If it's on the level, we look elsewhere. I'm going to talk to the cops again, and we'll see what happens. I'll keep you posted."

"Mr. MacLeish, is Dominic going to be safe with you?"

"I'm working on it. I haven't quite figured out what to do with him. I'll get back to you. In the meantime you might want to get in touch with his father. But why don't you get on to the school first? I'm going to make new arrangements for Dominic. I'll call you back in half an hour or so."

After he hung up Cooper looked at the boy across the room. "Do you have a teacher named Stevens or Stevenson?"

Dominic stared blankly for a moment and said, "No. How come?"

"I think your grandma gave away our position. I'm going to move you. I don't think you should stay here another day. And you know what would be best?"

"What?"

"I think you should fly to New York and stay with your father a while."

Dominic's face relapsed slowly into abstraction. Cooper waited for a reply of some kind but it didn't come. He picked up the phone again and dialed Diana's number.

"Hi, it's Cooper. Sorry if I woke you up. Can I park Dominic with you for a day or so?"

Diana was still shaking off sleep. "Here? Why?"

"I think somebody's trying to kill him. They know he's staying here."

After a silence Diana said, "Come on over. It sounds like I'm going to need some coffee to handle this."

Cooper hung up. "Pack up your stuff. You're moving," he said to Dominic.

Ten minutes later they were in Diana's living room. Diana was still in her robe, her hair hastily pinned up with stray locks dangling and her look skeptical. "You have a talent for this, don't you?" she said when Cooper had told her the story. "What do you do, walk around with a bull's-eye pinned to your back?"

"I think they were shooting at Dominic, and that's why he's here. Give us two days. Then he'll be out of here."

"Fine." She stood with her arms folded, looking speculatively at the boy. "You know how to cook? 'Cause it's up to you. I'm never here in the evening."

"He'll manage," said Cooper. "Mostly he'll just need to crash here."

"If it's too much trouble I can go somewhere else," said Dominic unexpectedly, sullen behind his forelock. "I have other friends."

"And whoever shot at us last night can find them easier than he can find Diana. You're better off here. You supposed to work tonight?"

Dominic blinked at him. "Tomorrow."

"All right. You're probably OK there. I don't think they could know about that. Now let's talk to Shostak." Cooper strode to the phone, checked his notebook, and dialed the number Shostak had given him. He was told the detective was off-duty. Cooper left his name, asking the detective to call him, then hung up and dialed Mrs. Horstmann's number.

When she came on the line he could hear the strain in her voice.

"You were right. Nobody from the school has called, and they don't have anyone named either Stevens or Stevenson. I . . . well, you can imagine how I feel. Mr. MacLeish, Dominic is in danger, isn't he?"

"For the moment he's safe. I've found a new place for him. Now I'd like you to call his father and bring him up to date if you will. I don't think anyone's in immediate danger. I'm trying to get in touch with the detectives I talked with. I hope in a few hours we'll have the police back in on this full force."

After he hung up Cooper turned to the boy. "All right. Dominic, why don't you lie low here? I've got four hours left to make money with that cab, and I haven't broken even yet. If you go out, stay away from your usual hangouts. I'll keep trying to reach Shostak. You keep out of the cold and think about things. I still think we should put you on a plane to New York."

"He likes taking charge, doesn't he?" said Diana to Dominic. "It's the sergeant in him."

Nettled, Cooper said, "Anyone with better ideas, I'm listening."

She stood looking at him with her arms folded and the sadness in her eyes that never quite went away. "No, Cooper. You're the man with the ideas. I just hope they're good ones."

Cooper was waiting at the curb in front of the Palmer House, deep in thought, when a fat woman with a magnificent head of hair tore open the back door of his cab and said, "Get me to Midway and get me there fast!"

He didn't like her tone of voice and she had broken his train of thought. He checked the mirror and the street ahead, saw no cops, and peeled out from the curb with a screech that turned heads and froze pedestrians in their tracks. He slowed at Wabash, but the woman said, "You can let me out if you can't drive any better than that."

"You said fast."

"I said get me there."

"I'll get you there." The woman subsided into a nervous silence.

Cooper returned to his thoughts. He had just phoned Diana's hoping to find Dominic there, but there had been no answer. Cooper had decided to insist on sending the boy to New York. It was madness to let him hang around Chicago. Tonight, if possible, he would get in touch with Mrs. Horstmann and Nick Dennison and run Dominic out to the airport. There had to be a late flight to New York.

And there had to be rhyme and reason to things. Someone wanted the boy dead; someone had wanted his mother dead. Cooper realized that he had come around to full acceptance of the idea that Vivian Horstmann had been murdered. Flying lead had a way of making him take things seriously.

On his way home in the Valiant Cooper spotted Valenti sitting in a squad car under the Morse El viaduct. He pulled over just in front of the squad and got out. Valenti was sitting alone in the car writing on a clipboard. He looked up as Cooper approached and his face took on the tired, patient look of a keeper in the ape house with a gorilla tugging at his sleeve.

"Got a minute to talk?" said Cooper through the window. Valenti nodded and Cooper went around to the passenger side and got in.

"I heard you got shot at again," said Valenti. "You seem to have a way of antagonizing people."

"Just lucky, I guess. The guy grazed me, but I'm sure he was shooting at the boy."

"How come?"

"How come I'm sure or how come he was shooting at the boy?"

"Both."

"Why he was shooting at the kid, no idea. But I'm sure he was because one, if someone was shooting at me I think I'd know why, and two, because someone called his grandmother yesterday with a bullshit story to find out where he was staying. Not three weeks ago his mother winds up on the sidewalk twenty-three stories down under suspicious circumstances. Now somebody who knows the family well enough to call the grandmother wants the kid dead."

Valenti's eyes were narrowed. "It was you they hit, wasn't it?"

"Yeah. But how much imagination do you have to have to put it together and figure it was the kid they wanted to hit?"

Valenti stared at him, looking annoyed. "If I wanted the kid seriously dead, I'd do a hell of a lot better job than just driving by and squeezing off a round. I'd stop and make sure. I think this was some old pal of yours, pissed off about the money you took off him at pool or something."

"So who called the grandmother? Someone needed to find out where the kid was."

"I don't know. What the hell you telling me for? I got

nothing to do with homicides down in Area Six. Talk to Shostak.''

"I'm trying to get a hold of him. I just thought you'd be interested, since somebody took a shot at me up here in your neck of the woods.''

Valenti looked down at his clipboard, flipped over a page, and shook his head once. "I'm interested. But as far as anyone can tell, you were the victim of a random shooting. If you think there's a connection with the other thing, all I can say is talk to Shostak and keep your head down, 'cause if there is a connection, they'll be back, won't they?''

"Well son of a bitch. I think I've just been told I'm on my own.''

"No, you're not on your own. Anybody else takes a shot at you, we'll go after 'em provided you can give us a description. But I can't give you round-the-clock protection. You know that.''

"Yeah, I know. Just promise me one thing. If somebody does a better job next time, at least be a little suspicious, will you?'' Cooper pushed the door open and swung a leg out.

Valenti looked up at him. "I'll be suspicious, MacLeish. I promise. Shit, I get suspicious just seeing you drive by anymore.''

Dominic finally answered Diana's phone around eight. Cooper said, "Where you been all day?''

"I went out.''

"Yeah, I guessed. What'd you do?''

"I found a place to stay.''

"What?''

"An apartment. With two roommates. I went by the restaurant and Rose said she knew these people who were looking for a roommate. A guy and a girl. I talked to them and I can move in any time. They had another roommate but he like went to Tibet or some place like that and they have an empty room. A hundred and fifty a month. That's a pretty good deal, isn't it?''

"Uh, yeah. Who are these people?''

"Friends of Rose's. The girl waits tables at the restaurant. They seem really nice. My grandmother will pay the rent.''

"How old are these two?''

"Oh man, I knew it. Now you're starting to sound like my father. They're in college or something, I don't know. They're not going to give me drugs or anything. Ask Rose about them if you don't trust me."

"I was going to put you on a plane to New York tonight."

"I know. That's why I went out looking. Come on, Cooper. I don't want to go to New York. All my friends are here."

"Somebody's trying to kill you here, Dominic."

"I know. But they won't find me now, right?"

"I sure as hell hope not."

"They won't. You gotta let me stay here."

"If your father and grandmother agree."

"They'll agree if you do."

"We'll see. I'm going to talk to your grandmother now. When Diana gets home tell her I'll be over late, OK?"

Cooper hung up and then dialed the restaurant. He got Rose's assessment of Dominic's domestic arrangement and then sat thinking for a moment. He picked up the phone again and called Mrs. Horstmann.

When he identified himself she said, "Oh, Mr. MacLeish. I've been trying to reach you all day."

"Why, what's up?"

"I called Nick this morning. He's coming to get Dominic."

"When?"

"Right now. His flight will be in soon."

"Terrific."

Hearing his tone of voice, she hesitated. "Is that sarcasm?"

"I don't know. I'm glad he's coming, but I think he's going to have a fight on his hands. Dominic is determined to stay put. He's found himself a place with some roommates."

"I see. Well, that's for Nick to sort out, I suppose. I was wondering if you could bring Dominic here to meet him. Nick was intending to take a taxi here from O'Hare."

"What flight's he on? When does it get in?"

"Let me see . . . He's on United flight 87, arriving at nine-twenty."

Cooper looked at his watch. "I'll meet him. I can bring

him here directly to see Dominic, or bring them both up there if you want to be in on the meeting.''

''No, frankly, I'd just as soon stay out of it.'' There was real weariness in her voice. ''Do you think . . . I mean, from what Dominic has said to you, is there any chance of his softening toward his father?''

''I couldn't say. A chance, sure. There's always a chance.''

''Have you spoken with the police about last night?''

''I've spoken with a lieutenant in our district here. I'm still trying to locate the detectives who investigated your daughter's . . . death.''

There was a silence. Mrs. Horstmann said, ''What were you going to say, suicide or murder?'' She sounded tired and far away.

''I don't know what I was going to say. They're both pretty ugly words, aren't they?''

Cooper put on his jacket and slipped warily out the back door and down into the alley, just in case. On the expressway out to O'Hare he brooded on the idea of going to meet Nick Dennison to take him to his son. Their son. Somebody's son, anyway, whose he couldn't swear to. Probably only Vivian could have sworn to it.

Nick stopped short when he saw Cooper waiting for him at the arrival gate. He was wearing a tan overcoat and carrying a small leather travel bag; he was looking a bit haggard, showing some five-o'clock shadow and dark rings under the pale gray eyes. The rough nights had begun.

''Your mother-in-law sent me,'' Cooper said, sticking out his hand.

''Cooper.'' Nick squeezed it, giving him a cautious look.

''Dominic's fine. He's holed up with a friend of mine. I'm afraid he's determined to stay here in Chicago.'' As they walked to the car, Cooper briefed Nick on what had happened the previous night. Nick said little. In the car he finally said, ''I appreciate what you've done for Dominic.''

''It wasn't much.'' *I wonder if he knows,* Cooper thought suddenly. *If I am the father, Vivian might have told him.*

Launched on the expressway, Cooper said, ''I think the police are still inclined to think Vivian committed suicide. But I'm working on them.'' He told Nick of his dealings with Shostak.

"I talked to him by phone," Nick said. "He didn't seem to have much imagination."

"Or much time to speculate. But he'll listen."

"She didn't kill herself. She would never have done that."

"That's what Dominic said."

"I spent a week feeling so guilty I could hardly function. And then what I'd known all along asserted itself. She couldn't have killed herself." Cooper glanced at his profile, dark against the lights flying past outside. "We can't let them get away with it."

"Who are they?"

"I don't know. But this attack on Dominic is proof something's going on, isn't it?"

"That's what it looks like to me. It looks to me like somebody thinks Dominic knows too much, or knows the wrong things. What you need to do is have a long talk with these detectives. You know more about Vivian's affairs than anyone, probably. Whatever the hell's going on, it must have something to do with what was happening in her life recently."

"That's the problem. I don't know much about her affairs since we split up."

"Still, you'd know more than anyone."

"Mm. I guess I'll get on the phone again tomorrow, see if I still have any clout, get some people off their asses."

They were silent after that, two strangers in a car with nothing to say to each other. As he pulled up in front of Diana's place Cooper said, "I'll take you up and leave you. He doesn't know you're coming. I'll wait down here in the car. OK?"

He could just see Nick's face in the sickly glow of the streetlights. "Does he still hate me?" Nick said.

"No more than a lot of fourteen-year-olds hate their fathers, or think they do." Cooper pulled on the door handle, paused, and looked at the other man. "He's not a bad kid really."

Nick's look was inscrutable. Cooper pushed open the door and they got out of the car. Cooper rang Diana's bell and led Nick upstairs. Dominic opened the door when they were halfway up and called out timidly, "Who is it?"

"Me," said Cooper. When they reached the landing and

Dominic saw Nick behind Cooper, he stiffened and said, "What are you doing here?"

"He's here to bury the hatchet," Cooper said. "Talk to him, will you? I'll be outside." He slipped past Nick and went back out to the car.

For an hour Cooper sat and chewed on a thumbnail and ran the heater intermittently and thought. He thought about Vivian and he thought about Dominic and he wondered why, if relief was uppermost in his reaction to the thought of Nick's taking him away, there was also regret at seeing him go.

He was startled when Nick opened the door on the passenger's side and slid in. Nick moved slowly, as if with great fatigue. He closed the door and sat still for several seconds. Finally he said, "Do you really think Dominic is safe here?"

"I thought you were taking him back."

Nick nodded. "I was. But that kid is as stubborn as they come. We hashed things out. More or less made peace, I guess. But he's determined to stay here. I guess I can see that he would be miserable in New York. His friends are here, his grandmother's here."

"And somebody here is trying to kill him," Cooper said.

"I know. I reminded him of that. I don't think he quite realizes what that means. He's only fourteen, remember. Anyway, that's why I'm asking you if he's safe here."

Cooper let out a long breath. "For the moment, yeah, I think so. But hell, I can't guarantee it. He'd be better off out of town."

Nick nodded slowly. "I haven't been able to make that boy do anything for two or three years. Maybe because I didn't put my foot down enough when he was little. I've always been too damn busy to be his father. But if I take him to New York now, it'll mean dragging him by the scruff of the neck. And here at least he seems to have found himself a job and a place to stay, and that's good. That's more initiative than I've seen in him in a while. So I said he could stay."

Nick was staring out the windshield, hands in the pockets of his overcoat, slumping a little. Cooper sat trying to sort out his feelings. He was mildly surprised to find that he felt sorry for Nick. Mostly, though, he felt uneasy.

"I can't guarantee his safety," he said.

"I know. But as you described it, whoever shot at him

knows the family. So they could track him down all the same if I took him to New York, couldn't they? He might in fact be better off here, living away from the family. Especially if the police know what's going on.''

Cooper frowned into the darkness. ''Maybe.''

Nick shifted on the seat and sighed. ''I'll talk to this Shostak again tomorrow morning. They can't just give up on this thing.''

Cooper saw responsibility for Dominic being thrown right back into his lap. He shrugged and reached for the keys in the ignition. ''Where can I drop you?''

''Don't bother. I called a taxi from inside. It should be here any second. I'm going back out to the Hilton, at O'Hare. I'll do my phoning from there tomorrow and then I have to hustle back to New York.''

They sat without speaking until a taxi came slowly along the street and eased to a halt in front of Diana's. Nick held out his hand. ''Thank you, Cooper. I mean it.'' He held Cooper's hand firmly and then got out and walked over to the cab. Cooper watched him go, thinking of the bluff, confident Nick Dennison he had hated fifteen years before. That one was long gone.

Cooper and Diana lay in the dark and whispered so as not to disturb Dominic out on the sofa. ''If I was his father I *would* drag him back by the scruff of the neck,'' Diana said. ''The kid's his responsibility, not yours. Sounds to me like he really is too busy to be a father.''

''Maybe.'' Cooper listened to cars whispering by, out in the night. A girl laughed, just below the window, and walked on. ''I got the feeling he wants to reclaim Dominic but just doesn't quite know how.''

Diana lay silent for a moment before saying, ''You're not making it any easier for him. How do you think he feels about you?''

''I don't know.''

''You think she told him you're the father?'' She rolled onto her side, her face close to his. He could feel her breath on his ear.

''I was just wondering that tonight.''

''If she did, the guy probably hates your guts.''

Cooper gave a shake of the head. "I don't know. Maybe. He did the decent thing, marrying her. He must have really loved her."

"She seems to have had that effect on men." The dryness came through Diana's whisper.

"Jealous again?"

"I thought we didn't have that kind of relationship."

Cooper had no answer for that, and after a while he began to drift off. Near sleep, he was pulled back awake for a moment by the clear vision of two men in an old seventies-era Camaro, quietly cruising the streets, somewhere near at hand.

9

THE PHONE WAS ringing when Cooper came in his door the next morning. When he answered it he heard the patient voice of Detective Shostak at the other end of the line.

"I understand you've been trying to call me."

"Yes. You might be interested in knowing that someone tried to kill Vivian Horstmann's son the other night."

"So I hear. From Vivian Horstmann's ex-husband, the guy who thinks he has clout. He's been on the phone again."

"Yeah, he's in town."

"So what happened the other night?"

"Somebody shot at us as we were going into my building. Two pistol shots. They missed, but not by a lot."

"And that has to have something to do with his mother's suicide."

"Or her murder."

"It still smells like a suicide to me."

"Have it your way. Still. Somebody pretending to be a teacher called the grandmother to find out where the boy was. We checked with the school and they never made the call. The next day someone shoots at us. It's a little hard to believe in coincidence here, isn't it?"

After a second or two Shostak said, "Somebody was looking for him? That's interesting. We'll have a talk with the grandmother maybe."

"This is no suicide. People don't go around shooting at surviving relatives of suicides."

Cooper could hear the sigh over the phone. "Listen, my friend. We wrote off the Horstmann case and moved on. We've got a whole plate full of new and different dead people to deal with now. If there's anything in this incident we'll check it out. But I still haven't heard enough to make me think I was wrong—not yet."

120

* * *

Marsh poked a finger through the holes in the sleeve of Cooper's jacket. "You gotta do something about those moths, man. Or have you been picking up the wrong kind of people again?"

"What can I tell you?" said Cooper. "You know how these Latins are about their daughters."

Marsh laughed uncertainly, shaking his head. "You startin' to worry me, you know that, man? You get shot at more than any white person I know."

Cooper smiled and slapped Marsh on the shoulder. "Thanks for caring, pal."

"Don't stand so close to me," said Marsh, backing away. "I got a family to support."

Cooper had had a bum cab the last time out so he slipped Rooney a ten with the lease and told him he wanted a cab he didn't have to fight with. Rooney gave him a nice new Caprice and told him not to get any bullet holes in it, and Cooper headed out to cruise.

It was good to be in the cab, driving and chatting up passengers with one part of his mind and thinking with another. He'd been busy all morning; he had dropped Dominic off with his new roommates, seen him safely to work at the restaurant, and made arrangements to pick him up after work. Now it was time for some thinking. He fiddled around on the near North Side with a series of short runs for a while, then caught the perfect ride for thinking, a run out to O'Hare with a man in back who was more interested in the contents of his briefcase than in anything Cooper had to say.

Cooper wanted to start at the beginning and see what he knew. When he figured out what that was, he would find Shostak and Harrison and shake them by the lapels until they paid attention.

The beginning was Vivian Horstmann hitting the ground. Vivian had either killed herself or she hadn't. The note was a strong indication she had; it had convinced the police experts. Cooper had a reasonable respect for experts, but he also knew that there were people who made a living by producing forgeries that could give an expert a run for his money. Suspend judgment there, Cooper told himself. Accept the possibility of forgery if there are other indications that weaken the hypothesis of suicide.

Like Dominic's evidence. Cooper wouldn't have called it conclusive by any means; he could understand a detective's preference for the hard evidence of the note. Cooper himself had vacillated.

Until somebody had shot at the boy. Cooper had gone over it again and found no reason to suppose that he himself had been the target of those two shots, unless the shooting truly was random, and Cooper simply couldn't accept that. He was not a great believer in conspiracy theories, but when two unusual things happened close together, he was as inclined as anyone else to look for connections.

If Vivian's death was a suicide, there was no hypothesis Cooper could think of to explain the shots. If she had been murdered, the hypothesis that came to mind was that the person who had killed her wanted to stop the boy from talking. It was due to Dominic that Cooper had tried to bring the police back into the case.

The disturbing question that arose immediately was: How did the shooter know that Dominic had dangerous knowledge? Whom had Dominic talked to? Cooper himself. Mrs. Horstmann. Shostak. Who else had heard of his allegations? Valenti. Nick Dennison. Diana, for that matter. As far as Cooper could remember, that pretty much rounded out the circle of privileged information. And still, someone had called Mrs. Horstmann to find out where Dominic was, and then someone had shot at him. How had they found out that Dominic was talking?

Take a hard look at it. Mrs. Horstmann could have leaked it; he would have to ask her. Nick could have told someone, but probably only someone in New York. Valenti or Shostak or Harrison. Cops talked about cases, but how likely was it they would talk about them with the wrong people? Diana? No.

There was another hypothesis, Cooper realized. Dominic had disappeared immediately after Vivian's death and had resurfaced only recently. Perhaps someone had intended to kill him from the beginning, only to be foiled when he ran away. Perhaps the killer had realized from the start that Dominic could expose the faked suicide. The news of his reappearance would have put them back on his trail. If the killer was indeed someone who knew the family, or even only knew of the various family members, he could have heard of the boy's reappearance through any of a hundred channels.

Deep waters. Cooper knew he needed more before he could sit down with a world-wise cop and make him listen. He only hoped that Dominic stayed alive that long. He was still disturbed by Nick's failure to take the boy back to New York, though on reflection he found Nick's reasoning sound; if the killer was intent on finding Dominic, Nick's home in New York was no refuge.

So responsibility for Dominic was still squarely in his lap. Cooper had begun to feel less like the boy's father than ever, but he was a great believer in responsibility, and he had to accept the consequences of that tumble on the couch with Vivian Horstmann fifteen years before.

Cooper drove steady and hard until six in the evening, making money, getting hungry and a bit tired. At six he was out on Chicago Avenue having just delivered an old Eastern European grandma and a dozen packages to her home in what seemed to be a Mexican neighborhood, and he rolled back in along Chicago until he spotted a diner with a $3.50 dinner special. He sat at the counter and ate deep-fried fish and thought, watching the early evening traffic glide by outside. After he paid his check he stood looking at the phone in the back of the place next to the restroom, decided it was private enough, and went back and put in a quarter. He dialed Mrs. Horstmann's number.

She came on the line after four rings. Cooper mumbled through the greetings and said, "Did a detective call you today?"

"Yes. A man named Harrison. Asking about the caller who said he was from Dominic's school. I told him what happened and gave him the number of the school and that was about it. Do you think the police believe Vivian was killed now?"

"I don't know. I think it's hard for cops to change their minds. But at least they called you. Listen, the reason I called was, I was wondering if we could . . . uh, brainstorm or something I guess is what I'm getting at, since the cops don't seem to be doing anything more at the moment."

"I'm . . . not sure I understand what you mean, Mr. Mac-Leish."

"Well, for a start I was wondering if you could tell me something about Vivian's affairs. If you would. I mean, why? Why would anyone kill her? Who benefits?"

"I see." There was a pause.

"I know you might rather discuss this·with the police. I'm thinking if we can at least come up with some ideas we'll have something more concrete to interest them."

"I understand."

"Now I realize I'm an outsider. The only reason I'm presuming to pry into this is because I seem to have become Dominic's temporary guardian. And somebody did shoot at me."

"Certainly. I'd say that gives you the right to ask a few questions."

"I was wondering if you could just answer some obvious questions. Like whether anyone is likely to benefit financially from Vivian's death."

"That is an obvious question, isn't it? And easily answered. No, in a word. Vivian was in a good deal of debt when she died."

"I see. Because of the gallery?"

"Yes. She had inherited a legacy from my husband when he died and put it almost entirely into starting the gallery. Since then, however, the costs of running the place, rent and publicity and whatnot, had not come near being covered by her sales. She had taken out a loan to keep her going, but things had not gotten sufficiently better to even begin to pay it off. I understand it is a difficult business to break into. And I think Vivian's talents, as well as her passions, were more artistic than commercial. I'm afraid she had gotten in over her head. When she died she owed a good deal of money. The theory is, of course, that that was the reason for her suicide."

"Yeah . . . if she owed people money, that wouldn't be likely to provide a motive for murder. People keep debtors alive. She didn't have any partners in the gallery?"

"No, it was entirely her project."

"Uh-huh. So she was broke when she died. What on earth was she living on?"

"Partly the occasional sales from the gallery, partly the remnants of her settlement with Nick. She was hoping for better times. But also thinking of finding work if things didn't."

"She wasn't getting alimony or anything?"

"No. They had agreed on a lump sum settlement. And of course Nick was to pay for Dominic's schooling. Nick is rather a wealthy man, but Vivian was too proud to accept continuing support from him. She was determined to establish herself independently."

"I see. So nobody's going to inherit much of anything."

"I'm afraid not."

"What's going to happen to the gallery?"

"I suspect the bank will have a good deal to say about that. In any event if you're interested in the gallery you might speak to a woman named Melissa Wilkert. She was Vivian's only employee. I believe her number is listed."

"Mm." Cooper fished out his notebook and jotted down the name. "I wouldn't know what to ask her. I don't even know what I'm looking for. I was just wondering if there was something obvious out there crying to be looked at."

"Certainly not that I've thought of. And I've done a good deal of thinking late at night recently. Sleep hasn't come very easily in the past few weeks."

"No. I'm sure. Thanks for talking with me, Mrs. Horstmann. I'm sure if we put our heads together we can get the police moving on this."

"I hope so. Is Dominic with you?"

"He's at work. I'm picking him up later to see him home. I think he's as well as can be expected."

"I'm glad. Nick spoke to me before he went back to New York this morning. He said the boy seems to like you."

Cooper grunted, suddenly uncomfortable, and said, "Well, he's a good kid."

After he hung up, Cooper leaned on the wall for a moment, abstracted. A man came back to the restroom and pushed by him warily. Finally, with night fallen outside, Cooper went out and got in the cab again.

By midnight he'd made decent money and it was time to go pick up Dominic. He took the Drive north, pulled off Sheridan onto the quiet tree-lined streets away from the lake, and parked the cab as near as he could get to the restaurant. He sat for a moment in the cab, wondering again if there was any way the men in the Camaro could know about Dominic's working at the restaurant. He decided there wasn't, not unless he had led them there, and he couldn't see how anyone could have picked him up in the cab and tailed him all day without his noticing. He hadn't been near home, and that was the place where they would watch for him, if anywhere. Slowly, he got out of the cab and walked the half-block to the restaurant.

Dominic had punched out and was sitting with his hair hanging in his face at a table in the back of the dining room. Rose was there, and a couple of servers, looking wrung out from the Friday evening rush, sagging on their chairs. There were beers in front of them and the smell of marijuana in the air. The noise of pots clanging came from the kitchen. Dominic was damp with sweat and pale with fatigue. He avoided Cooper's eyes. Cooper sat at the table and chatted for a minute or two before he and Dominic left, Dominic marching behind him with his hands jammed in the pockets of his overcoat.

Walking to the cab, Cooper said, "How was it tonight?"

"It sucked." Dominic walked with his eyes on the ground.

"Hard work, huh?"

"Stupid work. A moron could do it."

"Yeah. Well, when you get a college degree you'll get something better than moron work."

"I can make money other ways. I don't need this shit."

"OK, you're on your own. You got rent to pay now. If you think you can do it without a job, go to it. Just make sure it's legal. Saves trouble."

In the cab Dominic leaned back against the seat with his eyes closed. After Cooper had driven a couple of blocks the boy said, "I mean, I like the people and stuff. It's just so boring."

"Moron jobs always are. Everybody needs to have a job like that for a while to remind themselves of why they're in school."

"I'm not in school. I'm not going back, either."

"You'll always have moron jobs, then."

"Abraham Lincoln educated himself. He didn't have to go to law school and all that."

"It was a different world then. They ask you for credentials now."

"I won't need credentials for what I'm going to do."

"What's that?"

"Split. See the world."

"Sounds good. Just do me a favor and read that Orwell book before you do. It'll take a little of the romance out of poverty for you."

After a minute Dominic said, "I just can't hack going back to school for a while."

"OK, I'm not going to argue with you. Like I said, you're on your own."

Dominic said nothing more until Cooper pulled up in front of his new place. Cooper looked over at the boy and in the light from the streetlamps he saw a trail of tears down the boy's cheek. Cooper cursed himself for those last callous words and sat in silence watching the boy cry. Finally he said, "I'm sorry, Dominic." He put a hand on the boy's shoulder. "You're only on your own if you want to be."

Dominic shrugged off his hand angrily and got out of the cab, slamming the door. Cooper watched him go into the building and sat for a moment longer, angry with himself for saying the wrong words and for doing the wrong things, from the start, the very start.

He was out early the next morning, wringing the last bucks from the cab before he had to turn it back in. It was slow most of the morning and then picked up. Around eleven he dropped a scholarly old man with the thickest glasses he'd ever seen at the Newberry Library. As he headed back down to Chicago Avenue, he paused at a light and it occurred to him that he was not too far from Vivian Horstmann's gallery on Superior.

There was no reason for him to go by there, but he was curious and he was his own boss. He vacillated while he waited for the light to change and finally gave in to the impulse just because he liked to give in to impulses occasionally.

Somebody with a bad case of Second City complex had

tried to call the area SuHu because most of the galleries were
on Superior and Huron, but River North was the name that
was catching on for the neighborhood. The dealers had bought
up the old workshops and done the usual gutting and refur-
bishing, and a stretch of several blocks of sturdy brick façade
was now festooned with banners bearing the names of the
galleries that overlooked the street. There were a few small
factories left, along with the upscale restaurants and bars that
had come in on the heels of the galleries, and even though it
was Saturday morning there were people out and about.

Cooper rolled along the street scanning the banners but
hadn't seen the name Horstmann by the time he got to Or-
leans. For a second he considered giving it up but then he
said what the hell. He parked the cab at the end of the block
and walked back, looking carefully. He spotted the blue ban-
ner with the name Horstmann hanging from the third floor
of a building next to the El tracks. He stood for a moment
looking at it and then went in the door.

There was a different gallery on each floor, visible through
the glass they'd put in when they tore out the old stairwell.
Cooper caught glimpses of paintings and sculptures as he
went slowly up the stairs; he saw three people in the gallery
on the second floor, standing in front of an enormous smeared
canvas in the diffident uncertain way people stand in muse-
ums.

On the third floor landing he stopped and looked at the
inscription on the glass door. THE HORSTMANN GALLERY it
said, with the hours posted underneath. No one was in sight
inside but according to the sign the place was open. Cooper
tried the door to find it locked and then noticed the bell and
the card saying PLEASE RING. He looked at it and hesitated;
he didn't really have any excuse to be here. He stood looking
through the glass. It was a small space that showed signs of
its industrial past, with the scarred and battered bare wood
floors that had been polished just enough to give them a shine,
the exposed wooden beams nearly two feet thick, the pipes
and ducts snaking along the ceiling. But the lighting was
warm and the solid white partitions spaced to give a comfortable intimacy. Cooper glanced at the paintings; he'd long
since decided that much of modern art was just Emperor's
New Clothes after all, and he didn't work too hard trying to

fathom it. These were square abstracts in mostly dark purples and grays; they reminded Cooper of a sweater he'd once had.

He stood in an odd sort of trance looking at this place where Vivian had moved and spoken and laughed and probably brooded about money. After a minute he decided he had satisfied his curiosity and was about to turn to the stairs again when movement in the shadows at the rear of the place caught his eye. A woman had appeared from behind a partition and was watching him. Cooper was caught by surprise but rather than flee he raised his hand to the button by the door and pushed it. The woman came toward the door, looking him up and down. Cooper recognized her; he'd seen her at the funeral. She looked to be in her mid-forties, with short brown hair cut in a style that had cost her money and a long wool skirt, high leather boots, and a black velvet jacket. She wasn't entirely sure what to make of Cooper, judging by the look on her face. Cooper gave her what he hoped was a disarming smile and wondered what the hell he was going to say to her.

She stopped at the desk which sat just inside the door and pressed a hidden button at its side. The lock clicked and Cooper pushed open the door. As he stepped inside the woman said, "I'm afraid we're not looking at any more slides right now."

Cooper stared for a moment before realizing she'd taken him for an artist. He groped a bit before saying, "That's OK. I don't have any slides. I just wanted to have a look."

With a wary expression that told him she was sure nobody who dressed like he did could be interested in buying art, she crossed her arms and stepped away from the desk. "Fine. There are brochures on the bench over there." She smiled a perfunctory smile. She had been pretty once, before lack of sleep or the cares of the world had put dark bags permanently under her eyes, and her voice, while high and soft, sounded as if a few thousand cigarettes had passed her lips. Cooper had turned toward the paintings, but he abandoned the pretense at once. He turned back and said to her, "Are you Melissa Wilkert?"

She stiffened for an instant. "Yes."

Cooper still didn't really know what he was doing there but he said, "My name's Cooper MacLeish. I was a friend of Vivian's."

Melissa Wilkert raised her chin a fraction and mouthed a silent "Ah." Here eyes fled his and then came back, expectant.

Cooper found nothing to say except, "I got your name from Vivian's mother."

"I see." She said it with a slightly interrogative tone.

"I was passing by and I decided to stop in."

Looking very skeptical, she said, "And what can I do for you?"

Cooper was a bit out of his depth but he figured the straightforward approach was best. "I wanted to talk about Vivian," he said.

She stood still for a while and Cooper thought she was going to ask him to leave, but finally she seemed to gather her wits and she said, "I see. Why don't you come back to the office?"

Cooper followed her back past the partition at the rear and found himself in a cluttered behind-the-scenes sort of space with a gray steel desk, filing cabinets, shelves holding a jumble of papers, magazines, and catalogues, a few canvases on the floor face to the wall, a couch, and a couple of chairs. Behind the desk was a closed door and on it was an ashtray with a half-smoked cigarette burning in it. Melissa Wilkert sat at the desk and diffidently pointed Cooper to a chair opposite it. She picked up the cigarette, tapped it with a finger, and took a drag. "You were at the funeral."

Cooper nodded. "I hadn't seen Vivian in a long time."

"How long?"

"Fifteen years or so."

She held the cigarette between long fingers with painted nails, supporting her right elbow in her left palm. Melissa Wilkert looked, in spite of her expensive clothes, as if she had not had a happy life. She had the tired look of someone who was used to being disappointed. She looked at Cooper for a long moment, making him uncomfortable. "She must have been very important to you."

"At one time."

She hesitated, her eyes refusing to settle on his face, and then said, "And what can I tell you about her?"

Cooper wasn't sure, so he asked a question of his own. "Have the police come to talk to you?"

"No. About what?"

"There's a possibility Vivian didn't kill herself."

She froze with the cigarette halfway to her mouth. "You must be joking."

"No. Her son and I have talked to them about it."

"Dominic?"

"Yes." Cooper crossed his legs, settling into the chair. "He was convinced there was someone there with her that night. I took him to talk to the cops. I don't think they were convinced until someone took a shot at the boy the other night."

She was gawking now, her mouth open. "Shot at him?"

"Uh-huh. Missed, fortunately."

"Why?"

"I don't know. Nobody knows. But the police are paying attention now, I think."

She closed her eyes briefly and put a hand to her temple. Finally she sagged a little in the chair and said, "Oh God. Somebody killed her?"

"It looks that way now."

"Buy why?" Her look was incredulous, appalled.

"I was sort of hoping you could throw some light on that."

She stared, her mouth open slightly, shaking her head in a half-conscious nervous way. Then she collected herself and her brows contracted. "May I ask how you come into all this?"

Cooper sat self-consciously opposite her, feeling as if he were being interviewed. "Out of left field. I had completely lost touch with Vivian. I read about her death in the paper and I showed up at the funeral, just because . . . for old times' sake, I guess. I found out Dominic had run away. I was interested and I started looking for him. With a little luck I found him."

She took a last pull on the cigarette and put it out slowly in the ashtray, then tossed her head as if to clear it. "And what on earth do you think I would know?"

"Mrs. Horstmann suggested you could tell me about Vivian's business affairs. Tell the police, that is. I think they'll be by before too long. You don't have to tell me anything. I'm just an old friend who can't leave it alone."

She stared at him a moment longer and then abruptly rose.

"Would you like some coffee?" He nodded and she went to a stand in the corner and uncapped a thermos. She filled a mug that had been sitting beside it and then produced a styrofoam cup from a paper bag for Cooper. She didn't ask him how he took his coffee. When she handed him the cup her hand was shaking. She went back behind the desk and sat down. "I've been thinking I was probably the last person to see her alive," she said, her voice lower, thicker. "She left here quite late on the night she died, saying she was going straight home. We'd been busy all day and evening and she looked exhausted. I've been thinking back ever since and reading signs of suicide into that, the way she looked and talked, reproaching myself for not seeing the signs, asking her what was wrong. Now . . . my God, I don't know if it's better or worse."

"You're not the only one who's had that thought."

For a moment she only looked at him in mute anguish. "Why in God's name would anybody kill Vivian?"

"If it had anything to do with her business, you'd know."

"Something to do with the business? With the gallery?"

"That's one thing the police are going to look at, probably."

"That's absolutely . . ." Suddenly she was pawing at the cigarettes again. "I'm sorry. This is very upsetting."

"I'm sorry to break it to you. I don't really know what the police are going to ask you. Probably they'll want to know if anyone stands to gain by her death."

Melissa Wilkert took a puff, drank some coffee, and seemed to stabilize a little. She gave Cooper a level look and said, "Well, I certainly don't stand to gain. She owed me two months' salary."

Cooper grunted in sympathy. "What's going to happen to the place now?"

"Unless the lawyers can sell it to somebody, I suppose it will just fold up. I'm not really up on all that. I'm just an employee, you see. I've kept the place open hoping to sell a few pictures and get some of my money. If that seems ghoulish I'm sorry, but I really need that two months' salary. I sold two pictures last week, because of the notoriety, no doubt. I'm hoping the lawyers will let me have some of the money."

Cooper drank some of the coffee. "Her mother tells me Vivian was in a good deal of debt."

"That's right. If the police are concerned about the gallery, it's much more likely to provide a motive for suicide than for murder." She tapped a painted nail nervously against the rim of the mug.

Cooper shifted on the chair. "So you didn't have any trouble accepting the idea of suicide when it first happened."

"My God, of course I had trouble accepting it. Vivian was the last person I would have expected to kill herself."

"Yeah, that's what everyone says."

She gave him a searching look. "Well, you knew her. What did you think?"

"What everyone else thought. I couldn't believe it. What I mean is, you were shocked maybe but you figured she had done it because she was depressed over money troubles?"

Melissa Wilkert frowned at him, cigarette in one hand and the other resting on the mug. She appeared to hesitate between the two, and finally put down the cigarette and let go of the mug. She clasped her hands, elbows on the desk, and said, "No. Vivian would never have killed herself over this place. She had her money invested here, but not . . . not herself. I thought there had to be something more. Something nobody could know. Suicide is a very mysterious thing. I thought Vivian was just one of those suicides no one would ever figure out. She was a very deep person. There was a lot to her. Intellectually, emotionally. A complex person, very complex. And sensitive. I think I finally decided it must have been that that killed her. She was . . . too sensitive."

After a moment Cooper said, "But she didn't kill herself."

Melissa Wilkert had to smoke before she could look at him, and when she did, the look was desolate. "So you say." Under Cooper's gaze, her head suddenly drooped and she covered her eyes with her free hand. They sat in silence for a few seconds and when Cooper heard a soft exhalation he realized she was crying. He waited, staring into his coffee, until she raised her head, eyes glistening.

"How well did you know Vivian?" she said.

Cooper returned her gaze and finally said, "I was in love with her once."

"Fifteen years ago?"

"Yeah."

"And you came to the funeral."

"She made quite an impression on me."

"She had a way of doing that, didn't she?" Melissa Wilkert set down the cigarette and heaved a sigh, a long sigh that ended in a harsh cough. She put a hand to her breast when she finished coughing and stared at the desktop for a moment, then wiped a tear from the corner of her eye. Cooper had the sudden impression that she had been not only pretty once but girlish, innocent; whatever had put the dark circles under her eyes had had trouble eradicating the last traces of that innocence.

"Let me tell you something about Vivian," she said. "Vivian was a friend of my ex-husband's. I only got to know her through him. Our social life tended to revolve around my husband's friends . . . as often happens with a certain type of man." Her eyes flicked to Cooper as if to assure him no offense was implied. "Anyway, when my husband decided he'd had enough of me and took up with a woman twenty years younger, all of his friends went with him. I was cut right out of their lives. Except for one person." She paused, and Cooper nodded, not needing to be told. "Vivian called me the day after she heard about . . . Phil running off with that girl and told me that she was outraged and that whatever kind of support I needed she would give. She took me out to dinner, she held my hand while I cried, she was an intermediary between me and Phil when I couldn't bear to face him. And then eventually she hired me to work here and we became good friends. Of all the crowd that Phil and I ran around with, Vivian was the only one who remembered I was alive after the divorce. That's the kind of person Vivian was." She picked up her cigarette and eyed it with distaste. "When her own marriage collapsed, I thought it was the cruelest thing that could happen to her."

Cooper swallowed some coffee and watched her smoke. After a moment he asked, "What happened with her marriage?"

Melissa Wilkert shrugged. "I think she simply decided she didn't want to stay married to a man who was more interested in money than in people. Nick's a decent man, basically, but his work was the big thing with him. He's going to be a very rich man someday, but even if Vivian were still alive it would be without her.''

"She was the one who wanted the divorce then."

"Yes. I don't think there was any . . . infidelity or anything. She just needed someone who cared for her. Nick just valued her as an ornament. She was a terrific wife for a high-powered investment banker to have. Smart, beautiful, and all that. But he didn't want all the other things Vivian was. Not until it was too late, anyway. A lot of husbands seem to be like that—they don't know what they've got till it's gone.'' Again there was a nervous glance at Cooper, who shrugged.

"A lot of people are like that."

"I suppose so. I'm sorry to be bitter. But Vivian and I both got sort of . . . soured on men in the past few years. No, that's not true. I did, maybe. But not Vivian. She didn't get soured on things. She got hurt but she didn't get bitter. I don't know how she did it.''

There was a silence while they both remembered, and then Cooper said, "So who would have killed her?"

She stared at him, rigid, fighting to keep control of her features, her eyes starting to brim again. "I don't know," she said softly. She closed her eyes and put a hand to her face. Cooper stirred, drank coffee, leaned forward with his elbows on his knees and thought of leaving.

Melissa Wilkert coughed violently, waved smoke out of her face, put out the cigarette. She settled back in her chair and blinked at Cooper. "I'll tell you who the police should talk to, though," she said.

"Who?"

"Vivian's lover."

Cooper stared, waiting for her to go on. Finally he said, "Who was her lover?"

"I don't know. But I know she had one."

"How do you know?"

"You can tell. When you work with somebody every day you know what's going on with them whether they tell you or not. Her manner changed.''

"What do you mean, her manner changed?"

"She got . . . brighter. Happier. You know, you can tell. Someone comes in smiling, humming, that kind of thing, after they've been down in the dumps for months. I could see it. She began to pay more attention to her clothes, things like that. Mind you, she always dressed well. But she started to put that little extra into it, a touch here and there. There was a definite change. She'd had an unhappy summer, with the divorce and all, and then suddenly she was like a girl, being courted again. And there were a few phone calls. I would answer and this man would ask for her and she would say she'd call him back. She seemed embarrassed about it. I put two and two together.''

''Huh. When was all this?''

''Not long ago. Only . . . I don't know, a few weeks, a month maybe before she died.''

''And she never told you who it was.''

''No. I was dying to find out but I thought she was being discreet, waiting to unveil him at some opportune moment. I didn't know that much about her social circles, really. She had a whole side of her life I wasn't involved with at all. And of course she wasn't one to brag about her conquests or anything. I just remember thinking it was good for her to have someone again.''

''She never said anything? Never let any remarks drop, anything that could tell who it was?''

''No. She was very coy about it. I wanted to ask her about it but . . . I don't know, she was secretive about it.''

Cooper nodded, abstracted. ''Well, see what you can remember. The cops are going to want to know about him.''

After a pause she said, ''Because he might have had something to do with her death, you mean.''

Cooper set the cup on the desk. ''I don't know. At least he may know something about what was going on with her.''

Melissa Wilkert stared at him for a long moment before she said, ''He killed her, didn't he?''

''We don't even know who he is.''

''If somebody killed her, it had to have been . . . in passion.''

''We don't know that.'' Cooper rose, frowning.

''There was no reason for it. It had to be like that. A crime of passion. She rejected him or something and he killed her.''

Cooper stood looking down at her as she started to cry again, tears welling gently in the corners of her eyes. ''Maybe,'' he said. ''But maybe not. Don't get carried away.

Just try to remember anything you can that might help the police."

"You weren't the only one who loved her," Melissa Wilkert said softly, wiping at her tears with long graceful fingers. "And you needn't get any dirty ideas. There's more than one kind of love."

Cooper wanted to tell her it was too bad she hadn't had enough of any kind of love, but he let it slide.

10

"I DON'T MUCH care how you do it," said the man in the phone booth. "Use your imagination."

"Oh man, I got a good imagination," said the Puerto Rican. "That's what gets me in trouble sometimes. I tell you about the guitar player in the joint I made sure won't play no more guitar?" Again the high wheezing laugh came over the line. "Have to play with his fuckin' toes now."

"Yeah, you told me. Stay out of trouble this time. Just find the kid." The Puerto Rican was drunk again, flapping his mouth. Maybe it was time to move him out of the bar.

"How about the dude?"

"What dude?"

"The dude we talkin' about. The taxi driver dude."

"What about him?"

"I mean what kind of shape you want him in?"

The man thought for a moment. "Like I said, I don't much care. Just remember the kid is the real job. Be careful."

"Oh yeah, baby, we'll be careful. The dude's gonna be real grateful, like, how careful we're gonna be."

Cooper left three messages with a pleasant-sounding youth at Dominic's new number before he finally got through to the boy late in the afternoon. "How you doing today, pal?" Cooper said.

Dominic's voice was subdued, whether through sullenness or depression or embarrassment about the night before, Cooper couldn't tell. "All right. Gordon said you called."

"Yeah. Where'd you go today?"

"Out with some of my friends. I don't have to like check in with you, do I?"

"No. But remember somebody's looking for you. You being careful when you go out?"

"Sure. But they don't know where to look for me now, do they?"

"I don't think so. But they might know your old hangouts. I'd steer clear of those if I were you."

"Uh, yeah, OK. Today me and this guy I know just went to a movie. That all right?"

"I guess so, if you got home in one piece. How's the new place?"

"Fine. Petra's fixing a big dinner tonight. We're having a bunch of people over."

"Sounds good. Listen, there was something I wanted to ask you."

"Uh-huh?"

"I talked to a lady named Melissa Wilkert today. At your mother's gallery. You know her?"

"Yeah, Melissa. I know her."

"Well, she said your mom had a . . . was . . . I guess she was going out with someone for a while before she died. You know who it was?"

There was a silence. "Going out with someone? No. Not that I know of. I mean, she would like flirt with these guys at parties and stuff, but that was all. She never . . . you know, she never like . . . she didn't have a boyfriend or anything."

"Huh. You don't know of anybody that liked her? Melissa said your mother's manner changed, about a month before she died. Her mood seemed to improve, she seemed to get happier. You notice anything like that?"

There was a silence. "No. Not really, not that I remember."

"She didn't mention any gentlemen friends, anything like that?"

"No. I mean, she had lots of friends and stuff, but . . ."

"She didn't get any mysterious phone calls from unknown men, no letters or anything?"

"I don't know. I didn't go around spying on her."

"Yeah, I know, OK. I'm just saying I think the police might be interested in anything you can think of. Here's an unknown person nobody has mentioned before."

There was silence over the line for a few seconds. "You mean like . . ."

"I don't know what I mean, Dominic. We just have to think of everything we can that might help the police."

"Yeah, all right. But I don't think she had any boyfriends. She was like . . . jeez, she was my mother."

"She was also still a young woman."

Cooper immediately feared he had made another wounding remark, but after a pause Dominic said merely, "That would have been weird for me to deal with."

"Maybe that's why she didn't tell you about it."

The silence was longer this time. "Maybe," said Dominic.

Cooper shoved the bookmark back in place and dumped *The Open Society and Its Enemies* on the desk. He drained his coffee cup and reflected that he was going to have to decide if he was writing only about American involvement in Vietnam, or about larger things, like open societies and their enemies. He kept finding he was attracted to the larger questions, which meant the work kept mushrooming and he'd probably never get the damn book finished. But then maybe Popper and other people had already written it, better than he ever could. And maybe going through with it for himself meant he'd get things figured out someday and stop being haunted by his participation in the enormously destructive and ultimately futile Southeast Asia War Games, 1965-1972, as a member of the second-place team.

Cooper took the empty cup into the kitchen and rinsed it out. Grinding through philosophy books was no way to spend a Saturday night. He had most of the evening left to kill before Diana would be off work and receiving at home. He'd tried to get Emilio on the phone to get up a game of pool but hadn't found him. There was nothing worthy of an intelligent person's attention on television. There was always Burk's, with plenty of beer and a good jukebox, but Cooper liked to steer clear of the place on weekends when it was crowded.

He was beginning to get seriously restless when the phone rang, promising escape. He picked up the receiver and said hello. He heard nothing but two seconds of silence and then the click of somebody hanging up.

"Nice talking to you, asshole," said Cooper aloud, and wandered back to the desk, wondering if he shouldn't soldier on a bit further with the books after all. He pulled out the chair and sat down, and then suddenly was seriously bothered. He stood up again and stared at the phone.

People hang up without saying anything if they have a wrong number. Or if they just want to see if you're home. And why would they want to see if you were home? Usually because they're hoping you aren't.

But maybe because they're hoping you are.

Cooper moved to the front window and pulled the shade aside. He looked up and down the block but he didn't see any old Camaros. Of course not. They wouldn't be here quite yet.

All right, am I being paranoid? Cooper asked himself. His upper arm was still bandaged and he touched it lightly just to remind himself that the bullet had been real.

Paranoid or not, Cooper decided, it might be a good time to slip out and spend the evening somewhere else. If that was a prospective burglar calling, he was welcome to the place.

Cooper pulled on his boots and took his jacket from the closet doorknob. He could kill a couple of hours in Burk's before going over to Diana's. He checked to see if he had money and then took one more look out the front window. Still nothing suspicious.

He felt a bit silly for a moment but then he remembered the shots. He went through the kitchen to the back door and took a look out. Nothing moving. Cooper slipped out and locked the door behind him. He stood listening for a moment and then went slowly down the stairs, stopping at the bottom to take another look. The alley was deserted and he hiked down to the end of the block, then came back around to his car parked fifty feet from his door. He was looking for the Camaro but he didn't see it. Cooper had one more moment of doubt, thinking that if he wasn't imagining things he should just call the cops and try and grab them when they showed up. Then he thought about trying to explain it all and decided to get the hell out of there.

He drove over to Glenwood and on up toward Burk's. After a minute in the safety of the old Valiant he was ready to laugh at himself for having found an excuse to leave the books and go drink beer and shoot pool. Then he looked in the mirror and saw what looked a hell of a lot like the front end of an old seventies-type Camaro about a block back.

"Shit." He nearly scraped a parked car on his right. He had almost reached Pratt, a main thoroughfare, and as he slowed he checked the mirror again. It still looked a lot like a Camaro, as best he could see in the yellow light from the sodium vapor street lamps. It had the same light color, maybe silver, as the car he'd gotten a brief look at three nights before speeding away toward Sheridan.

Cooper pulled up at the stop sign and thought hard for a second. The worst thing he could do was to lead them to Burk's, which was just around the corner from the restaurant where Dominic was working. He put on his turn signal and made a left.

He didn't go very fast, just wanting to see them again, wanting to make sure. When he had gone nearly a block he looked in the mirror and saw it, turning sure enough onto Pratt behind him, the old silver-gray Camaro. Cooper's heart had started to beat faster and he was angry now, angry that he'd let them flush him like this. That's what the phone call had been all about; they'd known it would work on his mind and he might decide to split. And they'd known he just might lead them to Dominic. They'd spotted his car and had been watching from the shadows under the trees, the Camaro out of sight around a corner somewhere.

At least he was thinking now and he wasn't going to lead them to the boy. He stopped at a red light at Clark Street and saw the Camaro pull over a block behind, not wanting to get too close. Cooper waited for the light to change and went through his options. He figured he could lose them easily enough but he wanted to do more: he wanted to identify them.

When the light changed he put the Valiant in gear and went through the intersection. The Camaro pulled away from the curb to follow him and Cooper started to see how it might work. Pratt ran downhill from Clark, under the train tracks and on up to Ridge with narrow residential streets to the right. Cooper took the slope at a leisurely pace, seeing the Camaro come over the crest of the hill behind him about three cars back, just keeping him in sight. Cooper knew those streets to the right and he thought they would do. He slowed and put on his right turn signal just past the train overpass and turned smoothly off Pratt onto the darker side street.

Immediately he saw that it wasn't going to work here, because the street was deserted ahead of him. The men in the Camaro would know right away that he had to have turned off. What Cooper needed was a street that had a quick turn-off, an alley or a driveway, and also enough traffic to keep his pursuers looking ahead for him. He swore and tried to think and kept going at any easy pace, rolling from stop sign to stop sign along the dark street with tree branches arching overhead, one pair of headlights still a block behind.

At Lunt he decided it would do. He stopped at the four-way sign and let one car go by with another one rolling up to the sign behind it. Cooper turned left and started looking for his hiding place. A hundred feet beyond the corner he saw it, the narrow driveway of a house on the left that was easy to miss if you weren't looking for it. Cooper knew he was out of sight of the Camaro for maybe five seconds more, and he put on a little speed and then braked and turned into the drive, cutting the lights. He pulled up into the shadow of the house, and looked back to his left, waiting. His heart was thumping.

He saw the Camaro come left at the stop sign and head up toward Ridge, following the cars that had preceded Cooper. He saw two men in the front seat as it went by but couldn't make out what they looked like. As soon as they passed he had the Valiant in reverse and was easing back onto the street, his lights still off. He straightened out and gave it some gas and ran up hard toward the Camaro's tail, determined to get within reading distance of the license plate before they could do anything about it.

They were already climbing the slope toward the cars stopped at the light at Ridge and they must have realized that he'd outfoxed them, because as Cooper got just close enough to chance a look down at the rear plates, the Camaro roared and shot forward, slewing into the left lane and forcing an oncoming car to the curb and leaving Cooper behind. He bore down on the gas and for a split second he had his mind made up to go after them, but as he saw them tear into the intersection against the light he knew he wasn't that crazy.

There were honks and a squeal of tires and then a crash as the Camaro clipped the front end of a desperately braking VW Rabbit and careened on through the light.

Cooper eased to a stop behind the other cars at the light. He swore again and slammed the steering wheel. He'd gotten just an impression of the prefix, maybe LR or LB, and that was all. He watched the shaken driver emerge from the Rabbit, then switched on his lights and turned right when the light changed. He wasn't sure if he'd made things better or worse; he'd given them notice he was watching now.

Cooper was in heaven; he had coffee aplenty, a stomach full of breakfast, and a spare chair for the Sunday paper. He finished the limpa toast and poured down some coffee on top of it, and held up his cup in salute to the photo on the wall above Diana's head. The photo showed the King of Sweden standing next to the owner of the restaurant. "These Nordic cultures," Cooper said. "Breakfast is the only meal they do well, but no one does it better." Diana made no reply, absorbed in the crossword puzzle, and Cooper fished through the rest of the paper. He decided he'd read all the interesting parts. He and Diana had lucked into the table by the window and he could watch the traffic out on Clark Street. After a while Diana looked up, watched him for a few seconds, and said, "Looking out for your friends in the Camaro?"

"Maybe I should get those glasses after all," said Cooper. "If my eyesight was ten feet better I'd have gotten that license number."

She gave him a blank look across the remains of eggs, sausage, and pancakes with lingonberries. "I didn't know they measured eyesight in feet," she said.

"You know what I mean. If I'd been able to read the thing ten feet farther back. What I need to figure out is what they'll do now. They know I've spotted them and they might think I got the number. Probably they'll ditch the car, get another one. Or maybe just give up. They've blown it now. We know they're watching and we'll be sure not to lead them to Dominic."

"But we still don't know who they are."

"No. But Shostak and Harrison might be able to do something with what we know. Detectives work their contacts on a thing like this, look for guys who have done this kind of thing before, ask around about who's driving a Camaro these days, that kind of thing. Something will turn up.''

"Preferably before someone shoots you," Diana said, with that quiet veiled look.

"It's the boy they want. And they won't get him. Unless he does something stupid. They can't know where he is now. I talked to him this morning, told him about last night. I think he took it to heart. He'll be careful.''

"Are you sure you're good enough at this to make sure nobody is following you around?''

Cooper frowned a little and shrugged. "I think so. I do that every day, drive around paying attention to what's behind me and in front of me. Besides, it takes a lot to really keep surveillance on somebody. They'd need whole teams of people around the clock to be sure of finding Dominic by following me. And I don't think these two sleazeballs in the Camaro are part of that kind of operation.''

Cooper waved at the waitress for some coffee. Diana put down the magazine and said, "You're having the time of your life, aren't you?''

Cooper sat still, trying to read her impassive, high-cheekboned face. "What do you mean?''

"I mean you really enjoy it, don't you, the chases and the narrow escapes and everything?''

"I wouldn't say I enjoyed being shot at," he said flatly.

"I wonder sometimes. Whenever you get into one of these scrapes, your eye gets brighter and your step gets livelier. Even the guy who almost killed you in the cab. You were shook, but you were really alive that night.''

"Yeah. That was the whole point. I was alive.''

"You're . . . what do they call it, a combat junkie.''

"Aw, bullshit. What magazine did you get that one out of?''

Diana leaned closer, her voice low and her dark eyes intent on him. "You need the danger, don't you? I mean, I think there's a fine line—maybe you don't really enjoy getting shot at, but you enjoy surviving, don't you? I mean you're not content just to *have* survived—you have to keep on surviving things.''

Cooper opened his mouth to reply but said nothing because

suddenly it struck him that that was just exactly it—she'd nailed it. After a moment Diana looked down at the crossword again and Cooper just sat watching her. The waitress came to pour him more coffee, and he drank it and kept looking at her, thinking about it.

He was no combat junkie, not like the real psychos who went off to Rhodesia looking for more firefights when it was all over in Vietnam. He'd known a couple who were headed in that direction, and he wasn't like them at all. For them that pure adrenaline high would always be a strong enough lure to make them forget the pain and fatigue and sheer degradation of the endeavor. Cooper couldn't forget those things.

But Diana had part of it right. While he didn't like pain and he didn't like fear, he did like moments like the one he'd had standing over the fallen stickup man, feeling that survival high and watching the son of a bitch hurt. He'd liked that, all right—as he'd like walking out of that house with Dominic, stepping over the legs of the bully with the bleached hair. Yeah, he liked that high all right.

He became aware that Diana was looking at him. "OK, I need it. What's wrong with that? There are plenty of assholes around to keep me busy, aren't there?"

"Yeah, it's not just the danger, is it? You could climb mountains or go hang gliding if it was just the danger. You need conflict too, don't you?"

"I don't go looking for it. There's plenty around."

"Yeah," she said softly, "isn't there?"

"You think I'm a sadist or something."

"No Coop, I don't think that. I don't think you necessarily like hurting people. But you don't mind a good fight, do you?"

"Have you ever known me to go around starting fights? Do I go looking to hurt people?"

"No, that's not what I'm saying." Her eyes held his. "But it doesn't bother you if you have to, does it?"

Cooper said quietly, "Should it? Should it have bothered me to run that guy over after he tried to kill me?"

"I don't know. That's for you to decide late some night." Diana had that look now, the sad look.

"Listen." Cooper leaned forward now, wanting desperately for her to understand. "Let me tell you what it really is. It's not hurting people. What I like is taking that look on some asshole's face, that look that says *I've got you by the balls, kid* and turning it right around, making him sweat for a change. I like that, I admit it. Because see, I just can't *stand* to let them get away with it. I just can't stand it. I got tired of standing it. When I was a kid it was all 'turn the other cheek,' that stuff. Well, turning the other cheek just means both your cheeks hurt then. I got tired of that.''

"You're still getting back at the big kids on the playground.''

"That's all you can say, huh? You think that's all it is.''

"Or getting back at your father.''

"Aw, Jesus.''

"But Coop, believe me . . . look at me now.'' She put a hand on Cooper's wrist and drew his eyes back to hers. "I'm not saying all this to make you feel bad about who you are, because I like who you are. The thing is, a person like you can be hard on people who . . . people who care about him. Roger was like you.''

That shut Cooper up; he'd learned that when Diana was thinking about Roger he just had to check out of her life for a little while. But Diana went on.

"He had the same thing. He needed that danger, too. God knows why—he never went through a war. Maybe it's just men.''

"Hey, let's not make it a male-female thing. I had enough of that with the Wilkert lady yesterday. There are women cops, too.''

"With me it's men. I keep running into men who love danger. Yeah, Roger loved it, putting on that uniform and getting out there, breaking up people's fights, chasing down the bad guys, getting in harm's way. For the same reasons you just gave. Right up to the day it killed him.''

Diana's gaze went away out the window. She'd shown Cooper one picture of Roger, a big strapping handsome blond with a wide smile and a bristling moustache. Diana had told him it had been a bad marriage from the start; she'd been fleeing the Puerto Rican half of herself by marrying the most Anglo guy she could lay her hands on. It would never have lasted, she said, but she had told Cooper she would have given a lot to go through the whole messy painful process of breaking up rather than stand there at that policeman's funeral being brave. She'd left Miami the week after that and never gone back.

"So what do you want me to say?" said Cooper quietly.

Diana looked back at him with those deep Iberian eyes and said, "How about 'I'll be careful'?"

"OK, I'll be careful." She gave him a faint smile then, closed her eyes briefly, and settled back in her chair. "I'll be real careful," he said.

True to his word, Cooper was careful going home. He spent five minutes checking not only his block but neighboring blocks before he parked the Valiant and slipped through the alley into his place by the back door. He often drove on Sundays but he had decided to give himself a break; he wasn't saving up for anything in particular and there was plenty in the bank to live on for the moment. Inside he flopped on the couch; he had housecleaning to do but he couldn't face it. The Bears were on TV, and he lay on the couch watching for a while with the sound down, but he wasn't that interested. He started thinking about Diana and then about Dominic and then Vivian. Soon he drifted off.

When the phone woke him up he checked his watch. It was only two and the Bears were still slugging it out in silence across the room. He picked up the phone and said hello.

"Cooper? It's me, Dominic."

"Hey, what's happening?"

"I'm down at my house, my mom's place I mean."

"Yeah?"

"Yeah. I was thinking about what you said. About my mom having a boyfriend and all."

"Uh-huh."

"And I decided to come down here and just like look around." Cooper was not quite awake and he couldn't find anything to say to that, although for some reason it bothered him. After a second Dominic went on. "My grandmother was going to clean the place out but she didn't get to it yet and everything's still here just like it was. I thought I would look at my mom's stuff and maybe find something to show who the guy was. I mean, if she was going out with somebody like you said."

"Yeah, yeah. Did you find anything?"

"I'm not sure. I found some stuff, but I'm not sure what it means. I wanted to ask you about it."

Cooper was awake now and he knew what was bothering him. "Listen, Dominic. Hold on a second. How'd you get down there?"

"I took the El, and then I walked. How come?"

"Look, I told you to watch your step. I don't want to scare you or anything, but these guys in the Camaro probably know where your mom's place is."

There was a pause. "Oh shit," said Dominic.

"OK, listen. You're probably OK there but don't move. Make sure the door's locked and wait for me to come and get you. I'll be right down."

"Hey, I don't think anyone followed me or anything."

"Probably not, but let's not take any chances."

"Yeah, all right. I'll wait for you."

"Don't open the door to anyone you don't know, OK? What do I do when I get down there, call up or what?"

"Yeah, from the desk."

"Give me twenty minutes."

It took Cooper less than that to make it out to the Drive and speed down to Belmont, but he took his time cruising the area, looking for the Camaro, looking for somebody sitting in a parked car, looking for he wasn't sure what. He had to park two blocks in from the Drive and walk to 3472 with a stiff breeze in his face, and he checked the street in front of the building again before going in. He thought about what Diana had said and decided that if there was any part of this he enjoyed, it certainly wasn't the feeling in the guts, the feeling that bad trouble could be just around the corner.

The lobby was empty except for the desk man, who was bored and marginally helpful in pointing Cooper to the phone. Cooper called up, heard Dominic's voice with relief, and was buzzed through to the elevators.

Again he was struck on entering the apartment by the way the lake dominated it, vast and luminous just beyond the windows, mirroring the cold somber sky. Dominic had on a sort of tunic buttoned tight up to his throat and baggy black pants and heavy black shoes and as he backed away from the door

Cooper thought he looked spooked, as if sitting alone in the place had gotten to him.

"Everything's cool, right? They're not like waiting outside or anything, are they?" the boy said.

"I didn't see anybody. But you got to figure they know where you used to live and if they want you badly enough, they'll start watching the place."

"OK. But come look what I found." Dominic was striding fast down the hallway to the right, leading Cooper into the little study with the ball and claw desk. Drawers had been pulled open, papers strewn on the desktop and on the floor.

Dominic snatched something from the desktop and handed it to Cooper. It was a square wooden box about three inches on a side and an inch deep, with inlay work in different shades of wood on the top. "I found this in one of the drawers."

Cooper blinked at it. "Nice. It looks Oriental or something." The inlay was intricate, a geometric pattern of light and dark in old varnished wood.

"Open it." Cooper fumbled at the clasp and got it open. The first thing he saw was a little slip of cream-colored notepaper, folded over once. He lifted it and beneath it, on a little velvet cushion, was a golden brooch in the form of a dragon, a winged dragon with scales and an undulating tail. "Read the note," Dominic said. Cooper unfolded the paper.

VIVIAN—BELIEVE IN MY LOVE. The words were written in black ink, in a careful printed hand that was almost calligraphy. The signature was a little stylized character, two horizontal strokes linked in the middle by a vertical one, with a little hook at the right end of the bottom line, suggesting the hook of a capital G.

Cooper looked at Dominic. The boy said, "What do you think?"

Cooper thought for a moment. Finally he said, "I think whoever gave it to her must have liked her a lot and had a fair amount of money. And I think it's too bad he couldn't have put it in one of those cheap cardboard boxes with the name of the store stamped on it, so the cops could trace it."

"What does that mark look like to you?"

"Like an I maybe? With a G? I.G. maybe? Or a J. Capital J and G back to back."

"Yeah, that's what I thought. I.G. or J.G. You think this is the guy?"

"Well, this is some guy anyway. Anybody you know have those initials?"

"I looked in her address book." Dominic nodded at it, open on the desk. "There's nobody under G with either of those initials except this old lady friend of my mother's."

"You never saw her wear this?"

"No. I don't think so. I think I'd recognize it. If she'd had it for a while, anyway."

"Mm-hm. So she might have gotten it recently." Cooper closed the box and handed it to Dominic. "Well, what's-her-name, Melissa was convinced your mom was . . . interested in somebody. Maybe this is the guy. But it seems to me you would have been the first to know, wouldn't you?"

Dominic stared at him gravely, arms akimbo, eyes wide, intent. "I thought so too. But I'm not sure. She went out a lot without me. She could have hung out with somebody without me knowing about it if she really wanted to keep it a secret. And she never . . . God, I can't believe I'm talking about my mother like this. She never brought anyone home or anything. Not while I was here."

Cooper nodded, musing. "But," he said.

"Yeah. But she could have that night, 'cause I was gone."

"The cops looked for traces of somebody else."

"Yeah, but how well? You know? I mean they were sure she killed herself before they came up here."

"What would you look for?"

"I don't know. I kind of looked around the bedroom a bit. You wanna look?"

Cooper shrugged and followed him out of the study and down the hall, Dominic moving with the awkward haste of a boy whose size was a bit ahead of his coordination. With a sense of trespassing, Cooper stepped into what had been Vivian's bedroom. Here also there were windows on the lake, but the curtains were almost completely closed and the light came feebly from a ceiling fixture and a lamp on the table by the bed. The room had been decorated to be light and open, and with the curtains drawn the effect was stifling, unhealthy. The bed was a blond wood affair with headboard and foot-board made of a single thin rail of wood curving over vertical bars. The bed was covered with a dark blue comforter, slightly rumpled as if someone had been sitting on it. The other furniture was all of the same light wood, including a tall armoire in one corner whose doors hung open, revealing colorful swatches of clothing hanging inside. There was a dressing table whose top bore a litter of cosmetics and jewelry spilling out of open boxes.

"I was looking for other stuff, stuff he gave her maybe," said Dominic. "But I didn't find anything else. No more notes or anything, I mean. I think that was all stuff she'd had for a while."

Cooper nodded, looking around the room. Since hearing of Vivian's death he had been feeling he was always just a step behind her, just about to catch up with her after fifteen years but always a little too late. His eyes came back to rest on the dressing table. "How come the pin was in the desk, instead of in here with the rest of her jewelry?"

Dominic looked at him blankly. "I don't know."

"Me neither." Cooper looked at the bed, sensing Vivian's presence, seeing her lying alone under that blue comforter, falling asleep in the dark, worrying about her business, about her son, perhaps feeling the same quiet creep of desolation Cooper had felt at times, heading toward forty without anybody to share that bed. And he wondered if she had always been alone. His eyes went to the bedside table, the dresser, the door to the bathroom.

"I looked," said Dominic. "I checked her drawers and stuff and I found her diaphragm." Cooper watched, shocked, as Dominic swept down on the bedside table and tore open a drawer. "Here it is. But there's no cream, whatever that stuff is you have to smear on it. I don't think she'd used this thing since she was still with my dad."

Cooper shook his head. "Jesus. When I was your age I didn't know what a rubber looked like."

Dominic tossed the diaphragm case back in the drawer and slammed it shut as if with distaste. "That's all I've been thinking about since I talked to you yesterday. It's weird to think about that, but if she was, you know, sleeping with someone here that night, that's probably who killed her, right?"

"Could be."

"Maybe she decided she didn't want to and he got pissed off, something like that."

"Maybe."

"I looked through her desk, looking for like letters he might have sent her, but I didn't find any love letters or anything."

"You've been hard at work."

"He killed my mother," Dominic said.

"Somebody did."

"Come on. That has to be it. We just have to find out who this guy was."

"Did you ask your grandmother about it? She might have known."

"Yeah, I did. She said Mom never told her about going out with anybody."

"Who's your mother's best friend?"

"Ellen Sims. I already called her."

"Man. You have been busy. What did she say?"

Dominic let out an exasperated breath. "She said Mom never mentioned anything about any guy. But she might not, not if she wanted to keep it a secret. I mean, she hadn't even told me."

Cooper looked at him, deep in thought. "You didn't know about any boyfriend. Your grandmother didn't know. Ellen didn't know. Melissa didn't even really know. She just suspected. Why would your mother keep it a secret? Maybe there was no boyfriend."

"So who did that pin come from?"

"There is that." Cooper left the bedroom and wandered down the hall and into the living room. He looked out at the lake, restless, gray, and chilling cold under the fall sky. Dominic trailed behind him. Cooper turned and swept his eyes over the room, the paintings on the wall, the handsome furniture, all silently collecting dust. "Here's what I think you should do," he said. "Go get the gift, bring it along. Make a list of your mother's closest friends, here in Chicago I mean, anyone who would be likely to know if she had a lover. Bring her address book, too. Get all that ready and we'll take it to the cops."

While Dominic went to gather the things, Cooper went to the phone in the kitchen and dialed Area Six. Neither Shostak nor Harrison was there and he left a message. He looked up to see Dominic stuffing the inlaid box and the address book into a manila envelope.

"They'll call back. We'll probably talk to them tomorrow."

Dominic stared, then nodded and blew out a long quivering breath. "I gotta get out of this place." His arms flew out in a gesture that took in the whole room, then flapped back to his side. "I keep thinking I'm gonna hear her key in the lock any minute and then it like hits me. She's never coming through that door again." His gaze held Cooper's for a moment, and in the boy's eyes Cooper saw the shadow, the shadow of that grief that was inside, waiting to steal out at night when Dominic was too tired to sit on it anymore.

Cooper had Dominic wait in the lobby while he scanned the street and slipped out to get the Valiant. He drew up in front and the boy ducked in. Cooper pulled away and headed down toward Belmont to get on the Drive, watching the mirror.

"Looking for that Camaro?" said Dominic.

"Looking for anybody pulling out behind me. They know I saw them last night. They've switched cars by now if they have any brains."

Dominic stared at him for a moment and then looked ahead. "This makes me nervous," he said.

"It should. If I were you I'd have been in New York days ago."

Dominic was silent after that, brooding in the corner of the front seat until Cooper drew up, sure no one had followed them, at Dominic's place.

"You have to work tonight?" said Cooper.

"Yeah." There was no enthusiasm in the boy's voice.

"I'll come by and see you. Put that stuff in a safe place."

"Why don't you keep it?"

" 'Cause they know where I live. If that stuff's important, they might be looking for it, too."

"So these guys who shot at us are working for the guy who gave my mother this pin."

"We don't know that. We don't know much of anything. Except that your mother probably didn't kill herself and that somebody's looking to put a bullet in you. What the connection is, your guess is as good as mine.''

Dominic stared out the windshield, nodded once, and got slowly out of the car, clutching the envelope. Cooper watched him walk into the building, looking like he was sleepwalking. Cooper stared at the door long after it closed behind the boy, wishing he knew what the hell he was doing.

11

VALENTI CALLED HIM late in the afternoon. "MacLeish. Decided to stay off the streets today, huh? Stay out of trouble for a change?"

"Yeah. You get my message?"

"I got it. And I looked at an interesting accident report today."

"No kidding. What happened?"

"There was a sharp-eyed old man with nothing in particular to do, standing at the corner of Lunt and Ridge last night. He saw some guy in a Camaro blow off the red light and sideswipe somebody and drive away."

"Funny, I saw the same accident."

"Yeah, I figured. The old-timer got the license number of the Camaro."

"He did? Thank God for sharp-eyed old men with nothing to do."

"Yeah. He also got the number of a dark green Valiant he said was chasing the Camaro."

"Ah. I can explain that. That's what I was calling about."

"Why can't you leave the Steve McQueen stuff to us? I hear about any more of this kind of shit, I'll bust you myself."

"Listen. They were tailing me, hoping I'd lead them to the kid. I spotted them and got behind them. All I was trying to do was get close enough to read their plates."

"How do you know they wanted you to lead them to the kid?"

"Because they were just following, not trying to draw a bead on me. I told you it was him they were shooting at."

"You're sure it was the same Camaro."

"Absolutely. It made all the turns I made. Had to be them."

"Could be."

"You're not going to tell me who the Camaro belongs to, are you?"

"We don't know who it belongs to. Those license plates were stolen off a broken-down Cadillac out on Augusta Boulevard two months ago."

"See? These are not just two dumb greasers shooting into the air."

"If you ask me, they're two total fuck-ups. Abbot and Costello could do better than these two."

"Yeah. But they still worry me. I got a crease in my arm I didn't have a week ago."

"Well, all I can tell you is keep your head down and don't do anything stupid. Maybe you scared 'em off last night."

"Yeah. Or maybe I just showed them they have to be more careful."

It was supposed to be eight ball only on Burk's table but since the bar was nearly empty and nobody else was waiting to play Cooper and Emilio had quietly agreed on nine ball, a little race to five for the price of the next round. At four games apiece and only the eight and the nine left on the table, Cooper knew he had to do it now, or Emilio would. The trouble was, with the eight across the table three inches from the rail just inside the kitchen and the nine sitting next to the side pocket at his right elbow, it was going to take a hell of a shot.

Bank it or cut it. The cue ball sat in the middle of the table a shade to the left of the eight ball. Try and bank it into the corner to the right, and a mistake of a single degree misses the shot. Cut it into the far corner opposite, and it has to be hard to kick it all the way down but calculated right to leave a shot on the nine.

Cut it. Cooper leaned over the table, feeling the shot more than seeing it, feeling the cue slide through his fingers, frictionless, anticipating the long smooth stroke. He exhaled and stroked it and the cue ball ticked the eight and came down hard off the rail, crossing the table as the eight rolled down toward the pocket and slowed, maybe too much but no, it was dropping, with the cue ball heading back to bounce off the far rail again, and yes, thank you Jesus, coming back just right to leave a straight-in shot on the nine. Cooper walked around the table and didn't let himself think before lining it up in a second or two and potting it.

"Nice," said Emilio.

Cooper straightened up, shook Emilio's hand, reached for his beer. "Take care of your stroke and it'll take care of you."

"Pressure shot. Ice water in the veins, the man has."

"Pressure." Cooper swallowed beer and laughed. "Shit, you think that's pressure, try sitting in a bunker with half the North Vietnamese Army coming out of the woods, looking out and seeing two little men in pith helmets about fifty yards away pointing an RPG at you. Now that's pressure. I knew I had about two seconds and I wasn't sure I had two rounds left in the magazine."

Emilio smiled at him for a second and said, "You made the shot, I guess."

"I'd be up on that big black wall in Washington if I hadn't." Cooper set his beer down with a clunk. Emilio went to buy the round, shaking his head as he walked away. Cooper dug out quarters for the next game, wondering why he'd felt compelled to tell Emilio the story. Cooper didn't tell many war stories, and he hated sounding cocky. Maybe the talk with Diana in the morning had stirred up the murky waters, and tonight with the three or four beers he'd had things were working their way to the surface. He was glad Diana hadn't been there to hear it; she would have thought he had enjoyed things like that.

Cooper leaned on the table waiting for Emilio and watched Lisa the barmaid with a distant detached lust. He realized he hadn't thought about Vivian Horstmann or her son for at least an hour. That was what Burk's was for, for forgetting things. Burk's was his bar, his second living room, a comfortably dark, comfortably shabby neighborhood tavern with a good jukebox and a pool table and a clientele like Cooper, not too prosperous and not too young.

Before Emilio got back three guys Cooper didn't know had come in and put their names up, so they went back to last pocket eight ball. Cooper got sloppy and blew an easy shot, and while Emilio dissected him Cooper mused. He watched smoke drift through the light over the table and then wan-

dered over to the booth to pick up his beer. There was a
painting hung on the wall over the booth that had been there
since the sixties, a stark black-and-white oil, a light-and-
shadow depiction of women's faces framed by long straight
hair in that old sixties style. Cooper had seen it a hundred
times but this time his eye lit on the artist's signature in the
corner and he suddenly remembered the note that was in the
box with the gold dragon pin.

Emilio was calling to him from the table; he'd missed sinking the eight ball but left it hanging on the lip and Cooper
knew it was hopeless. He forced himself to concentrate on
the game and managed to sink the rest of his balls but
scratched and lost trying to kick the eight out of the corner.
He slapped Emilio on the shoulder and sat in the booth drinking and looking at the painting and feeling sure it was an
artist who had given Vivian the pin. He thought there was a
chance Melissa Wilkert might be able to identify the signature. He smiled.

Cooper put his empty beer bottle on the bar, said good-
bye to Lisa and then he was standing in the doorway, looking
up and down the street, just making sure. He walked home
in the chill, passing the corner where Rose's restaurant stood,
where he'd ducked in to say hi to Dominic earlier. He had
promised to come pick the boy up at quitting time, but that
was three hours away. Cooper wanted to go home and pull
the armchair over by the window and put his feet up on the
sill and look out at the trees.

He remembered to take care again walking down his block,
looking for the Camaro, looking for any car parked near his
house with people in it who could be watching. He saw no
one in a quick pass along the street on the opposite side from
his building and he doubled back and went in the front door.
He saw that Mr. Kim had replaced the glass and stuffed plastic wood into the bullet hole in the doorjamb. Cooper had
never found where the other bullet had gone.

Upstairs, he hung his jacket on the closet doorknob, went
into the bathroom and pissed, then headed for the kitchen to
deal with a vague hunger. He stopped a few feet from the
doorway, looking into the dark kitchen. He had left the light
on, he was sure; it was his custom when going out in the
evening. He stood thinking back, unable to remember ex-

plicitly doing it this time; perhaps he was only sure because it was his custom. The bulb could have burned out, for that matter. Cooper knew that if circumstances had been normal he would not have thought twice about the darkened kitchen.

As it was he went forward cautiously, listening, his hand coming up slowly to reach around and try the switch. He had reached the point where he could see through the doorway to the broken pane in the back door, backlit from the alley, when something swept out of the darkness and hissed at him, and his eyes caught fire.

For a moment there was only pain, a searing agony that went right through his eyes into his brain, and then Cooper became aware that he had cried out and that he was twisting, falling. There were hands on him.

He was on the floor, shaking his head to get at the pain, and someone kicked him hard in the ribs. He cried out again and pressed a hand to his tightly shut eyes only to have it torn away from his face. He bucked, not in any conscious plan of defense, for the pain wouldn't let him think, but only by reflex, and then someone had both his arms and someone else was stuffing something into his mouth, and he was trying to shout again and his eyes were burning, burning, killing him.

He stabilized enough to realize what was happening as they wrapped the tape around his head to hold the gag in, someone pulling hard on his hair. He was blinded, he was trying to keep from choking on the gag, they were dragging him to his feet.

"Come on fucker, walk," said a low mean voice. They were dragging him forward and he roared through the rag in his mouth, trying to expiate the pain by screaming it out.

They slammed him face down on something, the table, and his arm was wrenched straight out and he roared again, trying to pull free, shaking his head like a madman to try and put the fire out, and something pricked the back of his hand splayed out on the table and there was a slamming noise and his hand hurt and *Oh Jesus Christ* Cooper knew they had just nailed his hand to the table.

"Sit." They rammed a chair against the back of his knees and his legs buckled. His head was down, he had nearly passed out but not quite, and he could feel his hand pinned in the center of the table and it hurt but not as badly as his eyes.

He was doing something between sobbing and gasping by this time, honking out through his nose uncontrollably. His right hand was free and he put it to his face reflexively though there was no way it could help the burning in his eyes.

"Listen." His head was snapped back by a strong grip in his hair. "Listen cocksucker, get a hold of yourself. I wanna talk to you."

Cooper retched, nearly threw up but suppressed it, knowing he would choke to death if he didn't. Every time he moved, his left hand tugged against the nail and hurt him. He kneaded at his eyes, feeling the stickiness, wondering what they'd sprayed him with.

"I'm gonna take the sock out if you promise to be good," the voice said. "You scream or any shit like that, we'll hurt you bad. You read me?"

Cooper fought for control and found enough to nod once. The tape was unwound in a fast couple of turns, tearing at his stubbled cheeks as it came off. The sock came out and he gasped, breathed freer, moaned with each exhalation. He was trying to sit still on the chair so he didn't tear up his hand, but the pain in his eyes made it hard.

"Now listen up. Listen good. We wanna know where the kid is, dig? Where's the kid?"

Cooper took a deep breath, his eyes squeezed shut, his right hand clenching and unclenching rhythmically. The pain was mainly in his left eye now; the left eye had taken the brunt of the spray. After a couple more breaths he sobbed out, "I don't know."

"Piece a' shit." The sock was rammed back into his mouth and he heard more tape coming off the roll and then he was being wrapped again. He made an effort and opened his right eye just a bit and saw light and shapes and not much more. Something bore down hard on his left arm and a hand was clawing at his, working it against the nail and hurting it, straightening out the fingers, and suddenly something tugged at the nail of his little finger and Cooper stiffened all over and bellowed through the gag, because he knew this was going to be the worst yet.

"Teach this cocksucker to lie to us," the voice said, and

a muffled scream came out of Cooper's throat as the nail was torn off, half of it anyway, in a fast jagged tear. His head went down toward his knees again, and there was nowhere to go from the pain.

"Sit up." Cooper didn't know how much time had gone by; not much, it seemed. "We're gonna give you another chance because we're in a good mood today." The hand grabbed his hair and pulled his head up. "We're gonna give you another chance. You're gonna tell us where the kid is and it's gonna be the truth this time or another fingernail comes off. We got nine nails to go, motherfucker. Shit, we'll give you nine more chances if you want. Now nod your head if you're ready to be straight with us."

Cooper sobbed through his nose and tried to think. He couldn't take any more nails coming off; he just couldn't take it. He nodded once and someone moved behind him and the tape was tugging at his hair and whiskers again. Cooper groped for strength and opened the right eye again and blinked through tears and fought to focus it; someone moved close in front of him and he made out a face before the pain became too much and he had to shut the eye again. A dark face, a beard, and something absurd, a hallucination. In that single agonizing second of sight Cooper saw a teardrop outlined impossibly in blue on the smooth brown cheek.

"That's it, man. Get your breath back." The sock was out and Cooper was breathing deeply again. "Take your time. We got all night. Now I'm gonna ask you again. Where's the kid? Where'd you take him?"

Tell them something. The pain had been with him long enough that, impossibly, he was starting to find control, to function in spite of it. "His father came to get him," he sobbed. "His father came to take him back to New York."

"When?"

"Yesterday."

"Prove it. You gotta prove it to us. Give us a phone number. I wanna dial his father's number and talk to him."

"I don't know his number in New York."

"You wanna lose another nail?"

"Wait!" *Think,* Cooper told himself. He exhaled, scrambled for a lie. "They might still be in Chicago. They were going to stay . . . a day or two. Out at O'Hare, the Hilton."

"Out at O'Hare at the Hilton. You wouldn't be shitting me now, would you fuckface?"

"No. I think they're there." Cooper knew he was only buying time, if that. He was going to have to think of something better.

"What's his father's name?"

"Nick Dennison."

"All right. I'll tell you what. We're gonna call the Hilton and check. And if you're telling us some kind of bullshit, we're gonna take the pliers to your other fingers and then start on your balls, and you only got two of them. So if you're lying to me, man, you better think about it and change your mind before we get through." His tone changed as he spoke to the other man. "Go call 'em. Get the number from four-one-one."

Cooper heard footsteps move through the dining room toward the living room. He had maybe a minute or two, he figured. *Think.*

"How about it, shithead? You telling the truth or not? We can make things just as hard as you want."

"I'm telling the truth." Cooper struggled to control his voice. His eyes hurt but not so badly anymore that he couldn't function. His hand hurt like hell, too, nailed to the table. Cooper heard the second man picking up the phone in the living room.

Cooper steeled himself, opened the right eye again, blinked, and looked at the table. He saw the claw hammer lying there next to his hand; he saw the head of the nail flush with the skin of the back of his hand, with a little collar of blood around it.

"You keep that eye closed or I'll give you another dose, motherfucker."

Cooper's head dropped again. That hand was going to have to come off the table, and that was about all there was to it. In the living room he heard the second man speaking quietly to the information operator in a low, indistinguishable mumble. The first man shifted position nearby, took a step or two.

The head of the nail couldn't do much more damage to his hand than a bullet, Cooper thought. The question was whether he had the strength to do it. It would have to be fast and brutal. He tensed his shoulders. Fast and hard and grab the hammer. He heard the man in the living room punching out a number.

"Last chance, man, if you want to change your story," said the man nearby. Cooper knew he couldn't judge his position accurately by his voice; he'd have to open his eye again.

Don't think about it. You have less than a minute. Just do it. He tensed his shoulders. It would take a quick hard jerk, straight upward to do as little damage as possible to his hand. *Oh Christ, was it going to hurt. Not if you go hard and fast,* he thought.

Rip it. Cooper coiled, growling as he tensed his legs and his shoulders, and then sprang, tearing his hand free of the table with a bellow and sweeping his right hand toward where he knew the hammer lay. He felt it and had it and then he had to look for the man with his one good eye, spotting him, a blur a yard away with his hand coming out of his pocket and then Cooper went at him with a blind hard backhand meant to kill and felt the hammer go THUNK as he hit something and strained to open the eye again and saw the man falling and the gun with him and heard steps in the living room, coming fast.

Cooper was on his hands and knees feeling blindly for the gun, hearing the footsteps, knowing he had to open that eye again to find the gun, almost panicking and running for the back door, getting his hand on the gun and picking it up, a revolver thank God so no fucking around with safeties and he brought the gun up and opened his eyes, both of them, just as the dim shape of a man appeared in the doorway, and Cooper fired at him, twice.

The man swore and ducked back into the dining room and Cooper was thinking again, diving under the kitchen table, his left hand hurting unbelievably, his eyes closed again, listening for footsteps. If they approached again he would look just long enough to fire. Until then, lie under the table and pant and try not to moan too loudly, with his eyes shut.

After a moment the footsteps sounded, but going away, toward the front door. Cooper heard them retreat and as he heard the front door being opened he was on his feet, charging out of the kitchen, navigating the familiar territory of the dining room with his eyes shut, saving energy for one last shot at the man.

Too late. He heard the footsteps out on the landing and then going down the stairs fast. He opened the right eye and saw the door standing open and then he was lurching across the living room and slamming the door, leaning on it, the gun in his right hand, realizing his left would be good for absolutely nothing for a while. He dropped the gun and locked both locks with his good hand, then retrieved the gun and, fighting hard to keep it together, went back to the kitchen. He took a quick look at the man lying unmoving on the floor and then made it back to the phone, where he punched out 911 by feel and gasped at the indifferent operator that there was a home invasion in progress and gave the address and told him to get someone there fast. Then he went to the kitchen sink, laid the gun on the counter, and turned on the cold water. He leaned over and put his face in the stream and waited for the water to put out the fire in his eyes, moaning a bit with each exhalation.

Cooper didn't pass out until he turned around and saw the nail sticking up out of the table in the center of a smear of blood, with little bits of flesh hanging on it.

"Easy-Off in the eyes. Vicious." The voice of the policeman sounded somewhere nearby. Light-headed, Cooper couldn't judge whether he was right next to him or across the room. He lay on the couch with a wet towel across his eyes and another one wrapped around his left hand. In the kitchen he could hear low urgent voices, the paramedics working on the man in there. A police radio crackled out on the landing; the door was open and Cooper could hear neighbors murmuring below.

"We gotta get you to a hospital," said the other cop. Cooper had looked at them briefly when they'd entered but hadn't looked at anything since. "Your towel's soaked through. You're bleeding all over yourself."

"They're about ready to go in there," said the other cop. "You can catch a ride."

"Don't put me in the same ambulance with him," said Cooper in a voice thick with pain. "I get a chance, I'll kill him."

There was an awkward silence. Footsteps came in from the landing and Valenti's voice said, "I'll take you in my squad if you try not to bleed on the seat.'' He came closer, walking slowly as always with his cop's swagger, and knelt by Cooper's head. "They came back, huh?'' he said softly.

"Yeah. They came back.'' Cooper couldn't manage much above a whisper.

"Go take a look at the kitchen table,'' said one of the cops.

Valenti was gone for a minute or so. Cooper heard him talking with the paramedics. When he came back he said, "What the fuck.''

"They nailed his hand to the table,'' said one of the other cops, in a tone of incredulity bordering on levity.

"With his own tools,'' said the other.

"His oven cleaner, too. These guys improvise,'' said the first one.

"Nice touch, the oven cleaner,'' Valenti said. "Better than a blindfold. You get any kind of a look at the one that got away?''

Cooper pressed the cool towel harder into his eyes, trying to ease the pain. "I saw one of them. What's the guy in there look like?''

"Blond, stringy hair. Little runt.''

"Then I saw the other one. Dark. Bearded. Hispanic maybe. And I think he's got a tattoo on his face.''

"On his face?''

"Yeah. I thought at first I hallucinated it, but I don't think so. He's got a teardrop tattooed on his cheekbone.''

"Christ. These dumb fucks go in for a life of crime and then go out of their way to make themselves conspicuous.''

"We should haul him in fast,'' said the first cop.

"Yeah. Well, you handled that one in there,'' Valenti said.

"I didn't hit him hard enough,'' Cooper said quietly, hurting all over.

"Naw, you hit him just right,'' Valenti said. "He's got a fractured skull but he'll live. If he died we wouldn't be able to talk to him, would we? This way he'll be able to tell us lots of interesting things.''

"I was stupid. I shouldn't have walked into it.''

"Hey. Who expects to get ambushed in their kitchen? Don't be too hard on yourself.''

"It was dumb. Fucking dumb.''

"OK, it was dumb. You're smarter now. Can you walk?''

Sitting up, Valenti's hand on his arm, Cooper said, "They asked where the kid was. That good enough for you?"

"Yeah. That's plenty good. I never said I didn't believe you."

"Do I get to talk to a detective now?"

"Yeah, MacLeish. You get to talk to a detective. Just tell me one thing."

"What?"

"How the hell did you get your hand loose?"

"You don't want to know."

Valenti helped him to his feet and paused and said, "You know something, MacLeish?"

"What?"

"You may be dumb, but you're for sure the toughest son of a bitch I ever ran across."

Cooper pressed the towel to his face. "I'll take smart any day, man. Any day of the week."

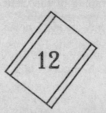

12

COOPER LAY WITH his eyes bandaged and listened to Harrison. "You damn near killed him, but he'll pull through," Harrison was saying. "They ID'ed him as Robert Murphy, professional tough guy in a small-time way and all-around asshole."

"The world's full of 'em," said Cooper.

"Yeah. Well, this guy spent one vacation in Menard for armed robbery and another in Stateville for aggravated battery. Must have been pretty aggravated—it's hard to get sent up for that. He's weaseled out of a couple of other raps by one means or another. He likes to hit women, for one thing. He makes a living more or less by getting involved in whatever shit is lying around on the street, especially in Uptown. Muscling people, collecting debts, that type of thing. Funny thing is, he's not that big, not like a lot of these intimidator types."

"He's got a certain flair all his own. Any luck with the other guy?"

"Not so far. But if he's got that tattoo he'll show up before too long, unless he's skipped town. But I don't think he has. We'll get him."

"Don't forget the business behind all this. The boy, his mother's death."

"We ain't forgettin' nothing. I'm talking to the grand-mother later today."

"Any chance the kid could get some protection?"

"Like a squad in front of his house? None. Best thing would be to get him out of town."

"I know. If he doesn't want to go with his father there's got to be some other relative somewhere he could put up with for a while. I'll work on him some more."

"Do that. But take it easy on yourself for a day or two."

Cooper heard the scraping of the chair as Harrison rose to go. "At least till you can see again."

When Harrison had gone Cooper heard Diana's footsteps come quietly over to the bed. Her hand ran gently through his hair. "Still hurting?"

"Not so bad. Now I'm hungry."

"That's a good sign. That's pretty normal for you."

"Yeah. And limp broccoli doesn't do it."

"Want me to get you a sandwich?"

"No. Just stay here a while if you can."

"I got all day."

"That's good."

His good hand slid across the blanket and he hooked his index finger through hers. They said nothing for a while and then Diana said, "I don't want to lose another one, Cooper. Being a widow sucks."

Cooper thought about all that Diana seemed to be implying and decided it was not the time to worry about it. "What do you say when I can see again we take off somewhere, get out of the city for a couple of days?"

"I can drive. Why wait till you can see?"

"There's a thought. Except I might enjoy the scenery more if I can see."

"And the minute you see something that needs fixing somewhere, there goes the vacation."

Cooper smiled. "I can't help it. There's a lot of things that need fixing."

He felt Diana disengage her finger, give the sheet a tug to straighten it. "How about we wait until this thing with Dominic is all over? I don't think you could tear yourself away anyway."

After a moment Cooper said, "No. Probably not."

In the evening, after Diana had gone, it got a little bit rough; not that the pain was so bad this time, not like in the hospital in Chu Lai during those long weeks, just that it's always tough to lie still when the body is hurting. The eyes were the worst; pain in the limbs was always easier to ignore somehow and the hand and the finger weren't badly hurt at all compared to the wounds he'd had back then. The shrapnel across the back, the 7.62 rounds in the leg and the ribs, those had hurt, a lot worse than his hand. But the eyes hurt now, especially the left one, and all he could do was lie there and take it, just like before. Those had been rough weeks in Chu Lai, lying in there through those endless nights hurting, hearing guys moaning softly somewhere off in the dark, each time knowing the wound wasn't quite bad enough to get him home, just bad enough to let him heal and get sent back out to the field. The one consolation had been that every day in the hospital was a day he wasn't in combat.

The memory of old pain helped take Cooper's mind off the present variety. His unseen roommate had the TV on for a while and then turned it off and apparently fell asleep, for the room was silent. Cooper lay and listened to faraway traffic and thought about Diana.

There was a soft knocking and someone came into the room. Cooper was lying on his side; he raised his head and said, "Hello?"

"Mr. MacLeish? It's Adelle Horstmann. Are you receiving visitors?"

Cooper scrambled to sit up. "Sure. Have a seat. I think there's one there, isn't there?"

"Yes, there is. I'm sorry if you were sleeping." Suddenly, eerily, the clear soft diction was Vivian's; she was there in the room with him.

Cooper shook his head slowly. "No, just killing time." He was fumbling blindly with his pillows; Mrs. Horstmann said, "Let me help you," and propped them up behind him so he could sit up.

"Thanks. With my eyes on the fritz, lying here thinking is about all the fun I can have." Cooper smiled in what he hoped was her direction; he heard a chair creak as she sat.

"Detective Harrison told me what happened. I'm very sorry. Since you were protecting my grandson I feel almost responsible." Her voice was quiet and uncertain.

"No, that's ridiculous. It's not your fault."

"Allow me to feel grateful then." She paused, and Cooper, at a loss, gave a little shrug. "I understand you resisted and . . . overpowered one of them."

"Yeah. I resisted. You talked to the detectives, then?"

"To Mr. Harrison, yes. He asked me about Vivian's affairs, much the sort of questions you were asking the other day.''

"Good. I think they may take us seriously now."

"I'm sorry this was the price you had to pay to get them to do so."

"I'm just glad I had the sense to get Dominic out of there."

There was a silence that went on until Cooper became uncomfortable. "Oh God," Mrs. Horstmann said quietly, and then Cooper stiffened as he heard her start to cry softly, sniffing once every few seconds, as he sat helpless, unable even to extend a hand. Without his sight he could only sit there and wish she would stop. He could hear her trying to repress it, only to have it break out in ragged bursts every now and again. He sat and remembered Dominic crying in the dark. When it sounded as if things were abating he said, "I think there's some water there somewhere," pointing toward the tray at the side of his bed.

She took a shuddering breath, let it go, and said, "Thank you. I'm so sorry. This has been very, very, very hard."

"Nobody should have to go through it."

He heard her scrabbling in her purse, blowing her nose. Composed, she said, "When Charles died I could accept it. He was sixty-four years old and had had a fair shot at things, as he said. But Vivian. That's not fair, not at all. They had no right. Nobody has the right to take my daughter." She breathed fiercely for a while and Cooper listened, listening for Vivian's voice. In a quiet steady tone Mrs. Horstmann went on. "When I thought she had killed herself there was no end to the pain. It just went deeper and deeper. There was no understanding it, no one to blame except her, except me. That was worse. You were right, Mr. MacLeish, that was much worse. This way I have anger, and anger helps."

"They'll get them. The police will get them," said Cooper.

"Let us hope so." She fell silent and Cooper put his hand to his eyes, pressing gently on the bandage, trying to ease the burning. His left hand was throbbing inside the cast.

After a moment Mrs. Horstmann said, "You loved Vivian, didn't you?"

Cooper turned his head toward her, surprised. "I was in love with her. I'm not sure that's the same thing."

"Perhaps not. But I'm glad you found Dominic."

"I had a reason to look for him." The words came out before Cooper could think about them. Under different circumstances, without the pain and the smell of grief still in the air, he might not have said anything. But it was suddenly important to tell her, not to let her go on wondering why he had an interest in the boy. He waited for her to ask but she said nothing. He groped for a way to phrase it right and after a long moment he said, "I think there's a good possibility that I'm Dominic's father."

A silence ensued and Cooper knew he had given her a jolt.

"You mean you don't *know* you are?" she said.

It was Cooper's turn to sit frozen. "No. Am I?"

"Of course you are. I saw it immediately when I met you at the funeral."

"You saw it?"

"The resemblance. Dominic looks like you."

Cooper let his head loll back on the pillow. He felt something coming loose, deep inside. "I can't see it. I was never sure."

"I thought you knew. I thought that's what was behind your finding him, taking care of him."

"I didn't know for sure. I thought he might be my son, just from the dates. I never knew he existed until Ellen Sims told me about him."

"You can be sure."

Cooper saw light dawning. "She told you."

"Of course. Daughters tell their mothers."

"She told you how it happened?"

"Yes. Vivian told me all about it."

Cooper exhaled, a long slow sigh. He remembered Vivian at the other end of a couch, long ago. "I didn't have that in mind when I went over there. I've felt bad about it for fifteen years."

"Vivian never held it against you. The initiative was hers, wasn't it?"

"Yes. I was angry with her for a long time because of that. That wasn't what I wanted from her. Not like that, anyway."

"You're not angry anymore?"

"No."

"I'm glad. She wouldn't have wanted you to stay angry."
She blew her nose again.

Cooper put his hands to his eyes again. He was very tired.
He said, "Nick knows, right?"

"Of course. Vivian told him everything, making her part
clear. I don't think he holds anything against you, either. And
I know he considers Dominic his son, fully. Nick is a driven
sort of man who has always put most of his energy into his
work, but he has great reserves of warmth, too. I know he
was devastated by the divorce. That's why I'm hoping he and
Dominic can be reconciled."

"Well, you don't have to worry about me. I was curious,
but I'm making no claims. He's Nick's boy."

"That also, I'm glad to hear. But I think perhaps you've
earned the right to a small share of Dominic, if a secret one.
Without you, we'd still be looking for him."

"He might be safer."

"I know how you protected him last night, Mr. MacLeish.
You've earned our gratitude."

Cooper let his hand fall back on the sheet. He was weary
and hurting and he wanted something to put him to sleep.
"Thank you for coming in, Mrs. Horstmann. And for telling
me."

"Why don't you call me Adelle?"

"OK. Make it Cooper for me then."

He heard her stand up, felt her take his good hand in hers
and squeeze it. "You have our thanks, Cooper. All of us,
including Vivian."

The next day Cooper left the hospital with one functioning
eye, a gauze patch over the other one, a cast on his left hand
and a bandage on the little finger sticking out of the cast.
Diana drove him to her place and made tea for him. They sat
together on the couch and read; eventually Cooper dozed a
little. Around three Diana put on her high-class waitress out-
fit and prepared to leave.

"Dominic called this morning," she said. "I told him
you'd call back." She stood looking down at Cooper on the
sofa with a distant expression.

"Yeah. I'll call. Thanks."

"Try and stay out of the cross fire today." Diana leaned over to kiss him lightly on the lips and was gone.

Cooper got Dominic at the other end of the line, after talking to a young woman who did not sound entirely awake and let the phone fall on the floor with a clunk.

"What's up?"

"Cooper! You out of the hospital?"

"Back in one piece."

"I wanted to come see you but Diana said it wouldn't be a good idea."

"No. Best to lie low. These guys are really after your scalp, pal."

There was a silence. "I talked to those detectives again. I gave them that stuff and told them what we thought about it and made that list and everything."

"That's good. Listen, I had an idea about that. I think maybe the mark on the note is an artist's signature. You know, a lot of them have stylized signatures they put on paintings, right?"

"Yeah, I thought of that too. The cops were gonna talk to Melissa about it."

"You're a step ahead of me again. Maybe we're starting to get somewhere. Listen, right now these guys don't know where you are. Let's keep it that way. You seeing any of your friends?"

"A couple."

"Don't meet them in a public place or go to their house. If you want to see them, figure out a way for them to sneak into your place. And don't go out alone. This is for real. Somebody wants you dead."

Another pause. "OK. I understand."

"And if you think of somebody in another city who might like to see you, take a little vacation. I'd still like to see you leave town for a while."

"Look, if someone killed your mother and people were like finally trying to do something about it, would you just leave?"

"No. Probably not. Unless someone was trying to kill me, too."

"Somebody did try to kill you. You're not running away."

"I'm older than you. And I'm used to this kind of shit."

"I'm not leaving. I'll be careful, but I'm not leaving."

"All right, all right. Listen, I'll come see you at the restaurant. When do you work next?"

"I don't work for a few days. Why don't you come over here tomorrow?"

"OK, maybe tomorrow morning. See you then."

"Hey, I found that book."

"What book?"

"Down and Out in Paris and London. It's pretty wild. I'm kind of getting into busing tables because of it."

"Well, hey. I hope it lasts. See you."

Cooper hung up and dialed again. He didn't expect to find Shostak or Harrison at Area Six, but he knew he could leave a message. He did so, and within a half hour the phone rang and it was Harrison.

"They let you out, huh?"

"Yeah. I insisted."

"Well, watch yourself. What can I do for you?"

"Just wondering if you got anything out of my friend with the dent in his head."

"Shit, the man's in critical condition. When he's conscious, we'll talk to him."

"All right. I understand you talked to the kid."

"Yeah."

"And he showed up with the gift, with the note?"

"Uh-huh."

"And you talked to a woman named Melissa Wilkert?"

"Yeah, we did that too."

"Well, what do you think?"

"You got all the ideas, let's hear 'em. What do you think's going on?"

"I don't know what's going on. But Melissa Wilkert thought Vivian started seeing someone, about a month before she died."

"Yeah, she thinks that's who did it."

"Yeah. So we thought maybe you could track him down. I mean, I know I'm an amateur, but if someone threw her over, it was probably someone she knew, right? There wasn't any forced entry, was there?"

"No. That makes sense. We were wondering about that too—if there was someone with her that night, who would it be? Who would be likely to be in her place, drinking with her, on a night her kid wasn't there, at two in the morning?"

"Were there any signs of someone else drinking there?"

"Of course not. That's why we thought suicide first. But any dumbass knows how to wash up a glass."

"So could Melissa identify the signature on the note?"

"Not for sure, no. But if she read the initials right there's a guy, an artist, whose initials match and who she says knew Vivian Horstmann."

"You talk to him?"

"You know, you have a way of getting on people's nerves."

"I'm sorry. I know you don't have to tell me all this."

"I don't have to tell you any of this. But hey, I guess I feel talkative today. No, we haven't talked to the guy because he's apparently left town."

"Oh yeah? That's interesting."

"Maybe. The neighbor doesn't know where he went and he's not sure when he left. Could have been as long as three months ago."

"In other words before Vivian died."

"Yeah. So we'll try and follow this up, but I wouldn't hold my breath."

"Yeah, OK. You talk to the grandmother?"

"Yeah, we talked to the grandmother."

"And his father? In New York?"

"Hey, MacLeish. We've done this before, you know."

"All right, I just want to make sure you know what all's involved here."

"Well, we appreciate that. You mentioned her ex. You think he killed her?"

"What? No. I just think he would know a lot about her. He was in New York when it happened, anyway."

"Uh-huh. That's what I hear."

"You don't believe it?"

"I didn't say that. I just got a nasty mind. See, in something like this the husband's the first guy I would look at."

"How come?"

"See it all the time. Guy's wife divorces him, he goes a little nuts."

"Except they don't usually send hit men after the kids too, do they?"

"All right, you got anything better?"

"Just the guy. The unknown lover. I figured Melissa Wilkert might be able to identify the signature on the note."

"Uh-huh. Well, we ain't done talking to people. If there was someone, he'll show up."

"Yeah." Cooper lay back on the couch with the phone to his ear, staring. "Thanks for calling. I know you're busy."

"Busy ain't the word for it. You know how many cases we're trying to handle right now?"

"Lots, I imagine."

"Lemme tell you. People keep on getting killed. And every time they do, we gotta drop what we're doing and go look at the new one, 'cause you gotta get 'em while they're fresh. Something like this Horstmann case, weeks old now, we squeeze it in when we can. Understand what I mean?"

"Yeah, I see."

"I made eight thousand bucks in overtime last year, and I'm ahead of that already this year. Murder in this city's gonna finance my retirement home in the Bahamas. Either that or a real nice funeral."

Cooper lay on the couch and thought until he dozed off. He got up after a while and pilfered Diana's larder and then napped some more. Sometime in the early evening he awoke in the dark and knew there were still things to think about. Other things. Old things. He had been penned up for several days and he needed to move, so he pulled his jacket on gingerly over the cast and went out, walking through the tree-lined streets toward the lake. Navigating with one eye was uncomfortable at first and the blind spot made him nervous; he moved with his head on a swivel.

His hand and his eye both hurt as he stopped at a liquor store on Jarvis and got a flask of Jack Daniel's. He brown-bagged it like a derelict as he walked toward the park. It was a chilly evening with a darting wind that had a hint of cold sharp rain in it.

When his wounds stopped hurting a fourth of the flask was gone and he was out at the end of the pier again, collar turned up against the wind and hands in his pockets, staring north along the shore of the lake and remembering 1973 again.

After a time he roused himself and made his way stiffly

back down the pier. Walking back to his place was a bit scary but he had to get back on the horse again; he wasn't going to let them make him an exile from his own home. He made two passes along the street and checked the alley behind. His courage bolstered a bit by the whiskey, he took a breath and went on in.

Upstairs he saw that the no doubt near-apoplectic Mr. Kim had boarded over the window in the back door but left the mess in the kitchen. The blood on the table and the trail of drops on the floor had dried dark brown.

Cooper called Adelle Horstmann and told her he needed to talk to her. She asked after his health and said he could come by. After he hung up he went into the bathroom and carefully peeled the gauze patch off his left eye; he wasn't going to try to drive one-eyed. He blinked, walked around the apartment for a while and decided his binocular vision was functional, just barely. The left eye wouldn't stop watering so he stuffed a supply of Kleenexes into his pocket. In the mirror he saw a long unshaven face with a drooping moustache and alarmingly red eyes. The busted hand and the whisky on his breath completed the impression of decrepitude, but Cooper decided it couldn't be helped.

He went out to find the Valiant and pointed it north. He followed Sheridan up along the lake into Evanston, driving carefully with his useless left hand resting on the crossbar of the steering wheel, blinking a lot. He wondered if they'd let him drive a cab with the cast on and decided that if they didn't he wouldn't mind much, except that it would be a lean month.

Charles Horstmann had made enough money as an eminent professor, author of textbooks, and shrewd investor to settle in a stolid three-story Victorian mansion on Forest Avenue in Evanston. Cooper drew up across the street and sat looking at lights behind closed curtains for a moment, thinking that this was where Vivian had grown up, feeling a distant echo of that ancient passion. He remembered standing under the sycamore across from another professor's house and for a few seconds he was very conscious of Vivian's presence in his life. She was a shadow, a whisper of sadness in his past, and a sudden new factor in his present, an enormous negative space in the composition.

It occurred to him then that whoever was trying to find Dominic could easily be watching his grandmother's house. He looked in his mirrors, put the car in gear, and drove slowly down to the end of the block, checking the cars. He turned around and came back just as slowly and drove on past the house. He parked in the next block and walked back, watching. By the time he reached the house he was confident he could walk up and stand under the porch light without getting shot at again.

He rang the bell and stood dabbing at his left eye with a Kleenex. There were footsteps and he saw Adelle peering at him through the beveled glass of the door. When she opened it she looked from the cast on his hand to his face but made no comment. She wore gray slacks and a roomy white wool sweater that looked hand-knitted.

"I look like hell, I know," said Cooper.

"You look as if you ought to still be in the hospital. Come in." She looked frankly apprehensive as she closed the door behind him. "Is there something new?" She stood with her arms folded, clasping her forearms in a gesture that betrayed tension.

"No, I don't have anything new. I'll leave that to the detectives. I wanted to ask you about something else." Afraid she was not going to invite him any farther in, Cooper cast a glance into the room opening to the left.

"Certainly. Please, come in." She led him into a living room to the left of the hall. There was dark wood everywhere, on the floors and framing the doorway into the darkened room to the right and around the fireplace opposite. There was solid furniture that had come *en mass* from someplace pricey, sitting on a carpet of deep, very old red. The curtains that hung over the front window were dark blue. The room was lit softly by two lamps, one standing in a corner and the other on a small table at the end of the striped damask sofa. The room had taken money and taste to decorate, but it was more than a showroom; there were magazines stacked sloppily on the shelves of a small end table and a hardcover novel lay open, face down, at one end of the sofa.

Adelle took his jacket and, after the slightest hesitation, said, "Can I get you something to drink?"

Cooper was starting to hurt again and he would have loved

more whiskey, but he said, "Some coffee or something would be great."

Adelle left by the hall door and Cooper explored the room, stepping gingerly, feeling like a tourist in a cathedral. He stopped in front of the mantelpiece and stood looking at a photograph, wiping the flow from his eye with the sodden Kleenex. The photograph showed Nick, Vivian, and Dominic in a family portrait, taken four or five years before from the look of it. Dominic was prepubescent, a serious-looking but handsome child, his large dark eyes not yet obscured by the forelock. Nick was prosperous and groomed as always, looking little different than he had when Cooper had first seen him.

And this was the Vivian that Cooper had missed, with the long undulating hair, cut to hang full about her face, but the same good will shining from her features, the full lips parted slightly in that smile, the one Cooper had never been able to picture in the depths of his infatuation. But this was a Vivian with the mellowing touch of the early thirties, the fulfilled beauty of the adult woman, the face a hint fuller, the eyes perhaps a shade less innocent but still kind.

Cooper heard footsteps in the hall and turned away. Adelle reappeared and said, "Sit down, Cooper. The furniture was made for it." Cooper smiled and took one end of the sofa while she moved the book and took the other. "What did you want to ask?" she said.

"Something I'm not sure you can answer, but if you can't, nobody can." Cooper leaned back and wiped his eye and marshalled his thoughts. "What we talked about last night— you said Vivian told you all about our sleeping together."

"Yes."

"Maybe you can tell me all about it then."

"What do you mean?"

Cooper took a breath and plunged. "Why did she do it? Why did Vivian sleep with me that night?" Adelle opened her mouth slightly, and Cooper thought she was going to reply, but she said nothing. Cooper went on. "You told me last night she never held it against me, that the initiative was hers. I almost asked you if you knew why she took the initiative, but I didn't." Cooper paused, waiting, but Adelle said nothing. "For her, that wasn't in character. Some women

might have played around when their fiancé was absent, but
not her. Other women might haul a guy onto a couch without
a thought to birth control, but not her. I knew her well enough
to know that. I thought for a long time it was because she
was drunk when I went over there that night, because her
inhibitions were gone and I'd been after her for so long and
she just gave in. But the question I never asked myself was
why she was drunk in the first place. That was out of character, too. I'd seen her drink, but not that much. The whole
thing that night was . . . just not like her.''

Adelle was looking at him gravely, sitting on the edge of
the couch. ''You're very perceptive,'' she said.

''And it's been bothering me all day. So I thought I would
go ahead and ask. Why did she do it? I thought maybe Vivian
had told you. Something a daughter might tell her mother.''

Adelle looked up at him and said, ''I think the coffee should
be ready.'' She rose and left the room. Cooper sat and listened to her footsteps fading away, then heard her making
small clattering noises in the kitchen. His eyes went to the
picture on the mantelpiece. Cars eased past the house outside.

She came back bearing a tray with a small carafe of coffee,
two cups on saucers, and milk and sugar. Her eyes were
downcast and she seemed glad to have the serving of the
coffee to absorb her. When they both sad holding the saucers,
she said, ''Why is it so important to you to know?''

Cooper had to think, blinking at her. ''It's always bothered
me. It would help lay her to rest for me.''

Adelle drank, stared into the cup for a moment, and set it
down on the saucer. ''I'm not sure you have the right to
know.''

Cooper nodded slowly. ''Maybe not. But here's another
thing that's been bothering me. Vivian was drunk the night
she died, too. Whatever happened to her that night, there she
was out of character again. I just wondered if knowing what
was going on with her the night I slept with her might cast
any light on what was going on with her the night she died.''

''I don't see how it could.'' Adelle spoke quietly; she
hadn't looked at Cooper since coming back with the coffee.

Cooper put the saucer down on the table. ''All right. I'm
sorry to have bothered you.''

"Please wait. I'm not clamming up just to be mysterious. You've disturbed me." Adelle was frowning at her coffee, her mouth slightly open again as if she were on the verge of speech. She was working hard at something, and Cooper knew he was going to have to wait it out. After a moment she spoke.

"Your connection between those two nights seems fanciful to me. I think Vivian did drink when she was very upset, yes. There were probably other occasions as well. What I can tell you about that night doesn't seem to have any possible bearing on the matter of her death. But you seem to be giving things a good deal of thought, and I suppose you are as involved as any of us now. In any case the confidence is now mine to betray." She set down her coffee and sat back, clasping her arms again. "I'm afraid what was bothering Vivian that night was something a mother told her daughter, not the other way around. You may recall that Charles and I had been visiting Vivian at that time."

"Yes."

"That day we had just told Vivian that Charles was not her real father."

Cooper waited. He nodded just once, slightly, to show he was listening.

"Do you need the whole story? Will it help you to know all about it?" She gave Cooper a fleeting look, pleading.

"I don't know. Tell me what you want to tell me and no more."

She nodded, took some coffee, and gave Cooper an appraising look. "Yes. Well. As I said, we told Vivian that day that Charles was not her real father. I'm afraid she took it very hard. I have always doubted the wisdom of telling her, in fact. It was Charles that insisted. Not from any desire to disclaim her. Certainly not. But he felt there was always the chance that her real father would . . . let the cat out of the bag, whether intentionally or not. He was . . . is a man given to demonstrations of one sort or another. Charles wanted Vivian to know the truth. We had agreed to tell her when she graduated from college."

Cooper feared that if he moved it would cause her to repent of telling him her secrets. His eye was still watering and he wiped at it gently with his sleeve.

"It was an extremely difficult scene for all of us. Actually Vivian seemed to take the news very well at first. She thanked us for telling her and said it made absolutely no difference. Which it didn't, of course. Charles was her father in any meaningful sense. Vivian seemed to understand that, and she . . . she clung to Charles and told him he was her father and nobody else." For the first time Adelle's voice wavered. She turned her head away from Cooper. "I think what bothered Vivian more than finding out that her father was not her father was finding that her mother was not the . . . the paragon of virtue she had always pretended to be."

Her voice was seizing up now, and Cooper waited while she composed herself. "I think that was devastating to her, to be told that she herself was a product of the sort of thing that her mother had always warned her about. And that we had lived a lie for twenty-two years. That, you see, was what ate away at Vivian's own principles, if only for that one night. The feeling that it was all a sham, this morality these people had preached at her. That everything was false. That she herself was not who she had always thought she was. That must have struck very deeply at her own sense of integrity. It was a real betrayal. I think she got over that in time, but that night was a very unfortunate time for you to come calling."

There was a tear now, a single tear tracking down her cheek. Cooper looked at the floor, understanding at last. It had been a fluke. On any other evening it wouldn't have happened. Cooper could hear the rolling of the cosmic dice.

After a moment Adelle continued, her voice steady again. "Vivian told me after she found out she was pregnant that when you came over that night her first impulse was to scream at you, tell you to leave her alone."

"I wish she had," said Cooper quietly.

"Well, she didn't. Instead she resisted the impulse and fell back on that generosity that was a reflex with her and took pity on you. And then things caved in and, as she put it to me later, she just wanted to taste what her mother had tasted, to find out what kind of act had led to her own creation. She told me that the thought of pregnancy went through her mind but that she thought it was unlikely because of the time of the month. And she said that the risk was intensely thrilling to her. All of this, of course, was aided and abetted and clouded by alcohol.''

The silence lasted until Cooper reached for his coffee cup. The coffee was black and bitter. He drank and set the cup back on the saucer and finally said, ''Huh.''

''And that, Mr. MacLeish, is what happened that night. History repeated itself, you see. In a way that would be too trite for fiction. I had slept with someone I didn't much care for and Vivian was the result. She did the same and Dominic was the result. Fortunately, in both cases there was a good man to take responsibility for the child. When Vivian realized she was pregnant she was in New York with Nick. She never considered abortion. She suffered terrifically with the guilt she felt, but she told Nick what had happened. I think it was hard for him, but he wasn't going to throw her over. I gained a good deal of respect for Nick in those days. He agreed to claim Dominic as his and married Vivian immediately, just as Charles had done with me. They had been intending to marry, of course, so it was in no sense a matter of dragging him to the altar, but my smiles were a bit forced that day. I couldn't believe it was happening again.''

There was a long silence. Cooper's eye seemed to have stopped watering at last. He wasn't sure he had the right to ask the next question. But he had a feeling it was sitting there waiting for him to ask. He finished his coffee and said, ''Who is Vivian's father?''

She didn't answer immediately and he turned to look at her. She was staring at him, looking weary, as if debating whether to tell him. ''Do you know who Alban Galloway is?''

Cooper frowned. ''The yacht-race guy?''

''He doesn't race anymore, actually, but yes. That's what he's best known for.''

''And he's Vivian's father.''

He abruptly regretted saying it, seeing Adelle nod with great composure.

''Yes. He's her father.'' She looked at him and he had a sudden vision of the woman she had been, close to forty years before, in a long silk dress and one of those Lauren Bacall hairdos maybe. She would have been very beautiful. ''It didn't happen very much as it happened with you and Vivian.

The seduction was more in the classic male to female direction. But I didn't fight very hard. I was young and Alban was a very charming, very much sought-after man. He'd come back from the war a hero and was already making himself a great deal of money. I had been seeing Charles but was not sure I really wanted to marry him, and suddenly one evening, at a very posh affair at a mansion on the lake shore, with champagne going to my head, there I was being pursued by Alban Galloway.'' She smiled faintly, wistfully perhaps. ''These things happened, of course, long before the sexual revolution. Unfortunately, in those days many of us were too prone to romanticism and utterly ignorant of contraceptive methods. Alban was very gallant, of course, when he found out I was pregnant. But by that time I had fled tearfully and guiltily to the safety of my Charles.''

Cooper sat for a while in silence, then passed his hand over his eyes. His head was beginning to ache. ''Huh,'' he said. ''That's a hell of a story.''

After a moment Adelle sighed and said, ''Yes, quite a story, isn't it?''

Cooper felt a need to move and he rose slowly and paced the room, padding softly over the carpet. His hand was throbbing. He stopped by the fireplace and turned to face Adelle. ''Alban Galloway is a very rich man, isn't he?''

''Yes. One of the wealthiest in Chicago. Charles used to tease me that I should have married him. As if Alban would have had me. When I say he was gallant I mean he offered to support the child, in a sort of grand Latin tradition I suppose. If he was going to sire an illegitimate child, he wanted it to be raised in style. But he certainly didn't want to be bothered by me anymore. I'm sure he was as glad as anyone that Charles was there to take me in.''

Cooper looked at her, seeing a life unfolded in her handsome features. He paced another couple of steps, put a hand to his aching temple. ''When you said Galloway was given to demonstrations, what did you mean?''

''Only that he has a reputation for flamboyance. And none for discretion. I think Charles was afraid he would try to give Vivian expensive gifts on the sly or something like that. That's why he wanted to tell her—so she would know why this man was interested in her.''

"Did he ever try anything like that?"

"Not to my knowledge. He inquired about her once or twice over the years, in a casual way. Even met her once, at some function or other. I think he was proud of our little secret, actually. Alban is not the humblest of men."

"So you saw him occasionally?"

"Not often. But we moved in the same circles to some extent. North Shore money circles, the set I was raised in and that Charles became accepted in over the years. I've seen Alban perhaps a dozen times since our . . . however you choose to describe it. My feelings toward him have always been ambiguous. I certainly never hated him or anything dramatic like that. But I grew more and more grateful that I had Charles. All of Alban's money couldn't have given me what Charles gave me. And all that money can't help him now."

"What do you mean?"

She looked up at Cooper, paused for just a moment. "Alban has had cancer for some time. He's dying."

13

COOPER HAD THE Dream again that night, for the first time in a while. He had his share of bad dreams, no more probably than anyone else who came out of the A Shau alive; most of the really bad ones had faded away with the years. But the Dream kept coming back; it was the only one he had again and again, and he had no idea what it meant. Why the image of a Vietnamese kid riding by on a bicycle against a background of jungle, smiling, should scare him so badly, he could never figure out. Perhaps it was because the wheels were turning backwards, like wagon wheels in an old western. Or maybe it was the sly smile, the promise of death coming from some angle Cooper hadn't even thought to check.

Cooper sat on the edge of the bed in the dark and listened to Diana's soft breathing behind him, feeling adrift and disoriented in her bedroom, but starting, as the minutes went by, to feel safe.

From the Dream he came back slowly to the Idea. He stood up, found his pants in the dark, and put them on, then his sweatshirt, easing it over the cast. Things still hurt, but not too badly. He found his way into the dark living room and sat on the sofa looking through the leaves of Diana's houseplants at the feverish light of the street lamps outside.

Who benefits if both Vivian and Dominic die? Nobody if Vivian dies in debt, unless there's a big unknown out there. Why Dominic? The Idea said killing Dominic wiped out the line.

The Idea was only half-formed. It was going to take some thought, and it was going to take some more asking around. It was just an idea.

* * *

Cooper was unable to get in touch with Shostak or Harrison in the morning. He wasn't sure he wanted to tell them about the Idea yet, but he did want to know if Murphy was in talking shape yet. He left a message at Area Six and then sat by the phone for a moment, pulling idly at the corners of his moustache and looking out at the gray flannel sky. Finally he pulled a small address book from his wallet, found a number and dialed again.

"Melvin Moreland," said a voice, snapping it as if it were a rebuff.

"Hey, Mel. What's the late-breaking news?"

"Reagan keeled over dead, the Pope came out of the closet, and New York seceded from the Union. Other than that it's a slow news day. Who the hell are you?"

"Cooper."

"MacLeish. Hell, I thought you died or something. Where you been?"

"Here and there. Making a buck or two."

"Well, you got me beat. What's going on?"

"They let people like you out for lunch?"

"People like me. I run the fuckin' paper now. I can take lunch any time I please."

"If you run the paper how come I still see your byline on articles about fun Polish restaurants on the southwest side?"

"That's where the news that matters is, man. Out where the little people live."

"What would you know about little people? Anyway, how about noon? I'll buy you lunch if you let me pump you for information."

"Aw, God. What are you on to now? I charge for stock tips, you know."

"That's what the lunch is. Payment. Just tell me where to meet you."

"How about the Pump Room?"

"You want to go to the Pump Room, fine. I'll be waiting someplace I can get lunch for under fifty bucks."

"All right. You like Thai food?"

"I can eat it."

"You can eat it. OK, there's a Thai place at Wabash and Hubbard. I forget the name but it's the only one there. The Bangkok or the Siam or the Mekong or something like that."

"No, it wouldn't be the Mekong."

"I guess not. But you can't miss it. I'll meet you there at
. . . make it twelve-thirty. I'm working on an exposé here
that'll blow the lid off Mother Theresa."

"Go easy on her, will you? The little people like her."

Melvin Moreland was the only newspaper reporter Cooper
knew. Moreland was an alumnus of the same little downstate
college, and he and Cooper had been occasional classmates
and pool-shooting antagonists, close enough acquaintances
that when Cooper had run into him in a Rush Street tavern
in 1983 they had reestablished the same sort of intermittent
friendship, based on pool and other sporting events and places
to drink.

Moreland was a couple of years younger than Cooper but
looked older with all the weight he'd put on and the dome
shining through the sparse hair on top. He seemed to work
hard but to lack either ambition or talent, since he had admitted to Cooper that he was never going to win a Pulitzer
or even, without a staggering stroke of good fortune, break
a particularly important story. He was divorced and appeared
to be sliding toward irrevocable bachelorhood. He loved to
eat.

"This stuff is about half as hot as they eat it," he was
saying with his mouth full of Pad Thai. "When they send the
customers home and it's time for the help to eat, they whip
up a batch of the real stuff and sit back there and eat till their
scalps steam."

"It's decent," said Cooper.

"Decent. You still got Hoosier tastes, don't you Mac-
Leish?"

"Hey, I said it was decent."

"Well, at least you're eating it. Now what did you want to
ask me?"

Cooper chewed for a while and took a drink of beer. "What
do you know about Alban Galloway?" he said.

Moreland frowned. "Alban Galloway? What do you mean,
what do I know about him? What everybody knows. He's
rich. He races boats. He has horses, too, I think. He bank-
rolls the city GOP, like a sap. What do you want to know?"

Cooper chewed slowly, not sure himself what he wanted to know. "How rich is he?"

"He's got lots of money. I mean a big chunk of money. He owns . . . let's see. Besides Alcorp, he owns the Barfield Building down there in the Loop, he's got a big share of a bank or two and he owns half of Lake County. That's just for starters. I won't go into the miscellany. I don't know half of it. But he's rich. He's real rich."

"Mm. Did you know he was dying?"

"I heard a couple of years ago he had cancer. I don't know how close to death he is."

"Close, according to what I heard."

"You heard, huh? Sounds like your informant is better informed than me. Why'd you come to me?"

"My informant knows some personal things. She doesn't know much about him business-wise."

"What are you checking up on Galloway for? He looking for a chauffeur?"

"Could be. What's his family life like?"

"His family life?" Moreland stared at Cooper for a few seconds, a smile spreading over his face. "Do I get to hear what you've got in mind?"

"I've got nothing in mind. I might, if you tell me what I'm buying you lunch to tell me."

Moreland shoved in another mouthful with his chopsticks, chewed it while staring at Cooper, and went on. "OK. He's on either his third or fourth wife, I don't remember. I think he wears 'em out with the racing and the politics and the screwing other people to the wall. Or maybe just screwing other people. His current wife used to be married to one of his partners. I saw her once at a party at the Yacht Club. She's got a face like my old ball glove, a voice like a fog-horn, and clothes that must cost about the entire GNP of Rwanda. She looks like an expensively attired mummy and she keeps herself well pickled judging from what I saw at the party. This the kind of stuff you want?"

"I guess. Go on."

"All right. Lemme think. His oldest daughter married one of William Rehnquist's law partners. Another one turns up about every other week in the *Tribune*'s INC. column on the

elbow of some rich ape in a tuxedo. You know the kind of
girl in high school who would fuck all the football players?
Put notches on the bedpost? Imagine her with an unlimited
allowance and you got Marilyn Galloway. I think that takes
care of the daughters. His son Billy's kind of a washout.
People still call him Billy even though he's gotta be over
thirty by now. They got him into Harvard or Princeton or one
of those places and he couldn't hack it. I think they wanted
him to take over the empire, but so far he seems more interested in spending it into the ground. How am I doing?''

"OK." Cooper ate and thought. "Tell me more about
Billy."

"What do you mean? The busts and stuff?"

"Yeah. The busts."

"OK. Billy seems to have that attitude. You know, the rich
kid attitude. I'm rich and that means I can do what I fucking
please. Trouble is, he's right. He can. He's been in and out
of court but never in jail. Daddy hires expensive lawyers.
And the judges all like Daddy.''

"What kind of stuff has Billy been up for?"

"Rich kid stuff. Beating up people he doesn't like. Hiring
people to beat up people he doesn't like. Torching a business
that was competing with one his Daddy gave him to play
with. Shit like that.''

"Jesus. And they never put him away?"

"Nope. He's a rich kid, like I say. So they never really
proved any of it, of course. Except minor shit that got him
probation. Real likable guy, huh?''

Cooper took a long drink of beer to quench the burning in
his mouth. "Yeah. I like Billy. I really do."

"You got a funny look on your face, MacLeish."

"Mm. How could I find out more about Junior? You got
files I could look through or something like that?''

Moreland shrugged, his jaws working. "I could dig up
some stuff and send it to you. For a couple of beers. And the
story.''

"Deal. When I figure out what the story is. What's the old
man like? You ever meet him?''

"No. Seen him. Distinguished. Craggy handsome type of
guy.''

"What's his reputation like? Sleazeball like his son?"

"No, I think he's pretty well regarded. Things between him and Billy are cool, they say."

"Where's he live?"

Moreland finished his beer and leaned back, his paunch straining at his shirt buttons. "Now why the hell would you want to know that? You're starting to worry me."

"I might want to talk to him."

"Talk to Alban Galloway? How come? Time to tell me what's going on, pal."

"I don't know what's going on. That's why I want to talk to him."

Moreland was silent for a while, the little smile playing over his lips. "I don't know exactly where he lives. Somewhere up on the North Shore I hear, Kenilworth or Glencoe or someplace."

"I guess I can find it."

"You're just going to walk up and ring the doorbell? You won't get in."

"Maybe not."

The waitress came by, a tiny Thai girl of stunning beauty, black-eyed and honey-skinned, and Cooper asked for the check. When he looked back at Moreland he saw the reporter's eyes flick toward the cast on his wrist.

"It's got something to do with the way you look today, doesn't it?" Cooper didn't answer and Moreland smiled his knowing smile again. "What kind of a fight was it, really?"

"It wasn't a fight. I was pulling your leg. It was a carpentry accident."

Moreland shook his head slowly. "Must have been a hell of an accident."

"It was. I'll be more careful next time, you can bet on that."

There was a demonstration of some sort at the base of the Picasso in Daley Plaza; Cooper didn't bother to wander over and look. Somebody was being strident through a megaphone and his companions stood around with placards hanging from their necks, looking cold and a bit embarrassed.

Cooper went into the Daley Center. He couldn't remember

whether the law library was on the twenty-seventh or twenty-ninth floor and he asked the guard at the metal detector. It was twenty-nine and he went in search of an express elevator.

The Cook County law library occupied the whole floor and provided fine views of the city in three directions through the floor-to-ceiling windows. Cooper walked past the long circulation desk thronged with haggard law students and went into the reading room. He had been there only once before and he wasn't sure he could orient himself. He collared an old man in a gray smock who was reshelving books and asked for help. The man listened to what he wanted with an aggrieved expression and then told him in a loud voice that what he probably wanted was the Smith-Hurd Annotated Statutes and directed him to a row of shelves.

It took Cooper forever to figure out the indexing scheme of the much-handled, maroon-bound volumes, but he was not going to ask for assistance again if he could help it. Finally he tracked down a volume that looked promising and took it to the southeast corner of the room, where there was a vacant table right by the window, screened by a row of shelves from the suspicious gazes of the lawyers reading at the long tables in the middle of the room. Cooper looked out at the slate-gray lake beyond the immense sculpture garden of the Loop, exhaled, and opened the book.

Again he had trouble navigating the sections and subsections and paragraphs, but eventually he found what he wanted: something labeled 110½, 4-11, entitled "Legacy to a deceased legatee." He skimmed the various clauses first and then read slowly, hacking at the lawyers' prose.

Unless the testator expressly provides otherwise in his will, (a) if a legacy of a present or future interest is to a descendant of the testator who dies before or after the testator, the descendants of the legatee living when the legacy is to take effect in possession or enjoyment, take per stirpes the estate so bequeathed . . .

Cooper stared down at an El train threading through the gloom far below. After a moment he looked back at the book and turned over pages slowly. There were notes and comments following the text of the statute. Most seemed irrele-

vant to what he was looking for, but he went patiently through
the small print. The comments seemed to be much like the
Approved Rulings at the back of the Official Baseball Rules;
Cooper remembered searching feverishly through them once
to convince the ump he could steal on a foul tip.

He brought his attention back to the matter at hand. Several pages on he stared hard at a paragraph and read it again.

Where gift to beneficiary under will lapsed because beneficiary
predeceased testatrix, share of such beneficiary passed as part of
the residuary estate of testatrix.

Cooper looked far out over the lake and thought, hoping
this proved the Idea made sense. He'd have to kick it around
with somebody who knew, but it looked all right to him down
there in black-and-white, in more or less plain English.

He took the book back to the Xerox machines, found he
didn't have change, had to wrestle some out of a clerk at the
desk, and waited patiently in line behind a kid who looked
about sixteen but had on a three-piece suit. He copied the
relevant pages and left the book there to be reshelved. Then
he left the library and stood waiting for an elevator, looking
out the window at the end of the hall down at the remote
scurrying in the Plaza, wondering if he could possibly find
Alban Galloway's house.

As it turned out, all Cooper had to do was follow Sheridan
Road north, on through Evanston and into the wooded towns
where Money lived, in big silent houses tucked back from
the road behind trees. He stopped at a 76 station in Wilmette
to ask after the Galloway place and was told to keep going.
Sheridan became more bucolic and snaked through ravines
and provided glimpses of the lake at the end of private drives.

He wasn't sure whether he was in Winnetka or Kenilworth
or Glencoe when he came to the long pale brick wall fronting
the road; they didn't seem to be real towns anyway, just col-
lections of expensive houses. The wall ran for at least a hundred yards along the road before it was interrupted by the
gate; beyond it Cooper could see trees, big trees: firs, oaks,
spruce. He could see a long black roof in the distance.

He turned in at the imposing entrance, guarded by two

copper-roofed blockhouses which presented blank façades to the road, with a single window high up in each one. The drive was flanked by tall columns surmounted by what appeared to be enormous bronze pine cones. A pair of iron gates barred the drive. Cooper stopped and stared through the gates at the house, at the end of a long straight avenue lined by trees. Someone had given thought to the prospect, to the view of the house framed by the gates, by the perspective of the trees.

The place fit the description given him at the gas station. Cooper wasn't even sure Galloway would be here; for all he knew the old man was in a hospital or an expensive sanatorium somewhere. Even if he was here, Cooper was by no means certain of being admitted. He had debated waiting to speak to Adelle again, asking her to intercede, but had decided to take a stab at going straight to the source. If the Idea was completely harebrained, it would be best to have it dealt with quickly in a tête-à-tête and consigned to oblivion.

Cooper looked for a button to push, a phone to lift, any means of communication with the interior, and found none. He honked once. After a few seconds a man came out of a door in the right-hand blockhouse and ambled up to the gate. He stood waiting while Cooper got out of the car and went to meet him. The man was old and red-faced and irascible-looking. He wore a green windbreaker.

Through the bars of the gate Cooper said, "This the Galloway place?"

"You got it," said the man.

"I'd like to speak to Alban Galloway."

The man looked at Cooper and then looked at the old Valiant and said, "He expecting you?"

"No. But you can tell him I'm a friend of Vivian Horstmann's."

"He ain't seeing nobody these days."

"Could you tell him what I said? Vivian Horstmann. If he needs my name, it's MacLeish."

The man shrugged and trudged back to the blockhouse. Cooper went back to the car and got in and waited. He turned off the ignition and waited for a long time, looking at the house made of gold and pink brick with its broad black front door and dark trim around the windows. He had almost decided that he had been snubbed when the man came back out of the guardhouse and pulled back the bolt on the gates.

Cooper started up and crept forward as the man pulled the gates open. The man waved him to a halt as he eased through; Cooper rolled down his window to hear the instructions. "Go on up and park at the side of the house. Somebody'll meet you there." Cooper nodded and thanked him.

The park was enormous and filled with trees. In summer it would be beautiful; now, with the brown grass and black and spiny trees against the gray sky, it was somber. There was a greenhouse to the right of the gate, and other low brick outbuildings tucked among the shrubbery in the distance. The house itself had three stories and a broad front; wings with at least a dozen large windows in a line spread out grandly on either side of the front door. The drive skirted the steps at the door and swept to the left. Cooper followed it all the way down to the side, where it turned the corner and went under a covered carport. In front of him Cooper suddenly saw the lake, just beyond a garden and a screen of trees and a narrow beach.

A man was waiting at the side door. He wore the trousers and vest to a nice navy blue suit, but not the jacket. Cooper stopped the car and got out.

"Mr. MacLeish?" said the man.

"Yes." Cooper walked up the steps and shook his hand. The man was about his age, tall and bony, with brown hair going gray very nicely around the big ears, a long nose that ended at a carefully tended moustache, and a prominent dimpled chin. He looked fit, like a just-retired basketball player perhaps. He gave Cooper a look of polite distrust as he shook his hand, taking in the cast on the hand and the still-red eyes.

"Jack Lime. I'm Mr. Galloway's assistant. I understand you're a friend of Vivian's?"

"That's right."

"I was sorry to hear about her death."

"You knew her?"

"Yes." Lime was leading him down a long hallway tiled in black-and-white checkerboard fashion. "I hadn't seen her in some time, not since she and her husband split up, but I was certainly sorry to hear it. A very nice lady. A very sad thing."

"I'd like to speak to Mr. Galloway about her if possible."

Lime frowned and made no answer. They passed several closed doors in the long hallway. The vast house was silent; Cooper had expected bustling domestics, butlers and maids at every turn. He saw no one besides Lime and heard nothing more than their own footsteps on the tile floor, reverberating down the hall. Ahead the hall seemed to end at a sort of gallery, with large windows that gave onto a garden or courtyard.

Lime stopped at a door on the right and ushered Cooper into the room ahead of him. It was a study, filled with light from one of the broad windows in the front of the house. To the left of the window and sitting obliquely to it there was a desk of dark wood. The desktop had a phone, a lamp, a litter of files, memo pads, and loose sheets of paper. Along one wall were shelves bearing law books and journals. Oak filing cabinets lined the opposite wall. Lime pointed Cooper to a leather armchair at the corner of the desk and took his own seat behind the desk. He rested his elbows on the arms of the chair, clasped his hands, and gave Cooper a challenging look.

"Mr. Galloway is not in the best of shape and won't be able to see you, I'm afraid. Now you mentioned Vivian Horstmann. Mr. Galloway didn't even know Vivian Horstmann. What's on your mind?"

Cooper settled onto the chair. "He knew her. Did you tell him I was here? Give him the message?"

Lime was unperturbed. "I'm his . . . you might call me his chief of staff. I don't bother him, especially in his present condition, unless I'm sure he needs to hear it."

Cooper nodded gravely, showing he was aware of the awesome responsibilities of Lime's job. "I'm sorry to seem mysterious. But what I have to say is for Mr. Galloway only. If you'll tell him it concerns Vivian, he'll either say yes or no. If it's no, I'll leave."

Lime gave him a stone face for a few seconds and then raised his chin a degree, perhaps two. "I handle Mr. Galloway's affairs. Personal affairs as well as business ones. You can count on it remaining confidential, whatever it is. I admit I'm curious. But in addition it's my job to screen people who want to talk to him. If you can't tell me, odds are Mr. Galloway won't want to hear it."

Somewhere in the house a door shut a bit too hard and the boom reverberated down another long hallway. Cooper waited a moment and said, "Why don't we let him be the judge of that? Just tell him I want to talk to him about Vivian."

Lime frowned at his desk and reached forward to pick up a pencil. "Mr. Galloway is a sick man. I don't like bothering him with riddles. Since we both seem to have known Vivian Horstmann, I suggest you tell me what's on your mind."

Cooper stood up slowly. He walked to the window and looked out at the leaf-strewn expanse of the park. It was a bleak gray afternoon and all the money in the world couldn't brighten it up. Part of Cooper wanted to tell Lime what he'd come to ask about, as long as he'd gotten this far. The rest of him said walk out and let Lime wonder for the rest of the day what that was all about. He turned toward the desk.

"Is your boss still capable of using a telephone?"

"Of course."

"Then if you've got a piece of paper I can write down my phone number and he can call me. Just tell him what I said, will you?"

Lime shrugged very slightly. "I think we can spare you a piece of paper." With a bit of frost in his manner he shoved a yellow memo pad toward Cooper and laid the pencil beside it. Cooper printed his name and number on the pad and straightened up.

"Thanks for your time. I think I can find my way out."

"Straight down the hall." Lime's tone was light but he was still frowning. As Cooper made for the door Lime said, "Can I ask you something?"

"Sure." Cooper turned to see him toying with the pencil, brows lowered.

"Why did Vivian kill herself? I wouldn't ever have thought she would."

Cooper had to think about his answer. He stood in the doorway looking at Lime and after a few seconds he said, "I was hoping Mr. Galloway could tell me that." He figured it was a good exit line and he left, hiking back down the hall, spooked a bit by the big empty house.

He turned the Valiant around in the garage yard at the rear of the house, glimpsing what looked like a Jaguar in an open stall, and drove carefully out the long drive. He honked again and the red-faced man opened the gates to let him out.

Cooper drove back along Sheridan on autopilot, wondering what it meant, if anything, that Jack Lime had known Vivian Horstmann. When he got to Evanston he stopped at Adelle Horstmann's place, but there was no answer when he rang the doorbell. He stood on the porch a moment, watching the street and thinking, before walking slowly back to the car.

He camped at Diana's all afternoon, dozing. In the evening he reached Adelle on the phone. He heard the old note of caution, apprehension perhaps, when he identified himself. She couldn't look forward to his calls very much, it occurred to him.

"Do you know a man named Jack Lime?" he said.

"Jack Lime?" she said slowly, as if fearing a trap. "No. I don't think so."

"He works for Alban Galloway. He says he knew Vivian."

"I'm afraid I've never heard of him. What . . . how did you meet him?"

"I went to Alban Galloway's house today, to try to talk to him."

There was a silence. "What on earth for?"

"Just an idea. Vivian's name was enough to get me in the gate, but I never got past this Lime character. He wanted to know what I had to say to Galloway and I wouldn't tell him."

"May I ask what you had to say to Alban?" There was a bit of ice in her voice.

"I wanted to ask him something. I wanted to ask him if by any chance he was intending to leave some kind of bequest to Vivian."

The silence this time was longer. "I see," Adelle said.

"I was thinking you might have better luck getting in to see Galloway."

"Why should I want to see him?"

"To find out if he did in fact plan to leave something to Vivian."

"I'm not sure I'm following you, Cooper. You think this is germane to . . . to Vivian's death?"

"I think it might be. I think if he did leave her something it might be wise to tell the police."

"This makes no sense to me."

"I'd be happy to come by and lay it all out for you."

"I'm not sure you should bother until I understand a little better what you want."

"All I'd like you to do is to ask him a couple of questions. About his will."

"If this is really connected to Vivian's death, shouldn't we let the police handle it?"

"Maybe. We will if we have to. But I'm not sure there's enough of an idea yet to bring in the cops. And people like Alban Galloway don't like to talk to cops. He might be more willing to talk to you."

"I can't imagine he'd be too anxious to discuss his private affairs with me."

"Tell him what happened. Tell him about Vivian, about Dominic. If he cared about Vivian he'll want to help."

Cooper could just make out her breathing over the line as she thought. Finally she said, "I understand Alban is very ill now."

"All the more reason to hurry," said Cooper.

"Things are coming to a head," said the man in the phone booth.

"Talkin' about head, I could really use some, you know what I mean? There's this blond in here right now, man, sitting down at the end of the bar, and she got those kind of lips you know man, that look like they . . . "

"Listen up, goddammit. I don't pay you to sit in there and get wasted."

"Hey, you know, I'm getting real anxious to talk to you face to face. I been takin' a lot of shit from you, man."

"And a lot of money. For no results."

"My partner got his head broke open trying to get you some results."

"Well, I'm still waiting."

"You didn't tell me the taxi dude was a fucking maniac."

"A maniac, huh? That's what I thought you were. But forget it. You want another shot at him?"

"A real shot this time? No fuckin' around?"

"A real shot. But you're going to have to be on standby. Things are getting interesting. I got a different place lined up for you, and starting tomorrow I want you available more often.''

''What kind of money we talkin'?''

''The best kind, amigo. The green kind. The only kind.''

14

SHOSTAK SOUNDED TIRED; Cooper wondered if he always sounded that way, even after a good night's sleep, or if he just never got a good night's sleep. "They won't let us talk to him yet, but he's going to live. You cracked him pretty good. As soon as the doctors let us, we'll sit down with him and see what he has to say for himself. Get them in a hospital bed and they talk. I think they feel vulnerable or something."

"What about the other guy?" said Cooper.

"We think we've got a name for him, but we can't find him. Yet. We talked to Murphy's mother. Can you believe a guy like that still lives with his mother? She says the guy with the teardrop is a PR called Richie. We think he's Ricardo Flores, a guy that goes way back with the Kings, Humboldt Park and around in there, did some time for holding a match to a guy who couldn't come up with the scratch for some stuff he'd taken on consignment."

"Holding a match to him?"

"Yeah. After his partners had poured gasoline on him."

"Jesus."

"The guy lived. Richie got back on the street last year."

"I guess he wasn't quite rehabilitated."

"No. Not quite. We're hoping we run him down before too long."

"Not as much as I'm hoping. Listen, can I ask what's happening on the other front? I mean with the Vivian Horstmann end of things."

"We're working on it. We found Jesse Goddard's wife."

"Wait a second. Who's Jesse Goddard?"

"The guy who gave Vivian the gold pin."

"Huh. Your partner never gave me a name. That's for sure, is it?"

"Yeah. We matched the signature on the card with some

of his paintings. His wife doesn't seem to like the guy much, says they've been separated for a while. Called him a philandering son of a bitch in fact. She said she suspected Vivian Horstmann was one of the other women. According to her, Goddard's in Mexico. He called her in late September and told her he was taking off. But she doesn't know exactly when he left. They didn't communicate too well, seems like.''

"Huh. You think it's worth trying to find him?"

"Worth it, yeah. Possible, who the hell knows? We've talked to the federal police down there but if they find him it'll be lucky. Meantime, there's plenty of work.''

"Yeah, I'm sure.''

"We're talking to everybody who knew her. Looking for motive, whatever. There's a million different things to consider. Including the possibility that she really did kill herself. See, I still like that note. I can't see how you could fake it.''

Cooper was silent, thinking. "But if she killed herself, how come they're trying to kill the kid?''

"I don't know. When we figure it out we'll let you know.''

"Huh." Cooper hesitated. He was within a hair of dropping the bombshell on Shostak, telling him that Vivian was really Alban Galloway's daughter, but he checked himself. Before he went betraying confidences he wanted to hear what Adelle Horstmann would have to say. "Thanks," he said.

"Is the kid in a safe place?" asked Shostak.

"More or less. I can't get him to leave town but he's lying low.''

"What about you? You watching your back?''

"All the time. Front, back, you name it. I'm watching.''

Dominic's apartment was a long two-bedroom occupying the whole second floor of a three-flat a couple of blocks from the lake. Dominic introduced Cooper to one of his roommates, a lissome ash-blond with a haircut like the ones Cooper's father had given him with the clippers when he was six years old. Her name was Petra and after flashing a nervous smile at Cooper she disappeared in a cloud of cigarette smoke into the front room while Dominic led Cooper toward the back of the apartment. The boy was wearing a pair of loose cotton trousers dyed purple and a T-shirt that said "Sometimes it's worse in the Bahamas."

"Here's my room," he said, pushing open a door. It was a small room with a single window giving onto the alley; there was a mattress on the floor with a jumble of sheets on it, a slab of plywood on two old milk crates serving as a table, a floor lamp with a frayed wicker shade on it, and a stained and battered recliner armchair upholstered in canary yellow in the corner. The floor was covered with flecks of white paint.

"Gordon and I found all this stuff in the alley. It's like unbelievable what people throw away in this society."

"You're sleeping on a mattress you found in an alley?"

"It was in good shape. I got the sheets and stuff at a resale shop. Cost me five bucks for all this stuff."

Cooper shook his head. "You made out pretty well."

"Come on back." Dominic took him back to the dining room, a large luminous room with a bare wood floor glowing in the late-morning sunlight. There was a table with four unmatched chairs, an enormous tropical-looking plant standing in the corner by the window, and a life-sized cutout of Arnold Schwarzenegger.

"They stole that from a video store. Want some tea?"

"Sure." Cooper sat down at the table, shoving aside a bag of marijuana and an ashtray with a roach still in the clip. There was an open copy of *Mother Jones* on the table. "What do your roommates do?"

Dominic answered from the kitchen over the clattering noises he was making. "Gordon goes to Northwestern and Petra works at the restaurant. They're really neat people."

"What do you do with yourself all day?"

"I read or listen to music or go over to the restaurant and just like sit around and talk with people. Man, I've met some really interesting people. There's one guy Petra knows who went all over India on a bicycle. This guy knows all about Eastern religions, Hinduism and stuff. I'm learning a lot."

"That's good. You watch it when you go out? Look out for two guys in a Camaro, for example?"

"You think they're still after me? I thought you put them in the hospital."

"One of them. The other one's still out there. And I think he may be after you for a little bit yet."

Dominic sat still across from Cooper, suddenly subdued. "Those detective guys talked to me again."

"Yeah? What'd they have to say?"

"They asked me all about my mom's personal life and stuff. About if I knew this artist guy. I told them about how I just found the note but they wanted me to try and remember if I'd ever seen him, stuff like that. They asked me to describe all the guys she knew and we went through her address book and everything."

"Hm." Cooper stared at the patch of sunlight on the floor. "Was one of her friends tall, six-five or so, dark hair and moustache?"

"I don't know. She knew a whole bunch of people. That doesn't sound like familiar or anything. How come?"

"Just a hunch. Somebody I met who said he knew your mother."

The gentle whistle of a kettle boiling rose from the kitchen. Dominic went to attend to the tea while Cooper looked around the room, toyed with the ashtray, thought.

"I've been talking to my father," Dominic said, bringing in two mugs with steam rising through the sunlight. "He calls me a lot."

"That's good. I guess. How does it feel?"

Dominic sat down and stared into his tea. "All right. It's getting easier. I think he's really trying. To understand me, I mean."

"How about you? You trying?"

"Sure."

" 'Cause it takes two. I found that out with my own father."

"Yeah?"

"Yeah. I never realized how much I hurt my father by running off to join the Army. And when I came back I could tell he didn't much like what I'd become, and I held it against him for a long time." Cooper paused, remembering. "I used to accuse him of wishing I'd been killed over there. I think it was partly true—in a way he would have found it easier to deal with the memory of a son he'd loved than to deal with the person I was after that. But it was unfair. It took me a while to catch on, but I did."

Dominic stared at him, not understanding, Cooper was sure. "Do you get along with him now?"

"We're getting there. It takes a long time sometimes. But it's worth the effort."

Dominic held his hands at the sides of the mug, warming them. He looked younger than fourteen; he looked like boyhood stretched too soon into uncertain adolescence. Cooper was already feeling faintly embarrassed by his confession; he spoke of his father to almost no one.

"I might go to New York in January after all," said Dominic quietly.

Cooper nodded slowly and reached for his mug. He wondered why the news gave him that faint, distant pang. He started to say he would miss the boy, but stopped because he wasn't sure it was true. He took a tentative sip of the scalding tea and decided that the truth was that he wanted a son, and this was the only son he was ever going to have—and he couldn't even have him.

Diana had called it stupid, but Cooper would admit only to stubborn; he wasn't going to give up his home. His previous visit had given him confidence and he needed to get clean clothes and clean the place up and he just couldn't believe they'd come back in broad daylight. He sat in the Valiant and watched for a while before going inside.

The phone rang around six, as he was sitting at the old oak desk staring at his notes, wondering if the struggle was worth it. He fled to the phone in relief. It was Adelle Horstmann.

"I've been to see Alban Galloway."

"You have. Did you have any trouble getting in to see him?"

"No. Not once I had succeeded in reaching him by phone. That was the hard part."

"Did you have to go through this guy Lime?"

"I may have spoken to him on the phone, but I didn't tell him what I wanted to see Alban about. When I went out there I saw no one except Alban and a few attendants. Alban is not in very good shape, I'm afraid. I got the impression he's mostly bed-ridden now, though he did meet me in a sitting room. He's very gaunt, very weak. And of course his hair is nearly gone, from the chemical treatments I suppose. He had magnificent hair before." She paused and Cooper was left hanging for a moment.

"He was surprised to see me, of course. But he seemed glad. I think he thought at first I'd come for . . . you know, some belated declaration of love or something. When I explained what I wanted he was quite taken aback, I think. And a bit confused. I think he's in a good deal of pain, and that must affect his concentration. In any event, I had to tell him about Vivian's death. He hadn't heard. I don't think he's had much interest in the news recently. I told him about Dominic. And then I told him what you suspected, just as you explained it to me last night."

She paused as if expecting some reaction. Cooper said, "I wouldn't say suspected so much as just wondered, but anyway. What did he say?"

"You were right." Adelle's voice was suddenly cold. "Alban told me his will contains a legacy to Vivian. Securities worth something over five hundred thousand dollars."

Cooper grunted, intent. "What happens to the bequest now that Vivian's dead?"

"Unless he changes the will, which he said he saw no reason to do, it passes automatically to Dominic."

"And what happens to it if both Vivian and Dominic die before he does?"

"There is a residuary clause. It would pass with the bulk of the estate to his son William."

"Did he draw the same conclusion I did?"

"He thought the idea was ridiculous, of course. For one thing, he pointed out that William's inheritance from him will total in the millions. He asked, quite naturally, I thought, why William would risk murdering two people for an insignificant five hundred thousand."

"I don't know. I don't know that he would." Cooper leaned back on the couch, frowning out the window. "But the only person I can see who benefits from killing both Vivian and Dominic is Billy Galloway. And from everything I've heard, Billy likes to take things. He might do it just for the sport."

After a moment Adelle said, "Isn't there the danger that you might become a bit . . . you know, fixated on this idea?"

"There's always that danger, I guess. I'm willing to listen to other ideas."

"Well I certainly don't have any. I think the question is whether this is substantial enough to take to the police."

"Yeah. That is the question. I say it can't hurt."

There was a silence. "Perhaps not. Except I'd feel I was betraying Alban's confidence."

"You told him why you wanted to know, right? He gave you the information of his own free will. Don't you think he'd understand?"

"The terms of a person's will are confidential. I couldn't go straight from Alban to the police with private knowledge he had entrusted me with."

"Then why did you ask him in the first place? You were convinced enough by the scenario I laid out to go talk to him. Are you less convinced now?"

He heard Adelle's breathing while she considered; she was not about to let herself be bullied. Finally she said, "I suppose you're right."

"I'll talk to the cops. I'll try and keep you out of it. I'll tell them I got it out of Jack Lime or something."

"No. I'll answer to Alban if necessary. Tell them the truth."

Cooper took a deep breath and let it out. "Thank you. This may all be horse . . . uh, this may be nonsense. And it may get us knocked off Alban Galloway's Christmas list. But at least we're trying."

Adelle was silent for a moment. "Of course you're right. Believe me, I care much less about Alban Galloway's feelings than about finding out who murdered my daughter. And . . . I'm glad you're taking a hand in the matter."

"Well, I've got a stake in it too," said Cooper. "Whoever they are, I don't think they're very happy with me still walking around breathing."

Cooper had no food in the house, so he went out for a gyro at a Greek place on Morse. While he ate he looked out the window, watching the laundromat parking lot across the street, watching the delivery drivers hanging out in front of the pizza place, watching for anyone who could be watching for him. Coming home, he made one pass down the block and then walked back toward his place. There were a couple of beers in the refrigerator and he wanted to go on reclaiming his place, spend the evening with his feet up on the window-sill, thinking, until it was time to head over to Diana's.

He had his mind on those things and it wasn't until he was about to turn up the short concrete walk to his door that he noticed the two men sitting in the white Porsche across the street. He might not have noticed them if it hadn't been for the glow of a cigarette in the dark car. As it was, when his mind kicked in he was already halfway up the walk. The back of his neck prickled a bit as he pushed into the lighted foyer and began fumbling for his keys. He self-consciously moved as far to one side of the little space as possible, out of the direct line of fire, and took a look. He couldn't make out much through the panel of glass with the reflection of the inside light on it, and he quickly got the right key in his hand and stepped to the door and let himself in.

Two guys waiting in a parked car—under the circumstances it made Cooper nervous. He trotted up the stairs, stopped at his door to listen, opened it, and stepped in warily. He'd taken to leaving all the lights on when he wasn't there; they were all still on and things looked OK, but he had the wind up and he picked up the Slugger from its new home by the door and walked to the lamp by the front window. He switched it off and pulled the blind aside an inch or two and looked down into the street.

He could see the Porsche through the bare branches of the tree looming outside the window. The doors of the Porsche came open and a cigarette butt shot through the dark like a meteor and died on the asphalt in the middle of the street. The two men stepped into the light of the street lamps. They looked sizable and purposeful and they started walking to-ward the door of Cooper's building.

Cooper didn't wait. He strode back through the house, through the kitchen to the back door. He decided he wouldn't need the bat if he moved fast, and he laid it on the counter. He undid the deadbolt and slipped out onto the porch, closing and locking the door behind him. He cast an eye up and down the alley and went as quietly as possible down the wooden steps. Skirting the trash dumpsters, he moved along to the gangway between his building and the next and stepped lightly toward the front. He slowed as he approached the street and crept the last ten feet with his hand on the rough brick of the wall to steady himself. His heart was pounding; he could feel it in his guts now, the fear of getting torn up again, or worse. Suddenly he wished he'd brought the bat with him after all.

He put his head around cautiously and looked; the men were nowhere in sight and Cooper knew they were in the foyer. They were ringing his doorbell, or no—ringing a neighbor's to get inside without alerting him. Then they could be through the flimsy door to his place in a couple of seconds and on him. Now was the time to slip across the street, check the license plates on the Porsche, and split.

The door opened and the men came back out onto the front steps. Cooper pulled back and listened. They were talking in low voices. ". . . that's the guy?" Cooper heard. All he heard of the answer was "cast on his hand." They had marked him. The next words he heard were clearer and a lot scarier.

"Check around back."

He waited to be sure, then heard their footsteps coming across the grass toward the gangway. He took a frantic look behind him, prepared to run for it. Fifteen or twenty feet back there was a recess in the wall of the next building, a little bay designed to maximize the exposure to light of the side rooms, a strategy that had failed when Cooper's building had gone up to block the sun. Cooper took quick quiet steps back to the bay and slid into it just before the men turned the corner.

He stood waiting as they came slowly down the gangway, back to the wall, hoping the darkness between the buildings would shelter him, telling himself that if they saw him it would be time for a quick blow or two and then a dash.

They went by in the dark without turning their heads and all he could see of them was that they were large, over six feet and broad in the beam. He waited until their footsteps sounded in the alley behind and started to die away, and then he came out and walked fast, out from between the buildings and across the street to the Porsche. He bent down to check the rear plate and then took off for the corner where he'd parked.

He sat in the car swearing quietly for a moment, then started it up and drove up to the 7-Eleven where there were pay phones outside. He dialed the 24th District and asked for

Valenti. Cooper expected to be told that the lieutenant wasn't there but he was asked for his name and in a minute or so Valenti came on the line.

"MacLeish. They let you loose, huh? How's your eyesight?"

"Good enough to see two guys getting out of a Porsche in front of my house and coming after me."

There was a pause. Valenti said, "What, like the other night?"

"Yeah, like the other night."

"You mean they chased you? They shot at you? What happened?"

"I ducked out the back when I saw them get out of the car. But they were looking for me, for sure. I went around and heard them talking about me. And they weren't Jehovah's Witnesses."

There was another pause. "So what do you want me to do?"

"Send someone over. They might hang around for a bit."

"Send someone over to do what? Arrest them for first-degree sitting around in expensive cars?"

"For Christ's sake use your imagination. You saw what happened to me the other night."

"There's no such thing as preventive detention in this country, MacLeish. Did you talk to these guys? Ask what they wanted?"

"All right, I was spooked. Fuck it. I got their license number. You can check it out, can't you?"

"Check it out for what?"

"For anything. Like if the owner has a record for aggravated assault, for example."

"Jesus. OK, tell you what. It's almost dinnertime. Meet me at the Jalisco in half an hour and we'll talk about it."

The Jalisco was the kind of Mexican restaurant where Mexicans ate, which meant it was cheap. The place had a dim green ambience due to the color of the walls and the greasy smoke from the grill at the rear. There were plants hanging in the front window and a Rand McNally road map of Mexico tacked on the wall and silent Mexicans taking refuge from the cold, dreaming of what they would do with their hard-won money back in the real Jalisco.

Valenti bit hard into a taco, chewed a few times and said, "Have something to eat, for Christ's sake. You make me nervous."

Cooper set down the coffee spoon with a clatter. "All right. I been patient for ten minutes. What'd you find out?"

"Not much. The car's not stolen." There was a loud splintering crack as Valenti attacked the taco again.

"Did you check out the owner?"

"Yeah. I checked him out." Valenti chewed and looked at Cooper impassively.

"What, and it's top secret?"

"No, it's not a secret particularly. But then you don't have any particular right to know, do you?"

"It was me they came after."

"You still don't know if they wanted to beat you up or sell you magazine subscriptions."

"You're just playing dumb. I know it comes easy, but shit. Look at this cast on my hand and tell me I got nothing to worry about."

"Now don't start trying to piss me off, MacLeish. I've been a cop too long. I don't piss off easy."

"All right. If you won't tell me, call Shostak and Harrison, tell them."

"I didn't say I wasn't gonna tell you. But before I do I want to know you aren't gonna run off and do something stupid, like go after them with a beer bottle or something."

"You ever know me to do anything like that?"

Valenti ignored him and ate some more. After a while he said, "The name William Galloway mean anything to you?"

Cooper stared at him for a few seconds and then his mouth widened slowly in a smile. "The Porsche's registered to William Galloway?"

"You know the guy?"

Cooper drank some coffee, sat back in his chair, and said, "Let me tell you a story."

"If it's got anything to do with Billy Galloway I've probably heard it."

"You haven't heard this one. It starts with Alban Galloway. And Vivian Horstmann's mother."

Valenti's eyebrows rose just enough to show he was caught by surprise. "I'm listening."

Cooper told him. Valenti ate steadily, grunting once in a while. When Cooper finished telling him what Adelle Horstmann had learned, Valenti said, "So you got it all figured out."

"I don't know. What do you think?"

"I think Billy Galloway has too much money to worry about a stray half million. I also think that even if Billy Galloway had nothing to do with this he'd probably come looking to talk to you if he heard you were spreading the story."

"OK, maybe. I still think Shostak and Harrison should hear it. Don't you?"

Valenti shrugged. "Sure. Tell 'em. But don't tell anyone else. You get the Galloways mad at you, you'll have lawyers coming out of the bushes after you."

"Lawyers don't bother me. I don't have enough money to be scared by lawyers. People with guns scare me, though, and people who hire them."

Valenti took a drink of water and leaned back. "He works fast, huh? The Horstmann lady talks to his old man this afternoon, and tonight he's sitting outside your door. How'd he find out?"

"His father probably called him."

"Uh-huh." Valenti paused, frowning at Cooper. "You think the lady's safe?"

"Jesus. I hadn't thought about it."

"If Billy's trying to cover things up, where would he start? She's the one who went to the old man with the story."

"Christ." Cooper was appalled.

"Save it. Think for a second. If your idea is right, the old man knows now. You think he'd help cover up?"

"He doesn't have to know. Billy could be going off on his own."

"Naw, MacLeish, it doesn't work that way. If Billy's old man comes to him and says 'Hey, these people think you killed somebody,' what does he do if he really did? Start killing everyone who might know? No, he starts working on a good alibi or he jumps on the next flight to Rio. Too many people could know by now to start killing them off. Now if it's all bullshit, what does he do? He finds out where the guy who started the story lives, and he goes over to talk to the son of a bitch, see what the hell's going on."

Cooper stared hard at Valenti for a few seconds. "So it's all bullshit."

"I think so."

"I hope you're right, I really do. But I'm still going to call Shostak and Harrison and tell them about it."

Valenti shrugged and waved a hand at the stout Mexican woman who waited tables. He belched softly and said, "I don't know why I eat here. This stuff goes down like lead."

"You got sour cream in your moustache," said Cooper pensively.

They had a hockey game on the TV at Burk's and Cooper stared at it, mesmerized by the movement across the bright ice, listening to Aretha on the jukebox. *Just a little bit, just a little bit.* Burk set a beer in front of him, and he drank from the bottle and thought about Billy Galloway. He'd never met the man, but he didn't have to to know he'd hate him, even if he didn't kill Vivian.

Cooper was having trouble deciding if he was glad to be wrong about Billy Galloway, or disappointed. He'd been proud of himself for figuring it out. And it would have been nice to nail somebody like Billy Galloway, a rich kid who thought he could do anything he pleased.

On the phone Adelle Horstmann had agreed with Valenti; she'd never believed in the whole thing anyway. Even so Cooper had told her to lock her doors, then regretted sounding so dramatic.

Still, how reassuring could he be? Someone had killed her daughter, tried to kill her grandson. Somebody was still out there, waiting. If it wasn't Billy Galloway, Cooper was stumped. He'd given it his best shot and he didn't have any more ideas in him, not tonight.

Cooper drank beer and considered. He knew he ought to go home and work, tackle the big ideas again and take his mind off people dying, but there were nights when the long polished wood bar at Burk's was just where he wanted to be and this was one of them. Nobody demanded anything of him here; there was beer and music he knew and not too much light and as much talk or as much privacy as he wanted.

The song ended, and in the sudden quiet talk filled the space around him. Butch the Indian was there, somewhere to his left, the nasal voice loud and clear as always. "Bitter? Shit no, I ain't bitter. My fuckin' twin brother runs off with my wife, would you be bitter?" Cooper had heard the story before. He twirled the beer bottle slowly in front of him and looked to his right. The back that had been turned to him, blocking his view, moved away and there was Big Tim, ebony black and solid as a rock, all chest and no neck and fortunately for all one of the gentlest natures on earth. He raised a chin at Cooper in greeting and went on listening to the man at his shoulder, a long-faced, ponytailed kid Cooper didn't know. Behind him he heard Butch say, "Be like shootin' myself in the fuckin' mirror."

No, you ain't bitter, Cooper thought. He drank. "Skinheads," Big Tim was saying. "Saw one of them walking up Glenwood the other day. Big black boots, spiky leather all over, shaved head, something tattooed on his scalp. Looked like a Confederate flag or something. Funny thing was, the guy he was walking with was black. You tell me what's going on there."

"Tattooed on his head?" Ponytail said.

"On his head. You think that's weird, there was a guy used to be around the neighborhood, haven't seen him in a long time. Weirdest guy I ever saw around here. Had green thunderbolts tattooed on his forehead. Swear to God. Right down out of the roots of his hair onto his forehead, kind of converging at the bridge of his nose."

"Jesus, you gotta wonder."

"Yeah, like what kind of social life does this man have? What does he say to women in bars?"

"Well shit, did you see the guy that was in here earlier, with the little teardrop on his cheek?"

A chord crashed as the jukebox kicked in again. Cooper had frozen, clutching the cool wet beer bottle, staring at the TV; after a second he snapped his head to the right and looked. He could see Ponytail's lips moving but couldn't make out the words. After another couple of seconds he let go of the bottle and reached out and grabbed Ponytail's arm, sliding off the stool, moving closer to be able to hear him. Ponytail had stopped with his mouth open, gawking at Cooper.

"What guy?" Cooper said, over the noise of the box.

"Shit, my beer."

"I'm sorry. The guy. What'd he look like?"

"What the fuck?" Ponytail was backing away, indignant. Big Tim was staring at Cooper with big round eyes.

"You said you saw a guy with a teardrop tattooed on his cheek in here."

"What's your problem, man?"

Cooper held up his cast. "If it's the same guy, he did this. Now what'd he look like?"

Ponytail stared for a moment. "How'd he do that?"

"Will you listen to me? If this is the guy I think it is, he's bad trouble. And he's not finished with me. Now what the hell did he look like?"

"Shit—black hair, beard, I don't know. Looked Spanish to me."

"Christ. Is he still in here?" Cooper was looking into the dark recesses of the bar, suddenly aware of how he'd been sitting with his back to anyone who cared to walk up behind him.

"Naw, he left. I think. Jesus, you ain't kidding, are you?"

"No. You *think* he left?"

"Yeah, yeah, I saw him go out," said Big Tim.

"How long ago?"

"I don't know. Half hour, maybe."

"Did you see which way he went when he left?"

"Uh-uh. I just saw him go out the door. I don't think he went far, 'cause he had a beer in his hand. Hey, you in trouble, man?"

Cooper stared at him, trying to think. "Somebody is," he said, and wheeled and made for the door.

It was cold outside, and Cooper was grateful for it. Wake-up time. Burk's was a hole in the wall in a street that ran up one side of the El line; opposite the door was the blank concrete wall of the embankment with tree branches hanging down from the slope above. Cooper took a quick look left and saw no one, then looked right, trying desperately to remember if Dominic was working tonight, just around the corner at the restaurant. He came out of Burk's doorway and started walking fast, then trotting, down to the corner. He started to make the turn to duck into the restaurant but checked himself and went on across the street instead, into the gloom under the trees on the other side, his heart beating.

It brought back old memories of walking into bad places, staring hard into the shadows, hoping he saw what he was looking for before it saw him. He went down the block a ways, looking into the parked cars, looking into the narrow gangways between the houses. He saw no one so he cut across the street and came back toward the restaurant, still watching, feeling the ache in his left hand.

It was nearly ten and the restaurant was empty, only a few late customers lingering. Cooper gave them all a good look and then saw Dominic, shifting bus trays at the counter in back. Dominic looked up as he approached and smiled.

"I don't get off for another hour at least," he said. "Clean-up and stuff."

"Go punch out now," Cooper said softly. "I'll clear it with Rose."

Dominic stared at him. "What's up?"

"Tell you in the car. Where's Rose?"

"In the office, I guess. What's going on?"

Cooper stuck his head in the office and Rose looked up from the closeout sheet. "Can somebody cover for Dominic?" he said. "I want to get him home."

"He'll be out of here as soon as he gets done with clean-up. Can't you . . ."

"I got a little emergency here, Rose. Cover for him." Cooper didn't wait for argument; he went back into the dish-room, where Dominic stood uncertainly, waiting for orders. "Get the apron off and let's get going." Cooper stopped and stared at the back door, next to the sink. The latest in a line of Salvadoran refugee dishwashers watched him uncomprehending.

Out back, thought Cooper. *That's where he'd wait. He'll wait for Dominic to come out there, taking out the trash or whatever. And if Dominic hasn't come out by the time the customers leave and the place gets quiet, he comes in.* Cooper walked to the door, remembering what was behind it: a narrow gangway that led to the left and then made a ninety-degree turn to the right and ran behind Burk's to connect with the alley where the trash dumpsters were. The space would be filled with junk unless they had cleaned it up and there would be a lot of places to hide. Cooper had his hand on the door, pulling it open, and then he stopped. If Teardrop was out there in the dark, it was time to think twice about heroics.

Behind him Dominic said, in a small voice, "What's going on? Are *they* out there?"

"I don't know," said Cooper, unable to pull the door open any farther.

I'm afraid, he told himself. *Afraid to walk out there and see.*

Cooper remembered being afraid, a lot of times. And he remembered what had to be done when you were afraid. You had to go do it, just jump off and go do it, knowing there weren't any guarantees but it had to be done. He pulled the door open and saw the brick wall in front of him and the passage leading off to the left, dimly lit.

For God's sake use your head, he told himself. This time he wasn't on his own out there in the elephant grass a million miles from anywhere, and he had more choices. He could play it smarter now. Cooper shut the door and picked up the two-by-four that barred it after closing and slid it through the brackets. He stalked back across the room, saying to Dominic, "Get ready to go. Go sit in the office and wait for me. Or no—" Cooper had remembered that the office had a window that gave on to the passage out back. "Stay out of the office. Go sit in the john or something. Have somebody tell you when they see the Valiant out front and then come directly out."

Rose was in the doorway, arms folded, looking indignant. "I'm starting to remember why we didn't get along," she said.

"You got to take my word for this one. We might have trouble here." Cooper was keeping his voice calm, not wanting to panic anybody.

"Then why don't we call the cops?"

"I got nothing to tell them except suspicions. They won't send a car for that. Not fast enough to do us any good."

"Suspicions of what?" She and Dominic both waited for his answer.

"The guy that jumped me the other night was in Burk's about half an hour ago. Now get into the john and stay there until I pull up out front. Watch for me, Rose." Dominic looked at him for one second, wide-eyed, and then nodded and started moving. Rose just stared as Cooper brushed past her.

Cooper wondered for a moment, hustling up the street back past Burk's to where he'd left the car under the viaduct, if he was panicking for no reason. But how many guys with a teardrop tattooed on their cheek could there be?

He started the car and hesitated, drumming a thumb nervously on the wheel. If he just spirited Dominic away, they would miss any chance there might be to collar Teardrop. But if he called the cops they would laugh at him. He wasn't even sure it was the same guy, wasn't sure he was still around. But just the possibility that he was was reason enough to get the boy away fast. Dominic's safety had to be paramount.

Does he have a gun? Cooper put the car in gear and turned down the narrow lane with the El embankment on his left. It had been Murphy who'd shot at him, whose gun he'd taken away in his kitchen. If Teardrop had had a piece, wouldn't he have pulled it instead of running when Cooper shot at him from the kitchen floor?

No guarantees. If he was there to kill the boy, the assumption had to be he was suitably equipped. Cooper had almost reached the alley which connected with the passage behind the restaurant. Suddenly he knew he had to at least try for an ID before running away. He braked and whipped the wheel to the right.

His headlights swept over the trash dumpsters and the ancient graffiti on the dark brick, and he was rolling slowly toward the mouth of the passage. He was hunched over the wheel, tensed, looking at the shadows at the edges of the light. He turned slowly into the space that ran behind Burk's to the back of the restaurant.

They hadn't cleaned it up. There were stacks of boxes, old shelves, a battered old stainless steel milk cooler. There was something under a tarp that looked like it might be a boat and something Cooper had to stare at a second before he identified it as a bathtub, with cornstalks growing out of it.

Nothing was moving, in the glare of the headlights or in the darkness at either side. Cooper sat rigid, trying to scan it all. There was a six-foot chain-link fence that separated the space from the gangway of the big apartment house to the right. Cooper's eyes ran down the fence until they lit on the bottle.

A beer bottle, of clear glass, with two inches of beer left shining amber in the light, sitting on the corner of the milk cooler. Cooper stared at it. Over the soft idle of the Valiant he could just make out the muffled distant sound of the jukebox in Burk's.

Something moved in the rearview mirror outside Cooper's window. His heart leapt and he slammed the Valiant into reverse and gunned it, straight back, leaning over to the right just like before but trying to keep the wheel straight because he knew he had no room to maneuver here. The tires screamed and out of the corner of his eye Cooper saw a dark shape rush by the window and then he knew he was almost out of room and he braked hard and came upright, putting it in drive, ready to smear the son of a bitch along the wall if he had to.

In the headlights he saw the white apron and the big white eyes of the Salvadoran dishwasher, stiff against the wall, one hand frozen halfway up to shield his eyes, looking like a deer caught in the headlights, scared to death. Cooper swore and gaped at him for a second, then checked both his mirrors and looked at where he was. He was sitting square across the alley, his rear bumper almost touching the wall of the building behind. In front of him the dishwasher lowered his hand, still staring into the light.

"Sorry, pal," Cooper breathed out loud. "Where the *hell* did you come from?" He eased off the brake and started to turn toward the street, slowly. The Salvadoran peeled himself off the wall and moved back toward the restaurant, the scared look starting to give way to one of affront.

Cooper gained the street again, his heart thumping. OK, maybe. If that's his beer, he's sitting back there in the dark and I'm sure as hell not going to root him out. Time to get Dominic clear.

He reached the corner and stopped, remembering the gangway on the other side of the building. A six-foot fence was easily scaled and he didn't want Teardrop slipping through to the front to surprise them. He double-parked right there at the corner, took a look around, and got out and went into the restaurant. Rose met him with a bewildered look. "What's going on out there?" she said.

"Nothing. Get the kid and we'll try and keep it that way." Rose disappeared through the kitchen door and a few seconds later Dominic emerged, pulling on his coat.

"Francisco says someone's acting real weird out there in the alley," he said.

"That was me. We scared the shit out of each other. Apologize to him tomorrow for me."

"Is that guy out there?"

"I don't know. He might be. I just don't want to take any chances. Right now we're going to sit and wait until those people at the register are finished paying and then we'll go out the door right behind them and get in the car, at the corner there." Dominic nodded, a bit pale but looking game.

They slipped out in the wake of a party of five that had dawdled interminably at the register, drawing a couple of stares from them for treading on their heels. Outside the door they veered off and Cooper shepherded the boy to the car and they moved away down the street, Cooper feeling the weight lift as they left the place behind.

"Aren't you gonna like tell the cops?" Dominic said.

"Yeah, I'll tell them. There's nothing they can do about it now, though. I don't even know if the guy was actually around." Cooper remembered the beer bottle in the glare of the headlights and wondered. He wished suddenly he'd had a gun, a big .44 special or better yet a sixteen, just like old times. Shove in a magazine, put it on full automatic and he wouldn't have been scared to go down that alley then. He was starting to get over the fright and get angry again.

Dominic stared straight ahead and said nothing until after they turned right onto Morse Avenue, broad and as bright as day after the narrow bricked street in the shadow of the El line. "At least this gets me off work a little early," he said with a whiff of laughter.

"There's that." Cooper was calming down, reassured by the lights and the people moving lazily along the sidewalks. "Listen, isn't this starting to get on your nerves a bit? If I were you I'd have left town a week ago."

"I told you. I . . ."

Cooper hit the brakes, slowing abruptly and pulling over. They had just rolled through a green light at Ashland.

"What?" said Dominic, clutching at the door handle.

"See him? Up there toward Clark Street. He just came out of the street by the Korean church up there." Cooper spoke quietly, tensed again.

He and Dominic watched as the old Camaro climbed the gentle rise toward Clark Street a block and a half ahead, drifted to a stop at the traffic light, then made a left as the light changed and disappeared, going south.

"You're sure it was the same guy?" Diana said.

"I'd bet on it. It was the same car. I'm amazed the guy's still driving it around. He's got to know the cops are watching for it now, because of the stolen plates."

"Maybe he's got new plates now."

"Maybe."

"How'd Dominic take it?"

"I think he was scared, but he's hanging tough. The scary part was getting him home. I made him duck down on the seat while I scouted the block and the alley behind, then walked him up the back way and made sure his roommates were there and everything was cool before I let him go in. I don't think these guys could know where he's living, but then I didn't think they could know about him working at the restaurant, either."

She was silent for a while, watching him from the end of the sofa, then said, "Food for thought."

"Yeah. Worry, even. I think I must have led someone to the restaurant somehow. When, I don't know. I've tried to be careful. But that's the only way I can figure it. I mean, who that's involved in this knows about the restaurant? Where it is and everything? You, me, Rose. Period. Nobody could have given it away. I had to have led them there somehow. Unless it was just coincidence the guy chose Burk's to have a drink in tonight."

"Dominic knows where the restaurant is."

Cooper stared at her. "Well of course. What's that supposed to mean?"

"Did you ask him who he's told about it?"

"No, but I'm sure he hasn't gone broadcasting it to stray hit men and millionaire's sons."

Diana shrugged, sipped her wine, tucked her feet under her. "No, but he might have told some of these friends he keeps mentioning. You ever met any of them?"

"His school friends? No. But they're just kids he's gone to school with, kids he's known for years. They couldn't have any connection with this."

"Maybe not. But my bet would be he's told somebody about working at the restaurant and it got to the wrong people. I mean, you said you'd spot someone trying to follow you, right?"

"I would think so, yeah." Cooper rubbed at his brow, tired and disturbed.

"You didn't lead anybody here, did you?"

"No. I made sure."

"There's a lot I don't understand about this. Like, who are the guys in the Camaro? Who are they working for?"

"Whoever killed Vivian. Billy Galloway, I thought."

"Then who were the two guys in the Porsche?"

"Billy himself, I guess. And a friend."

"Why the visit?"

"If Valenti's right, just to find out what's going on. If I'm right, to warn me off. Rough me up a bit."

"He's got Teardrop to do the rough stuff. Why come himself?"

"OK, Valenti's right. They're working for someone else."

"Someone who found out where Dominic was working. How?"

"I don't know how. I don't understand a damn thing right now."

A silence followed. Cooper slouched with his eyes closed, wishing he'd never come across the news of Vivian's death. He heard Diana rise, pace softly around the room. After a while she spoke. "Maybe the guy wasn't looking for Dominic tonight. Maybe he was looking for you."

Cooper opened his eyes. Diana was standing with her arms folded, watching him with her impassive gaze. "Why?" said Cooper.

"Why do you think? After you put his partner in the hospital he'd want to settle up."

Cooper considered for a moment. "So he knew where I hang out. He followed me, like I said. Not tonight, but some other time."

"Or maybe it was you who told the wrong thing to the wrong person sometime."

After a moment Cooper said, "I'm too tired to figure this all out right now."

"Me too. But we better figure it out soon."

"We will. All the doors locked?"

"Always."

"Then let's forget it for tonight."

In the bedroom Diana was golden in the muted light from the single lamp by the bed; her hair hung loose about her round face, shifting highlights of flame showing as she moved. She slipped out of her robe and Cooper watched her, lean and tawny, as she lifted the blanket and slid in beside him. He watched the movement of her muscles beneath the freckled skin of her shoulders and then she was under the covers, the long smooth warm length of her nestling against his side, her head tucked into the crook of his arm. He pursed his lips gently against the crown of her head, amidst the auburn hair. She exhaled and the breath warmed his chest.

"I'm glad you didn't walk down that alley tonight," she said.

"Me too."

"I saw you lying there in that hospital bed. And I remember how it felt when they called to tell me Roger had been shot." Cooper just lay there, holding her close. "Don't get yourself shot, Cooper. I wouldn't like it at all." Diana's voice was languorous and tired and far away against his neck.

He lay for a while looking at the ceiling and then hoisted himself up on his elbow and looked down into her face, which bore all the traces of her varied ancestry: the honeyed cast of hair and skin, the dark Latin eyes, the faint Mongol tilt to the cheekbones. She stared back at him in mute remoteness and he wondered if this was another relationship that was going to slip out of his control and get messy; he wondered why it was that he couldn't just feel comfortable with her and not worry about where it was going. He wanted to caress her face but with the cast on his hand he could only run a finger clumsily down her cheek.

She put her hand to the back of his neck, twining his hair through her fingers, and pulled him gently downward. "We talk too much," she whispered, her features inscrutable. "Let's get back to what we got together for." She brushed his lips lightly with hers and then her tongue was there and Cooper was holding her tight and wondering why it had been so long.

15

DIANA INSISTED. IF Cooper was going to risk going to his apartment again, she was coming along. "We'll get your books, clothes, whatever you need, bring them back to my place," she said. "Why should you sit in there waiting for somebody to come shoot you?"

"OK, sounds good. But there's no reason for you to come along."

"I'm coming. If that guy comes back I'll show him how nasty a Puerto Rican can be. He thinks he's seen it all, I'll show him."

"Diana. If he comes back he'll have a gun."

"Two's still better than one. Just for watching if nothing else. I'm not letting you go alone."

Cooper shrugged and said fine, grateful for her spirit but fervently hoping he was right about Teardrop not trying it again. He couldn't imagine anybody keeping a permanent watch on his place, but then he wouldn't have thought they'd look for him at Burk's either. One thing Cooper wanted to do today was sit someplace and think it all out, figure out what the hell was happening and why. But first, a shower and a change of clothes.

It was routine by now, checking the block and the alley behind before he even thought about getting out of the car. Everything looked normal but Cooper realized he could never be sure and he was really depending on the odds, the odds against Teardrop trying the same thing twice. They went up the back and checked that the door hadn't been tampered with again, they went into the kitchen carefully, listening. Cooper had cleaned up but left the nail sticking in the kitchen table, and Diana looked at it with distaste. "You going to leave that there?"

226

"For a while," Cooper said. "Just a reminder." Diana shook her head.

Cooper showered and then he and Diana packed him a bag for a couple of days' stay at her place. Cooper wanted to make some sort of crack about moving in with her to make it clear he wasn't really, but he couldn't think of just exactly what he wanted to convey so he kept quiet. The doorbell rang while he was gathering his books and notes from the desktop.

He looked at Diana.

"Don't open it," she said. "If it's not the Jehovah's Witnesses, it's the Moonies."

"Maybe." Cooper went to the door. "Or maybe it's Opportunity, and that's the only time he's going to ring." He hesitated for a second and pressed the button that buzzed people in, hearing the latch go and the door swing open below. He opened the door and stepped out onto the landing and leaned on the rail, hearing slow footsteps coming up the carpeted stairs. If it was Teardrop he'd have time to duck back inside and bar the door, unless of course the guy had automatic weapons now and fired a burst up through the landing. Cooper was trying to convince himself that that was unlikely when the man hove into view on the steps below.

He had gray hair; that was the first thing Cooper saw. As he made the turn in the stairwell Cooper saw the face upturned—middle-aged, ruddy, and bearded. The man wore a tan suede jacket and his hands were stuffed in the pockets. Cooper nodded at him and he said a diffident hello and came up the last flight slowly, watching Cooper. "I'm looking for Cooper MacLeish," he said, and stopped three steps from the top.

"You found him," said Cooper. "What can I do for you?"

"I'd like to talk with you if I may. My name is Jesse Goddard," the man said.

Cooper just stared at him for a moment. The face was long and melancholy and handsome in an autumnal past-the-prime sort of way. Cooper put him in the late forties or early fifties. The beard came to a nice point and the hair was rumpled but under control. The eyes were big and soulful, eyes that would hold a woman's glance. "Come on in," Cooper said, starting to recover. "I've heard your name."

Goddard came up the last two steps, sized Cooper up, and

gave him a quick half-smile. Cooper flapped a hand toward the apartment to usher him in. As Goddard stepped tentatively inside, hands still in his pockets, Cooper looked past him and caught sight of the anxious look on Diana's face. Cooper came in behind Goddard and reached down for the Slugger before he even closed the door. He said, "I'd be happy to talk to you, but you have to do me a favor first."

"What's that?" Goddard had half turned; he was looking at the bat as Cooper brought it up, in his right hand, choked up far enough to swing it one-handed.

"Stand perfectly still while my friend here searches you. Move and I'll brain you." Cooper had the bat above his shoulder, ready to crack his skull if one hand came out of the pocket too fast. He saw the blood go out of Goddard's face and the shock creep over it, the lips parted just a bit. As Diana came across the floor Cooper looked Goddard in the eye, not frowning, just looking, shifting his weight, ready to swing.

"Feel in his pockets," Cooper said to Diana. "From behind. Make sure his hands are empty." She stood close behind Goddard and reached around as if embracing him and felt in the pockets and then pulled his hands out, showing them to be clenched into fists but empty. Goddard's brow had just begun to contract, passing from shock to anger. "Now pat him down, under the arms, around the waist. Around at the small of his back, too." While Diana obeyed, Cooper kept looking right into Goddard's eyes. "If I'm wrong about this I apologize, and you'll just have to forgive me. But I've had a rough week and I'm not taking any more chances."

Diana stepped away and shot Cooper a look. "Nothing, I don't think," she said in a tight voice, with just a hint of that accent.

"Now the legs," Cooper said. "Check the ankles for sure."

As Diana knelt, Goddard found his voice. He cleared his throat softly and said, "Am I allowed to ask what I've done?" He was angry now, glaring at Cooper.

"Sure," said Cooper. "Maybe nothing. But then maybe you killed Vivian Horstmann, too. The cops think it's possible."

The jaw slackened again and the shock was back in God-

dard's face as Diana stood up, shaking her head. Cooper said,
"OK, Mr. Goddard. Take off your jacket and hand it to her.
Slowly."

Working hard to maintain his dignity, Goddard obeyed.
Under the suede jacket was a blue-striped rugby shirt and no
weapons visible. Diana took the jacket and Goddard rallied,
drawing himself up to full height and trying to get a handle
on his frown again. "Would you like me to strip?" he said,
aiming for acid urbanity and not quite making it because of
the quaver in his voice.

Cooper let the bat drop to his side. "This'll do, I think."
He relaxed, feeling how ready he'd been to club him. "Like
I say, I've had a rough week. The police want to talk to you,
you know."

"No, I wouldn't know. I've been out of the country."
Goddard's eyes were still wary, flicking to the bat and back
to Cooper's face.

"Yeah, I heard. In Mexico." Cooper set the bat back by
the door and waved at the couch. "Have a seat."

Goddard just stared for a few seconds, rigid, before he
finally turned and looked at Diana draping his jacket on
the back of the director's chair. Then with a little shake of
the head he walked slowly to the couch and sat down gingerly
on the edge. Diana moved to the window and sat on the sill.

"How the hell did you end up here?" Cooper said, making
his way to the director's chair.

Goddard watched him sit down, still unable to get the frown
working, looking a bit dazed. "Melissa Wilkert gave me your
name. I looked you up in the phone book." His voice was
deep, his enunciation careful. He spoke like a man impressed
by the sound of his own voice.

"Uh-huh. When did you get back from Mexico?"

"Yesterday."

"Why'd you come back?"

Goddard finally managed a full-blooded glare. "With the
reception you just gave me, I don't think I owe you any answers."

Cooper leaned back in his chair, his tension easing. "I
know my manners have deteriorated in the last week, but I've
got an excuse. People keep trying to kill me. And your name
came up in conversation. So bear with me. The police want

to talk to you because they think you might have been with Vivian the night she died. Were you?''

Visibly working to control his anger, Goddard settled back onto the couch and crossed his legs, taking a look around the room for the first time. ''I've already been through this with Melissa. I was in Mexico when Vivian died. I only heard of her death by phone the day before yesterday. I came back to find out what in God's name had happened to her. Melissa tells me she was murdered.''

''So it seems. Can you prove you were in Mexico?''

''I don't believe I have to prove anything to you.''

''No, but you'll have to prove it to the cops.''

''I can prove it.''

''When did you go down there?''

''Almost two months ago.''

''And you've been down there all this time.''

''That's right. Near Oaxaca. I can find plenty of people to testify to that.''

''OK. I'm sorry about the reception. Things have been a little wild here.''

Goddard's expression passed slowly from indignant to confused. He blinked and said cautiously, ''Melissa said you could tell me more than she could.''

''What do you want to know?''

''Who killed Vivian?''

''Nobody knows. Not me, not the cops. Not yet. Go see them so they can cross you off the list.''

''They seriously think I killed her?''

''They look for the lover in a case like this. It looks like Vivian knew whoever killed her.''

The point of Goddard's beard sagged onto his chest and he closed his eyes. ''Her lover.''

''Yeah,'' said Cooper quietly, looking at him with distaste. ''Isn't that what you were?''

When Goddard opened his eyes it was to stare out the front windows, shaking his head just a little. ''I wish,'' he said simply. ''Melissa told you I was?''

''We found the pin you gave Vivian. With the note. 'Believe in my love.' Melissa identified your signature, that's all.''

A smile, of defeat perhaps, moved Goddard's lips. "Ah, yes. My gift to her. She never even acknowledged it."

Cooper looked at him for a moment, obscurely relieved. "You never were her lover?"

"No." A short hiss of laughter came from Goddard and he shook his head. "No, Vivian wouldn't have that."

After a moment Cooper said, "It was unrequited, huh? You gave her gifts and things and she rejected you."

Goddard looked sullenly from Diana to Cooper. "I'm not sure my personal affairs are any of your business."

"Or the cops' either, but they're going to want to know. They're going to want to know when you left for Mexico and if you could have been angry enough at Vivian for being rejected to kill her."

"I've already told you I can prove when I left for Mexico. And just to set you straight, mister, she didn't outright reject me. She basically strung me along for months until I got tired of it."

"She strung you along? That doesn't sound like her."

Another bitter laugh escaped Goddard. "How well did you know her? Vivian was capable of great . . . inconstancy, let's say, when she wanted to be. She could be the world's greatest tease."

Cooper frowned. "So you gave up on her and left. Why'd you come back?"

Goddard just looked at him for a few seconds in discomfort. "See if you can figure that one out on your own," he said.

"You must have had it bad," Cooper said.

"It's an easy thing to mock, isn't it?" Goddard said quietly.

"I'm not mocking. I know how it goes," said Cooper. He drummed a thumb on the arm of the chair in irritation. "What do you mean she strung you along? Were there other men in the picture?"

"Your curiosity is insatiable."

"I'm not asking because I give a damn about your love life. I'm asking because I want to know who killed Vivian."

Goddard wet his lips with his tongue and appeared to make a decision. "There was nobody that I knew of. That wasn't the problem." Again he gave vent to the little bitter laugh.

"The problem was that Vivian could never make up her mind whether or not it was a sin to give in to her carnal desires." Goddard was giving the acid another try, with more success now.

"You make her sound like an eighteen-year-old."

"Oh no, she was an adult all right. And she gave me plenty of reason to believe, at first at least, that she wanted the same thing I did."

"So what happened?"

"Her conscience got the better of her. At least that's what I surmise. We met last year when she showed my work and I thought there was some attraction there. Last spring she was going through the divorce and she gave every sign of wanting to break free of all that. By that time I was . . . a bit smitten, and as I say she gave me some encouragement. But she drew back as soon as things got to a point where . . . where things naturally get between two adults."

Goddard paused, perhaps hoping Cooper was going to let him off the hook. Cooper said, "Why do you think she drew back?"

"She said she didn't like it that I hadn't divorced my wife. My marriage has been dead for years, but we haven't yet taken the trouble to wipe it off the books. Vivian put great stress on that point, but I think she was just . . . just hesitant. I think under the sophisticated exterior she was still a good Catholic girl."

"That's an easy thing to mock too, isn't it?" said Cooper.

"I'm not mocking any more than you are. But it certainly complicates adult relations."

"Yeah, I think that's the idea. How long did all this go on?"

Goddard shot him another look, ready to protest, and then took a deep breath and went on. "Most of the summer. By August I was reduced to pleading, and she had taken to avoiding me. I started to get angry—not enough to do her harm, if that's what leaps to your mind—and then I decided I had better things to do with my life than chase her around like a lovesick teenager. So I left for Mexico. There's a place near Oaxaca where I go and paint. The other day I called a friend of mine here to get some things I needed sent down, and he told me about Vivian."

Cooper sat frowning, abstracted. Diana slipped off the windowsill and walked slowly out of the room, back to the kitchen. Cooper looked at Goddard and said, "I think you should talk to the police."

Goddard heaved a great sigh. "I think I'll let them find me."

"No you won't. That would be failure to cooperate in an investigation, and they don't like that. I'll give you the names of the investigating officers and the number to call. You can call them right now." Cooper rose and went to where his jacket was hanging on the closet doorknob and pulled his notebook out of the pocket. He found the number at Area Six and went to the phone and dialed it, and then handed the receiver to Goddard, who gave him a sullen look but took it. "Ask for Detective Shostak or Harrison. They probably won't be there, but you can leave a message. Just tell them you want to talk about Vivian and they'll get right back to you."

Cooper went back to the kitchen to join Diana while Goddard spoke into the phone. Diana had put water to boil on the stove and was spooning coffee into a filter.

"Convinced him, huh?" she said.

"Looks like it. I guess this means he didn't kill her."

"I guess so. You don't like him, do you?"

"Shows, huh?"

"The preacher's son started coming out a little bit."

"He's always there somewhere."

"Someday I'd like to hear what he thinks about *our* adult relations." She stood with her arms folded over her maroon pullover, a faint smile touching her lips.

"I'll ask him sometime," said Cooper.

They could hear Goddard speaking, leaving the message as Cooper had told him. When he hung up Cooper went back out to the living room. Goddard was on his feet, putting on his jacket.

"Thanks," said Cooper. "I'm sorry about the baseball bat."

"Well, it seems to have worked. You got a confession, though not the one you wanted, perhaps." One eyebrow was raised, Goddard's dignity fighting back.

Cooper shrugged. "I never really thought you killed her."

Goddard stood watching as Cooper collapsed into the director's chair. "You said somebody tried to kill you," he said. "Was that connected with Vivian's death?"

"Yeah. How, I don't know. But I'll figure it out. The cops can tell you all about it."

After a pause Goddard said, "What was Vivian to you?"

"Nothing. I knew her a long time ago."

Goddard nodded, his hands in his pockets, skepticism settling in on his features. "I see. Well, I don't really think I can thank you for your hospitality, but I suppose I can thank you for not braining me."

"Don't mention it. I hope the cops let you get back to Mexico before too long."

When Goddard had gone Diana came out of the kitchen with two cups of coffee and they sat on the couch. "So much for that suspect," Diana said. "There was no lover after all."

"Huh. So why did Vivian start paying more attention to her appearance, how come her mood changed for the better? Melissa Wilkert was sure. There had to have been somebody."

"Not necessarily. Her mood changed because Goddard gave up and left town after hounding her all summer. Get him and Melissa together and compare dates and I bet you find she brightened up about the time he left. And then she was free to start looking nice again. If somebody you don't like is always around wanting to drag you into the sack, you don't feel much like dressing up, believe me. It can have a real depressing effect on your life-style. I can well imagine her breathing a sigh of relief and hauling out the makeup kit again. That's my vote. There wasn't any lover."

"Jesus, I should have brought you in on this from the start. Yeah. I should have figured it out. That's why the pin was in her desk drawer instead of with the rest of the jewelry. She never accepted the gift. She was probably planning to send it back with a frosty letter or something. This secret lover business was all smoke. She couldn't stand the guy."

"Sounds to me like she gave him some encouragement, at first at least."

"Maybe. But she would have seen through him before too long."

"You're relieved, huh? Still jealous after all these years?"

"No more than you."

"I admit it's pretty hard to keep hearing about Vivian the irresistible."

"I bet you've had at least two guys fall in love with you in your life."

"Yeah. But I keep hearing what a saint she was, too. For God's sake, she must have had a few stains on her character."

"She did. She got drunk sometimes and slept with people she shouldn't have, her marriage fell apart, and she almost got involved with a philandering son of a bitch. She wasn't perfect. But she was a good person, yeah. No doubt about that."

"OK, I'm not running her down. I shouldn't have said anything. I'll just be glad when this is laid to rest."

"You and me both."

They listened as a car or two went by outside. A faint honking came drifting over from Sheridan Road. Cooper picked up his coffee and leaned back and hoisted his feet up on the steamer trunk. He stared out the window at bare branches until the phone rang. Diana handed him the receiver.

"Hi, Cooper. It's me, Dominic."

"Hey, what's going on?"

"The detectives came back." Dominic's voice had a touch of the plaintive over the phone.

"They did, huh? What'd they want to know?"

"I don't think they believe me. I told them about last night and they practically said they thought we were imagining things. They asked me all the same questions like a zillion times, like they were trying to trap me."

"They're trying to make sure they get things right," Cooper said. "They have to get things nailed down pretty solidly."

"They scared the shit out of Petra. She hates cops."

"At least they're working on the case. They're taking it seriously."

"I just wish they believed me."

"They probably did. Cops work like that. They don't cozy up to you. They go after you."

"They're coming to see you next. They're on their way."

"Great. We just made some coffee."

"You know what the problem is? They won't believe anything a kid says. I could tell by the way they were looking at me. If you're under twenty-one they like despise you.''

''Now you're getting paranoid. Don't let them get under your skin.''

''You weren't there, but anyway. Uh . . . the other reason I called is because my father's coming into town tonight. He wants to take us out to dinner.''

''What, both of us?''

''Yeah. He wants to thank you. For taking care of me and stuff, I guess.''

''OK. When and where?''

''I don't know. He's gonna call when he gets here.''

''All right. I'll be around. See you.'' Cooper handed the phone back to Diana. ''The kid says the cops are coming over to see me. Those two detectives.''

''The Dragnet guys? This should be interesting.''

''Yeah. We can tell them about Goddard. And I want to tell them about Billy.''

''I bet they tell you the same thing Valenti told you.''

''Maybe.'' Cooper watched as Diana rose and wandered slowly to the front windows and looked out into the street. ''What do you think is going on?'' he said.

''I don't know. But I have a feeling we could figure it out if we thought hard enough.''

The doorbell rang shortly after that, and when Cooper stepped out onto the landing and looked down he saw Shostak and Harrison trudging up the stairs. Shostak was wearing a raincoat over a tan suit with a dark blue tie. Harrison brought up the rear, apparently warm enough in the autumn chill in a dapper gray pin-striped suit with a red tie. They were both big men and they took over Cooper's living room effortlessly, assuming command by virtue of their size and the watchful way they moved to opposite sides of the room, Harrison by the window, Shostak toward the dining room, nodding as Diana appeared in the doorway. ''We got your message,'' said Shostak.

''Your latest message,'' said Harrison.

''Thanks for coming by. Want some coffee?'' said Cooper.

''No thanks.'' Shostak looked if anything more fatigued and morose than before. He turned from the dining room and stood with his hands on his hips, looking Cooper up and down.

"I'll take some," said Harrison cheerfully. "How you doin'?" he said to Diana. "Make it black, black as you can." He spotted the director's chair and sat down, hoisting his right leg up on the left thigh. Cooper sat on the couch and watched Shostak complete his tour of the room and come to a halt looking at the books on the shelves opposite the window.

Cooper said. "You just missed Jesse Goddard."

Shostak snapped a look at him. "He was here?"

"Yeah. He showed up out of the blue. He just got in from Mexico, and Melissa Wilkert pointed him in my direction. He says he's been out of the country for two months and can prove it. I had him call and leave a message for you."

Shostak grunted and looked at Harrison, who shook his head once and said, "Hm."

"You have a way of being in the middle of things, don't you?" Shostak said.

"That's not all. I think I saw Flores last night."

"Yeah, the kid told us," Shostak said. "You saw his car, anyway."

"OK, I saw his car. And he was spotted in the bar next to the restaurant."

"Uh-huh. Think he was laying for the kid?"

"Well what do you think?"

"I don't know." Shostak looked at him blankly for a couple of seconds and then watched as Diana came in and handed a mug to Harrison. He gave her a smile and thanked her and Diana retreated to the doorway into the dining room, where she stood leaning against the doorframe. Shostak said, "Your message mentioned an idea."

"Yeah, I had an idea."

"I'm glad somebody does. Let's hear it."

Cooper told them, starting with what Adelle Horstmann had told him about Vivian's parentage. He took them through it as he had told it to Valenti, including the attempted visit of Billy Galloway. Shostak interrupted him occasionally to ask a question; Harrison sipped his coffee and listened.

Cooper wound it up. "Lieutenant Valenti said it didn't sound likely to him. Maybe it isn't. But I thought you should hear it. It's the only idea I could come up with that explains why someone would want to kill both Vivian and her son.''

There was a silence while Shostak and Harrison looked at one another. Cooper looked for some expression on their faces but saw none.

"It's new," said Shostak.

"New and different," said Harrison. "And original." He drained his coffee and set the mug on the windowsill.

"Does it make sense?" Cooper said, like a kid begging for approval.

"I don't know," said Shostak, still prowling the room, hands in his trouser pockets now. "We'll have to check it out, I guess." He sounded as if the prospect depressed him.

"We'll have to talk to some mighty high-powered people, sounds like," said Harrison, studying his thumbnail. "But that's OK. We like talking to high-powered people. Makes a change."

"Right offhand," said Shostak, "I'd say your idea has a couple of problems."

"I know. Like the fact that Billy Galloway's going to inherit millions anyway," said Cooper.

"Yeah. Maybe that's a problem. I was thinking something else." Shostak stood at the corner of the oak desk, looking down at Cooper's books and notes, apparently absorbed. "I was thinking that if someone like Billy Galloway wants some violence done, he doesn't hire people like Murphy. He can afford to get real professional hard people, the kind of person who doesn't do things crudely and doesn't fuck up the job."

"OK, fine. At least you can give Billy a call and ask him what he was doing around here last night, can't you?"

"Sure. We can do that." The two detectives exchanged another look. Harrison looked bored; Shostak looked thoughtful. He flicked a glance at Diana at the rear of the room and then looked back at Cooper and said, "Got any more ideas?"

Cooper blinked at him. "Not really. Have you talked to Murphy yet?"

There was a pause and then Harrison said, "That's our big treat for the day. The hospital says we can see him this afternoon."

Cooper nodded slowly. "Should be interesting."

"We hope so. We'll try and squeeze him in, somewhere between Papa Galloway and little Billy."

Cooper stared at him and felt his stomach tightening with anger. "I didn't make this shit up just to waste your time," he said.

"We're not saying you did," said Shostak in his slow patient way. "We're just a little . . . concerned, that's all."

"Concerned about what?"

Harrison answered. "Concerned about the fact that everything that says that this death might be a murder comes from the kid. Or from you."

There was a long silence while Cooper looked from one man to the other and let it sink in. "Uh-huh," he said finally. "You think we're making it up."

Shostak gave a little shake of the head, a raising of the eyebrows, to suggest innocent bewilderment. "We don't know what to think."

"See," Harrison said, "this would have been closed weeks ago. Lady dead on the ground, suicide note up in her place, medical examiner says the fall and nothing else killed her . . . man, that looks like a suicide to me. Except you bring the kid around and he says uh-uh, she wasn't alone up there 'cause this and that and she didn't have no paper like that around and all the rest. OK, we look again and then somebody shoots at you and jumps you and all that and we look at everything again and look for homicidal boyfriends and shady stuff and it still looks like a suicide, and now suddenly you got this new theory."

Cooper was frowning, chewing at his lip. He said, "You think I staged this?" He held up the cast. "You think I had some guy nail my hand to the fucking table to pull the wool over your eyes?"

"Naw, I don't think that. I just think we don't really know what's going on. I think we don't really now what the attacks on you have to do with Vivian Horstmann going out the window."

The detectives were motionless, watching him, Shostak erect by the desk, Harrison sitting back in the chair with his hands clasped on his stomach. Cooper let the hand with the cast fall back at his side and stared blankly at them. Behind him he heard Diana shift position slightly with a rustle of clothing.

Shostak moved, stepping slowly away from the desk. "We went back and looked at the copies of the note and the writing samples again. We took 'em to a different handwriting guy and made him look at them. He said the same thing—the note was written by Vivian Horstmann. You can fake a signature so it'll pass but fakes of something like that are almost impossible except for a real artist. And even then an expert can usually tell. I think we've got to say this one's genuine." Shostak came to a halt in front of the bookshelves again and put out a hand and rested it lightly on the top shelf, reading the titles.

"Did the kid say anything more to you about why he's sure his mother didn't kill herself?" said Harrison.

Cooper shook his head. "No. Just what he told you that first day."

"Mm-hm. Does he talk a lot about it? Does he have his own theories?"

"I haven't been spending a lot of time with him, to tell you the truth."

The silence lasted for several seconds. Finally Harrison said, "Maybe you should start. He might tell you some more things."

Cooper looked at him; he was looking at his thumbnail again.

"I'll tell you another thing you should do," said Shostak. "As long as you're thinking of theories. You should think up a scenario that involves Vivian Horstmann killing herself, 'cause that's what she did." Cooper looked up to find his hard eyes fixed on him. "Figure out how that fits in with the rest and give us a call. We'd love to hear it."

Harrison put his hands on his knees and stood up and said, "Or maybe we'll give you a call later, after we talk to Murphy. You gonna be around?"

"Probably." Cooper hadn't moved; he was still perched at the end of the couch, frowning at them.

The two detectives were making for the door. "Thanks for the coffee," said Harrison, nodding at Diana.

Shostak had the door open. He paused on the threshold

and looked at Cooper and said, "Try and figure out something else, too."

"What's that?" said Cooper.

"Try and figure out how much of what the kid says is true." He went out and Harrison followed, pulling the door to behind him.

Cooper sat still. After a moment he heard Diana come slowly across the floor and sit on the couch beside him. He turned his head to see her biting softly at the inside of her lower lip, watching him. They sat for a moment longer without speaking.

"Huh," said Cooper finally.

"What do you think they know that we don't know?" Diana said.

"Something. I have a bad feeling it's something I should have figured out by now."

"If they've figured it out, why didn't they just tell you?"

"They can't have figured it all out or they wouldn't have come. I think they have a few pieces and we just have to fit 'em together."

"So let's fit 'em together."

Normally Cooper would have gone to work; he liked to drive and sometimes the job was just the background he needed to get some thinking done. Today, however, he knew they wouldn't let him take out a cab with the cast on his hand. At other times when he needed to think he would go to the pool hall on Sheridan Road and run through rack after rack of balls, bending over the table in the cone of light that isolated him from the rest of the large cool dark room. With both of those alternatives closed off, and with Diana determined to bodyguard him, he took her in tow and headed for the lake.

It was a cool clear day with an edge to it, a fine autumn day with a reminder of winter coming. Cooper and Diana made their way out along the pier and stood at the end looking south at the skyline, with gentle swells coming in from the far reaches of the lake to lap at the concrete six feet below them. Diana laid her gloved hands on the restraining cable, the chill breeze blowing her hair gently about her face above the fleece collar of her jacket, strong blue-jeaned legs planted firmly on the concrete.

"All right, let's look it in the eye." Cooper faced her squarely, hands jammed in the jacket pockets. "I like to think I'm a rationalist and I'm tough enough to abandon a pet theory when the universe refuses to cooperate. Back to square one."

"And square one is?"

"Vivian Horstmann killed herself." Cooper stared south at the distant cluster of skyscrapers sharply delineated in the sunlight. "I accepted the idea at first and it stood up to scrutiny. Let's take that as the axiom and see where it leads."

"OK. Start with suicide and what do we have?"

"A traumatized son who's certain his mother couldn't have killed herself. And who showed convincing proof, I thought."

"But how convincing was it really?"

"Convincing enough to get the police back on the job."

"Except it wasn't, not really. It was the attacks on you that got their attention, wasn't it?"

"Yeah, I guess so. Shostak considered Dominic's evidence and rejected it."

"So like they said, everything that says this death might be a murder comes from the kid."

"Or from me. And what have I really established? Motive. Period. A possible motive. For someone who may never even have heard of Vivian Horstmann."

"So it really did all come from Dominic. The open curtains, the pad of yellow paper, everything."

Cooper's grip on the cable tightened. "Looking at it now, I'm amazed I ever bought it. I guess I wanted as badly as Dominic to believe that Vivian would never have killed herself."

"That's understandable."

"I still have trouble with it." Cooper tried to see it, to see the Vivian he had known, drunk enough and despairing enough and tired enough to stagger out to that wrought iron balcony railing, to look out into the vast murmuring night, climb clumsily over and let go. "She had to have changed a lot."

"That happens."

Cooper resisted the tide of sadness he felt rising and forced his mind back to the facts. "All right, Vivian killed herself. And somebody's trying to kill the boy. And me, but probably just incidentally. How could her suicide possibly make the attacks on us logical? 'Find a scenario that fits,' Shostak said. OK, I'm trying."

"Does every scenario that explains the need to kill Dominic have to do with inheritance? You got your idea about Billy Galloway from learning about Vivian's real father, but are there other ideas out there? Inheritance isn't the only reason people get murdered."

"Yeah, there are other reasons. To shut them up, for instance. What does Dominic know that can't be said?"

"For that matter, what does the need to kill Dominic have to do with Vivian's death in the first place? Like the guy said, we don't really know what the attacks on you have to do with Vivian going out the window."

Stuffing his hands in his pockets and hunching his chin into the collar of his jacket against a devious wind, Cooper tried to clear his mind of prejudice and think it through. "I was proud of my idea, and it's tough to ignore it now."

"I know. A possible motive for a character like Billy Galloway must be very hard to ignore."

"Especially since, even though Billy might never have heard of Vivian Horstmann, Jack Lime has. I wonder why that son of a bitch bothers me. I keep having the feeling that Jack Lime knew Vivian better than he let on."

Diana was silent, looking out over the restless lake. "Figure out how much of what the kid says is true," she said at last.

"Yeah, I guess it's time to consider that last piece of advice." Cooper turned around slowly, taking a sweeping look out over the deep gray shimmer of the lake and then coming back to shore, seeing the bare trees in the park and the dull gray and brown of the city beyond. "I'm going to need to walk to think this all through."

"Well, if I'm going to walk my ten miles at work tonight, I'm not walking with you. I'll be home with my feet up. Thinking." She smiled at Cooper, that crooked little smile that dimpled one corner of her mouth. "I guess you're safer on the streets than sitting at home. But don't walk down any blind alleys. And if you see that Camaro, don't walk, run. OK?''

"Yeah, OK. Don't worry. These boots were made for flying.''

He walked for a long time, down Sheridan and then Broadway and into the quiet neighborhoods to the south and west, where there were lots of one-family houses and black trees hanging over the street. He walked down to Bryn Mawr and back over to Broadway, where he sat in a coffee shop with fogged windows under the El and drank bad coffee and kept thinking. He hopped the El back north and went home, watchful but too tired and irritable to think seriously about somebody trying it again. He slipped in through the back and put his feet up on the windowsill. He was tired and he had a headache and his hand hurt. He was also more confused than when he had started thinking.

The telephone rang. Cooper went wearily across the room and picked up the receiver.

"Yeah," he said.

"Cooper MacLeish," said a voice, a neutral man's voice.

"Yeah."

"I want to talk to you.''

There was a silence. This wasn't Shostak or Harrison; Cooper wondered what other cops they might have decided to throw at him. "Who are you?'' he said.

"My name's Bill Galloway. I understand you've been talking about me to people.''

Cooper stood still, his mind racing, trying to catch up. The voice had had the feigned boredom used in making threats, and after the first moment Cooper stood waiting for the threat to come. But nothing came over the line for a few seconds except faint breathing. "I might have mentioned you," Cooper finally said, lamely.

"That's what I want to talk about.''

Cooper sat down on the couch. "So talk.''

"I don't like talking about things like this on the phone. I like talking to people face to face.''

"The phone's good enough for me.''

There was a little exhalation at the other end of the line. "Look. You got nervous last night and ran away, OK. I should have called before I sent my people. But this kind of business, we gotta sit down across a table from one another, have some drinks and talk. On the phone, I can't see you, you can't see me, I can't see who's in the room with you and vice-a-versa. Right?''

After a moment Cooper said, ''I'm not sure I see what we have to talk about.''

''You don't? Somebody starts spreading rumors about me, you don't see why I might want to have a talk with him, find out who put the bug up his ass?''

Cooper remembered Valenti explaining things to him the night before. ''Yeah, I guess.''

''I don't take it personally, but you gotta understand I can't take it lying down, right?''

''It was just an idea. The cops don't buy it anyway.'' Cooper felt craven saying it.

''Well I'm certainly glad to hear that. I'd still like to have you over for a couple of beers and work it all out. I'd like to make sure we lay this little bit of business to rest. You understand?''

''Yeah.'' Cooper was staring hard out the window, with the feeling things were going too fast for him.

''Good. Now why don't you come down and see me at my place? I don't want to scare you again, sending around two big guys like that. You know where Harbor Point Tower is?''

''Uh, sure.''

''Then why don't you come on down here and we'll get things straightened out, OK?''

''What, right away?''

''Why not?''

''I can't make it. I got business to attend to.''

''All right, attend to your business. Talk to whoever you have to talk to. Bring a friend if you like. The more the merrier. How much time do you need?''

Cooper thought frantically. He didn't know how to get in touch with Shostak and Harrison at short notice. ''I don't know. Maybe the rest of the afternoon.''

''OK. How about six o'clock? That give you enough time?''

''Yeah, that should do it.''

''All right, see you then. Try not to be late, OK?''

After he hung up Cooper sat still for a while, recovering from the surprise and trying to figure just what was going on. After a while he reached for the phone again.

He talked to a cop at Area Six who was having a bad day and was irritated to have to spend time on the phone with people like Cooper. Cooper outlasted him and managed to leave a message for Shostak and Harrison to call him. He hung up and stared at the phone for a second and then dialed the 24th District and asked for Valenti, to be told that the Lieutenant wouldn't be on for another hour. Cooper hung up without even leaving his name.

If Valenti was right, he didn't really have anything to worry about. He'd tell Billy—or Bill, apparently—what had given him the idea, reassure him that the cops thought it was non-sense, apologize, say good night. If Valenti was right.

Cooper went and got a beer out of the refrigerator. It was a bitch to open because he could only grasp it with one hand. He swore at it and finally got it open by sitting and holding the bottle between his thighs. He went back to the living room and sat on the couch and drank it. Outside, the sun was beginning to decline.

What if he just didn't show? Billy would send someone after him again, for sure. Was there really any danger?

For insurance, he'd tell a few people where he was going tonight. A few key people, like the detectives. Valenti, too. Diana, anybody who would listen. Would Billy Galloway invite him down to Harbor Point if he was planning to kill him?

Cooper drank half the beer and thought about it all, and decided the answer was no. Valenti had to be right.

He had sat next to the phone and when it rang again all he had to do was put the beer between his legs and stretch out his good hand. Dominic said, "Hey, where you been? We've been trying to call you."

"I had stuff to do. What's going on?"

"We're down at the Hyatt, you know on Wacker?"

"Yeah."

"My dad's staying here. We thought you could come down and meet us here and then we could go out for dinner or something."

"Uh . . . sounds good."

"Are you OK? You sound kind of weird."

"I'm just tired. I'll be ready this evening, don't worry."

"OK. My dad says how about six o'clock?"

"Make it . . . let's say seven. I got something else to do at six." Lay a trail, Cooper thought suddenly. "I have to go see a guy at Harbor Point Tower. That's not too far from the Hyatt. I should be able to get done and get over to the hotel by seven. If I'm late, you could always call over there. The guy's name is Galloway. Billy Galloway."

"Billy Galloway?"

"Yeah. Call over if it gets late. Harbor Point Tower. But I should be out of there by seven."

"Man, you really sound tired. You sure you're not . . . I mean, you're not hurting too much or anything?"

"No, I'm fine. I'll get in a nap and be all set. What's your dad's room number?"

"Uh . . . three sixty-one. We're gonna go out again in a while, but we'll be back before seven. OK?"

"Cool. See you then."

Cooper finished the beer. He wanted a nap, but he knew he wouldn't sleep with things on his mind. He kicked the things around a little more, then gave up.

With all the coming and going through the alley, Cooper hadn't picked up his mail in a couple of days. He needed something to distract him, and he was able to muster the energy to go down and fish a handful of envelopes from the mailbox.

Three of them were junkmail and one was a bill. The big manila envelope had the name M. Moreland in the corner. Upstairs Cooper threw the other envelopes on the steamer trunk and sat down on the couch, tearing open the manila envelope and sliding out the sheets inside.

They were photocopies of articles from Moreland's paper, with dates from the late seventies through 1982. Cooper leafed through them once just looking at the headlines: NORTH SHORE VANDALS NABBED, GALLOWAY SON HELD IN BEATING, BARRINGTON DRUG RAID NETS SEVEN, PROBATION FOR GALLOWAY IN DRUG CASE, CHARGES DROPPED IN '81 ARSON SCHEME . . . Cooper could see from the headlines that a fair amount of Galloway money had gone to get good lawyers for Billy. He went back to the beginning and started skimming.

Galloway apparently became incensed when his car was struck
from behind by Werner's truck. According to witnesses Galloway
then produced tire chains with which he allegedly assaulted Werner . . . Among those arrested in the sweep was William Galloway, 24, son of Chicago millionaire Alban Galloway . . . State's
attorneys expressed anger at the judge's refusal to allow the evidence of Pilarski, which they said was crucial to their prosecution
of Galloway . . . Donaldson had requested a restraining order to
protect her from Galloway . . .

Cooper sifted slowly through the pages, grimacing, holding them as if they were soaked in filth. Finally he slapped
them down on the steamer trunk and they fanned out over the
top. Cooper sat with his elbows on his knees, glaring at them.
    Billy Galloway, the son of a bitch. He hadn't liked the way
he'd sounded on the phone, hadn't liked anything at all about
him since Moreland had first mentioned him. And he was
going to have to walk into his place tonight and be polite to
him.
    It would have been nice to nail him. But the idea seemed
to have gone south, like Flores's Camaro the night before.
    Ricardo Flores, 23. The name was there, in black-and-
white, near the end of a column of type. Cooper stared at it
for a second or two and then pounced on the paper. He
snatched it from the sheaf and stared at the headline: GUILTY
PLEA IN RUSH ST. BEATING. Cooper started reading and then
had to start over again because he was too excited to understand what he was seeing.

A Humboldt Park man was given probation Monday in the beating of Los Angeles businessman Howard Strachan behind a Rush
St. tavern in March . . . Ricardo Flores, 23, pleaded guilty to a
charge of battery . . . Strachan had maintained in his deposition
to police that the beating was ordered by William Galloway, a
former business associate and son of transportation magnate Alban Galloway . . . Prosecutors declined to bring charges against
Galloway, saying no evidence had been presented to support Strachan's allegations . . .

Cooper read it through again, then stood slowly, brandish-
ing the paper to an invisible audience. He carried the paper

over to the window and read the article again. He stared out at the stripped trees, the paper in his hand dangling at his side.

Proof. Of what?

That Teardrop was on Billy Galloway's payroll.

Meaning?

Meaning I was right. About everything?

Find a scenario that fits. Find one that involves Vivian Horstmann killing herself, 'cause that's what she did.

All right, there it is. There it was all the time. All the time you were walking around trying to think it through, like a two-bit Sherlock Holmes.

Even if Vivian did kill herself, Billy still has the motive. Whether or not he killed Vivian, it's still to his advantage if Dominic dies before the old man. Maybe it was Vivian's death that put the idea into his head in the first place. He could have known about his old man's will. They'd be grooming him to take over when Alban died; Billy would know about his affairs.

And no matter how much Billy stood to make already, the Billy depicted in these clippings would see a chance to reap a few hundred thousand more, just for the sport.

Billy would have known of Vivian, for sure. Jack Lime had known her, and Billy would talk to Jack Lime. Maybe his dad had even told him about that fling with Adelle. When Billy heard about Vivian killing herself, the light would go on. Billy wouldn't even have to know the details of the will. He would just have to know or suspect that his father intended to leave something to Vivian, and have a nasty mind.

Billy did have a nasty mind, judging from the times he'd shown up in the news. And he knew nasty people like Flores who did nasty little jobs for him.

Cooper tried the phone again, even though it had been only a few minutes. He left another message for Shostak and Harrison and left one for Valenti this time, to call him.

Before he went calling on Billy Galloway, he wanted to talk to some policemen.

16

WHEN THE PHONE woke him the room was dark and his mouth was dry. He scrambled to sit up and reach for the phone at the other end of the couch. A glance at his watch showed five-thirty. He answered and heard Valenti say, "Let me guess. Somebody in a BMW drove really fast down your block and gave you the finger."

"Hey, listen. A lot's happened since I saw you last night. I saw the guy with the teardrop, hanging around the neighborhood. And today Billy Galloway called me."

"Yeah? What'd he say?"

"He wants me to come see him."

"Well, that should be fun. I hear his guests snort only the finest. Let me know how it goes."

"Listen to me. I found out Flores did some work for Galloway once."

"Who's Flores?"

"The guy with the teardrop."

"What kind of work?"

"He beat a guy up. Back in '81. The guy claimed Galloway ordered it but it was never proved."

"No shit. That's interesting."

"Yeah. What do you think now?"

"About what?"

"About Galloway being behind this. Even if Vivian Horstmann killed herself, Billy still has a strong interest in seeing Dominic dead before his old man is. That's a motive, now we have a link between him and Teardrop, shit. What do you want?"

"You talk to Shostak?"

"I left a message for him. Look, my ass may be on the line here. Don't you think Galloway's at least a bit . . . shady?"

"Hell yes, he's shady. For a lot more things than you know about. But what do you want me to do about it? I'm not a homicide detective anymore."

"You're the only cop I could get a hold of. Look, in half an hour I'm supposed to go talk to him about all the rumors I've been starting. I have a feeling if I don't show up he'll just come get me. I don't know if he's likely to try and kill me when I walk in the door or what. What I'm asking is what I should do. Go talk to him? Take along a bodyguard? Flee the country? What?"

Cooper expected a flip answer but Valenti was silent for a moment before asking, "Where does he want you to meet him?"

"At his place. Harbor Point Tower."

"His place? Hell, he wouldn't invite you to his place if he wanted to kill you. What's he gonna do, saw you up and flush you down the toilet?"

"That's what I thought. So what exactly does he want?"

"What I told you last night. He wants to find out what's going on."

"But what if he really is trying to kill the kid?"

"Then for Christ's sake don't tell him you know about Flores. If he really is the guy, he's trying to find out how much you know. Tell him it came to you in a dream but when you woke up it all sounded like bullshit."

"I told him on the phone you all think it's bullshit."

"Fine. Tell him we know where you are, too. Tell him a hundred people know where you are. The more the better."

"Yeah, I already figured I'd do that."

"And tell Shostak about the connection between him and Flores. Maybe that is important, I don't know."

"You're still skeptical, huh?"

"I just can't see somebody with that much money worrying about the sum we're talking about here. I just don't see it. What I think is maybe whoever is trying to kill the kid knows about the connection and got in touch with Flores to make it look like Billy was behind it. I don't know. I got my own worries here."

"OK." Cooper exhaled, staring at the news clips spread out across the trunk. "I'll go reassure Billy. Just remember where I went if you hear I've gone missing."

"Don't worry, MacLeish. If Billy wanted you dead you'd be dead by now."

"That's a comfort. Thanks."

Time to get going. Cooper got up and went to the bathroom and pissed. He drank some water and combed his hair, then went out into the dark living room and stood at the window, watching the night descend.

He wondered if it was insane to go down there and meet Billy, unarmed. For a second or two he thought about weapons, wondering if he could get some ordnance on short notice. Somebody he knew had to have a piece he could take along, just for comfort. Finally Cooper decided that that would just be raising the stakes; if he was seriously worried about the danger he shouldn't even go.

He wished the detectives would call him. He'd feel better having talked to them before walking into Billy Galloway's lair. With the certainty now that Galloway had hired Flores, the picture was nice and sharp. Galloway wanted Dominic dead; he had tracked him down to the restaurant and was still tracking him. But as soon as Shostak and Harrison got Cooper's message it would be over. They had enough now.

In the meantime he had to stall. If he just gave it a miss tonight, Galloway's gorillas would be back in force. They wouldn't want Cooper on the loose, spreading loose talk. So he had to show up and buy time. Thinking it through, Cooper decided that Valenti was right. Galloway was after reassurance; he wanted to find out what Cooper knew. So Cooper would tell him: not much. Just an idea, so much bullshit. He'd back down, scrape and shuffle a bit. And walk out alive.

Still, it would be nice to tell someone else where he was going. Diana was at work. Cooper thought for a minute and decided he'd already told the people who really counted, the cops. He took a deep breath and picked up his jacket.

Wrestling the Valiant down Lake Shore Drive, hampered by the cast, he passed the building where Vivian had lived and then died, giving it a brief glance as he went by. Twenty-three stories was a long, long way to fall, a bad way for anybody to end, a bad way especially for somebody you had loved to wind up.

Harbor Point Tower was a sleek black shaft of a high-rise that stood with a couple of lesser mates out at the end of

Randolph Street, all the more isolated since they'd fixed the S-curve and rerouted Lake Shore Drive around the complex. Cooper wasn't sure where the hell to park; he went down Randolph to the end and drove up the little street they'd put in just for the tower, seeing nothing but No Parking signs and watchful doormen. He decided he'd have to put the Valiant in one of the pay lots on the lower level and went all the way back to get on Lower Randolph and head back out in the fluorescent-lit netherworld two stories below street level.

There was a pay lot in the basement of one of the other high-rises where he could get away for three bucks if he was no more than an hour. He put it there and then had to walk back outside, climb the steps all the way to street level and go up the block to Harbor Point Tower.

The wind was coming in off the lake like a knife in the dark. Cooper walked up the drive past the little private park with the tower looming above him, black steel and opaque glass, lights glowing dimly behind windows high in the rounded corners. The doorman looked like an organ grinder's monkey in his uniform but it didn't stop him from looking at Cooper as if he were embarrassing everybody by walking in the door. Cooper made sure to say Billy, not Bill, when he asked at the long desk in the lobby. The man by the phone gave him a polite smile, called upstairs in a low discreet voice, and pointed Cooper to an elevator.

The elevator was as quiet and discreet as the man at the desk. It took Cooper up seventeen floors in a whisper. Cooper stepped out into a hallway with no decoration whatsoever, just long expanses of white wall above gold carpet, and looked for 1732, the year of George Washington's birth and the number of Billy Galloway's suite.

When he reached it he paused, wondering if he really wanted to walk into the lion's den. Play it dumb, he reminded himself, and then knocked three times, ignoring the doorbell set into the woodwork. After a few seconds the door was opened by one of the men who had come to see Cooper the night before.

He was as big as Cooper remembered, fullback- or linebacker-sized with a scar at the bridge of his nose that could have been left by a football helmet. He was over the hill now, the muscle starting to go and the belly starting to strain against the electric blue shirt under the cream sport jacket. He took a look at Cooper and stood aside without comment, watching him with dispassionate stone-colored eyes.

Cooper nodded at him. "Billy Galloway at home?" he said.

The fullback nodded once in the direction of the windows that had already caught Cooper's attention through the doorway to the left. Cooper took a few wary steps into the living room, taking in the broad sweep of distant lights at a glance and then seeing the man rising from the couch that faced the windows.

He was a big man but not hard like the fullback; he had been given a large frame but wasted it, just eaten and drunk until it was rounded off, hung with forty pounds or so of fat. Even so he was reasonably handsome in an arrogant sort of way, with a jutting chin that rescued the heavy jowls somewhat and a curving nose and blue eyes that didn't look stupid. His hair was a dull blond and there was plenty of it sweeping at an angle over his forehead and over the tops of his ears. He had on a bright orange Hawaiian shirt with a green pattern, the shirttail hanging out over white deck pants. He had a glass in his hand and he stood looking at Cooper with the chin in the air for a moment before saying, "You're Mac-Leish, huh?"

"I'm MacLeish." Cooper gave back his stare. He was conscious of the fullback behind him, moving softly. That made him uncomfortable and his eyes flicked to the windows, trying to find him in the reflections there.

"Hell of a view, isn't it?" said Billy Galloway.

"Yeah." The room was in the round corner of the building and the windows covered a full ninety degrees of arc. Cooper's gaze took in the view and also the furniture that looked as if it had come direct from a showroom in the Merchandise Mart. In front of the camelback sofa Galloway had risen from was a cocktail table that consisted of a thick slab of glass on a couple of black marble pedestals. That would be hell to shift if he ever decided to move, Cooper thought. There was a bottle of Chivas on the table and a bucket of ice.

"What happened to your hand?" Galloway said.

"Long story," said Cooper.

Galloway shook his head. "Sit down." He pointed to a chair at the end of the sofa. The chair was upholstered in finely striped fabric, had flare arms, and was so thickly padded that Cooper knew he'd be practically immobilized when he sat down in it. Cooper had gathered there would be no shaking of hands and he made his way to the chair slowly and perched on the edge, elbows on his knees. Galloway took a sip of his scotch, still standing, and said, "Want a drink? I can give you a beer or whatever else you have a taste for."

"Beer's fine," said Cooper, meeting the stare.

Galloway gave in first and turned to the fullback and said, "Get him some of that Japanese beer why don't you?" Then he sat down, setting his drink on the glass table. The fullback disappeared through the doorway. Galloway sat back on the sofa, getting comfortable. "Nobody calls me Billy anymore," he said.

"Sorry."

"That's OK." He looked at Cooper a moment longer and said, "Who told you to call me Billy?"

Cooper twined his fingers and frowned a bit. "Everybody I talked to calls you Billy."

"My friends call me Bill. I guess you've been talking to my enemies."

Cooper blinked at him, thinking. "I'd call them neutral observers," he said.

"Who are they?" Billy's chin jutted a bit as he asked the question.

"A newspaper reporter and a couple of cops."

Billy leaned forward to pick up his glass. "A reporter." He took a drink and stared out the window into the night. "Shit."

"He did all the talking," Cooper said. "I'd never heard of you before he told me about you."

Billy watched him for a moment and then drained the glass and set it down. "I could have just sent a platoon of lawyers over to talk to you, you know."

"That would probably cost you more than it would cost me."

"Mm-hm, that's what I figured. Besides, I'd just as soon things didn't get out of hand. And I bet that's what you're counting on too, isn't it?" Not understanding, Cooper just looked at him. Billy shook his head and breathed a little sigh. "OK, what is all this shit, anyway?"

The fullback came up softly behind Cooper and set down a beer bottle on the table at his elbow, a smaller version of the one in front of the couch. Cooper had the impression the man didn't much like playing butler. Galloway leaned back and said, "I mean, who the hell are you and why is it worth your while to make up stories about me and tell them to cops?"

Cooper looked at the beer bottle but didn't pick it up. He had decided in the car coming down to tell it more or less as it had come to him, only not all of it. "About a month ago," he said, "a woman named Vivian Horstmann killed herself. She jumped off her balcony onto Lake Shore Drive. I used to know her." He looked at Galloway, hoping to see reaction, but Billy was just staring at him with hard blue eyes. "I heard she had a son and I had reason to think he might be mine. I tracked the kid down and he told me he didn't think she had killed herself. He thought somebody helped her. I didn't believe him until somebody shot at us one night, and then two guys jumped me and tried to make me tell them where the kid was. That convinced me and I started wondering why someone would want both him and his mother dead." Cooper paused, waiting for comment if it was going to come and organizing his thoughts. "I started asking around. It turns out Vivian was your half-sister."

"No shit." If Billy was surprised, he gave no sign beyond the words.

After a moment Cooper went on. "I talked to her mother and she told me the story and we managed to find out that your father left Vivian a lot of money in his will. And it occurred to me that if both Vivian and her son were dead before your father, the money he left Vivian reverts to you. That's where the idea came from. That's all. I told the cops who were working on Vivian's death about it and I told one other cop, too, a friend of mine. That's all the people I've told and they think it's horseshit. So I don't think you have much to worry about."

"What about you? You think it's horseshit?"

A penetrating question, Cooper thought. He smiled and said, "I'd be a fool to say anything but yes, wouldn't I?"

Galloway shrugged. "What do you think I'm gonna do, kill you because you've got a vivid imagination? You're entitled to your fantasies. The only thing that bothers me, see, is if you start spreading them around. 'Cause even bullshit can hurt somebody like me."

"Yeah, I can see that."

"But before we talk about that, let me ask you this. How much do you think my old man left her?"

"About five hundred thousand, I heard."

Galloway laughed and shook his head. He laughed a little harder and looked over his shoulder to where the fullback was sitting on a hard chair in the dining alcove. "Hear that, Don? This guy thinks I'm gonna kill some lady for half a million bucks."

"Pretty funny," said the fullback morosely. He had lit himself a cigarette and he took a long drag on it.

"Yeah, pretty funny." Galloway looked at Cooper for a moment, shaking his head. "The furniture in this place is worth more than that. I want five hundred thousand bucks, I can raise it in half an hour. Nobody's gonna believe I would kill the lady for five hundred thousand bucks."

"OK. Nobody will believe it. I guess I was wrong." Cooper put his hands on his knees, starting to rise. "Sorry to take your time."

"Wait a second. Don't be so anxious to run off. Drink your beer. Hey, what's the matter, you think we're gonna poison you? Don, get the man another beer and don't open it until you bring it to him, OK? He doesn't trust us."

There was a pause. Cooper settled back onto the edge of the chair and waited. He was on the verge of saying not to bother with another beer but he wanted to see if the fullback would do as he was told. After a short delay Cooper heard the chair in the dining room scrape and then heard the fullback walk slowly into the kitchen. Galloway poured more scotch into his glass and crossed his legs, getting comfortable and lowering his eyebrows at Cooper, getting intense.

"So the story is horseshit. You know it's horseshit and the cops know it's horseshit and the papers are gonna know it's horseshit. So why am I worried?" He waited for Cooper to answer.

After a moment Cooper said, "I can see why you'd be

pissed off. But worried, no. I don't think you have to be worried."

"But I am. 'Cause you see—innuendo, baby. Innuendo can do a lot of damage to a person in my position.'Specially 'cause I did have my run-ins with the law when I was younger. Hell, who didn't? Maybe I had too much leeway, too much money for a kid to have. OK, I can see that. But you think other people would have made the papers like I did with the things that happened? Fuck, no. But me, Alban Galloway's boy, hell, they splashed it all over. It's taken me a while to live some of that shit down." Cooper just watched him, thinking of Flores kicking the hell out of people for Billy Galloway.

"Must have been rough," he said.

Billy gave him a sharp look. "OK, I can hear you thinking. 'What's this rich kid got to complain about?' You think growing up with millions of bucks means no problems. Well all right, not the kind of problems other people have, maybe. But it ain't easy, pal, let me tell you. That money just lays there on top of you, all the time. Sometimes all I wanted was to be a normal kid, but hey—that's Alban Galloway's boy, you know, the rich kid. And they never let you forget it."

There were soft footsteps behind Cooper and the fullback was there at his elbow again, with a bottle of beer and an opener. The cigarette hung from the corner of his mouth. He looked very bored. He held the bottle up for Cooper to see, opened it, and set it down with a lightly louder clunk. He picked up the cap and the first bottle and walked back toward the dining room.

"Have a drink for Christ's sake," said Galloway. Cooper slowly leaned back in the chair, sinking into its depths, and reached for the beer. It had a picture of a Japanese woman in a black dress on the label and it tasted vaguely woody.

"That's better. Cheers." Billy took a drink and went on. "Let me give you an example. When I was eighteen I wanted to join the Marines. I was ready, man. I'd gone down and talked to the recruiters and everything. Soon as I had that diploma I was headed for Parris Island. I wasn't gonna have to listen to any more of that rich kid shit ever again. And you know what? I told my old man what I was gonna do and he said if I did I could kiss my inheritance good-bye. He wasn't going to have his heir down there in the dirt with all the other grunts. He said if I wanted I could go in as an officer, after college. He had everything all set up for me at Princeton and nothing was gonna fuck up the plans. He tried to bribe me and then practically kidnapped me, had his people cart me off to the Bahamas to keep me from joining up. Good-bye, Marines.''

Cooper took a slow pull on the beer and said, "You didn't miss much.''

"Maybe not. But all that's just by way of saying your life isn't always your own when you've got a lot of money. Know what I mean?''

Cooper thought for a moment and decided he couldn't resist, just couldn't resist saying it. "You could have kissed your inheritance good-bye.''

Billy stared at him for a moment and then laughed, one harsh bitter laugh. "That's easy for you to say, pal. That's very easy for you to say.''

Cooper shrugged. "Forget it then.''

Billy shook his head slowly. "I thought I was starting to get a little respect, you know? So now what do I hear? I hear some lady comes talking to my old man, some guy's sold her a story about my killing somebody. Killing somebody, for Christ's sake, for pocket change. Pocket change, chump change. Making me out to be not only greedy, but *stupid.*'' He drank and set his glass back down on the table. "Shit.''

Cooper said nothing. Billy studied him for a moment and then pointed a finger at him.

"Now listen. I don't want to hear any more bullshit.'' He paused, waiting for a response again, and Cooper nodded.

"All right,'' he said. "Like I say, the cops thought it was ridiculous from the beginning.''

"I don't mean that,'' said Galloway, holding out a hand in a stop-right-there gesture and firming his lips. "I mean about how you got the bright idea and all. I know somebody's made it worth your while to have this bright idea, and that's OK. That's how the game works. But it stops here. I can be as nice a guy or as hard a guy as you want. Carrot and stick, baby.''

Cooper stared at him, mystified. He tilted his head slightly in perplexity and took another drink of beer. Galloway went on.

"Carrot and stick. How much did they give you?"

Cooper swallowed slowly and frowned at Galloway. "Who?"

Billy Galloway seemed to sag on the couch. He shook his head sadly. "Look, I wasn't born yesterday. We're all adults in this room. You did your bit. I don't hold it against you. But it's over. You want the carrot, you got it. Provided one thing. Provided you get amnesia when you walk out that door. You forget you know any reporters, you forget you talked to any cops. You forget you ever heard of me. You go back to jockeying that cab all over town. Yeah, I did a little research on you. You go back to driving a cab and if they got any more propositions for you, you tell 'em you're spoken for. Understand?"

Cooper stared hard at him for a moment, feeling like a six-year-old in the oversized chair, and then nodded. "Got it."

"If not, there's always the stick," said Galloway. His eyes went toward the dining room and settled on the fullback, just for a moment. "Lawyer pressure doesn't mean much to you, maybe his kind of pressure will. You ever see him take out a quarterback?"

So he was a linebacker, not a fullback, Cooper knew he should have recognized Don by now but he wasn't that keen a football fan. He just nodded.

"OK. So you don't want to wind up like Joe Theismann or somebody, you get out of the rumor business. Right?"

Cooper drank more beer and thought. His eyes went to the windows and he looked out at the lights. He could see the vast bejeweled sprawl of the South Side stretching away into the night and the empty harbor running south to the planetarium out on its lonely spit of land in the impenetrable black of the lake. He thought a moment longer and said, "How big a carrot are we talking about?"

Galloway's lips went grim again, as if he were disappointed. "Big enough for you, small-timer." His hand went to the pocket of his Hawaiian shirt and he pulled out a thick sheaf of bills, folded in half. He leaned forward and tossed them on the end of the cocktail table in front of Cooper. "That's a one-time payment. A generous payment. You get

greedy, try and come back for another touch, remember two things. One, you can't blackmail me with bullshit. Two, I walk softly but I have a big stick sitting in my dining room."
He looked at the man in the dining room and smiled. Cooper looked too. The old football player was carefully tapping his cigarette on the side of an ashtray, absorbed in the task.

Cooper set down the beer and leaned forward with some effort and picked up the sheaf of bills. They were hundreds, with Ben Franklin looking up at him pleasantly. He counted them; there were twenty-five of them. He squared their edges and folded them in half again and stood up.

"I understand," he said. He took a couple of steps so he was standing directly in front of Galloway, looking down at him, holding the wad in his hand. Cooper hoped he had read everything right; he wasn't entirely sure what was going on but he had a feeling that he was in the driver's seat.

"Who do you think put me up to it?" he said.

Galloway just looked at him, blinking slowly. "To tell you the truth, I don't really give a shit," he said. "Just make sure it never hits the papers, not even speculation. I'd be real unhappy if it did."

Cooper nodded and looked down at the money in his hand, more cash than he'd ever held at one time. He hadn't been shot or poisoned and he had taken Billy Galloway for twenty-five hundred tax-free dollars. He smiled.

"You don't have anything to worry about," he said.

Billy Galloway hauled himself up off the couch. "I better not," he said slowly, facing Cooper, looking at him with heavy-lidded eyes.

Cooper reached out and stuffed the wad back in Billy's shirt pocket. "Far as I'm concerned, I never heard of you or your father or Vivian what's-her-name. But keep your money. You might need it when Jeeves over there asks you for a raise." Cooper stepped around the table and skirted the sofa and made for the door. Galloway let him get almost there before he spoke.

"This is not an option I'm offering you. Take the money or not, but your mouth stays shut. I want that clear before you walk out of here."

Cooper stopped and turned to face him. "I've said all I'm

going to say to anybody about it. But if my mouth stays shut it won't be because you want it to."

In the elevator going down, Cooper shook his head. He had a feeling he hadn't left the right impression with Billy Galloway.

Outside the wind was still feinting and thrusting. Cooper turned up his collar and marched toward the stairs that led down to the parking garage. He realized suddenly that he had forgotten to tell Billy about all the people who knew where he was. He laughed, feeling the tension in his jaws and in his stomach ease a little. He'd made it out in one piece.

Going down the steps to the lower level, he checked his watch; he hadn't even been up there fifteen minutes. The Hyatt was right across the way, almost within walking distance; he'd be early for his date with Dominic. Parking near the Hyatt would be a bitch and for a second he considered just leaving the Valiant in the garage and hiking over to the hotel, but he'd just have to hike back later and he had confidence in his ability to muscle into a semilegal place somewhere.

At the bottom of the steps he swept a quick look around the eerily lit underworld, with massive beams holding up the overpasses above, basement loading docks for the high-rises, and cars parked in the gloom along both sides of the street.

"Hey, buddy." Facing him was a beat-up light green Dodge Econoline van parked at the curb by the foot of the steps, idling. Inside, a man had a road map spread out over the steering wheel. He was looking at Cooper through the windshield, beckoning to him with an impatient gesture. "Help me out a second, would you?" He had short black hair and a moustache and he looked irritated. Cooper took a couple of steps toward the van, seeing the man lean over the seat to talk to him through the window on the passenger side, illuminated by the interior light of the van. Cooper had almost reached the window when he focused on the little blue teardrop on the man's left cheek, and by then the hand that had gone down to the seat was coming up with a gun in it.

Every crisis system in him kicked in at once and he was away, running past the back of the van as the muzzle flashed. The detonation filled his head and he felt the shock of the bullet going past his ear. After a half second he realized he was still alive. He'd run blindly, just trying to get away from the gun, but in the right direction. The drive that led to the parking garage was a hundred feet ahead. He ran propelled by the surging energy of fear.

Behind him the van was slapped into gear and tires screeched. Cooper had almost reached the drive when he realized that the van was in reverse, coming after him. He made the corner of the building and saw sky above where a vast tract of empty ground stretched out to the river. The lighted garage entrance in the blank wall of the high-rise was just ahead on the right and he had enough of a lead that he should make it inside before the van could come down the drive after him.

Except that as he cut left on the gravel at the end of the sidewalk his feet went out from under him. He hit the ground and rolled, stunned, pain shooting up his arm from his injured hand. He picked himself up and scrambled ahead after a second or two but by the time he gained his footing on the asphalt the van had reached the head of the drive. After a moment of wrestling with the gears Teardrop pointed the van down the alley and came after him. Cooper was fifty feet from the door to the garage when he took a look back and saw the van bearing down on him, headlights off.

With the instinct for survival that is the infantryman's God, he knew the only way to go was to the right, to keep Teardrop and the gun on the opposite side of the van from him. Cooper veered, twisted to look, saw the van swerve over right on top of him, about half a second from running him over.

He dived for the side of the drive, hit grass and rolled. Brakes squealed. He came up to his knees and looked, that clean, hard adrenaline high in place of the fear now, primed. The van had overshot him and stopped with its front wheels off the drive twenty feet ahead. Cooper was to the right rear of the van and he knew Teardrop could see him in the mirror. His first reflex was to turn around and run for the street, but he knew there was no help that way and the van could move a lot faster than he could. As the engine roared and the van reversed back onto the drive, turning to bring the front end around to face him, Cooper decided he had to go forward.

He charged, keeping low, as the van wheeled around and the headlights came on. Before they could catch him Cooper dived again, to the left, past the right front of the van, trying to keep out of Teardrop's line of sight. He jolted hard on the asphalt and came up in a crouch at the side of the van while it jerked forward, halted, rocked in place.

And Cooper realized he didn't have to make it into the garage. To his left was maybe five acres of undeveloped unlit wasteland, just beyond the end of the drive, beyond a low bank of gravel that would keep the van from coming after him. He got his balance and was starting to rise, knowing Teardrop would never be able to come around and get off an effective shot before he was out into the darkness, when suddenly the front wheels of the van twisted to the left and came slicing toward him in reverse.

The fender slammed into his hip and the right front wheel burned his right thigh as it swept past. He remembered what his taxi had done to the stickup man and saw the van jerk to a halt again just in front of him, the wheels turning again, straightening out to crush him with the next rush.

He scrambled desperately to the right as the van leapt forward and he tried to flatten himself into the drive as the front end came screaming over him, feeling something scrape over his back, seeing the tire roar past his face with his cheek pressed to the asphalt. He raised his head to look frantically for the back wheels, just in time to hear the brakes squeal again and see the left rear tire slew toward him. He had no room to roll and he had to use every muscle he had to scoot sideways out of its path.

The van stopped and Cooper could see that dark vacant land ahead, the promised land. He started to wriggle forward to get out from under the back of the van but it was reversing again, in the same madhouse whine of engine and tire on asphalt, and he was twisting to see where the next wheel was going to catch him. The van swerved and then the brakes were jammed on again and suddenly everything was quiet because the engine had died.

Cooper lay in that utter quiet with his feet out from under the van, about even with the driver's door, still alive. As he heard the ignition laboring to turn over he had the kind of inspiration that keeps soldiers alive and he was suddenly backing out from under the left side of the van with all the speed he could muster because he had realized that Teardrop couldn't turn the ignition key and hold the gun at the same time.

The engine roared back to life as Cooper emerged from beneath the van, hoping he wasn't too late. He knew he wouldn't have time to fumble at the door with the cast on his hand; it would have to be through the window. He rose to his feet to see Teardrop with his hand on the gear lever; when he saw Cooper he made a swipe for the gun on the dashboard but Cooper had a handful of black hair in his good hand by that time and he pulled with all his weight, slamming Teardrop's head down against the window frame and coming away with a loose tuft of hair. Then he went for the door handle and got it open and pulled the man out before he could collect himself. Teardrop had the gun in his hand and he fired one shot into the night sky as he fell to the asphalt, but then Cooper wound up and place-kicked Teardrop's face about fifty yards with a deep satisfying whack. Teardrop made a grunting noise and was still. Blood seeped from his nostrils as the gun slipped gently from his fingers onto the asphalt. Cooper wound up again and kicked him a second time with all the force of his terror and rage and the head flew back. He saw only the whites of Teardrop's eyes and he knew he shouldn't kick him again or he'd kill him. He bent down and picked up the gun. It was a Ruger revolver, maybe a .38. Cooper pointed it at Teardrop's head and held it there for a moment, just enjoying the view beyond the sights, before letting his hand fall to his side.

Cooper stood panting, leaning on the side of the van, looking down at the man with the teardrop tattooed on his face and waiting for people to come running. He stood like that for what seemed a long time and then swore out loud and wondered where in the hell people were and how anybody could get away with loosing off shots in the middle of a city without anyone taking notice.

Cooper roused himself, stepped around the man on the asphalt and walked toward the entrance to the garage. He had the aftershakes now; he made himself breathe deeply and slowly to get rid of them. He slipped the revolver into the pocket of his jacket. He was going to find someone and wake them up and tell them to get a fucking policeman down here.

Except that as he walked the screaming adrenaline high

subsided and his mind started to work again. Something replaced the terror: something called anger, very deep anger. He stopped outside the pedestrian entrance to the garage, wondering if he shouldn't just go right back up to Billy Galloway's place and put a couple of rounds into his head, spill some blood on his fancy furniture.

No, hold him. Put him and his washed-up football player at gunpoint and let them stare down the muzzle while he called the cops and told them how Billy Galloway had set him up, tied him up in a package for his man Flores.

Only Billy probably had his own ordnance up there and with two of them to watch it could get tricky. The first order of business was to get a cop down here and tell him what was going on. Cooper couldn't believe no one had come out of the garage yet to see what the commotion was about; were they asleep in there?

Cooper stood at the door to the garage and thought of spending half the night trying to explain everything to the bored cops who would come around in a squad car after a few minutes if there was nothing more urgent happening. He turned around and looked at Teardrop lying in a heap with blood running out of his nose onto the asphalt beside the gently idling van. He thought hard for a moment and decided he needed to get Shostak or Harrison or both of them on the line because only they would know enough about what was going on to hustle down here and stick a gaff in Billy Galloway before he swam off somewhere.

Cooper took a deep breath, brushed gravel off his torn jeans, and went into the garage. The attendant in the glassed-in booth to the left of the door was a plump blond woman in a security guard's uniform. She looked up from a magazine when he approached the window and held out her hand for the ticket he shoved at her. He watched her ring it up.

"What the hell's going on outside?" he asked.

"I don't know," she said. "I thought I heard something funny."

"Somebody's lying out there on the drive. He looks hurt. Maybe you should go take a look."

She looked at him to see if he was joking and took his five and gave him change. "I can't leave my position," she said.

"You ought to use that telephone then. The guy's not moving." She frowned at him and he was about to ask her if there was a pay phone he could use, but he decided he wanted to be gone when the cops got here and he nodded at her and went off to find his car, leaving her staring after him.

He drove out the exit on the far side and as he came around back past the drive he saw a car halted there, its headlights illuminating the still unmoving figure of Teardrop, the driver out and leaning over him. Cooper figured Teardrop would be in good hands soon and it was time to find a phone he could use.

His hand was throbbing again and he was still shaking a bit, seeing and feeling it all over again, and he got mixed up in the maze of underground streets. By the time he got himself sorted out he was north of the river and on Grand Avenue. He looked for a phone booth but didn't see one. Finally he spotted a garish little hot dog place with broad red stripes painted on the walls and a phone at the end of the counter. He parked by a fire hydrant and went in and plugged a quarter in the phone. There were no customers in the place and the little bent man behind the counter looked at him with great sadness when he realized he wasn't going to buy a hot dog. Cooper read the number at Area Six off his notebook and punched it in, realizing he was unlikely to find the detectives there but determined to have somebody put him in touch with them no matter what it took.

As it turned out it took nothing more than mentioning their names. There was a wait during which Cooper looked at the damage he'd done to his knee and to the heel of his good hand falling on the gravel, and then Harrison's voice came on the line.

"MacLeish. Tried to call you earlier. You were out."

"Yeah, listen. Can you and Shostak get downtown right away?"

"No, we can't get downtown right away. We ain't slept in more than twenty-four hours and we go back on duty tonight. Only place I'm going is home."

"Listen. Billy Galloway hired the guy with the teardrop to kill me. Richie Flores. He just tried it, just now, and he didn't miss by much. I can prove the guy was working for Galloway. He's worked for him before. I got proof. Now for

Christ's sake get down here and pick me up and let's go get
Galloway.''

"Ho, hold on a minute, man. What do you mean he just
tried?''

"I mean he just damn near blew my fucking head off. I
managed to make him miss and I kicked his face in, but the
point is Galloway set me up. He called me up and . . .''

"Whoa. Shut up a minute. Where are you?''

"I don't know. Grand Avenue somewhere. Grand and Wabash or some fucking place.''

"Where's Flores?''

"Outside a parking garage on Lower Randolph.
Somebody's probably called the police by now.''

"You mean you didn't?''

"I had to talk to you. I start trying to explain things to
some guy who knows nothing about this, I'll be there all
night. We have to get Galloway.''

"You kicked his face in and you ran off and left him.''

"Yeah, now listen.''

"No man, you listen. You get back there and tell the officers on the spot what happened.''

"All right, shit. What about you? You going to arrest Galloway or not?''

"How come you're so sure it was Galloway set you up?''

"Because Flores was waiting for me by the only place I
could have parked around there. Galloway called me and told
me to come down and see him at six. He must have told Flores
to be waiting. All he had to do was wait up by Galloway's
place somewhere, see me make a pass looking for parking,
follow me down to the garage, and go to a phone. After I
talked to Galloway, he called down to Flores to tell him I
was leaving. Son of a bitch, man, what do you want?''

"MacLeish, get a hold of yourself. You got a hold of
yourself? You breathing OK and everything?''

"Yeah, yeah. I'm fine. What?''

"MacLeish, you know why we tried to call you earlier?''
Cooper paused, took a deep breath. "Why?''

"We talked to Murphy this afternoon.''

"Jesus, have you been listening to me? Richie fucking Flores just tried to kill me.''

"Yeah, and you kicked his ass, I know.''

"After he fucking near killed me. You ever had a .38 go off in your face? Try it sometime, then we can just sit around and shoot the shit."

"You're getting testy, man. Maybe I should hang up the phone and not do you a favor after all, let you get yourself arrested."

"What are you talking about?"

"I mean you shouldn't have just run off. Now listen, where are you? I'm gonna call this in for you and have somebody come pick you up."

"What about Billy Galloway?"

"Billy Galloway will keep. He ain't going nowhere. If he set you up, he thinks you're dead, right? Now I want you to get a grip on yourself and keep it this time."

Cooper took another breath. He looked at the floor. He looked at the little bent man behind the counter, who was wiping up spills, pretending not to listen. "All right, I got a grip on myself."

"Cool. Now where are you?"

Cooper looked at the little bent man. "What's the name of this place?"

The man looked at him, sadly. "Rico's," he said. "That's me, Rico."

"Place called Rico's, on Grand, little hole-in-the-wall place," Cooper said into the phone. He saw the little bent man turn away, shaking his head.

"All right. I'll have 'em come get you. Now don't you want to hear what your pal Murphy had to say?"

"Am I going to find it interesting?"

"Yeah, I think you will. Murphy and us had a nice little talk. He's conscious, and man, is he pissed off. He can't believe he let you take him."

"Well, you tell him I'm sorry he woke up."

"I think he is too, with the headache he's got. He had some interesting things to say, once we got a lawyer in there to hold his hand and convinced him that talking was his best bet if he wanted to walk around outside anytime before the twenty-first century."

"All right, what did he say?"

"First of all he asked if we were gonna charge you for clobbering him."

"He what?"

"Don't worry, we said no. With a few other words thrown in. Then I asked him the big question and guess what? He says he doesn't know who hired him."

"He doesn't know?"

"The bad part is, I think he's telling the truth. He says it was Flores came to him with the job, and Flores told him he didn't know either. He was hired by phone, just a voice, took all his instructions by phone and got paid by mail. He threw the envelopes away but of course they wouldn't have told us anything anyway."

"And you believe this guy."

"I think if he knew who hired him he'd tell us to save his own worthless ass. I think he really doesn't know. Flores might, but I wouldn't get my hopes up. It's happened before. If you know the right people you can hire yourself some muscle without meeting anybody face to face. You get a reference, you call 'em up, they give you an address to send the money to. You go through a cutout, slip in an extra hundred for the guy who handles the mail. Be careful with the envelopes and they'll never trace you. These guys took calls at a bar out on Milwaukee. After they got a sort of retainer at first they were supposed to be at the bar at certain times twice a week to pick up the pay phone when it rang."

"Why are you telling me all this now?"

"Because I want you to have the big picture. I want you to understand things, so you don't run around getting hysterical. Now listen, I haven't told you the best part yet."

"OK, what's the best part?"

"You wanna know what Murphy said when we asked him just what his instructions were?"

"What?"

"Check this out. He said the first time, when the guy on the phone told him to shoot at you in front of your house, the instructions were to scare you, but above all *not to hurt the kid.*"

After a second or two Cooper said, "Not to hurt him?"

"He said make it look like he was shooting at the kid but above all, not to hurt him."

Cooper stood still for a long moment.

"You still there?" said Harrison.

"Yeah."

"Now get this. The second time, when they jumped you inside your house, they were supposed to do anything they had to do to find out where the kid was, but when they did, all they were supposed to do was wait for the next phone call and let the guy know where he was."

"Huh."

"Now, I think that's real interesting, don't you?"

"Yeah. I think that's interesting. I'm not sure I see what it means."

"Shit. I was hoping you'd have some ideas. I'll tell you one thing it means, though."

"What's that?"

"It means when you get done telling the officers who come and get you there about Flores, you should go home and get a good night's sleep, because we want you and the kid to come down to Area Six and see us tomorrow morning. Shostak and me would like to have a nice long talk with you both. We'd do it tonight except if we don't get some sleep before we go back on duty they won't be able to tell us from the dead people. And we want to be nice and fresh for our talk. I'm sure you do, too."

"Yeah, sure." Cooper was rubbing his eyes with the tips of his fingers sticking out of the cast, suddenly deathly tired.

"You got any idea where the kid is? We been trying to call him."

"He's at the Hyatt, downtown here. His dad's in town for the weekend."

"Hey, that's nice. Why don't you bring the dad along tomorrow? Say around nine o'clock. You know the place."

"Yeah. We'll be there."

"I hope so. See you then."

"Wait a minute."

"Yeah."

"What are you going to do about Billy Galloway?"

"MacLeish, you sit down, have a drink, and wait for the squad to come. Think about all this and when you figure out what to do about Billy you can tell us tomorrow, when you come in with the kid. OK?"

Cooper watched a cockroach crawling slowly up the wall, crossing from a red stripe to a white one. "OK."

"Now I'm going home and get my usual four hours of sleep. See you tomorrow."

Cooper slumped on a stool at the counter. The little bent man said diffidently, "Having trouble?"

Cooper looked at him for a long moment, standing there bent over with his soiled rag in his hand, and then he started to laugh. He laughed for a few seconds, sagging back against the counter, and said, "Yeah. Having a little trouble."

"You want something to eat?"

"No. Maybe a cup of coffee."

Cooper rubbed his good hand over his face and shook his head. The shakes were gone and the pain was subsiding but he was tired, dead tired. He dug out a dollar to pay for the coffee but he didn't drink any of it; he just sat on the stool with his back to the little man, staring out at the street, waiting for policemen to come and take him away, and thinking.

He thought until it was all clear, and then he knew he wasn't going to wait for the cops to come. He had someplace to go and something to do. He stood up and walked out of the place, leaving his change on the counter. Rico called after him but Cooper was too intent to answer.

17

T HE HYATT REGENCY consisted of a pair of tall brick tow-
ers, two of a cluster of new high-rises perched on the
south bank of the river. Cooper was in no mood to cruise
patiently looking for parking; he turned off Michigan onto
East Lake and climbed the short block to Stetson, which ran
by a couple of construction sites behind the hotel. He dumped
the Valiant there, hiked up the block to the hotel, and went
into the east tower, not really knowing where he was going,
wondering if he was right.

By the time he saw a bank of phones Cooper had figured
out what to do. He still needed police, but not just any police. Shostak and Harrison would have left Area Six by this
time, so that left Valenti. He dug in his pocket and came up
with only a nickel and three pennies; he bummed a quarter
from a woman in a blue suit and jammed it in the phone.
Cooper dialed the 24th District; he had finally learned the
number by heart.

"I need to talk to Valenti," he said to the cop who answered.

"The lieutenant's out on the street."

"You can get him on the radio, right? Tell him MacLeish
needs help. Tell him to call me at Nick Dennison's room at
the Hyatt downtown."

"I can't . . ."

"Tell him Teardrop tried to kill MacLeish again. Have him
call MacLeish in Nick Dennison's room at the Hyatt. Got
it?" Cooper hung up in his ear.

He had forgotten the number of Nick's room and he
couldn't figure out how the hotel was laid out, but he finally
got someone to direct him to reception, a long counter over-
looking the bogus pool-and-garden landscape of the glassed-
in atrium. A young woman looked up at his approach and

Cooper said, "I'm here to see Nick Dennison. I don't know the room number."

She gave him a wary look and nodded and went off to check. Cooper looked out over the atrium and watched people drinking and laughing and refusing to believe how close death was to all of them.

"We have a *Dominic* Dennison," the woman said uncertainly at his elbow.

Cooper stared at her for a moment. "Yeah. That'll be the room."

Halfway to the elevators, Cooper stopped. It was the last piece; he knew it all now.

Three sixty-one was near the end of the corridor. Cooper knocked and listened; he heard the television going inside. The door was pulled open and Dominic stood there looking at him. Cooper could only look back for a moment, only stand and feel the horror.

"Cooper, hi. We saved you some champagne." Dominic had on his black suit coat over an army green T-shirt. He had a tulip glass in his hand and his hair was flopping in his face and his eyes were bright and his cheeks were red. He looked to Cooper about twelve years old. "I know I'm underage but Dad said it was a special occasion." He stood aside and Cooper came into the room, taking in the view north over the river, the lamplit pastel colors, and Nick straightening up after having turned off the TV.

"Hello, Nick," Cooper said.

"Cooper, good to see you." Nick stepped forward to hold out his hand. He was casually dressed tonight, in a tan sweater and designer jeans. He looked Cooper up and down and the expression on his face was uncertain, as if he were reconsidering the wisdom of having invited him along.

"What happened to you?" Dominic asked. "You look like you been rolling around in the dirt."

"I have." Cooper moved over to the window and stared out at the floodlit Wrigley Building shining white and massive above the dark river. "Nice room," he said. He turned from the window and saw the stand with the room service tray on it, an open champagne bottle in an ice bucket.

"What happened?" said Nick. He and Dominic were both staring at him with startled, concerned looks now.

Cooper walked slowly to the armchair in the corner and sat down heavily. "I had a little trouble over at Harbor Point," he said.

"What kind of trouble?" said Dominic. "Like before, you mean?"

"Yeah, like before." Cooper pulled back the edge of the tear in his jeans with a finger, looking at the abraded flesh inside. "Same guy in fact."

After a silence Nick said, "Did you call the police?"

"No. Not about that."

The silence was longer. Dominic and his father stood very still, and then exchanged one glance. Dominic said, "What are you talking about?"

"Sit down, both of you." Cooper crossed his legs and settled back in the chair. "Go ahead, sit down. I want you both to be comfortable." Dominic was still holding the empty glass in his hand, frozen, staring. "Sit down," said Cooper more loudly. Dominic sank onto the bed; Nick very carefully pulled the chair out from the desk and sat on it, looking at Cooper like a restaurant patron watching someone at the next table being sick.

"Dominic," said Cooper.

"Huh?" The boy's voice was strangled; he had caught the full scent of Cooper's rage.

"What did your mother call your father when she wanted to have a really serious talk with him?" Cooper's eyes flicked once to Nick while he waited for the boy to answer.

"What do you mean?" said Dominic quietly.

"I mean did she always call him Nick? Or when she was mad at him or having a serious talk, did she ever call him by his full name?"

The silence this time stretched out for long seconds. Very slowly Dominic turned his head to look at Nick. Cooper watched the boy and felt sick at heart, sick to death. "She gave you his name, didn't she? You're Dominic Junior, aren't you? Nick is short for Dominic, not Nicholas. Right?"

Dominic Junior looked at Cooper and shook his head, unable to understand.

"You were right about the yellow paper. Your mother never had any around the house. But I bet your Dad had some in his place in New York."

Dominic's eyes snapped back to Nick this time. Nick was looking at Cooper, frowning faintly. "You're out of your mind," Nick said in a tone of wonderment.

"When your mother went to see him in New York last spring, that was when she told him she wanted a divorce, wasn't it? You know how she told him? She wrote him a note, maybe just before she left, at the end of a long argument when they were too tired to fight anymore, I don't know. Anyway, he saved the note. Remember the wording?"

Cooper could see Dominic remembering it and he could see Nick starting to calculate chances. Abruptly Nick stood up. Calmly, softly he said, "Dominic, this man is dangerous. I think we should get out of here and get some help." He took a step toward Dominic, raising a fatherly hand.

Cooper slipped his hand into his jacket pocket and brought out the Ruger. He trained it at Nick and said, "You try and leave this room and I'll put four holes in you. That's how many rounds are left after your muscle shot at me."

Nick stiffened and his hand dropped to his side. "You've really lost it, haven't you?" he said.

"I thought Billy Galloway set me up at first. But I was wrong. Who else knew I was going to Harbor Point, Nick? I told Dominic and I told a cop. I think we can rule them out. Dominic, you told your dad I was going over there, didn't you? Did he make any phone calls this afternoon that you couldn't overhear? Slip away to a pay phone for a few minutes or something?"

Dominic said nothing, but Cooper only had to see the way he looked at Nick to get the answer.

"Now sit down, Nick."

"You're crazy. He's crazy, Dominic."

Dominic hadn't moved from the bed. He looked helplessly from Cooper to Nick, the champagne glass held loosely in his fingers, lolling on its side in his lap. Cooper avoided looking at Dominic's face because it hurt so much. He spoke to Nick again.

"Put your ass on that chair unless you want a bullet in your thigh. That's better. Now don't move. Dominic, your mother used to drink a lot when she was really upset, right? Did she ever drink when she argued with your Dad?" There was no answer. "I bet she did. I bet she argued with him that night. Here's another question. Did he still have all his keys from your place here? Could he have let himself in? Come in through a back way or through the garage or something, so the guy at the front desk wouldn't have seen him?''

Out of the corner of his eye Cooper saw Dominic set the tulip glass on the bedside stand, moving very slowly. Cooper was watching Nick, watching him think fast, watching him figure the angles.

''I wasn't even in Chicago that night, Dominic. You don't believe this crap, do you? This is crazy-man stuff. This guy used to be in love with your mother, you know that? He always hated my guts. That's where this is coming from.'' Nick was controlling his voice, keeping it as low and calm as Cooper's, but his eyes were flicking back and forth, from Cooper to Dominic and back, very quickly.

''The cops said your mother wasn't found for a couple of hours after she died.'' Cooper lowered the gun just a bit so he could rest his forearm on the arm of the chair and went on. ''Maybe enough time for Nick to get out to the airport and on a flight back to New York so he could answer the phone when they got around to calling him. Your grandmother called him, didn't she? We'll have to ask her what time it was when she did. Say eight or nine in the morning, maybe. Our time, that is. Already four or five hours after she died. Probably just enough time for him to make it. He must have done a lot of flying back and forth for that twelve hours or so. The airline records ought to show it.''

Nick sat back a bit. ''They can check the airline records all they want. This man's raving, Dominic. I'm sorry you have to listen to this.''

''I'm sorry he has to listen to it, too. So you used a false name for the midnight flights. That's probably easy enough to do. Maybe you got yourself a credit card in a fake name. That should be easy for someone like you. Or you just paid cash. I don't know how hard it is to fly under a fake name. The cops'll sort it out.''

''So what are you saying?'' Nick leaned forward with sudden intensity. ''That I made this . . . this clandestine journey, slipped into the apartment, and strangled her or something, and then dropped her off the balcony to make it look like suicide? That's insane. I'll talk to any cops you want about this.''

"No, you didn't strangle her. You didn't have to. She was drunk. Really drunk, like she got only rarely, when things were really bad for her. I saw her like that once. I can imagine you wearing her down, pouring her more drinks, whatever you did. Maybe you told her you wanted to get back together, badgered her for a few hours, I don't know. But all you had to do was wait her out. You knew Dominic wouldn't be there that night. She'd probably told you about the field trip a while before that. I bet that's when you saw your opportunity and set things up. Put the note in an envelope, brought along the pad to plant it on her desk. The risk would be if someone else was there that night, but you knew it wasn't likely. She didn't have any lovers. She wouldn't, not for a long time after the divorce. You figured you could slip in that evening and surprise her. You probably got there before she did—she came in late that night. You were waiting for her. And then all you had to do was badger her, wear her down, wait her out.''

"MacLeish, for Christ's sake. Look at what you're doing to the boy.''

"You did it, Nick. You're the one who hurt him. You waited until Vivian was too drunk to put up any fight and then you picked her up in your arms, maybe told her you were going to put her to bed, just like old times.''

"Stop it.''

"You carried her to that balcony and got the door open and took her out there . . .''

"Shut it, MacLeish.'' The voice was louder suddenly.

"Nobody could see you out there. You hoisted her up over the rail . . .''

"Dammit!''

"And you threw her over. You probably watched her all the way down.''

Cooper raised the gun and Nick sank back onto the chair. Everybody sat still for a few seconds. Cooper chanced a look at the boy and saw him staring at Nick, just staring, frozen.

"Why?'' Nick's chin jutted, challenging. "Why would I have killed her? I loved her. She was the one who wanted the divorce.''

"Why? For half a million bucks." Cooper let that sink in, seeing Dominic turn slowly toward him, before going on. "Five hundred thousand dollars and revenge on the fiancée who betrayed you and the kid you never wanted. Shut up and let me spell it out. Dominic, did you know your mother was an illegitimate child? Your real grandfather is a man named Alban Galloway. He's as rich as they come and he's dying. He left your mother a fortune, a small one maybe but still a fortune. With your mother dead, you get it—if he dies before you do. That's why you were never in danger. Your daddy here has to keep you alive until Alban Galloway dies. Then, of course, he gets to administer the fortune as your guardian. And maybe down the road a few years you have an accident and he gets it for good."

"Jesus Christ. You're a madman."

"Not me, Nick. Dominic, you know those guys that came after us? You know what the cops say their instructions were? Not to harm you. Above all not to harm you. That's what finally kicked in, finally let me see what was going on. As long as it looked like they were trying to kill you, suspicion had to fall on Galloway's son, 'cause he gets it all if you die before Galloway. But they weren't trying to kill you. They were just trying to make it look like they wanted to. You gave this a lot of thought, didn't you Nick? Went to a lot of trouble, coming into town to hunt up just the right couple of no-goods to do the rough stuff, arranging the phone numbers and the payments and . . ."

The phone rang.

"That's for me," Cooper said. He rose from the chair and motioned Nick away from the desk with the gun. "Move." Nick stood up and backed slowly away, for the first time starting to look frightened. Cooper walked to the desk and twisted to reach across for the phone with his left hand. He could just get a grip on it with his fingertips despite the cast. As he was raising it to his ear, he fumbled it and it thumped onto the desk. Cooper pawed at it and out of the corner of his eye saw Nick moving and whirled to bring the gun to bear on him but not fast enough.

The champagne bottle caught him square on the cheekbone and his head was filled with light and the loud muffled crack of bone breaking. Cooper was falling back helpless knowing

there was something he should be paying attention to but not
knowing what it was besides this pain all through his head.
Then he hit the floor and somebody was rushing toward him
out of somewhere close by and Cooper remembered that it
was the gun he had to hold onto but it was too late.

He came out of it enough to see Nick through the red haze
of pain, drawing back from him with the gun in his hand.
Cooper had enough there to kick out with both feet and send
Nick sprawling backwards, and then Cooper was struggling
to pull himself up with a hand on the chair and keep his eyes
focused and Nick was levelling the .38 at him. Cooper
jumped sideways as Nick fired. He felt the old familiar punch
of lead slamming into his body and he was back against a
wall and trying to get up again and his shoulder had that
feeling, that numb shocked feeling of traumatized flesh and
Cooper knew that even Nick couldn't miss the second time.

"Dominic, don't let him kill me," Cooper managed to
say, his mouth filling with blood.

Nick was so high above him, taller than Cooper remembered, a step or two closer and aiming the gun, close enough
to choose the spot. There was a little cry coming from someone's throat and somebody came flying across the room and
took Nick from behind with a tackle. Cooper leveled himself
up the wall, the pain starting to drown him, knowing he had
to get over there and help.

Things were making crashing noises and Nick and the boy
were on the floor in a tangle and Cooper pitched over on
them and managed to get his left arm with the cast around
Nick's neck and squeeze for dear life. It felt as if he had only
one arm; he just couldn't bring the other one into play. His
eyes were squeezed shut and he hurt with every jolt as the
three of them thrashed; then Nick twisted too violently for
Cooper to hold him and suddenly the three of them were
apart and Dominic was scrambling to his feet.

"No," said Nick distinctly. Cooper managed to focus on
him, on his ass scooting back toward the window, and on
Dominic, standing by the bed with the gun in his hands.
Cooper had never seen a look of pain like the one on the
boy's face.

"Don't do it, Dominic," he said, with great effort.

Dominic fired once and the look of pain was replaced by

one of deep and guileless astonishment. He looked down at the gun and then back at Nick, and Cooper looked too and saw the shock on Nick's face and the hole in his tan sweater in the middle of his chest. Nick slumped back against the windowsill and gasped, once, hoarsely.

"Oh my God!" It was a little boy's wail, coming out in a voice just past breaking, appalled. "I just shot my father!"

"No you didn't." Fighting the pain with the last dregs of willpower, Cooper pulled himself up and made it over to the boy and untangled the revolver from his fingers. He let it drop and pulled Dominic close to him with his one good arm and squeezed, holding fast to his boy. "You saved his life."

18

O NCE THE FIRST people burst in, the room filled up quickly with paramedics and police. Cooper hurt too much to really follow the comings and goings but at some point he became aware that Valenti was there, bending over him where he lay on the bed.

"Jesus Christ, you're busy tonight. You're responsible for the guy over on Randolph too, aren't you?"

Cooper spat blood onto the towel and closed his eyes again because it was too painful to keep them open. "What are you doing here?"

"I broke all the records getting down here after I heard you say 'Don't let him kill me.' It's nice to have that blue light on top sometimes. And the radio. I got 'em in here as fast as I could."

"Thanks. How's the boy?" Cooper said.

"He's OK. Who shot Dennison?"

"I did."

"That's funny. The boy says he shot him."

"I did it."

"Yeah, OK. I should have stayed on the phone. We'll sort it out later."

"Is he dead?"

"No. They just wheeled him out in a hurry. They don't move so fast if they're dead."

"Good. I want to see him on trial. He killed his wife."

"No shit. You finally figured that out, huh?"

Cooper opened his eyes again. "What?"

Valenti shook his head. "When you told me the story, I called Shostak and talked it over with him. Even without talking to Murphy it was pretty obvious they had to take another look at Dennison. They were gonna get someone to talk to him in New York, but he saved 'em the trouble by showing up here, I guess.

I talked to Shostak just now and he said they had decided to come see him tonight. But then you came along and fucked everything up. You know, you gotta learn to leave this stuff to the pros.''

"The pros, huh? Where were you when the guy over on Randolph jumped me?''

"We can't cover all the angles, pal. It's a good thing you can take care of yourself.''

"Shit.'' Cooper had been fighting to keep it together but he could feel shock starting to come on and he hoped the paramedics got to him before too long. "Care like this, who needs abuse?''

Valenti gave a little grunt of laughter. "And no Purple Heart this time, either. Must be rough. But I'll tell you what, MacLeish.''

"What?'' Cooper said softly, starting to fade.

"When you get out of the hospital I'll take you to a place on Taylor Street where they got veal parmesan like you wouldn't believe.''

They took him back to the VA hospital, and when Cooper was not too fuzzy with painkillers he could look around the room, watch TV, and see his visitors. Among the first were Shostak and Harrison.

"You look like somebody danced on your face for a while,'' said Harrison. "I don't think steaks are enough for those shiners. You need a whole side of beef, man.''

Shostak looked at him in his morose way and shook his head. "I hope you're putting your time in here to good use. Like thinking what you're going to tell the court.''

"The truth. You got the story from Dominic, right? What's wrong with it?''

"What's wrong with it is we haven't got a case.''

"What do you mean, no case?''

"I mean there's no way we can convict Dennison on what you came up with. We would never have arrested him on the strength of that.''

"The guy tried to kill me. You can arrest him for that, can't you?''

"Maybe, with what Valenti heard over the phone. But remember, you pulled a gun on the man. He got it away from you and defended himself. When he's strong enough to start making charges, they're going to get you for unlawful restraint, at least.''

"I was making a citizen's arrest."

"Man, try that out on a judge. I want to see that. But you're not the only one in trouble. They could get the kid for shooting him."

"I'm the one that shot him, not the kid. And it was self-defense."

"Be interesting to see who Dennison says shot him when he's ready to talk."

"OK," said Harrison, "you shot him in self-defense. After he shot you in self-defense. One gun, two guys get shot. Must have been kinda wild."

"Don't you believe Dennison did it?"

"Oh yeah," said Harrison. "You had most of it right, seems like. We looked at the airline records and found one guy who flew New York to Chicago and back that same night. He paid cash and the address he gave doesn't exist. We haven't talked to the plane crews yet, but we're hoping to find somebody who remembers him and can finger him. And we're gonna have to keep working on the Murphy and Flores part of it. We'll link 'em up somehow."

"Right now though, we've just got no case, that's all," said Shostak, passing a hand over his face, looking fatigued. "Nothing we could take to a state's attorney. We had high hopes for the note but at this point there are no clear prints on it except for the grandma's. Even if we establish all this stuff, flying back and forth and all, it's all circumstantial. I can't see how to convict the guy. And your scenario has one big hole in it, you know."

"What's that?"

"How in the hell did Dennison find out about the will? None of it holds together unless he could get that information."

"I think I know," said Cooper. "Jack Lime. I had it all wrong, putting him together for some reason with the idea of Vivian's secret lover that people kept going on about. When I talked to Jesse Goddard, that finally put all that nonsense out of my mind and I could get back to what was bothering me. What bothered me about Lime was he lied to me. He told me Galloway didn't know Vivian. But once I found out I was right about Galloway leaving her money, I realized Lime had to know about that. As the right-hand man of a dying millionaire he would be familiar with the will. I couldn't figure out why he would lie. I kept thinking about him and I finally realized that he and Nick must have been pals. Lime said he hadn't seen Vivian since her divorce. Why do you stop seeing someone when they get a divorce? Because it was the spouse you were friends with. Check it out— I bet he and Nick were in law school together or something, and they got drunk one night a while back and he let Nick know his boss had left Nick's wife a chunk of money.''

The detectives exchanged one of their looks. ''Boy, if that's true, that's gonna be one lawyer out of a job fast,'' said Harrison. ''I can't wait to talk to the guy.''

''And it bothered him,'' said Cooper. ''He realized it was an indiscretion, and when I showed up wanting to talk to Galloway about Vivian it must have been a shock, since the link between those two was supposed to be a secret. He first denied Galloway knew her and then I bet he called Nick. If Nick was the only person he'd told about the bequest, he'd think first that Nick had let it leak out. So he called Nick and asked if he knew who the hell this guy MacLeish was. I don't know what Nick said—probably just that he knew of me but didn't know what I was up to. I don't know how much it would have bothered Nick to know I'd made the connection. He was planning to throw suspicion on Billy anyway and I was just doing his work for him. But then I think he wanted to make sure I wound up dead however things came out.''

''Yeah,'' said Harrison. ''I think he wanted you from the start. The night they nailed you to the furniture, I think their orders were to leave you cooling off on the floor, although Murphy won't admit it. Dennison didn't need to know where the kid was, of course. That was all for show, to get people thinking about Galloway. And I think when you saw Flores the other night up by the bar it was you he was looking for, not the kid.''

''Yeah, like Diana said. I had that figured all wrong. I thought I must have led them to the restaurant. But now I think Dominic told Nick where it was, and he just passed it on to those two. They picked us up there that first night, and

Flores went back there gunning for me because Dominic had told Nick I sometimes picked him up after work.''

"You been doing some thinking," said Harrison.

"Not much else to do in here.''

"All right, let's get back to Dennison," said Shostak. "We have motive and opportunity. That's not enough. Dennison's out of danger but he hasn't said a thing yet, and you've got to know he's going to have an expensive lawyer there before he does.''

Harrison snorted with laughter. "Too bad the kid didn't kill him. You could have stuck to the story that you shot him, and you probably wouldn't have any trouble making it self-defense, what with him chucking the wine bottle at you. Course, you'd have to explain the gun.''

"But he's going to live," said Shostak. "The best I can see happening is you accuse each other of starting it, you try and keep the kid out of it by saying you shot him, you both get probation for armed violence or something like that, and he walks on the murder charge. I just don't see how we can nail him.''

A silence followed and then Cooper said, "At least he's going to be walking around under a cloud for the rest of his life. Everybody's going to know he killed her. And there's got to be a way to get him dumped as Dominic's guardian, so there's no way he can get his hands on the money.''

"Let's hope," said Harrison. "Still, that guy's gotta have enough money anyway to buy a lot of sunshine.''

"Maybe not," said Shostak. "I spent a half hour on the phone with the head of his office in New York. Found out a couple of things. One, Dennison got hurt bad in the crash in '87. It was an open secret around the office he was walking wounded from all that. He needed something to get his ass out of hock. Two, you know the securities Galloway left Vivian Horstmann? I found out from her mother they were Alcorp stock. Well, according to Dennison's boss, Alcorp is hanging out there on the line, waiting for a takeover just as soon as the old man dies. Happens whenever the undisputed number-one guy of a corporation croaks, apparently. They think Billy's going to bail out and somebody's going to eat up Alcorp. The stock's been undervalued anyway, according to this guy, and with a takeover it's going to go through the roof. Dennison saw a chance to get control of a pretty good nest egg, get himself out of trouble, and set up for life.''

After a moment Cooper said, ''That was enough of a motive, I guess. But I think the main thing was he just started to hate her and the boy. God knows, he might have tried at first. Adelle Horstmann thinks he really cared for Dominic, at least when he was little. But when the kid started acting like a teenager, when things went bad between him and Vivian, that's when I think he started to hate them. Neither of them was his anymore.'' Cooper closed his eyes. ''And I was responsible for that.''

''Yeah, I don't think he was real fond of you,'' said Harrison. ''He really wanted you bad.''

''Yeah. Know what really scares me, though? The kind of mind that could see that note she left him and think of using it as a suicide note.''

''That was his chance,'' Shostak said. ''There was no reason for her to die before Galloway, of course, except that it would have looked a hell of a lot more suspicious if she and the kid both had accidents in quick succession after she came into the money. This way the pattern was less obvious. He's a smart son of a bitch. The most dangerous kind of a son of a bitch.'' There was a silence for a moment.

''Christ, my head hurts,'' said Cooper.

''Want me to call the nurse?'' said Shostak.

''Later. What about Flores and Murphy? Can you get them?''

Harrison had turned on the TV and was flipping channels with the sound down low. ''We may have a little trouble with Flores, at least for the business at the garage. You shouldn't have run off and left him. Especially with the gun. If you'da waited for the squad like I told you, we might have gotten him for jumping you. He'll probably walk on that, but we'll get him for nailing your hand to the table.''

''Great. And he'll go away for another six months or so.''

''Naw, you don't know all of it. Guess what we found when we looked at his aunt's place.''

''What?''

''A scalp, man. A bona fide human scalp, wrapped up in plastic in the freezer.''

After a long moment Cooper said, ''Jesus Christ.''

"Yeah. He's a fine human being, ain't he?" Harrison shook his head and flicked the channel selector again.

"The Uptown murder."

"You got it. We'll get 'em both off the streets permanently this time. Him and the runt. Man, nothing but game shows on this time of day."

"Tell me something," said Shostak. "How did you come up with the Galloway idea, anyway?"

"I don't know. It was just there once I found out about Vivian being Galloway's daughter. I wasn't all wrong, was I?"

"No, you were almost there. That was the right idea to get."

"Except Billy Galloway was just a big red herring, wasn't he?"

"Yeah. All Billy wanted was to find out how the rumor started. He figured it was a political tactic."

"Political?"

"Yeah. Billy's gone straight, you see. He wants to get into politics."

"Politics? With his record?"

"This ain't Minneapolis, MacLeish. This is Chicago. Billy's thinking of running for the county board. He must have figured one of his potential opponents paid you to discredit him. That's why he thought he could just offer you more money to shut you up."

"But if it didn't work he was prepared to sic his strongarm guy on me."

"Yeah, probably. Like I say, this is Chicago."

"Jesus. Something else I've been thinking about. All this business with Murphy and Flores was kind of . . . overelaborate, wasn't it? Didn't it just increase Nick's chances of getting caught?"

"Maybe," said Shostak. "But he wasn't going to use them unless he thought somebody was on his trail. He hoped to make the suicide convincing, and he did a damn good job, actually. But he was smart enough to know that anything like that has a chance of falling apart, and so he came up with the backup plan in case people started using the word murder. By the dates Murphy gave us, it seems like Dennison didn't set them going until after you brought the kid to us. He must have started to worry then.''

Cooper thought for a moment. "Yeah. Dominic called him and told him we were going to solve the murder, something like that.''

"He probably came into town and set the whole thing up weeks ago. He knew that seeming to go for the kid would put suspicion on Billy, especially with the old connection with Flores.''

"We're working on that part of it, the contact with Flores,'' said Shostak. "There's the weak link. Dennison talked to somebody to get in touch with him. Whoever it was, there has to be a trace.''

Harrison turned from the TV for a moment to say, "My guess is he went through a skip chaser or something, had a collection agency track him down. Gave 'em a phony name and story, something like that. If we can get on to the intermediary he used to contact Flores, we'll have him. When Flores feels a little better we'll hear what he has to say. If we can get Dennison for anything, it'll probably be for hiring them to come after you.''

"But here's what I mean,'' said Cooper. "If he was going to go to the trouble of planting a red herring in the first place, why plant one that would lead to the Galloway connection? I mean, that was close to the real motive. Why didn't he work up one that led in a completely false direction?''

Shostak answered, rubbing at his brow in concentration or perhaps only fatigue. "God knows what went through his mind, but I can guess. If the suicide scenario fell through, it was going to be clear this was no ordinary killing, lovers' quarrel or whatever. Not with the faked note and everything. Now the Galloway connection wasn't obvious at all. But once anyone started digging there was always the possibility it'd show up. And if it did, he wanted things to point to Billy, not him. See, the nice part for Dennison was that even with Flores running around, that didn't necessarily point to the Galloway business. Hell, we'd never have found the connection if you hadn't come up with it. All that did, faking the shots at the boy and all, was to muddy the waters. But *if,* if somebody did dig down deep enough and find the connection, then it would look like Billy had to be behind it, because Dennison's interest was to keep the boy alive, not kill him.''

"Yeah, I see. Still, in his place I think I'd have left well enough alone. You would have written it off as suicide long ago, like you said."

"Except for you. What he was afraid of happened. Somebody came along and started digging. So it might have been elaborate, but he hasn't come out of it too badly,'' said Shostak, the picture of gloom. "We can't convict him."

Cooper closed his eyes and got back to the old business of dealing with the pain. Someday he might get good at it, but he was tired of all the practice he was getting. Harrison gave up on the TV and Shostak rose from the chair and pulled on his raincoat. "All right, we'll let you get back to your headache," he said. "I imagine we'll be back. I think you're gonna have a legal mess on your hands. I hope you know a good cheap lawyer."

"Worry about that tomorrow," said Harrison. "Just lie here and let her take care of you for a while." He nodded at the figure in the corner.

When the detectives had left, Diana moved to the bedside and took up her post again, silently. She gave Cooper her distant patient look and he could hardly tell she had been crying.

Two days later Cooper was feeling better, but he still had trouble answering the phone with his left hand in a cast and his right arm strapped to his body. He managed to get the phone to his ear with his left hand and said, "Yeah."

"MacLeish, Harrison here. How you doing?"

"Better. What's the good news today?"

"Couple things. First, you were right about Lime. We talked to him yesterday. I never saw the starch go out of a guy so fast. I mean, the man was scared when we walked out of there. But he can breathe a little easier today. He won't have to testify."

"How come?"

"Nick Dennison killed himself this morning."

Several seconds passed and Cooper said, "How, for Christ's sake? I thought he was in intensive care."

"No, he got out of there yesterday. This morning he was

in a regular room. They don't know quite how he did it, as weak as he was, but somehow he got out of bed, tubes and all, and made it over to the window and got it open. A nurse came in just in time to see him go out. He was on the seventh floor.''

Cooper lay on his back and looked at the ceiling and felt his stomach turn over. "That's not as high as the twenty-third, but it'll do, I guess."

"It did, all right. Stupid shit, he would have beat the murder charge."

"Huh." Cooper breathed a long slow sigh, thinking of the first time he'd ever seen Nick Dennison, with Vivian, a long time before. "Maybe he woke up in the middle of the night and remembered loving Vivian."

There was silence over the line and then Harrison said, "And maybe he remembered he was broke. I don't think people like him deal with that too well."

"Whatever. I can't say I'm real sorry, not about Nick anyway."

"Me neither, man, me neither. This is one I'm gonna be real glad to wipe off the slate. And hey, I don't think you'll be needing a lawyer after all."

The long cold fall had given way to the deepening chill of December and the earth lay silent under the gray sky. There was a little snow left on the ground from the first dusting of the winter and the wind by the lake was bitter. From where he stood Cooper could just make out the light at the end of the Farwell pier three miles to the south. "It's funny to see it from way up here," he said. "That's where I usually go when I have thinking to do."

Beside him Dominic shivered. The boy had no hat on, only the old black overcoat he had worn when Cooper had first seen him. He stared out over the lake, choppy and sullen in the early winter gloom.

"Come on, let's get back. It's too cold to talk out here," Cooper said. They turned and walked back toward Forest Avenue, the wind raising wisps of snow about their feet. Cooper pulled up the collar of his jacket with his good hand, the left one, finally free of its cast. His right arm was still in the sling, bunched under the flight jacket. The park was deserted except for him and Dominic. They walked in silence.

"I have to start driving again," Cooper said. "Get the Valiant out of the pound where they towed it. You can get old just waiting for an El train. And I'm flat broke. I need to get back in the cab. Sling comes off next week, they tell me."

They walked up the steps to the porch of Adelle Horstmann's house and Cooper stopped Dominic with a hand on his arm. The boy turned to look at him, hair hanging in his thin bony face, his breath streaming out into the cold. He blinked at Cooper a few times but didn't even ask what was on his mind; he just stared.

"I know it's cold out here, but it's not that cold," said Cooper. "You got to talk to people, Dominic. Just to say hello, ask the time of day at least. Even if you got nothing else to say. You start wrapping yourself up like that and before too long you'll find you can't get unwrapped again."

He let his hand fall back and waited. Dominic shivered and said, "I don't care."

"Listen to me." Cooper stuffed his free hand in the pocket of his jacket, thinking hard, wanting to get it right. "You've been through more shit than most people ever have to deal with, I know that. But other people go through shit, too. When I was twenty years old, man, I had just spent a year seeing and doing the worst, the very worst people can do to each other. Man, I was ready to write off the whole fucking human race, deep-six 'em all and have the planet to myself. I wanted to be left alone and not do one damn thing ever again I didn't want to do and just drink myself to sleep every night for a while. And there's a hell of a lot of men came back and did just that, and you see them sitting around in bars and not looking at anybody. Or you see them in hospitals and dying in alleys. Know what kept me from that? Two things. One was staying in the Army for a while, with the discipline keeping me on the rails when I might have gone off. And the other one was meeting your mother."

Dominic's eyes flicked back from far out to light on Cooper's face. "Yeah. I had come through it OK, all things considered, but I needed something else. I needed to see something in people I had forgotten all about. I needed to see goodness. And your mother had it, and that's why I fell in love with her, and that's part of why you're in the world. Now, I know that what happened to you is a lot worse in some ways than what happened to me. What happened to you is you found out your whole life was based on a bunch of lies. And the person who was truest, who really honest-to-God loved you, was taken away from you. I can't think of much worse that could happen to a person. But you can't give up on them, Dominic, not yet. You have to fight it, 'cause if you think it's cold out here now, you should feel the cold when you've written everybody off. Now that is cold, believe me. I know. You got to fight it until you meet somebody that shows you the goodness again. You have to let someone do that for you.''

Dominic's gaze was away again, impenetrable. Cooper opened his mouth, hesitated, and went on. ''You got a right to be suspicious of fathers. I'm a piss-poor excuse for a father, I know. But I'm here. And I'm willing to try . . .''

Shit, thought Cooper, *here it comes.* His throat was constricting. ''I'm willing to be however much of a father you . . .''

Shit, all of a sudden he couldn't talk.

''Dominic . . . if you want another father you got me.'' Cooper threw his arm around the boy and reeled him in in a brief hard embrace and then left him standing on the porch. He marched down the steps, wiping furiously at his eyes, trudging away up the street. When he had gone about a hundred feet he stopped and took a look back and saw the kid standing there, just standing on the porch in the cold. Cooper raised a hand and after a second he saw Dominic raise his in response, wave once, and let the hand fall back to his side. Cooper turned and started walking again. The tears were turning to ice at the corners of his eyes.

It was a long walk to the El. He stood frozen on the platform looking at the gunmetal sky and thinking of Vivian. He got on the train and kept thinking of her all the way home, back into the city, into the crumbling littered streets, into the gray dirty evening. He thought perhaps it was time to close the book on Vivian Horstmann.

He thought of what he'd told Dominic and decided that was how he should remember Vivian. And close the book. Every other woman he'd tried to love had fallen short of the ideal, the Vivian that Cooper had chased and never won. It was time to learn that loving was not solely a function of the beauty of the object, that loving came from wanting to love as well.

Cooper leaned on Diana's doorbell, hoping she would be at home on an evening off. When he trudged up the stairs and saw her waiting, feline and golden in the open doorway, he said nothing, but held out his one good arm and folded her into his embrace, feeling her stiff with surprise at first and then sliding her arms around him, softening.

"I love you," he said.

POLICE THRILLERS by
"THE ACKNOWLEDGED MASTER"
Newsweek

ED McBAIN

CALYPSO	70591-5/$4.50 US/$5.50 Can
DOLL	70082-4/$4.50 US/$5.50 Can
HE WHO HESITATES	70084-0/$4.50 US/$5.50 Can
ICE	67108-5/$4.99 US/$5.99 Can
KILLER'S CHOICE	70083-2/$4.50 US/$5.50 Can
BREAD	70368-8/$4.50 US/$5.50 Can
80 MILLION EYES	70367-X/$4.50 US/$5.50 Can
HAIL TO THE CHIEF	70370-X/$4.50 US/$5.50 Can
LONG TIME NO SEE	70369-6/$4.50 US/$5.50 Can

Don't Miss These Other Exciting Novels

WHERE THERE'S SMOKE	70372-6/$3.50 US/$4.50 Can
GUNS	70373-4/$3.99 US/$4.99 Can
VANISHING LADIES	71121-4/$4.50 US/$5.50 Can
BIG MAN	71123-0/$4.50 US/$5.50 Can
DEATH OF A NURSE	71125-7/$4.50 US/$5.50 Can

Buy these books at your local bookstore or use this coupon for ordering:

Mail to: Avon Books, Dept BP, Box 767, Rte 2, Dresden, TN 38225   B
Please send me the book(s) I have checked above.
☐ My check or money order—no cash or CODs please—for $_____ is enclosed
(please add $1.50 to cover postage and handling for each book ordered—Canadian
residents add 7% GST).
☐ Charge my VISA/MC Acct#_____Exp Date_____
Phone No_____Minimum credit card order is $6.00 (please add postage
and handling charge of $2.00 plus 50 cents per title after the first two books to a maximum
of six dollars—Canadian residents add 7% GST). For faster service, call 1-800-762-0779.
Residents of Tennessee, please call 1-800-633-1607. Prices and numbers are subject to
change without notice. Please allow six to eight weeks for delivery.

Name_____

Address _____

City_____ State/Zip_____

EMB   0392